BROKEN GAME

A DARK COLLEGE HOCKEY ROMANCE

KINGS OF REINA UNIVERSITY
BOOK 1

JO BRENNER

HIGH RISE PUBLISHING, LLC

Editing provided by Surey Rodriguez-Cortes.

Hockey consulting by Chasing Books PR.

Photography provided by Michelle Lancaster.

Cover design provided by Qamber Designs.

Illustration provided by A'Reayon Smith.

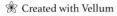 Created with Vellum

For everyone who daydreams about being spanked with a hockey stick...

ALSO BY JO BRENNER

Bad Heroes

You Can Follow Me

Lose Me In The Shadows

Meet Me In The Dark

Tabb U

Butterfly: a dark college hockey romance

NEWSLETTER AND BONUS EPILOGUE

Want to read the bonus epilogue? Join my newsletter for the epilogue, updates, and other goodies! **Click the link below to join and read the bonus epilogue.**

Download Here

BRUTAL GAMES PLAYLIST

Shove It
Santigold
Novocaine
The Unlikely Candidates
Pumpkin Soup
Kate Nash
Kiss with a Fist
Florence + the Machine
Anything Could Happen
Ellie Goulding
Psycho
Amy Shark
I See Red
Everybody Loves an Outlaw
Toxic
Yael Naim
Lose Control
Shanna Sascha
Aviation High
Semi Precious Weapons

Red Lips
Sky Ferreira
Blue Jeans
Lana Del Rey
Feel It Still
Portugal. The Man
Gold
Kiiara
Hunger
Florence + the Machine
Womanizer
Britney Spears
Front Row
Toby Lightman
21 Questions
50 Cent
bad guy
Billie Eilish
Mr. Rattlebone
Matt Maeson
6 Underground
Sneaker Pimps
Hush
The Marías
Hallucinogenics
Matt Maeson
i hope ur miserable until ur dead
Nessa Barrett
I WANNA BE YOUR SLAVE
Måneskin
Monsters
All Time Low
Paradise Circus

Massive Attack
You Got Me All Wrong
Dios Malos
Fuck Feelings
Olivia O'Brien
My Love
Florence + the Machine
Crazy in Love
Beyoncé
Love Is Blindness
Jack White
Don't Blame Me
Taylor Swift
Skin and Bones
David Kushner
Wild Horses
Bishop Briggs
DARKSIDE
Neoni
The Fire
Bishop Briggs
Yes I'm a Mess
AJR
Too Sweet
Hozier
Apologize
OneRepublic
Lust for Life
Lana Del Rey
1:5
CHINCHILLA
Little Talks
Of Monsters and Men

No Light, No Light
Florence + the Machine
Blood // Water
grandson
Burn It Down
Daughter
Mastermind
Taylor Swift
Who We Are
Hozier
Vigilante Shit
Taylor Swift
One Of The Girls
The Weeknd, JENNIE & Lily Rose Depp
Northern Attitude
Noah Kahan & Hozier
Aphrodite
Sam Short
Work Song
Hozier
Record Player
Daisy the Great & AJR
bury a friend
Billie Eilish
Gravedigger
Matt Maeson
Daylight
Matt and Kim
Gimme Sympathy
Metric

CONTENT NOTE! PLEASE READ!

This is a dark bully romance, with dark themes and plot points that may be sensitive to some.

Please, please, please read the content warnings on my website, jobrenner.com. I'd add them here, but the River Platform (IYKYK) could get big mad if it sees the list, and then bye bye, book.

Joking aside, please do visit my website. Your health—mental, physical, spiritual, emotional—matters.

1

Aviva

"Are you sure you want to do this?" Tovah, my best friend, partner in crime, and guide to the madness in front of us, asked. We stood, shoulder to shoulder, staring up at the big, ivy-covered colonial that housed the star players of Reina University's hockey team.

Music blasted from the windows and the open front door, where students—excited about the start of the school year—spilled out, half naked, drunk, and laughing. They were squeezing out the last bit of summer. I envied them for a moment, the easy joy in their lives. They were happy to be at the hockey house. And why shouldn't they be? They didn't know about the darker side of the sport it represented.

I, however, did.

If I got my way, they'd know about its darker side sooner rather than later. And I was determined to get my way.

"We can call Plan B off. Plan A, too. Go back to our

apartment and take off this fucking makeup and put on sweats and watch *Ted Lasso*," Tovah suggested.

And yeah, it sounded tempting to abandon my mission. But I owed it to my brother, Asher, to see this through. To get him justice. And that meant checking out my competition—and making inroads with the hockey players who might be allies.

I rubbed at the scar on my chest as I considered. The scar, hidden under a sleeveless crop top turtleneck, was a reminder of everything I'd lost, and why I was here.

For Asher.

"And you love Ted Lasso," she added hopefully.

I tugged up my black skirt to cover my round stomach and tugged down my bike shorts, flipped back my curly brown hair, and squared my shoulders. I was what people politely referred to as "curvy," "mid-size," or "a bigger girl," and I was mostly happy with it. Mostly comfortable in the size and shape of my body, with its rolls and curves and dimples and stretch marks. Mostly okay with having to wear bike shorts under skirts and dresses to avoid thigh chafe. Mostly invulnerable to the way fatphobic people judged my body—and me. Because fuck them.

Again, *mostly*. Sometimes it got to me. But not tonight. I had more important things to worry about, like my mission.

Spying on the hockey team to figure out who my "in" might be was risky. But I loved my brother. Hated how he'd retreated into himself, how he'd ripped the Wayne Gretsky poster off his bedroom wall. How he'd stopped caring if I brought home no-pulp orange juice by mistake. I'd risk anything to bring that crooked smile back to his face.

"We're doing this," I told her.

She sighed, linking arms with me. "You're lucky I'm a

good investigative journalist—and that I love you. Let's do this."

Together, we entered the house.

The party was in full swing: to the left, a group of girls were dancing on tables. To the right, a group of four students sat on the spiral stairs, passing a joint between them and laughing hysterically.

"Let's go find the Core Four." Tovah tugged me forward.

"The Core Four?" I asked, bemused.

"The four best hockey players at Reina. I don't remember who nicknamed them that, but it stuck. And you're about to see why."

She led me through a sea of strangers my age who eyed me with a mix of curiosity and distrust. I didn't blame them. I was new—a transfer student to Reina U as a senior—and therefore a complete unknown, when most of them had known each other for years. Moreover, they were right not to trust me.

As the saying went, I wasn't here to make friends.

I was here to get justice for my brother.

Period.

We entered the kitchen, where four guys were holding court.

The Core Four.

I immediately picked up on why. Even surrounded by people, the four guys were intimidating, aloof. They towered over everyone else, and not just physically. I could feel their presence, even from the doorway.

Did any of them know about what had really happened to my brother? Did they care? Had they been hurt in the same way?

Tovah cleared her throat, bringing my attention back to her.

"Okay, so, the twins are Levi and Judah Wasserman. They're both first line defensemen. The one with the glasses and the super serious look in his eyes? That's Levi. Judah's the one with the man bun; he thinks he and his hair are god's gifts to women." She rolled her eyes. "Separately, they're like, the brain and the brawns. Together..." she shivered. "Well, obviously I've never experienced it, but I've heard through the grapevine that they like to share."

I raised my eyebrows. "That's new."

Tovah shrugged. "Things at Reina U can get a little... wild. You'll see."

With that ominous statement, she turned her head, then scowled. "The curly-haired flirt with the dimples and smirk is Isaac Jones. He's a player. Probably a talker in bed, so maybe he's your in if Plan A fails..."

"Do you not like him?"

She shook her head, her curly hair—dyed purple this month—flying every which way. "I don't anything him. He doesn't matter."

I raised an eyebrow, briefly distracted by her denial. "Maybe we should talk about why you feel that way."

Tovah rolled her eyes. "Don't therapize me right now, *Dr. Gold*. I swear, you've been doing it since we met."

"Future Dr. Gold," I corrected. Hopefully I would become Dr. Gold one day. When my parents died and Great Aunt Gladys took us in, she'd sent us to a psychologist for grief counseling. The psychologist, Abby, was kind and wise and patient with us, and the only reason Asher and I managed to grieve healthily and heal *at all* from the trauma of losing them. Ever since, I'd wanted to be a psychologist, and help other people the way she'd helped me. For now, all I could do was be there for Asher while he saw a real, licensed therapist.

"Whatever." Tovah cleared her throat, her eyes catching on a tall, built guy with dark, straight hair. "And *that*, well, that's Jack. He's hockey captain, king of the Kings, king of everything, really. He's not only scored the most goals for the Kings, he's had the most assists in the league. The sports department at the Daily Queen nicknamed him 'Jack Hat Trick Feldman.' Everyone knows Jack. Everyone *wants* Jack, or at least wants to rub shoulders with him, in case some of his power will rub off. And in turn, Jack knows *everything* that happens on Reina's campus, and controls everything, down to who deals Vice and Vixen."

Confused, I opened my mouth to ask what Vice and Vixen were, but at that moment, the guy with dark hair— Jack—turned around.

His eyes, a dark, magnetic gray, locked on mine.

I swallowed, my mouth and throat suddenly dry. The room disappeared, the people disappeared, until it might as well have just been him and me, alone in space, no gravity, no nothing. The only thing keeping me from floating away was the heat of his gaze on mine.

I don't know if you've ever been truly noticed by someone before. It's...disconcerting, to say the least. It's like your clothing, your makeup, your armor, the cover-up you religiously paint over your scar—all the ways you try to fade into the background ...they just fall away. And suddenly there's a spotlight on you.

I'd never had someone's complete and undivided attention before. That it was the 'king of the Kings' made it especially disturbing, but I couldn't stop watching him.

He looked and looked, and even though other people were trying to get his attention, he didn't take his eyes off me. Like even if the house burned down, he'd still notice the slightest change to my expression. It made my breath leave my lungs, being noticed like that. Made me forget everyone and everything, including Asher, including my mission to get vengeance and take this whole fucking team and institution down.

Until all that was left was *him*.

Or would've been, because then the asshole winked at me.

Winked.

My own eyes narrowed, the room and the people and my mission reappearing around me with a pop of reality. If Jack "Hat Trick" Feldman knew everything that happened at Reina U, then he probably knew what his horrible coach had done to my brother.

A girl standing next to him whispered something in his ear, and he laughed, but he was still staring at me.

The asshole winked again.

I straightened my shoulders for the second time that night, determination filling me with steel.

Jack Feldman might be my way in.

But I doubted I could trust him. I wasn't sure I could trust any of them. And that meant that whatever had just happened between us was completely meaningless.

If only my racing heart believed that.

2

Jack

I was bored.

These days, boredom was my constant companion. People were all the same—easily read and manipulated. Classes no longer felt challenging, especially because my professors gave me automatic A's for playing on the Kings. Coach said I was too smart for my own good.

The only thing that kept my interest was being on the ice, and even that was starting to feel mundane. Usually, the feeling of being a well-oiled machine with my team, the moment my stick touched the puck, outmaneuvering my opponents, *winning*...all of it made me feel alive.

But now it didn't. It felt like the world was muted, quiet, almost still...like *my world* was waiting for something.

"Feldman, you asshole. What are you brooding about?" Judah nudged my shoulder with his cold can of beer, not bothering to lower his voice.

I glanced at one of the Kings' two defensemen. Judah—and his stupid man bun—was a pain in my ass, because he always spoke his mind without tact or care for who else might be listening. He was a loud dick and most people, including his professors, thought he was an idiot—that his twin, Levi, had all the brains. Judah liked it that way. The fucker was secretly insightful, which sometimes I was grateful for.

Not now though.

I glanced at him. "Not brooding."

He snorted. "Sure."

"Jack doesn't brood, he plots." Levi rolled his eyes at his brother.

"Same fucking difference," Judah said. "You think you know more than me because of those stupid glasses you barely need."

"And you think you're prettier than me because of that ridiculous hair," Levi countered.

Before they could squabble more, Marnie sidled up to us.

"Who plots?" she asked as she placed her hand on me, red nails gleaming in the kitchen's light. I'd fucked her a few times, and we were friends, but I didn't want her near me.

Gently lifting her hand off my shoulder, I smiled down at her. "No one, sweetheart."

This time, Isaac interceded. The flirt put a hand around Marnie's waist, pulling her toward him. "C'mon gorgeous, let's shake our booties on the dance floor."

Giggling, Marnie leaned into him. Isaac and I exchanged a look, me expressing my gratitude and Isaac accepting it. Isaac was known as a player—even more than me—but the four of us knew the truth: sometimes he took one for the team.

So to speak.

"You obvious asshole," Judah said. "Sending Dr. Dimples off to do your dirty work."

I laughed, lifting my beer to my lips—and froze.

Someone was staring at me. Not unfamiliar; people stared a lot. It came with the territory, and I didn't mind.

This felt different. My back almost burned from their gaze on me, and some instinct I didn't understand warned me to ignore them. Like if I turned around, everything would change.

So I turned around.

And saw *her*.

And suddenly, all the boredom and fucking ennui I'd been feeling for so long disappeared as if it never existed. I inhaled sharply, like someone had slammed me into the boards.

Her curly brown hair with glints of red was down, falling over bare arms. She wore a tight, sleeveless black turtleneck and a tiny black skirt, both emphasizing a round stomach and soft, rolling curves I could and would happily get lost in. Some guys might call her fat. I'd beat up every fucking one of them. Because I didn't care how she was labeled—to me, she was a stunning, gorgeous goddess. Period.

Thick thighs and long legs led down to a pair of scuffed up, sparkly sneakers. It was hot for early October, unseasonably so, which made the turtleneck an intriguing choice.

I'd seen a lot of pretty girls. Girls who cheered my name and wanted me to sign their tits after a game. This one wasn't even smiling. In fact, she was glaring at me.

But her eyes...

Dark, mysterious, a little angry, a little haunted, a little turned on. As I watched her, every single one of those pretty girls ceased to exist. They didn't fucking compare. Staring at her, seeing her stare back—it unlocked something inside of me. Something I hadn't known existed. Something that, when opened, released an unfamiliar word:

Mine.

I'd never thought of anyone as mine before.

Hockey was *mine.* Ruthlessness was *mine.* Social status, and sponsorships, and likely being number one in the NHL draft...all of that was mine. But a person? After growing up in *my* family, after having been betrayed and abandoned, first by my parents and then by my older brother, after watching all of my other siblings run away or drift off to do their own thing...it was clear a person would never be mine. That meant keeping them, and I didn't want that. Not when everyone left. Not when I couldn't trust anyone outside of the team.

No, I'd never had a mine.

Until right the fuck now.

She was still staring at me.

Go ahead, princess, stare all you want.

But her glare grew. I could feel loathing from where she stood in the doorway. Women rarely glared at me. Even the ones I kicked out of my bed post-orgasm didn't get mad. I didn't know who this girl was. I didn't know why she was pissed at me. I didn't care.

Especially when Noah Hawthorne, some douchebag in Sig Nu who hadn't made the team and never would, approached her, leaning down to whisper something in her ear.

Mine.

With a growl I couldn't control, I shoved my barely-touched beer at Judah, making my way toward them. If she wanted to flirt with someone, she could flirt with me. And if that jackass touched her, I was punching a hole through his head with my already clenched fist.

Halfway across the room, I stopped, and forced myself to inhale. I could hear my older brother, Micah, in my head, telling me to rein in my temper and *think*. And the genius hacker was right. My temper got me into trouble a lot, a switch I was trying to control better.

Your emotions don't help you control the situation. Other people's do. If you're too caught up in your anger, you won't see the threads to pull.

A cool head is the head that wins. My half-brother, Marcus, the cold, emotionless billionaire.

Alright, I could play this situation better. I didn't know this girl, but picking her up in my arms and carrying her upstairs like an unwilling bride most likely wouldn't go over well.

I continued my way across the room, swaggering slowly without a care in the world, a half-smile on my face as I scouted my prey.

"...Never seen you at one of these parties before, cutie. I'm happy to show you around, show you the ropes," Noah was saying as he handed Tovah Kaufman, senior sports editor at The Daily Queen, a beer.

The girl I'd locked onto immediately grabbed the beer out of Tovah's hand, testing the cap to make sure it was properly sealed before handing it back to her. *Damn.* She was smart enough to make sure it hadn't been tampered with—a good idea when Vice and Vixen ran rampant around campus, even if we didn't allow it at hockey parties. Not only that, she clearly cared enough about her friend that ensuring her safety was second nature. What would it be like, to matter so much to someone that caring for you was like muscle memory to them?

Who was this girl? She had to be visiting Tovah from somewhere else. If she was a student here, there was no way

I would've missed her. Reaching them, I raised my chin at Noah.

He glared at me.

I jerked my head to the side.

Face turning a satisfying shade of red, Noah muttered, "asshole," and walked away.

The girl had watched our mostly silent interaction, eyebrow raised. Once he was gone, her glare returned.

"What's with the glare, princess?" I asked.

"Uh oh," Tovah Kaufman said. Even though the rumor was that she got around, she stayed away from the team. So why was she here tonight?

"Don't call me princess," the girl said automatically.

"Aviva..." Tovah trailed off.

Aviva.

It was the perfect name for her. The three syllables settled themselves deep in my chest and made a home there.

"What's wrong with princess, princess?" I asked, tugging on one of her curls.

Aviva shifted away from me, but the look in her eyes briefly shifted from loathing to lust. Eyes wide, lips parted, blush spreading across her cheeks—a rosy pink color I wanted to see *everyfuckingwhere* on her.

Capitalizing on the moment, I took her hand, slowly turning it so it was palm up and bending over it to drop a light kiss on her wrist. Her rosy skin was so soft and vulnerable here, and as I brushed my lips over it, I caught her scent: tart and sweet like apples and honey.

Mine. The word echoed in my head. I didn't fight it.

I felt her shiver, heard her interrupted gasp as she tried to control herself. I couldn't help the smile the sound brought to my lips.

She tugged on her hand. I didn't release it.

"I'm Jack," I informed her.

She practically spat at me. "I know. It's hard *not* to know that."

"Aviva," Tovah interjected. "Maybe we should—"

I rubbed my thumb over her rapidly beating pulse. "Oh, and what else do you know?"

"About you?" She pretended to think. "Only that everyone here thinks you walk on water."

The mockery in her voice rubbed me the wrong way.

"And what about you, princess?"

"Verdict pending."

This was not going as easily as I'd assumed it would. Part of me was annoyed. Part of me was impressed that she *wasn't* impressed. I wasn't used to girls not falling at my feet. I kind of liked it.

"Have a problem with hockey players?"

"Not with individual players—usually. Have a problem with the institution at large." She watched me as she said the last, like she was looking for some...hint of something.

The back of my neck went hot. I resisted the urge to rub it. Hockey had given me everything: a way out from under my father's thumb and the stiflingly insular community I'd been raised in. Friends and a makeshift family. A purpose. And the closest thing to a father figure I'd ever had in Coach. Someone shitting on it was like someone shitting on me and everything that mattered.

I wanted this girl. Badly. But now I wanted her on her knees in front of me, mascara running down her face as she put that bratty mouth to good use.

"If you have a problem with hockey, why are you at a hockey party?" I countered.

Aviva hesitated.

"I dragged her here," Tovah said quickly, moving between us, likely to get her friend out of the line of fire.

Lie.

I could usually tell if people were lying. It was like an alarm that went off in my head.

And I hated liars. They were weak, cowardly, and would always betray you.

Was Aviva lying, too? Why couldn't I get a real sense of her the way I could everyone else? Why did she feel like such a mystery?

I moved around Tovah to Aviva's side. The beautiful brunette turned, keeping her gaze on me the way prey tracked their predators.

Smart. She *was* prey. My prey. I hadn't decided how I would devour her yet.

"Why are you here, princess?"

She looked past me. "Wanted to see how the other half lives."

I glanced at her sharply, looking her over again. Before, I'd been so caught up in her face and body, I hadn't truly taken her clothes into account. Now I saw it: pilling on her sleeveless turtleneck, a loose thread on the seam of her black skirt, rubber sole splitting from the canvas of her left sneaker.

Unlike most of the students at Reina, Aviva clearly did not come from money. Neither had I, technically. It was not inexpensive to raise six children on a single salary in Teaneck, New Jersey. My father was a "man of the book," and focused on religious studies. My mother worked as the receptionist at a doctor's office, and the rest of our income came from wealthier people in the community who would throw us a bone every once in a while.

I'd made my own future—first through my hockey

scholarship, and then via various sponsorships. That, with the likelihood of being drafted first, meant I didn't have to worry about me. But then my half-brother Marcus entered stage right. He was a billionaire on some sort of apology tour, and even though I refused to move out of the hockey house, he'd started a trust fund for me and my other siblings. It meant I'd never have to work again, but I didn't care—hockey was my life.

Aviva's money situation was clearly different.

No wonder she hated "princess."

Didn't mean I'd stop. It was fun making her face turn red.

"Are you always this angry, *princess*?" I drew the word out, just to see her eyes light with fire.

"Only when I have a good reason," she said.

"Aviva, let's go," Tovah said.

"Let's not," I said. "How about I show you how the other half dances?"

Still holding Aviva's wrist, I tugged her out of the kitchen and into the living room, where our second line had set up a makeshift dancefloor for us. I wove between the bodies of friends and classmates and girls I'd probably fucked at some point, until we were in the center of the space, surrounded, but somehow also alone.

"I have no idea why I'm letting you drag me around," she muttered, once we'd left her friend behind.

I grinned at her. "Because you're attracted to me."

"I'm not attracted to bossy guys."

Her body said otherwise. Especially when the song changed, to something low, sexy, dark, and kind of angry.

"I love this song."

"Yeah?"

Tell me what else you love.

I pulled her against me, wrapping my arms around her waist and lining her up against my hardening cock, not even bothering to ease her into it. She stiffened immediately.

"Relax, princess," I told her. "We're just dancing. I promise."

For now.

"Don't call me princess."

But her eyes dilated, and her body became pliant in my arms. Her submission was a turn on. If she liked me bossing her, I couldn't wait to show her just how dominant I could be. I moved my hips to the music and she followed my lead. Her scent flooded my senses again. I'd never even been a fan of apples before, but I knew I was going to become familiar with their taste, and my mouth watered at the thought.

"I'm going to ask you another question," I murmured into her ear.

She shivered. "Is that a statement or request?"

I chuckled. "I don't make requests. Better you know that now."

Her body softened even further into mine. She fucking liked that.

Fuck, I wanted this girl.

"Why are you here?" I asked again.

"You know, Jack Feldman, you have a lot of questions."

Avoidance.

"I do," I admitted.

"Why?"

I couldn't say...because you're a mystery when no one else is, and I want to know everything about you, from the color of your panties to your nightmares. Because the minute someone knows who I am, they'll do anything to please me because they want to use me, but you don't. Because you checked your friend's beer bottle without having to think about it. Because you seem to hate me, and it pisses me off but only makes me want you more.

Aviva was overwhelmed by me, and the only thing keeping her from fleeing was the thick attraction between us. She was intrigued, despite herself, and I had to rein in my impulse to steamroll her, or she'd be gone.

I like a chase, don't get me wrong.

But I preferred having her within my grasp.

So I ignored her question, asking the one that was really plaguing me. "Is scoring a hockey player on your bucket list?" The thought pissed me off...that I might be inter-changeable to her.

Rising onto her toes, Aviva wrapped her arms around my neck, and whispered in my ear. "There's only one thing on my bucket list, Jack Feldman. But even if it were a mile long, hockey players wouldn't be on it. *Ever.*"

Her honest answer was equally relieving and aggravating. I needed to know what that one thing was—and then I needed to get rid of it so her one thing was *me.*

"Then why are you dancing with me?" I asked.

"I'm not dancing with you."

I tightened my grip on her hips. "Feels like it to me."

"You forced me to."

I laughed again. She could've fought me harder, if she really wasn't interested.

"Princess, I think you like being forced."

Her gasp was quick, short, and made my cock go so thick and hard it hurt.

"Don't—"

But she smelled like apples and honey, and she was soft and warm and round, and so I didn't really care what protest she'd come up with next, or why she was anti-hockey, or why she seemed to both be drawn to me and hate me.

Nothing had ever felt as good as Aviva's body in my arms, tight, trapped—and I was going to take what I'd wanted since I'd first seen her.

Releasing her waist with one hand, I gripped the back of her neck to keep her from escaping, and lowered my mouth to hers.

She resisted at first, but the feel of her soft lips on mine, the sexy, surprised moan, it all made me want to push her harder. I took her mouth in a brutal, claiming, almost punishing kiss, forcing her lips open to take my tongue, got lost in the taste of her, the heat of her, the sound and smell and feel of her. She squirmed against me; I refused to let her go.

And then when she moaned again and softened into my arms, lowering her arms to wrap around my waist, well. That was it.

I was a motherfucking goner.

The world shifted on its axis. Even fucking gravity disappeared. The people around us certainly disappeared. Just me and her and this raging satisfaction.

Mine.

And then she bit my lip, hard. I pulled back.

"What the fuck? You want to play rough, princess?"

She raised a hand to her mouth, and the dazed look in her eyes didn't match her tone when she said, "I don't want to play rough. I don't want to play at all."

The lie pissed me off.

"Bullshit."

I leaned back in for more, but she was too fast for me, ducking underneath my arm and, with one final look at me, dashing out of the living room, out of the house—and, if she got her say, out of my life.

Too bad she'd caught the attention of a predator.

Like I said—I love a good chase.

So I followed her out the door, ignoring the surprise of the people around me. I had a princess to hunt, after all. And unlike Cinderella, she hadn't left me with a glass slipper.

Once outside, I saw her disappear around the corner of the block. Deciding to follow her by car, I reached into my pocket for my keys —only to discover that Cinderella hadn't left me a souvenir—she'd taken one.

My wallet, to be precise.

What the actual fuck?

Had she been playing me the whole time? Had the *innocent, I hate hockey players, especially you* thing been an act? Did she just want my wallet? If so, why? She was smart enough to know I'd cancel my credit cards immediately, so it couldn't be for money.

I touched my fingers to my lip. It was cut, and wet with blood.

Annoyed that she'd gotten one over on me—and equally intrigued that *anyone* had managed to steal from me without me realizing—I got in my car and followed her from a distance with the lights off. Aviva was up to no good, and I was going to be the one to catch her in her next act— whatever that happened to be.

She'd bit me.

Broken skin.

Made me bleed.

Two could play at that game. And when it came to games, I always won.

3

Aviva

I had absolutely no idea what I was doing. No fucking idea.

Shit.

As I slowed to a walk a few blocks from the hockey house, I took deep breaths, trying to clear my head.

That had not gone to plan. Not that my plans were airtight, but that had turned into a complete, confusing, frustratingly hot, sexy-ass shit show.

I'd had a Plan A and Plan B to seek justice for Asher.

Plan A: Break into the hockey team's locker room, get into Coach Joshua Jensen's secondary office, and see if I could track down the videos Asher said he'd taken when Jensen sexually assaulted him.

Plan B: Get to know some of Asher's teammates, and wile my way into their good graces, on the off chance that I could find out who else Jensen was abusing—if anyone—or knew what he'd done.

Plan B was why I'd transferred from Stanford to Reina.

After all, I needed to approach the plan sensitively: I'd learned in some of my psych classes that abuse victims, especially ones who'd been sexually abused, felt misplaced shame. And people in tightknit groups—like a hockey team —would feel pressured to keep silent or risk exile. And in this case, any player who spoke up might lose their place on the team as well.

Which was why I preferred Plan A. If I had tangible evidence, I could get my brother justice immediately—and get him back his spot on the team, his hockey scholarship, and his future. He'd lost all of it when he'd reported Coach Jensen to the university's administration.

If Plan A didn't work, I'd work on the hockey team to get the information I needed.

Asher wasn't a great font of information these days. He'd completely shut down when he'd quit the team and dropped out of school. Currently, he was living in our now-deceased great aunt's house, either working out aggressively, or hiding in his room, playing video games. He had no idea about my plans to expose his coach. He didn't even know I'd transferred. If he did, he'd be pissed. He certainly wouldn't tell me which other players knew about the abuse, and had sworn me to secrecy over the whole thing, out of his own misplaced shame. Shame that made me want to kill some-one, that filled me with so much helpless rage, I didn't have enough room to house it.

Sometimes, the unfairness of it all, seeing him in pain, made me feel like I was on fire. I would happily let the world burn, if it made him better or brought him any peace.

Thus, plans A and B.

But as they say: make plans, and the universe laughs.

I had not expected Jack Feldman. I had not expected to be so attracted to Jack Feldman—or for a gorgeous athletic deity to even notice my existence, much less zero in on me, flirt with me, dance with me...

...and kiss me.

I could count the decent kisses I'd had on one hand. And I'd never had a great kiss until now. He'd conquered me, and I'd let him, and god, it had felt so fucking good to let someone else be in charge for once, even just for a moment. To feel like someone else saw me, and liked what they saw. To be wanted, so badly.

And it was more than that. He smelled like—well, I couldn't describe what he smelled like, but whatever it was, it was *good*. Like my own personal temptation. His mouth had been warm and hard and punishing, the grip of his hand on the back of my neck menacing, but I got lost in him, anyway.

Until I'd wrapped my arms around his waist, slipped my thumb into his pocket—and felt his wallet.

A wallet that—just as I'd guessed—contained his ID card.

An ID card that probably had 24/7 access to the arena and locker room.

It had woken me up out of my Jack-Feldman-lust-daze. Here was my best shot. And sure, I hadn't planned for it, but that didn't mean I wasn't going to take advantage of the opportunity.

Also, I was pissed at myself for getting sucked into his current. So I'd bitten his lip, used the distraction, and ran. I could still taste his blood in my mouth. It tasted like rage and desire.

Something was seriously, seriously wrong with me. Maybe it was time for me to see a counselor, too.

Another block, and I'd reached campus. For a moment, it felt like there was someone behind me, watching me. But when I turned around, the only shadows came from the trees.

A text popped up on my phone. It was from Asher.

> How's the first week back?

I swallowed. That was just like him: Even though he was struggling with his own pain, he still checked in. Still cared about my life, about making sure *I* was okay.

I felt guilty for lying to him about where I was. He had no idea I'd transferred; I'd hidden any paperwork at the house and had kept it off social media. But he didn't need to know. If he did, he'd be worried, and demand I stop. And I wasn't going to stop. I wanted him to have his life back. Coach Jensen had made sure Asher couldn't get a hockey scholarship *anywhere*. No way for my brother to start over.

I responded.

> Fine. Same as always.

I paused, then added.

> How's therapy going?

> Fine. Same as always. #twinning

He was teasing, but I could feel his sadness through the phone. But what was there to say? At least he was going. I'd hated leaving him alone, but knowing he had a professional working with him made it a little easier.

> Good. Let me know if you need anything, okay?

Dots appeared and disappeared as he typed. Finally he responded with:

> You got it, kiddo.

Kiddo. It was our running joke. Even though I'd been born a minute before him, he liked to pretend he was older. He was trying to alleviate my worry, but I was still worried.

Which was why I had to stay focused on Plan A.

I pulled open Reina U's app on my phone and tapped on the map so I could figure out where the hell I was going.

During the day, Reina's campus—with its beautiful old brick buildings, covered in ivy, archways, and perfectly cared for grass, blanketed with leaves signifying the beginning of fall—was intimidating. At night, it was menacing, unearthly. Statues of founders and board members and other semi-famous, dead white men loomed above, casting shadows over the path. I hurried on my way, focusing on the plan. I wasn't positive that the coach would have recordings in his office, but I had to try. If not, there might be a spare set of keys to his house somewhere, or some other incriminating evidence. Although I really, really wanted those videos. They'd prove everything, without Asher having to say a word.

After our parents were murdered in a robbery gone wrong, and I'd gotten my scar, Asher had become everything to me. Great Aunt Gladys had taken us in when none of the wealthy Golds would even talk to us, and I was grateful to her. But after she died, it was Asher and I against the world. His wellbeing was my everything—and anyone who fucked with that...well.

I wasn't *actually* going to commit murder, but I was going

to destroy Coach Jensen's life. And anyone else's who'd stood by and let him harm Asher.

With that thought, I reached the arena. It was huge, and dark, and locked—until I tapped Jack's ID against the card reader.

With a click, the door opened.

As I strode down the corridor, lights flickered on, one after another. It smelled like sweat and ice and victory, and I hated it. It was too much of a reminder of the way Asher had been *before*, when Aunt Gladys and I had saved every cent to finance Asher's dream. He had been going somewhere in his life—*was* going somewhere, and I was going to get my brother back.

I *would*.

Reaching the locker room, I tapped the card against the card reader, opening the door—and wrinkled my nose the moment I stepped inside.

God, hockey locker rooms fucking stunk. I knew this well; I'd washed Asher's gear for him over the years, but it had been a while since I'd been so...surrounded by it. I wandered through, trailing my hand over the cubbies.

And felt like my heart was stabbed by an empty one that still read *Asher Gold* on the top in gold letters. Blinking away angry tears, I continued through the cubbies, passing a cubby with a jersey hanging: Wasserson, 69, and snorted, and then stopped at the last.

Feldman, 1.

Unable to stop myself, I traced a hand over the name and number, imagining I could smell that particular Jack scent, and sighed. I hated that he'd gotten to me the way he had, but he *had*. At twenty-one, I hadn't had much experience with guys. Hadn't really had the time, or the interest. Mostly the time. As a scholarship student at my old university, and now Reina, I had to work to cover food and books, as well as pay rent for the tiny apartment I now shared with Tovah. Between that and my psychology classes, I didn't have time for guys who probably would take one look at my scar and run away.

My one and only boyfriend, Tom, had been awful about it. We'd made out a lot—subpar kisses, I'd now realized. When I'd finally been ready to lose my virginity to him, he'd taken off my shirt, seen my scar—and had been disgusted. So disgusted, he blamed me for not being able to stay hard. I'd immediately dumped him.

After that, I had no interest in having sex. All my orgasms would continue to be courtesy of my own hand. I tried not to be ashamed of the scar, but Tom had done a number on me. I was never letting anyone see it, ever again. After all, it was an ugly reminder of the night Asher's and my life had gone to hell.

Releasing Jack's jersey, I turned, ready to focus on figuring out how to get into Coach Jensen's office.

Which was when someone grabbed me from behind.

I tried to scream, but their big hand covered my mouth as they dragged me backward. Terrified, I fought against them.

"Maybe instead of princess, I should've nicknamed you thief," Jack murmured in my ear.

Jack was here, holding me, surrounding me. And from his tone, he sounded like he wanted to kill me. I struggled against him, hitting and kicking and scratching wherever I could. It didn't matter. He just stood there, batting away my arms and legs like I was a kitten, waiting until I tired out.

Which I did, finally. As I breathed heavily, I realized he was as hard and thick as he'd been at the party. And, oh god, it shouldn't have, *it shouldn't have*. But knowing my fighting had made him hard, the feeling of him pressed against my ass, just his jeans and my skirt and our underwear the only barriers between us...it made me wet.

He wasn't done with his questions.

"Maybe I should've nicknamed you spy. Which is it, Aviva? What the hell are you doing in here?"

"None of your business," I tried to say against his hand, but it just came out as a mumble.

Angrily, I bit him for the second time that night.

"Careful there, little spy," he said, jerking me back against him harder. "I bite back."

Turning me around in his arms, he looked down at me, his dark eyes threatening to swallow me whole.

His *angry* dark eyes.

"How did you find me?" I gasped.

He backed me up against the wall between his and Judah's lockers, wrapping his huge hand around my throat. Panicking, I tried to fight him off, but he didn't release his grip. I could breathe fine, but the threat was there: if he wanted to cut off my air, he could. If he wanted to crush my throat, he could. I couldn't fight him, was helpless against him.

What was it like, to have that much power?

"I'm the one asking the questions now," he said. "Who the hell are you really, Aviva, and what are you doing on my campus, in my arena, in my locker room? What are you looking for?"

I couldn't tell him. I didn't know him and didn't trust him. And I'd made Asher a promise not to tell anyone what had happened to him—I wasn't going to risk informing Jack if he didn't already know. After all, nothing about our interaction, at the party or now, screamed "trustworthy" or "good guy."

So I kept my mouth shut.

This pissed him off.

"Are you a student at Tabb?" he asked, naming their rival school. "Trying to do hockey recon for their team?"

I snorted. "Like I give a shit about who wins a hockey game."

"Then what? Getting some scoop for a story for your journalist friend, Tovah?"

Despite the threat he posed, my ears perked up. "What kind of scoop?"

"Nuh uh," he said. "If you're trying to expose me— expose my *team* for Vi—" he cut himself off.

What had he been about to say? Did it have anything to do with his coach? Asher?

"What is there for me to expose?" I prodded. "Do you have any secrets, Jack Feldman?"

"Do you?" he countered, stroking a thumb up and down my pulse point.

I trembled from his touch.

"You do. I'll promise you this much—I'm going to find out every. Last. One."

4

Jack

She'd lied to me.
   Stolen from me.
   Ran from me.

And now she was trying to find dirt on me. Why else would she have broken into our locker room, and be hovering over my cubby? Aviva had secrets. Before, I'd only *wanted* to learn them. Now I needed to. To keep myself, my dreams, and my teammates safe.

Vice and Vixen were two black market aphrodisiacs that had flooded college campuses around the country this past year. And while neither I nor my teammates dealt Vice and Vixen, I was the guy who kept an eye on it at Reina and nearby schools for the dynastic family that ran the whole show—the Silvers. Sometimes, my teammates helped out. The police were in the Silvers' pocket, so there wasn't much worry there—but if Coach Jensen or the NCAA found out, I could say goodbye to my future.

And Coach would never look at me the same way again. Just the thought of his disappointment made me sick.

If Aviva wasn't here to steal info for a rival team, then she had to be searching for evidence about Vice and Vixen. And if not that, what could it possibly be? What was her agenda?

This girl who I had wanted so goddamned badly could potentially destroy everything that mattered to me. I had to resist squeezing her throat tighter. I didn't actually want to kill her, I wanted to find out what it was she was looking for. My baser instincts reared up, dark parts of myself I'd buried. I felt out of control with desire and it scared me. I wanted her, yes: to debase her, humiliate her, show her who was in charge.

What could she possibly be trying to find?

I needed to know. Needed her on her knees in front of me, sobbing, throat sore from my cock, face and tits covered in my come, and then I wanted to tease her and deny her and make her need me so badly, she'd talk.

I'd find out what she was here for, sate my curiosity, protect my team.

And then I'd be done with her. Done with this insane fucking infatuation.

Done with feeling powerless over my feelings for a complete stranger.

Releasing her neck, I started lifting up her shirt, determined to get my eyes and then my mouth and teeth on her tits. She cried out, covering her chest and turning away from me.

"What the hell are you doing?"

I caught her hands in one of mine, lifting them up over her head and pressing them back against the locker. "I told you, princess, I'm asking the questions now."

I worked my free hand up under her shirt, momentarily

distracted by the softness of her skin and stomach. She fought me like a bat out of hell, harder than she had when I'd first snuck up behind her, like she would die if I took her top off and saw her tits.

Just how innocent was she?

"Are you a virgin?" I asked casually, as I trailed my fingers upward.

"What does that have to do with anything?" she spat, raising a leg.

I caught the action before she could knee me in the nuts, easily sidestepping her. "Answer the question."

"No."

"No, you're not a virgin, or no, you won't answer me?"

"None of your business," she said through gritted teeth.

I hated the idea that she might not be a virgin. That some other man or men had gotten their hands on her, had been inside her. The possibility made me crueler than perhaps I would've been otherwise. In punishment, I pinched her nipple, so hard and so tight she shrieked.

The action must have offended her so much, she regained her strength, ripping her wrists out of my hand and slapping me across the face.

"Don't you fucking touch me," she gasped.

My right cheek burned where she'd hit me. She was feisty and brave, that was for sure. I tried to get myself under control, tried to think of what Micah or Marcus would say.

Eh, fuck that.

Grabbing her by the arms, I shoved her down so hard, her knees hit the hardwood floor.

"Damn, that sounded painful," I said. "Now, princess, you've got two options. One: You tell me why you stole my wallet and broke into the locker room. Two: I take off your shirt and see what you're really hiding." A thought occurred.

"Is it a wire?" It seemed a little absurd, but then so was finding a stranger in my locker room.

"It's not a wire," she cried, gripping the bottom of her shirt like it was a lifeline. "Jack, just let me go."

Why did keeping her shirt on matter so much to her?

I shook my head, annoyed at myself. I wanted to know everything about her, when I shouldn't care at all. "Talk."

I watched as she considered it. Whatever she was hiding was almost as important as her secret. Finally, she shook her head.

"I don't care what you do to me, you asshole. I'm not telling you *jack* shit," she said.

"Cute," I said. "But the next time you open that pretty mouth, it's either to give me answers, or to take my cock down your tight little throat." I squeezed her shoulder. "You hear me?"

She glared up at me, but didn't speak.

That wouldn't do.

I rubbed my cheek, eyes on the beautiful temptress kneeling in front of me, filled with dark, depraved thoughts. It was as if I were two men: One, completely shocked by my behavior—I should've called Coach and reported her, and he'd deal with it. The other, thrilled by what had fallen into my lap. I hated her for trying to fuck with my team, but I also wanted her. She was furious, and stunning, and I was going to do whatever I had to to get my power back.

Everything had been boring. Sex was boring. But this? This was as far from boring as you could get.

I grinned at her, fully aware of how menacing I looked as I slowly unbuttoned my jeans, pulling my cock out.

"Ever seen one this big before, princess? Do you even know what to do with it?"

She glared at me.

I opened my mouth to embarrass her further when I caught her pressing her thighs together.

She was turned on by this. By the humiliation, degradation, forcefulness, and the sight of my cock. She was my perfect girl—and might also be the enemy.

"Time to open up."

She shook her head, long dark brown hair flying everywhere. I wanted to see those rich brown curls spread across my pillow. For now, I'd content myself with using it as a rope to control her.

In a moment.

"Nowhere to go, no place to hide. Forced to submit to a *hockey player* you hate and his fat cock. Not much of a fairytale, is it, princess?"

Her eyes were filled with helpless rage.

Cock in one hand, I pinched her nose closed with the other. As I'd expected, her mouth popped open, and I took the opportunity to slide in deep.

"No teeth," I warned. "Or I'm ripping that shirt off your body, taking photos, and posting them on every social media site I can think of. Now, suck like a good girl."

She hesitated, like she was considering fighting me again.

"All over social media," I warned. "I'll send it to your family, too."

That must have done it. Staring up at me, eyes wet, mascara running down her face just like I'd imagined, she hollowed her cheeks and sucked. It was sloppy, messy. It was obvious she hadn't had much experience, and that calmed me. Maybe I didn't have to kill anyone. And her uncertainty and innocence, the heat of her mouth—I reveled in every second.

So did my cock. I had to resist coming immediately, and

try not to get lost in the feel of her mouth. Her hopefully innocent, seemingly inexperienced, now-mine mouth.

Pulling back and then thrusting deeper, I hit the opening to her throat. She gagged, and the sensation made me groan.

"Oh, fuck, Aviva, that's so good."

Once again, she tried to back up, but she had nowhere to go. I grabbed her hair, twisting it up into a ponytail and using it like reins to direct her mouth where I wanted it, tilting her head back so my cock could slide into her throat.

That felt *amazing*. She choked as I held myself there, enjoying the feeling of her throat bulging and working my cock as she tried to suck in air.

"I could keep you like this forever," I mused, my words no more than a growl. "Tie you up here in the locker room, get a ring gag, and use your mouth whenever I wanted. Leave you here for my teammates to find, let them take turns."

Tears streamed down her face, maybe from my words, maybe from her lack of air. Taking pity on her, I slid back, so it was only my crown between her lips, giving her space to breathe.

She gasped, inhaling before I shoved back into her mouth and throat, holding her in place so she could barely breathe again.

"How about it, Aviva? Want to be my little sex doll forever? You know, you can end this at any moment if you tell me what you're doing here and what you're looking to find."

She tried to say something around my cock, sending shivers up my spine.

Fuck, I was close to coming.

I pulled out again, squeezing the base of my cock to keep myself from finishing too soon.

"What was that, Aviva?"

"Go to fucking hell."

Damn.

I was annoyed, because I wanted answers, but also impressed. Anyone else would've cracked by now. This girl was made of iron and fire.

Part of me was relieved she wasn't answering me because I wasn't done playing with her. Cock painfully hard, I released her hair and mouth. Grabbing her around the ribs, I hoisted her up, carrying her backwards toward the bench in the center of the locker room and laying her flat on it. She still fought me, but she was losing steam. I lifted my shirt off my body, satisfied by the way her eyes tracked my stomach, abs, and pecs as they were revealed.

Whipping my shirt around until it resembled a rope, I used it to tie her wrists together, and then tie the ends around the top right leg of the bench, before straddling her legs to keep her from kicking me.

Trapped.

Perfect.

Slowly, carefully, I dragged her skirt down, ensuring maximum humiliation for her. Her breath grew ragged, but she didn't—couldn't—stop me. As I pulled them down, I became fixated on her simple black underwear, the dimples in her thighs, the constellation of freckles on her left hip. Barely able to control myself, I inched the tight skirt down, down, down, beyond triumphant when I saw the wet spot darkening her panties.

"This turns you on, princess? Being forced and humiliated?"

"Why, does it turn you on to force someone half your size?" she spat. "Make you feel big and strong, tough guy?"

But her hips jerked when I rested my palm above her pussy.

Her heat was so incredible, I almost forgot why we were here.

"You know," I mused, stroking her, satisfaction filling me when she jerked again, "I never thought it would turn me on, but I guess there's a first time for everything."

"Fuck you," she said again, rage turning her beautiful brown eyes dark.

"Oh, you're gonna," I promised her. "Just wait."

Leaving her skirt to gather between her ankles to help aid in restraining her, I slipped off her panties, down her legs, over one foot and then the other, before balling them up and pocketing them. The idea of gagging her with them was appealing, but I still had a purpose here—torture her into telling me the truth.

Seeing her body stretched out on the bench, her wet, barely touched, rose-pink pussy with its short curls protecting what was inside...fuck. I squeezed the base of my cock again, determined not to come yet. Nah, I was saving that for the finale.

"One more chance, Aviva. Tell me why you're here."

"Telling you isn't going to help, Jack. You'll hate the truth more than you hate not knowing," she said.

I almost flinched from her words. I couldn't imagine anything this girl could know that could be that scary. But a small part of me—the same part that had warned me not to turn around at the party—whispered, *don't let her drop this bomb on you.*

I didn't listen to it.

I was too motherfucking excited about what I was gonna do to her next.

Time to play.

5

Aviva

Don't cry. Whatever you do, don't cry.
And don't come, either.

I was enraged, humiliated, and so turned on I wanted to die. I'd never had an orgasm with someone else, never been this aroused, never had a *man's dick in my mouth*, and now I was half-naked and restrained by this jackass bully of a hockey player who thought he was god's gift to the world. Was I about to have my first orgasm with another person? *I didn't want it.* How the hell had I gotten here? How had things gone so wrong, so fast?

And why did they feel so right? Why did having zero control make me feel so...free?

I'd always been in control of everything. Aunt Gladys had been ill the whole time we'd lived with her, and so Asher and I had to step up. I wanted him to focus on hockey, so I'd taken care of everything: the house, the finances, food. Everything. I got so used to being in control, it never occurred to me that not having it could feel *good*.

Which was a horrifying thought. I couldn't like this. Couldn't enjoy being forced. How depraved was I?

Not nearly as depraved as Jack, at least. He stood in front of me, straddling the bench and my thighs, his cock so hard the head was purple and pressing up against his abs. My jaw hurt. My throat *ached*. I could still taste him.

And oh god, what was wrong with me? Because I wanted *more.*

Jack rested his huge hand on my pussy again. I clenched.

"This is too easy," he told me conversationally as he started tapping his fingers against the seam of my pussy and slowly working his dick with his other hand.

I whimpered.

A drop of precum appeared at the tip of his dick.

"That pathetic little sound makes me so hard, Aviva," he said. "Let's see if you'll make it again."

And then he started tracing little circles over my pussy, again and again, over and over, avoiding my clit but touching me everywhere else. Featherlight touches on my thighs, my hips, my mound. It took every last ounce of strength not to buck and chase his fingers and the pleasure they brought.

"Stop," I begged.

He paused. "Are you going to tell me why you're here?"

When I didn't respond, he started tracing little patterns again, making everything in me wind tighter.

"You know what I think? I think you aren't telling me because you don't want me to stop, not really. I think this tight little good girl pussy is secretly a greedy slut. She's the most honest part of you. I think—" he moved his fingers higher, higher, oh god, higher— "you want this, don't you?"

A circle and a tap, right on my clit.

I cried out, wound tight, so tight, terrified and exhilarated and ashamed of what would happen next—

—and then he removed his hand.

I trembled.

Relieved.

Disappointed.

For a moment, and then his fingers were back.

"Has anyone ever gotten you off, princess?"

He didn't deserve an answer.

"Didn't think so."

He slowly pushed one inside of me, and I jolted. Lifting his finger—his middle finger—up, he showed it to me.

"Look how fucking wet you are," Jack said, and if I didn't know better, if I didn't know how much he already hated me, I'd have thought he said it with awe. "Barely touched you, and you covered my finger." He watched me as he slid his finger into his mouth, sucking it.

"Guess even thieving, conniving little pussies taste good."

He sounded frustrated. He *was* frustrated. Because the next thing he did was shove two fingers inside of me this time, fast and hard. His fingers were long and thick and even as wet as I was, it hurt. The only fingers that had ever been inside of me were my own.

"Jack, please," I begged.

"Tell me why you're here."

If I told him, he might tip off Joshua Jensen and put him on his guard. I needed the element of surprise and secrecy, or I'd never get justice for my brother.

I inhaled slowly, trying to ignore him, his hard chest, his huge, angry cock, his fingers. He was torturing me to try to get me to talk, but he wouldn't win.

I closed my eyes to shut him out, and in punishment, he shoved three fingers inside of me this time.

Too much.

I screamed.

"Wonder if I could fit my whole fist inside you."

My eyes flew open as I bucked underneath him. "No!"

"Then talk."

But I couldn't.

Terrified, I shut my eyes again and braced myself for the pain that was sure to come next, which is why I was surprised when his fingers disappeared, and so did his body.

And then I was being dragged down the bench, my thighs spread open wide. I opened my eyes again, only to see his head descend between my legs. He licked me, once, twice, three times, and the threat of orgasm that had faded away came roaring back. I couldn't buck him off, he was gripping my thighs too hard with his big hands.

I was about to come this way, wasn't I? My first orgasm from someone else, and it was happening without my consent, tied to a bench in a locker room that stunk of pheromones and long-stale sweat. It felt so good and I hated it, hated him...

Pain, sharp and shocking. Jack had bitten my clit, and he wasn't letting go.

I shrieked, so loud the whole campus must have heard me.

It hurt so bad.

It felt so good.

Finally, Jack lifted his head, his lips wet—with me.

"Talk," he said. "Or this is going to get worse."

"Fine, then do your worst," I gasped.

"With pleasure."

He lowered his head, licking and sucking and biting—

my pussy, my inner thighs, my clit. Each time I thought I would come, each time he stopped just before it happened. Each time, he demanded I tell him the truth—each time, it got more and more difficult to keep silent. Time blurred, or maybe paused, I wasn't sure. Overwhelmed, overwrought, I sobbed, my cries mixing with Jack's groans and the slapping sound of his hand on his own cock as he took turns punishing me and pleasing himself.

Finally, he stopped. I opened my eyes, afraid of what I would see. His own dark eyes were almost black with lust and anger as he released my weakened legs and rose to his feet in front of me. In that moment, I understood why he was treated like a god here.

"Poor little princess," he crooned in a voice thick with mockery and desire he didn't even bother to hide. "So desperate and so afraid. Just waiting for my cock to rip you apart."

"Jack," I whimpered, begging. "Please…"

"Please what. Please stop, or please make you come?"

I didn't know the answer.

Growling, he used one hand to spread me wide, and with the other, guided his cock forward, the crown pressing against me, seeking an opening. The sensation was too much—too terrifying, too goddamned good. I couldn't take anymore. I couldn't lose my virginity this way. I refused.

"Stop, Jack, please! Not like this! I'll tell you why I'm here, okay? Just please, don't do this to me."

Don't do this.

Don't make sex this humiliating and horrible.

He froze, his chest heaving, then released my hips and pulled away, slowly, almost reluctantly. Almost like he regretted winning.

But this was not a man who ever lost.

"I won't fuck you this time," he said. "But we aren't done here."

And then, just to reinforce his own words, he pumped his cock with his fist, hard and fast, eyes on mine, and that alone brought me closer to my own orgasm.

I shook, teeth clenched, trying so hard not to follow him over the cliff before me into an abyss I wasn't sure I'd ever be able to climb out of.

"Oh, you're going to come for me, princess," he promised.

I opened my mouth to disagree, just as he caught my clit between his thumb and finger and *pinched*—tossing me over the edge and sending me into freefall.

It was like nothing I'd felt before. Huge and powerful and overwhelmingly raw. I wanted to bask in it; I wanted to run from it.

Jack didn't give me a choice. With a strangled shout, he threw his head back and came. Wet heat splashed over me —my pussy, my bare stomach, my shirt. The shock of being used that way only seemed to draw out my orgasm, and I hung on for dear life.

Finally, he sighed.

"Fuuuuuuuck."

He leaned over me, wiping his wet hand over my lips, painting me with his release and my shame.

He moved his leg like he was dismounting a horse, kneeling in front of me as I shivered, overwrought.

"Now. Talk."

6

Aviva

Silently, Jack untied my arms from the bench before surprising me by rubbing life back into them. I lay there, panting, staring up at the ceiling, counting the white squares that decorated it like an empty Tic Tac Toe board. That was funny, because just like with Tic Tac Toe, there was no winning here.

I drew in a breath, and began, even as I regretted the words. I was breaking my promise to my brother by telling someone, and I couldn't tell if I was more ashamed of that or of what had just happened.

Either way, I was weak, and I hated myself for it.

"My last name is Gold. I'm Asher Gold's sister."

Nothing.

"Your head coach, Joshua Jensen? He abused him."

Jack rolled his eyes.

I narrowed my own. How dare he be so dismissive! "For two years, ever since Asher joined the Kings."

Jack snorted.

I turned my head to look at him. "You think that's funny?"

"Coach was right," he said.

"About what?"

Jack cleared his throat. "Asher's been playing like shit for a long time. Kept letting the puck past him. He's a weak link. Coach had to tell him he was being replaced as a starter. When your brother found out, he lost his mind—"

"That's a lie!"

"—Thought he could blackmail Coach by making false claims against him—"

"They're not false! They happened!" I practically yelled, I was so incensed.

"Bullshit," he scoffed.

I tried to control my anger. I didn't have to be a psych major to know he was deep in denial.

"Right," I said. "I bet you think that Boy Scout leaders, priests, and all men in positions of authority are good guys."

He pinched the bridge of his nose, like my words pained him. Well, they should.

"No, I know shit like this happens in the NCAA and on teams all the time. With *bad* coaches. But Coach—Josh—is a good man. The *best*."

"Maybe you think that, Jack, but I know my brother. I've seen his pain. He's—" I stopped myself. Jack didn't deserve to know how badly Asher was hurting. How he'd cut himself off from everything and everyone. Thrown out all of his hockey gear, his posters, everything. Gotten rid of our subscription to ESPN, stopped listening to Kendrick Lamar. He wasn't himself, and I was determined to change that.

But how could I, when Jack was in my way, and wouldn't listen to me?

He continued, speaking over me. "Your brother was

pissed, especially because there were big sponsorships on the line, so he threatened Coach: either he got to keep his spot, or he'd tell the faculty, the paper, everyone that Coach had assaulted him. Josh was concerned, and tried to get Asher the help he needed, financial and mental, but your brother is a greedy asshole with a huge ego and an axe to grind. Josh knew this was coming, and I—we—told him we'd back him up." He glanced at me, anger and revulsion in his eyes. "Had no idea that Asher had a greedy sister who was as conniving and fucked in the head as he is."

It was like he'd punched me in the gut, and I'd lost my ability to breathe. "I'm sorry, what?"

"It's obvious from your clothes. Asher was a scholarship student, and so are you. You don't have money, so you're desperate—and what better way than to lean on your brother and his sponsorships and future NHL contract? Hate to break it to you, princess, but you're going to be wearing those cheap clothes for a while. Asher's not going anywhere in life—he's lucky that Coach didn't take action against him."

Bile, sour and burning, rose in my already aching throat. I wanted to *kill* Joshua Jensen, and Jack, too.

"So what's your plan?" he asked. "Plant a confession in coach's office that says 'Yeah, I did it,' signed Joshua Jensen?"

"Hardly." This time it was my turn to snort. "I was looking for the videos."

"Videos?"

"Your sick fuck of a *coach* recorded every 'session' with my brother." Just saying the words made me want to throw something. Ideally at Jack.

Jack glared at me like I was vile. "My *coach* saved my goddamned life, Aviva. You don't know—" he paused. "It doesn't matter. You don't fucking deserve to know. He's a good guy whose only real fault is giving everything to his team and being too trusting. It bit him in the ass with your brother; I won't let it happen to him again."

"But the videos—"

"There are no videos, unless your plan was to plant them."

I glared. "Do I look like I'm hiding videos anywhere?"

Waving this off, he said, "My brother's a computer genius. I know you can plant shit digitally."

He grabbed my wrist, dragging me off the bench without much care. I grabbed my skirt, trying to pull it up my shaking legs, but Jack had no regard for my comfort. He tugged me forward, even though I had one leg in my skirt, one out. I tripped and would've fallen if he hadn't caught me with hard, cruel arms. "That is, unless you were planning on planting some doctored ones. Asher's a film major, right? Always thought that was weird, but it makes sense, now."

"Do you hear yourself? You're so desperate to keep your coach on his pedestal, you'll convince yourself of anything."

He laughed again, no humor in it. "I know when someone's lying, Aviva. I learned at a young age that people lie as easily as they breathe. You might have a cute pair of tits and a tight little cunt, but that won't fool me into falling for your bullshit and betraying the only real family I've ever had."

"Fine." I blinked away my tears, refusing to let the asshole see me cry. I was crying because I was angry, not because I was sad. "If you're determined to ignore the truth staring you in the face, then let me go."

"Nah," he said, keeping me locked in the cage of his arms. "You're not going anywhere."

7

Jack

Just like I'd thought: Aviva was a motherfucking liar.

I knew liars. Well. My eldest brother, Micah, had lied when he'd told me as a kid that he was coming back for me, that he wouldn't leave me with our abusive father.

My mother had lied when she said she'd protect us, no matter what.

My father had lied when he said he loved us. When he hadn't told us about his other family.

The only person who had never lied to me was Coach Jensen. He'd seen me skating on an ice rink at the age of thirteen, skated up to me, and said, "Kid, you've got real talent. Trust me, and I'll make sure you go far in life and get everything you want."

He'd kept his promise. Interceded with my parents, gave me a place to stay when shit at home got too horrible to be there, paid for all my hockey gear and training because god knew my father wouldn't fork over the money. He encouraged me, pushed me to be my best, and when he got the job at Reina, recruited me to come here. Together, we'd built a team, a family. I owed everything to him.

But as I stared down at the girl trapped in my arms, captivated by the angry tears sliding down her cheeks, I wondered—for just a moment—if I'd missed something. Because my internal lie detector was silent.

No. She was lying; I was too distracted by her pussy, that was all.

Some coaches were leeches who fucked with their athletes, but I *knew* Coach. He'd never once touched me, never even hinted at it. And Asher had always been sullen, angry, secretive. He'd had his own agenda. It stood to reason his fucking sister would be the same.

"Let me go," she repeated, bringing me back to the present.

I really should've. But despite her conniving bullshit, I wanted her. Her goddamned body, the sounds she'd made when she'd come, even her tears were a revelation. She smelled like sweat and fear and my come, like sex, sweet and tart. That goddamned apples and honey smell, it would haunt me forever.

I hadn't even gotten my cock in her tight pussy, and I wanted her more than I'd ever wanted anyone. It was like I was two men: one, feral, ravenous, determined to punish her and ruin her for anyone else. Turn her into my little fucktoy and humiliate her as I defiled every one of her holes. It was the least she deserved. The other, territorial and weirdly protective, like she belonged to me and I needed to keep her safe, be gentle around her inexperience.

I ignored that second man; it was an absurd impulse. I didn't want to protect her, I wanted to break her.

And I was going to. After all, she was mine to break.

"Here's what's going to happen," I informed her. "You have two choices. One option: I text Coach and tell him you broke into the arena, and he calls the police. You get arrested, you lose whatever scholarship you probably have, and get a permanent mark on your record. Say goodbye to your dreams and goals. On top of that, I'll make sure everyone here at Reina and in the hockey world at large knows your brother tried to blackmail the coach. The NHL doesn't take kindly to shit like that."

"They won't believe you," she argued.

"Oh, they'll believe me. You have no evidence. It's your word against mine. This university, this city, loves both of us. But you? You're an outsider, a stranger, trying to blow up the Frozen Four for us. Who do you think they'll listen to, Aviva? You and your loser brother, or Jack Hat Trick Feldman?"

Her shoulders slumped. She knew I was right.

So I continued. "Now, there is an option B: I don't tell Coach Jensen, I don't call the police. In return, you're mine. You're going to become my filthy little fucktoy. Whatever I want, you give me. Anytime, anywhere, any which way."

"Absolutely not."

God this woman. I couldn't help but admire her—here I was, threatening to destroy her life, and she still stood strong against me.

But as strong as she was, I was stronger.

I released her with one arm to pull my phone out of my pocket.

"Cool. I've got Gehenom PD's number saved in my phone. It comes in handy to have a few cops in your pocket."

Especially with my ties to Vixen and Vice. Getting the local police force to turn the other way and ignore what was happening on campus came in handy. So did having a billionaire half-brother with a guilt complex; Marcus might not agree with my tactics, but he'd keep me out of trouble.

Aviva grabbed for my phone, but it was easy to hold it over her head.

"Nuh uh, little thief," I scolded. "I won't fall for that pickpocket shit twice. Siri, call Gehenom PD."

The phone started to ring.

Once.

Twice.

Before it could ring a third time, Aviva spoke up. "Okay! Okay!"

Fuck yeah.

I pressed end on the call. "Okay, what?"

"Okay, I'll do it."

"You'll be my filthy little fucktoy?"

She nodded.

"Say it," I ordered.

"I'll be your f—" she stumbled over the words, her whole body trembling.

"Say it, or I call them back," I threatened.

"I'll be your *filthy little fucktoy.*" She spat out the words. If she could've killed me with her eyes alone, she would've. Her anger was stunning.

"Hearing you say that makes my cock hard." I shoved my hips against hers, grinding against her soft, bare stomach, so she could feel the evidence.

She was mine. For as long as I wanted her, I could do whatever the hell I wanted to her. Every dark impulse I'd ever had, everything I'd ever fantasized about, I could do to her perfect, soft body. And make sure she loved all of it, even as she hated me.

Mine.

Giving into impulse, I grabbed her hair, tugging her

head back, and kissed her. It was brutal, punishing, and at first, she resisted. I bit her lip as a reminder, and she opened her mouth. Taking advantage, I licked at her mouth, exploring her taste and reveling in her reluctant submission. I wanted to roar in triumph.

Instead, I broke the kiss. I had early morning practice, and besides, I was too tempted to fuck her pussy now, when what I really wanted to do was build the anticipation for me and the fear for her. I had all the time in the world.

"This is gonna be fun," I told her, releasing her and retrieving my shirt and the ID card she'd stolen from me.

Aviva stumbled backward and fell on her ass, and I had to force myself not to catch her.

Instead, with one long last look at her cowering, half naked on the floor, I turned to go.

"See you soon, princess," I promised, and, her panties in my pocket, I opened the door and exited, letting it swing shut on her furious sobs.

Aviva

Deviant Psychology and Divergent Behavior was my favorite class this semester. As a transfer, it had been hard to get into the senior seminar, but being a double major in premed and psychology had helped —as had my advisor.

It was taught by Dr. Dylan Johnathan, a psychologist rumored to be the cousin to three billionaire brothers—one of whom had died recently under mysterious circumstances. You couldn't tell he was grieving, though. He was charming, brilliant, and, if I had to be honest, attractive, with black hair that fell in his eyes and horn rimmed glasses he took off when he got really excited about a discussion topic.

As I walked into class on the Monday after Jack had caught me in the locker room, I wasn't thinking about class —or the fact that we were being assigned our semester long project and project partner today.

No, I was thinking about sex blackmail. The party, the locker room, Jack's interrogation, my confession—it had played on repeat in my mind all weekend. I swore I could still feel Jack's head between my legs, feel his cock in my throat.

After he'd left me in the locker room, I'd quickly dressed —without my underwear, because he'd stolen it—and snuck out of the arena. I'd called Tovah and she'd left the party to come get me. When we got back to the apartment and she'd seen me with my makeup all over my face, Jack's come drying on my top, she'd been near apoplectic, although she waited until I got out of the shower to start her own interrogation.

"What the hell happened to you?" she'd asked. "You were dancing with Jack Feldman, and then you disappeared. Did he do this?"

I hadn't been able to stop myself from crying.

"I'll fucking kill him," she said fiercely. "We need to go to the police."

But if Jack were telling the truth—and I figured he was —going to the police wouldn't solve anything. He had them in his pocket, and they wouldn't listen to me. Instead, Jack would fulfill his threat to tell said police *and* Reina University's administration that I'd broken into the hockey arena. I'd lose my scholarship, and the mark on my record would mean no grad school, no future in psychology. What was worse, he'd make sure Asher had no chance at a future as well.

I couldn't let that happen. I pleaded with Tovah, begging her not to tell anyone, aware that I was falling into the trap so many sexual assault survivors fell into, including my brother, but unable to do anything about it.

And that helplessness made me hate Jack most of all.

After she'd agreed to keep quiet, I'd gone to my room and stayed in bed for the remainder of the weekend.

But now it was Monday, I had class, and I was determined not to think about Jack Fucking Feldman. I hadn't heard from him, so hopefully he'd forgotten about me. I was going to focus in class, and then I was going to go to the tech support center, make friends with someone who worked there, and trick them into helping me figure out how to hack Joshua Jensen's login on Google drive.

Taking my usual seat at the conference table, I smiled distractedly at Dr. Johnathan. He looked up at me, slowly taking off his glasses and rubbing them on his shirt.

"Aviva! How was your weekend?"

How the hell did I answer that without blushing?

"Fine."

"Just fine?"

This time, my smile was a little forced. Dr. Johnathan seemed like a nice enough man, but he was in a position of authority—and I didn't trust men in positions of authority. Besides, I could hardly tell him what had happened to me in the middle of his classroom. "Just fine, Dr. Johnathan."

He rolled his eyes. "How many times can I ask you guys to call me Dylan?"

This time, I smiled for real. "Just fine, Dylan."

As I pulled my old and dented laptop from my bag, I felt heat at my side as someone dropped into the seat next to me. Dr. Johnathan—Dylan—cleared his throat.

"You guys, we have a new student in our class. I know it's a week after classes started, but even though he's a Classics major, he made a good argument for being included and well, I couldn't really turn it down." Dylan muttered something under his breath.

Curious, I turned to look at the newcomer. What was a Classics major doing in an advanced psychology seminar?

My heart got stuck in my throat.

Jack sat next to me, a smirk on his gorgeous face, turning the harshness of his chiseled face and square jaw almost warm with mischief.

I *hated* him.

"Surprised to see me, princess?" he asked.

"What are you doing here?" I hissed.

School was my safe place, where I could get lost in intellectualism and what Asher teasingly called "mental masturbation" and forget all of my stressors and worries for a bit. Where it didn't matter that I was one of the poorest students at this school, because all my professors cared about was my brain. I missed my old university, but I'd managed to carve out a small space for myself at Reina already, and didn't want to lose it. Or worse, have it taken from me.

Having Jack here was like reality forcing its way into my safe place—without my fucking consent.

"My independent study got canceled, so I needed a new elective." A private smile played across his lips. "Deviant psychology sounded...intriguing." He leered at me, lust and mockery turning his gray eyes silver.

"Bullshit," I snapped under my breath.

He nodded. "It's cute you thought I'd let you out of my sight."

The implication that he was following me made my cheeks go hot.

They turned hotter when he casually wrapped an arm around the back of my chair.

"Stop it!" I whispered, glancing around the room to see if anyone else was looking at us.

They all were. That's what happened when you were the target of the most popular, powerful guy on campus.

Fuck my life.

Some students had awed looks on their face, probably

from having Jack in their near vicinity. Some had lust in their eyes, which I wasn't going to hold against them. Not when Jack was in a gray t-shirt that strained over his abs, displaying a small sliver of his stomach and the beginnings of a treasure trail. Besides, they didn't know he was evil.

A couple had sour looks on their face—pointed at me. I resisted the temptation to curl up in my chair and hide from their scrutiny, making myself straighten my shoulders and lift my chin. It had an added benefit of creating a few inches of distance between my back and Jack's arm.

Tilting his head toward mine, Jack murmured, "Sit back and get comfortable. Whenever, wherever, whatever, remember?"

I froze, and then with a deep breath, forced myself to lean back against my chair and his arm.

"Good girl."

Even though the praise felt like an insult, it sparked unwanted arousal in my belly.

He raised his voice, looking around at the rest of the students in my—our—class.

"Hope you're all hockey fans." He bestowed a movie star smile on them, and they laughed in delight. I watched him, sensing that this was for show. It was common for predators —especially those who exhibited deviant behaviors—to hide their sociopathy or psychopathy behind a mask. Had anyone else seen what lay behind Jack's hockey king mask, or was it only me?

"Maybe we should start class? I know I have a lot to catch up on, and I can't wait," he said to Dylan. *That* seemed real. Pointed.

So did Dylan's barbed, "Of course. Happy you're here," as he stared sourly at Jack's hand on my arm. I had no idea what that was about, but it made me deeply uncomfortable.

Even more uncomfortable when Jack slid his hand up my arm and rested it on the back of my neck in a light but threatening grip. I felt like a fly in a spider's web.

Trapped.

Caught.

Just like in the locker room.

Breathe, Aviva. He can't do anything to you in front of your professor and nine other students.

But couldn't he? How far did Jack Feldman's power reach?

Dylan cleared his throat. "We've been talking for the past week about what deviant and divergent behaviors *are*, and how they're defined differently by sociologists, criminologists, and, of course, psychologists." He took an exaggerated bow and the class tittered.

Jack, however, didn't.

"We've talked about Merton's theory of deviance. Which is what, Aviva?"

"It's the tension between means and goals in a society—deviance is a way for people to achieve goals they couldn't through socially acceptable means," I responded.

He nodded, approval in his eyes. Jack tensed beside me.

"We've also talked about Freud's theories. Where does Freud think deviance comes from, Mr. Feldman?"

I startled. Dylan never called students by their last names, and it seemed a little...mean to ask a brand new student to define an unfamiliar theory. There was clearly a tension between the two men; but if so, why had Dylan let Jack into our class?

Along with that thought came another, scarier one: what was Jack's plan? He'd already proved on Friday night that he didn't believe in limits or the word "no." Just how far would he go, to get what he wanted? And what was it he wanted? I didn't believe for a second it was me, not really. I might hate him, but I also realized just how out of my league he was. He'd been surrounded by girls at the party.

A chuckle sounded next to me, almost in my ear. "Too much repression," Jack said, and the class laughed.

Dylan stiffened.

I blushed.

"Very good, Mr. Feldman," Dylan said, but it didn't sound like he thought it was very good.

He turned to the rest of us. "For the remainder of the semester, you're all going to pair up and find an example of deviance. This can be fictional, mythological, historical, even present day. And then what you're going to do is write a paper, part research, part argumentative, exploring whether the deviance fulfills Merton's theory...or Freud's."

One of the girls in class who'd been friendly with me, raised her hand. "But Dylan, there's an uneven number of us now."

Dylan nodded. "True. There's going to be one...three-some." He made a hammed-up look of disgust. "Please don't turn that into a joke. I expect more of you."

Everyone laughed again.

"And since you're adults, you can choose your own part-ners. I'll give you five minutes."

The girl turned to us. "How about it, you two?" she asked cheerfully.

Jack shook his head, looking bashful. "I'd say yes, but Aviva already claimed me as her partner." His smile turned sharklike. He covered his face with his hand, leaning forward and stage whispering, "She gets jealous."

She laughed. "No worries."

"What the hell are you doing?" I hissed at him. "I don't want to work with you."

Jack's gaze turned cool, but he leaned back into me, making sure no one could hear him but me. "You don't get to decide what you need anymore, princess. I don't think you get it. You're no longer in charge. You lost the privilege of making your own decisions when you tried to take down my team."

Before I could come up with something, Dylan cleared his throat. "Alright, looks like everyone's partnered up. Right?"

One guy—also wickedly attractive, wearing a pin of a rose with thorns—put his hand up.

"Sebastian, you need a group?" Dylan looked around the room, landing on me—and where Jack's arm still claimed my chair, and me, by proxy. "How about you join Aviva and Mr. Feldman?"

Jack stiffened. "Nope," he said, popping the 'p.'

Dylan's face reddened. "Mr. Feldman, last I checked, I'm the professor. And—"

"Nope," Jack repeated.

Dylan sighed. "Sebastian, you can partner up with Olivia and Annabelle."

With that, he started today's lecture.

"Let's talk some more about Freud today, and, 'repression.' As we all know, Freud is not beloved by modern day psychology, especially the...feminist branch..."

Pretending to take notes, I glanced over at Jack, who was watching our professor with an indiscernible look. "What was *that* about?"

Jack shrugged. "Not your business. Your only business from now on is keeping my cock happy."

I glanced around, terrified someone had heard, but everyone's eyes were on Dylan. None of them saw Jack as he gripped the back of my neck and held me in place. I tried to breathe regularly for the rest of class, ignore Jack's presence next to me, the threat of him, the sheer, brutal size of him, the knowledge that the nightmare hadn't ended like I'd hoped.

It had barely begun.

9

Aviva

When class ended, I expected Jack to release my neck and swagger off to wherever he came from—the pits of hell, most likely.

As the rest of the students filed out of the room, he released my neck, stretching out his own before standing up from his seat and holding out a hand.

"Shall we, princess?"

"Stop calling me that," I said. It was almost becoming automatic at this point. "And stop with this faux gallantry. I know who you really are."

Jack stood there patiently, waiting for Dylan to leave.

"Everything okay, Aviva?" Dylan asked, sounding concerned. I considered, for one moment, just one moment, telling him everything, but I knew nothing good would come of it. Jack's threats were clear: If I exposed him for assaulting me and blackmailing me, he would tell the administration I'd broken into the locker room—and the NHL that Asher had "falsely" accused Joshua Jensen of abuse and assault. I couldn't take that risk. No, I was putting up with this bullshit for Asher's future, and my own. Like it or not, Jack Feldman was right: he owned me. I just didn't have to make it easy for him.

"Everything's fine! See you next week!" I said.

"You sure?"

"You heard her," Jack said.

Dylan stiffened, glaring at Jack. But whatever power Jack had over him held. With one last glance at us, he left us alone in the room.

The moment our professor was gone, Jack's mask disappeared. He loomed over me, pushing a strand of my hair behind my ear and lingering there, the gentle motion at odds with his cold, hard expression. This was the real Jack Feldman, not the golden boy he played in public.

It was terrifying how gorgeous he was—short, dark hair, angry gray eyes framed by dark, thick lashes that would have almost made him look pretty if it weren't for the square, sculpted, currently tight jaw and beautifully cruel mouth. That mouth had been on me, had kissed me, had licked me and sucked me and briefly made me forget everything including who I was and what mattered to me. In some ways, it was good he hated me, because it would keep whatever happened between us as strictly blackmail. A kind, caring Jack Feldman? That had heartbreak written all over it.

Jack moved away from me, checking something on the door. Seemingly satisfied, he shut it and locked it. The click echoed in the small lecture room with a frightening finality. I jumped.

Grabbing Dylan's chair, he pulled it out from the table and placing it against the door before leaning back in it like he didn't have a care in the world.

"Come here," he ordered.

Everything in me screamed to disobey. I hadn't come this far in life to become some asshole jock's meaningless plaything.

"Aviva." Jack's voice was like a slap. "Come. Here."

Reluctantly, with daggers in my eyes, I rose and walked toward him.

"Such an angry little spy," he murmured, pulling me between his legs. "You must hate this: being forced, not having control. Or maybe you love it."

I stiffened at the jab.

He smirked at me. "Either way, don't worry: it's only going to get worse." His voice went hard. "Now, *strip.*"

Out of reflex, I covered my chest, leaning away from him.

"Lower your arms," he ordered.

I shook my head. Anything but that. I could handle a lot, but I couldn't handle the revulsion on Jack's face when he saw my scar.

"Not my shirt, Jack. *Please.*"

He considered, gazing up at me. My whole body tingled, the way it had at the party when we'd first looked at each other. Once again, it felt like he could see right through me, like all of me was bare. I forced myself to keep my head raised high.

Finally, he smirked. "Fine. But one of these days I'm going to rip off your top and look at your naked breasts. You won't know when it's coming, but I promise—it's coming."

Fear filled me, but I didn't argue. It wasn't worth it.

He jerked his chin at my jeans. "Get to it."

Standing so close to him, it was a struggle to unbutton them and shove them down my legs, especially since he didn't help, just watched me, a small smirk playing on his lips. Lifting one leg and the other, I kicked them away.

Eyes on my underwear, Jack's nostrils flared. And then he shocked me when he leaned forward, shoving his nose against my pussy.

Holy fucking shit, he was *smelling* me.

He dropped a soft kiss on my clit above my underwear, gazing up at me through his dark lashes. The tenderness of the action, which had to be fake, was belied by his words.

"Your little pussy smells so good. Already wet and ready for me. Raw and juicy and..." He kissed my clit again, and my thighs clenched. "Honest. Unlike the rest of you."

I protested before I could stop myself. "I'm not a liar."

"Aren't you?"

Silence stretched between us, his hot breath on me, his eyes on mine, unspoken words between us. Some language being spoken that I couldn't, *wouldn't* understand. I *refused* to. Jack couldn't see me, know me, and I didn't want to know him, either.

That way lay dragons.

He sat back, all business now. "Lose the panties."

I gulped, shoving them down my legs and kicking them out of the way.

His gray eyes were so dark, they were almost black. "So. Fucking. *Wet,*" he said, his words a sharp staccato that slapped the walls of the small seminar room.

"Take me out," he ordered. "And grab the condom out of my left pocket."

I balked. A blowjob was one thing, an orgasm...fine. Whatever. I'd survived it. But actual sex? When I'd never had sex before? Much less with someone who loathed me like Jack did? I wouldn't survive it.

"I'm not fucking you."

He raised an eyebrow. "Then pull my phone out instead. There are some calls I need to make."

"Fine," I spat.

"Now, that doesn't sound very enthusiastic," he mused. "I expect a little more eagerness from you, princess."

"Fine, *master*," I said sweetly, trying to burn him to ash with my eyes.

He chuckled. "Much better."

Reaching into his left pocket, my hand brushed against his cock, separated from the skin of my fingertips by threadbare fabric. He was already hard, and without thinking, I stroked him. Only once, but that was enough.

He groaned.

A thrill fluttered in my bones. Maybe I had some power, after all.

Locating the foil packet with its serrated edges, I pulled it out of his pocket.

Magnum. Figured.

I held it out for him to take.

He shook his head, once to the right, once to the left. "No, you're going to do the honors."

"So not only am I being forced to have sex with you against my will, I have to play a role in my own destruction?"

He grinned, wide and sharklike, his teeth flashing in the dim room. It had gotten late; I hadn't even realized. I'd been too swept up in Jack's perversions.

"Now you're getting it," he said.

Without any idea of what else to do with it, or where else to put it, I lifted the condom packet to my mouth, biting my teeth down on it to keep it in place. That taken care of, I focused on my task at hand, lowering my hands to Jack's waistband. I unbuttoned the top button of his jeans with jerky hands before gripping the zipper pull.

Jack put out a hand on mine to stop me. "Slow down, princess. Anticipation is the key to good sex. And," he grimaced, "I'd rather if you didn't catch my cock in the zipper."

"Wish I had thought of that," I muttered. "Although with my luck, you have analgesia." I was surprised by his low, husky laughter.

Jack looked as surprised by his response as I was. "You're funny. And clever."

"You know what that means?"

"The inability to feel pain." He winked at me. "I'm more than a pretty face."

Ugh.

I rolled my eyes, ignoring him. Slowly, I pulled his zipper down, revealing black boxer briefs, and the hard, thick outline of his cock. He inhaled, lifting his hips and helping me pull his jeans down before kicking them off and sending them to join my own clothes. Closing my eyes for one moment, just one moment, to center myself before what came next, I gently lifted the waistband of his boxers up and over his cock, revealing it as, once again, he lifted his hips and I pulled off the only remaining barrier between him, and me.

I stood before him, determined not to tremble but shaking regardless, eyes on his long, thick cock, which curved slightly to the left. He was circumcised, and even though his was only the second dick I'd ever seen, and the first I'd touched, it was so much better than Tom's uncut, skinny dick.

But why was I thinking about my tormentor's dick in positive terms?

Jack wrapped his big hand around his big cock and gave it a short, hard tug.

"Like what you see, princess? I guess I didn't give you much time to peruse the other night. Well, look your fill," he invited. "But I'm going to play while you get better acquainted."

He slipped his free hand between my thighs, gathering the wetness gathered there, dragging it up to my clit and circling, circling, circling. My whole body went tight and I gasped, writhing against his fingers, still captivated by the way he worked his cock with his other hand.

Slowly, he pushed one thick finger inside me, then two. He pushed them deep, curving them up in a come hither motion, and began rubbing them up against a part of me that had never been touched before. An unfamiliar sensation took over my body, demanding release. Over and over, pleasure spiraled inside of me, insistent and urgent with nowhere to go, until with a pop, it spilled over and with a shocked jerk and a cry, I came.

Everywhere.

The condom packet tumbled out of my mouth to the floor.

"Fuck, that was fast, princess. Feeling pretty needy, weren't you? And it looks like you squirted all over the floor." Jack watched me through slitted eyes. But as much as he tried to sound unaffected, I could hear how turned on he was through the growl in his voice.

I tried to slow down my heart rate and ignore the mess I made. I'd never, ever come like that before. I'd known it was possible, of course, but I hadn't thought it would be possible for *me*.

"I'd tell you to lick it up, but I'm not that cruel," Jack mused, before stroking his cock. "Pick up the condom and put it on me."

I hesitated.

"Condom, Aviva. Or I knock over your house of cards."

I looked down at the condom on the floor, and bent down to pick it up. I couldn't believe I was doing this.

There was a feather-light touch on my hip: Jack's hand. The gentleness scared me. I didn't believe in it for a second. Blinking away tears, refusing to look at my cruel tormentor, I ripped open the condom, removing it slowly. I pulled out the condom with my right hand, pinching the top like they'd taught us in sex ed, then paused, worried I was going to get it wrong and risk even bigger problems.

"What's wrong?" Jack asked, the gentleness in his touch reflected in his quiet voice. "Never put a condom on a cock before?"

I didn't trust it.

"Tom took care of it," I muttered.

Jack grabbed my right wrist, gripping it tightly. The condom hung there, between us.

"Who the *fuck* is Tom?"

10

Aviva

The gentleness in Jack's voice had disappeared. He was angry. Angry, and he had no right to be.

So I didn't answer him.

He gripped my wrist tighter, maybe in punishment. "Who is Tom, Aviva?"

"My ex-boyfriend." He didn't deserve to know that we hadn't gotten further than the condom.

Jack relaxed his hold but didn't release my wrist. "I'm going to make this clear, so there's no confusion: while you're my little filthy sex toy, there's no one else. No one touches this pussy, you hear me? You get permission from me if you need to see your fucking gynecologist. Understood?"

"Yes, master," I spat, enraged at the control he'd taken away from me.

He finally released my wrist, satisfied. "I like that. You can call me master whenever you want, *princess*." Sitting back, he crossed his arms behind his back. "You're holding it right. Just put it over the top of my cock and slowly roll it down."

Gritting my teeth, I placed the condom on top of his dick, trying not to react to how hard and hot it was. Slowly, carefully, I rolled the condom down the thick length, hating the way it felt in my hand, how I could still feel the ridges and curve through the latex. How gorgeous Jack looked when he closed his eyes and hummed at the feeling of my hand around him. His lashes were long, curly, black; his sculpted face with its hard, sharp angles more pronounced in his pleasure.

I hated him so much.

My body must not have agreed. I could feel wetness drip down my pussy to my thighs. I shouldn't have been this turned on again after coming already, but then what did I know about orgasms? What did I know about any of this?

Jack's eyes opened. They were a stormy, lust-clouded gray. The kind of eyes you could easily get lost in.

If the circumstances were different.

If he were a different sort of man.

"Climb on."

I stilled.

I'd assumed he'd fuck me in missionary the first time, maybe even from behind. But this, making me get on top... he really was making me play a role in my own demise. I hated it, hated him, but I had no choice. It was either this or saying goodbye to my dreams—and Asher's.

Awkward and embarrassingly shy, I put my hands on his shoulder for balance and lifted one leg over his spread ones, then the other, until I was straddling him, my thighs burning from the stretch. Jack didn't assist me, just held his cock in place as I hovered over him, avoiding contact with the tip of his cock.

"That won't do," he tsked. "Time is ticking; get to work."

Shutting my eyes, I tried to block everything out as I lowered myself onto him. It was a mistake. Closing my eyes only heightened the sensations: the feel of his crown pressing against my entrance, the tight, immediate pain as he entered me, the fullness as I let myself slide down. It *hurt*, having him inside me. And what was worse? The pain stirred something inside, a spark, a tingle of terrible pleasure.

Jack groaned, hard and deep, only making that pleasure worse. "Fuck, you're so goddamned tight. How long has it been?"

I didn't answer, because the answer was "forever." Not only had I never had sex before, I'd doubted I ever would. Tom's disgust with my scar had done a real number on me, and my insecurities piled up so high, I'd never thought I'd be in a relationship again.

This wasn't a relationship. This was prison.

As if Jack had heard me, he wrapped a hand around my throat. "Eyes on me, princess."

I obeyed him, and we stared at each other, his face tight. "You may be a little lying spy, but this cunt is honest. I can feel how wet you are, even through the condom. You like this, don't you? I'm barely inside you and you're already about to come again."

I opened my mouth to reject his words, only to lose them in his mouth. He was kissing me, no lead up or preamble, just his lips on mine, his tongue in my mouth, licking, tasting, owning me. Jack was evil, but he knew how to kiss. My pussy wasn't honest, but it was a traitor. It softened further, grew wetter, allowing me to sink down the last couple of inches until Jack was all the way inside me, so deep, I could feel him in my throat.

I cried out into his mouth, half in pain, half in pleasure, and he swallowed the sound whole.

Finally releasing my mouth, he whispered a low, guttural order into my ear, making me shiver.

"Move."

I raised up, his cock slowly sliding out of me, then lowered back down, still slowly but more easily this time. I was sure my movements were awkward, jerky. They couldn't have felt good but Jack's moans and groans and growls suggested differently.

I moved up and down, the movement becoming easier, smoother. Each time, the curve of his cock hit that same part of me he'd stroked with his fingers earlier. I couldn't control the sounds I was making.

"Fuck, that's right, princess. Keep whimpering like that. Keep proving how good this feels for you. You must hate it, something so bad feeling so good." Under his breath, he added, "I know I do."

So he hated me as much as I hated him.

With that, he fell silent, and it was just his eyes on mine, his loose grip on my neck, the feeling of him inside me, the sounds we made as I moved over him. Something was different. The night in the locker room had felt shocking, fast, like I couldn't keep up with what was happening. Today felt sharper, clearer; almost like every thrust, every grind, every groan, every whine happened in slow motion, and I was helpless to speed up my humiliation and instead had to experience every second of it as Jack reveled in my suffering. What's more, I couldn't distance myself from it. I was fully present for every moment.

Jack wasn't done verbally torturing me. "How does it feel, knowing you're doing all the work? I'm not fucking you, Aviva. You're the one fucking me. Your cunt is swallowing my cock every time, like a greedy little bitch. You're dripping all over me. Can't you smell it, how turned on you are? I can."

"Shut up," I told him.

He hummed. "Now, that's not very nice. Maybe I should've made you lick up your come from the floor. Maybe I'll make you lick up mine."

Oh, god.

I clenched around him.

His eyes went bright with triumph. "You like that? Like being humiliated? You are a dirty little princess, aren't you? Nothing more than my filthy sex toy." With his free hand, he slapped my ass. "Now, bounce. It's your job to get me off, and you need to work harder, or I'll fuck your little virgin asshole instead."

Oh god, oh god.

I clenched around him again.

He hummed. "Interesting."

Needing to shut him up, I started bouncing up and down on his cock, faster and faster. I already was close to the edge, and now an orgasm yawned before me, a deep, unfamiliar, terrifying abyss I was determined not to fall into.

"I don't want to come." The words popped out before I could stop them.

A slow grin spread across his face. "Too fucking bad."

He began slapping my ass, urging me on. I had no choice. He hadn't given me one, and neither would my body. Our skin slapped together, his balls against my ass. Trying to stave off the orgasm, I teetered on the edge, the spanking also urging me on.

Jack must have decided I wasn't moving fast enough. He released my throat, gripping my hips and taking over my movements, lifting me up and shoving me down so fast I couldn't track the movements anymore. Everything became a blur, my body moving over his, the feeling of his cock inside me; the only clear constant were his eyes as they grew darker, darker.

"I can feel you clenching around me. You're so close, aren't you? Come, Aviva. Fucking come, little spy, or you won't like what happens next."

With those words, he lifted his hips for the first time, thrusting up and in me, so deep, hitting me *just there, just right.* With a sound I didn't recognize, I came, the chasm welcoming me into its unfamiliar depths, a hole I might never find my way out of.

Jack growled, low and rough, holding my hips tight against his as he somehow shoved even deeper inside me, reaching a depth that hurt so good, I came again. Or maybe I had never stopped the first time. I felt heat through the condom.

"Fuuuuuuuuuck," he said, relaxing under me, his fingers stroking my hips in a soothing caress that made me want to recoil. I wasn't even sure he even knew he was doing it, but I didn't care.

I struggled to lift off of him.

He didn't release me.

"Not yet, little spy," he crooned. "I want to feel your after-shocks. Besides, haven't you heard of aftercare?"

"Have you?" I tried to retort, but my voice had taken on a soft, dreamlike quality.

He chuckled. "Look how sweet you are post orgasm. Like a small, defenseless kitten. You purr so nicely."

But he released my hips. Holding the condom in place, I raised my hips and his cock, now soft, slid out of me. I stood on shaky legs.

Jack looked down at his softened cock. His eyes went wide.

"Are you on your period or something?"

"Or something," I muttered, too tired and overwhelmed to bother to keep my virginity a secret from him any longer.

Ex-virginity, now.

"So you were a virgin," he said, and there was a look in his eyes I couldn't read.

But whatever it was, it scared me.

"I want to fuck you all over again," he groaned, dragging a finger through the blood on the condom.

And then, to my utter shock, he lifted his bloody finger to his mouth...

...and sucked.

"Such a fucking sweet cherry," he growled, and his eyes flashed silver. "And mine. All mine. You hear me, princess? This means you belong to me now. Some other asshole touches you, this *Tom* comes near you?" he sneered. "I'll motherfucking destroy him."

Standing, he disposed of the condom while I grabbed my clothes and pulled them on jerkily. I felt sick and elated, like I wanted to laugh or cry or scream, I wasn't sure. At least he hadn't taken my shirt off. At least my scar was still a secret from him.

I snorted to myself. What a pathetic silver lining.

Jack rose and dressed, but before I could follow suit, he was pulling me into his arms. Being held by him was disconcerting. Especially when he awkwardly rubbed my back and dropped a reluctant-seeming kiss on my forehead. The softness, the gentleness...it opened a gaping wound inside of me, because part of me longed for his tenderness to be real, even though I knew it was just one more way to mess with my head.

"What the hell are you doing?" I asked.

"Aftercare. You've never had sex before, it's right that I hold you," he muttered, although he sounded confused himself. Pulling back, he lifted my chin. "In fact, you're coming home with me, princess."

Oh, shit, what time was it? I swallowed, glancing around. It was dark out; the clock in the corner said 7 p.m. I had half an hour to get to the bar for my shift.

"I can't," I told him.

"What did I say about you telling me no?"

"I can't," I repeated, freaked out. "I have to go to work. Some of us need to work."

He glared. "You think hockey isn't work?"

"I don't want to talk about hockey right now. I need to go."

Surprisingly, he released me, watching as I gathered up my clothes and dressed.

"Where do you work? I can give you a ride." He grinned, standing and stretching. "Another one, I mean."

I'm sure he could. "None of your business."

Surprisingly, he let it go.

"Alright, Aviva. You can run away. I'll find you later."

With those foreboding words, I grabbed my bag and left the room, leaving Jack behind...

...for now.

11

Aviva

I was sweating by the time I got to The Stacks, the bar I worked at with Tovah. I dragged open the thick, wooden door with the tiny gold sign, aware that my hair was in complete, just-got-fucked disarray. At least I hadn't put on makeup today. I was already enough of a mess.

And I hadn't had a chance to go by the IT center and befriend a techie to help me hack into Joshua Jensen's cloud account, damn it.

Tomorrow, I promised myself. It would be my first priority tomorrow.

Alex, the bouncer, looked up when I entered. He was a big guy, on the wrestling team, and Tovah and I couldn't figure out if he needed the money or did the job for fun. Although I didn't know how fun it was, checking IDs and kicking out drunk and belligerent college students.

"You better watch out, Dick's on a rampage," he advised.

"I'm only a minute late," I said, sighing.

Alex raised an eyebrow. "Like that matters to the Weiner?"

I laughed, surprised anything was funny to me at the moment. But Alex had nicknamed Dick "the Weiner" one night when we were cleaning up the bar. Dick was the type to get as drunk and belligerent as our worst customers, often declaring himself a "big winner" and the rest of us "real losers."

"He's a 'weiner' alright," Alex had told me and Tovah as we set the bar back to rights. The nickname had stuck, even though Dick had no idea.

"Aviva!" the Weiner yelled, startling me and bringing me back to the present. I gritted my teeth. It took everything in me *not* to call Dick out for being a lousy boss, but I caught Tovah's wide eyes as she shook her head wildly.

Don't, she mouthed. *He threatened to fire you.*

"Aviva, you're late," Dick said. "Your shift already started. And I don't have time for irresponsible employees."

Barely.

Tovah shook her head again.

I didn't want to apologize, but I wanted to keep my job. Needed to keep it. My scholarship only covered tuition, and room and board. Books for class, food, transportation: all of that was on me. Not to mention paying the utility bills for Aunt Gladys's house now that Asher was back at home.

"I'm sorry." I forced out the words.

I was really sick of powerful men walking all over me. I was especially sick of the ways I gave in.

Like you gave in to Jack? my inner voice mused. I'd come today. *Twice.* Maybe even three times—that second orgasm lasted so long, it was difficult to tell. What the hell was wrong with me? My solo orgasms had never felt like that. What had made this so horribly pleasurable, when I hadn't even chosen to do it? I'd been forced. I had no choice. Before, sex had been fully consensual, and I hated it. Now, it was non-consensual, and I liked it—and hated myself.

"How sorry?" Dick leered.

Alex cleared his throat. Dick's face turned pink, but all he said was, "Go change and help Tovah."

Grabbing my uniform—tiny black shorts and the high-necked, tight black tank top that Dick had compromised with me on, I went to go change in the back room, making sure the door was locked. As I changed, I glanced over in the mirror, wincing at the faint bruises I saw on my hips, remembering the way Jack had gripped me while he'd forced me up and down on his cock...

I shook my head clear of the memory. Jack, and everything to do with Jack, belonged in a box. I needed to focus on work, school, and getting justice for my brother. That was it.

Unlocking the door and exiting the back room, I headed back to the bar, where Tovah was stacking clean glasses. Dick had disappeared, probably into his office to watch porn. I shuddered.

"Aviva, what is going on?" she whispered. "You're a mess —again. Did that asshole find you?" I glanced at her, biting my lip.

"Fuck," she swore. "Aviva, can we please go to the cops? Or let me write an exposé? We need to get you away from him."

I shook my head, adamant. "We can't, Tovah. I already told you. He'll make the NHL believe Asher's a liar, and ruin my life, while he's at it. Take any chance of getting a psychology degree away from me."

"You won't lose your chance to be a psychologist. And Asher won't care. I'm going to call him right now. He wouldn't want you doing this. Hell, he'd come here and fight Jack Feldman himself."

That's what I was afraid of.

She reached into her pocket, and I put out a hand to stop her.

"Please, Tovah. *Trust me.*"

She shook her head, curls—pink today—flying. "You know, you are absolutely the strongest, most selfless person I know. No one else could keep their shit together while being tormented the way Jack's clearly tormenting you, and no one else would put up with it—even for their family. I love you for it, but it scares me. How far are you going to let this go? I know after your parents were killed, all you had was each other. But when are you going to start protecting yourself, instead of him?"

I couldn't answer her. I didn't know how to.

She sighed. "What happened today?"

I cleared my throat. "We had sex."

"What?!" She yelled the word so loudly, Alex glanced up from his stool.

"Everything okay over there?" he asked.

I waved him off. "We're fine." Lowering my voice, I hissed at Tovah, "Shh. I don't want anyone to know."

Shame was a funny thing. It alienated, isolated, made us lie and obfuscate, all in order to protect ourselves from rejection—except all it did was keep us from the people and support we needed.

The thing was, I wasn't ashamed of having sex. I wasn't even ashamed of having been forced to: that wasn't my fault, that was Jack's. But I was ashamed of how much I'd liked it.

"Was it awful?" she asked quietly. "Do we need to go get you Plan B?"

I shook my head. "He used a condom. Tovah..." Tovah

didn't talk about sex much with me, but I knew she'd had it. "Have you ever...enjoyed not having the control? During sex?"

She inhaled, blushing. "Sure, I like CNC, as long as it's safe, sane, and consensual. But this is none of those things. Why, was it good?"

I nodded, looking away and busying myself with restocking the bar with glassware.

"Aviva, it's okay to not always want to be in control. Being submissive can be fun. And don't feel bad, if you liked it. I'm relieved, honestly. At least he didn't hurt you."

He had, and it had felt good.

He'd been tender after, and it had felt better.

Before I could tell her more, the door swung open, framing Jack in the dim, warm light of the bar. Isaac Jones stood at his side. Isaac smirked, his dimples showing, but Jack just looked...intense.

Then again, he always looked intense.

What the hell was he doing here? In the week since I'd started at The Stacks, I'd never once seen the Core Four at the bar. So was this a coincidence, or had he figured out where I worked that quickly? I felt heat rising to my chest, my face. He was looking at me like he was remembering my naked body, and he was planning on seeing it again—soon.

I hated him. I hated him for all he'd done to me, and I especially hated the way he made me feel like I was his sole focus. Like the world could end, and he'd stare at me the whole time. My agenda was better achieved in the dark.

He watched me, but he didn't *see* me. He thought I was a liar, and a conniving, manipulative, opportunistic bitch.

It hurt. I hated to admit it to myself, but it *hurt*.

Alex held out his hand for their IDs, checking them over, probably as a formality. He handed them back, and they bumped fists in some jock form of greeting that annoyed me. I wouldn't call Alex a friend, per se, but I'd at least trusted him a little. Now, I knew better.

Jack walked over to the bar, slowly, steadily, building fear and anticipation in me at his approach. Isaac swaggered after him.

"I got them," Tovah murmured. "Go handle the other end of the bar."

I did, making my way toward the two girls who stood at the back end of bar, eyeing Jack and Isaac.

"They're stupid hot," one whispered.

The other fanned herself. "I'd happily be in the middle of that sandwich."

"If you *want* to be in the middle of a sandwich, I hear the twins are game...but I'll take Jack Feldman. He's enough to handle."

"What are you drinking?" I asked.

If they were interested in Jack, they could have him. I'd happily let them take him off my hands.

They gave me their orders. As I took care of them, I eavesdropped on the other side of the bar.

"If it isn't the little journalist," Isaac greeted Tovah with a grin, dimples popping.

She rolled her eyes. "Isaac Jones, why are you such a pain in the ass?"

He laughed. "I guess a good girl like you probably doesn't know that sometimes a little pain in the ass is a good thing."

Tovah glared. "Do you two want drinks, or do you want to be assholes?"

Jack ignored her. "Aviva, come here," he called.

"I can take care of you," Tovah insisted.

"I bet you can," Isaac murmured.

"Aviva's going to take care of me," Jack informed her, but he was looking at me as he said it. "Aren't you, princess?"

Tovah mouthed the word princess, then tipped her head toward me, questions in her eyes. I knew what she was asking. *Why does he call you princess?* and *What do you want me to do?*

To the first, I had no answer, although I'm sure it was cruel and insulting. I answered the second out loud.

Popping the top off the hard seltzers the girls had ordered, I passed them over, taking their credit card and running it through the machine before handing it back.

"Switch with me," I called to Tovah, and as I headed the dreaded length of the bar back toward Jack, imagining how good it would feel to pour an entire pitcher of Blue Moon over his head, the girl who was interested in Jack said to the other, "He calls her *princess*?"

I had to resist telling her she didn't *want* Jack to call her princess. Not if it meant putting up with everything he'd done so far to *me*.

But maybe she'd like it like I did.

That thought pissed me off so much, I stomped the last few steps over to Jack.

"Fire in your eyes," he murmured. "Did I manage to piss you off, sweetheart?"

"Don't call me that," I told him, quietly but clearly. "Don't call me sweetheart, don't call me princess. Don't call me little thief or little spy or anything other than Aviva."

His own eyes went cold. "I'll call you anything I want to call you."

I shook my head. "Not in public you won't, unless you want Alex to boot you out of here and ban you for life."

Isaac whistled. "Not a great idea to make him angry."

"I'm going to remind you, *once*, who is calling the shots

here," Jack said, also quietly. His hand covered mine, and it might look sweet from other points of view, but I could feel the power and threat of his hand. He'd left fingerprints on my hips; he could do worse, I was sure of it. "It's obvious you don't like giving up control, but that's the game we're playing here. Got it?"

I shook my head. "My bar, my rules."

Jack stared at me for a long moment, his eyes searching mine. There was heat in them, heat that reminded my body of where it had been, only an hour ago. Heat and something else. Whatever he saw in my own eyes made him nod.

"I'll let you win this battle, *Aviva*. But don't mistake me: the war? It's mine. *And. So. Are. You.*"

"For now," I muttered.

He didn't dignify that with an answer as he lifted his hand. "Jack and Coke for me, Jack and Ginger for him."

"Cute," I said.

He winked at me. Like we were just two college students, flirting, and not a desperate-for-justice woman and her mercurial, enigmatic bully.

Who was Jack Feldman, really? And why had he chosen to torture me this way? I wanted answers. But I doubted I'd ever get them. If anything was clear to me, it was that the Kings' left wing carried his cards close to his chest. I shouldn't want to know him better, but I *did*. Mostly because knowledge was power, and if I did have his secrets, I might have leverage to use against him.

As I thought, I mixed his and Isaac's drinks. Isaac checked his phone while Jack watched me.

"Are you two even allowed to be drinking during the season?" I asked.

Jack shrugged. "I'm twenty-two; Isaac's twenty-one. Some players don't drink during the season, but I've never been that way, and I let the team do what they want, as long as they don't fuck up a game—or do anything stupid enough to get kicked off."

I ignored the jab. "Twenty-two?"

He nodded. "I red-shirted. Meaning—"

"Meaning you didn't play freshman year to give you four full years after. So you're a fifth year." I put down paper coasters and placed both drinks on top of them. Jack handed over his credit card.

It was a black Amex.

I swallowed, aware just how out of my depth I was with him. He didn't just have power over me as Reina's king and overlord. He was *wealthy*, powerful outside of this little college bubble, too. Once again, I wondered what it was like to have that much power. How safe it must feel, knowing if you fell, you'd always land on your feet—or if not, that someone would catch you. I'd never had that, not since I woke up to gunshots at the age of ten and discovered my parents, dead in their bedroom...

"Aviva." Jack's voice was sharp. "Where'd you go?"

I swallowed again. It was none of his business, but if I said that, he'd only push harder. "Why'd you redshirt?"

He raised an eyebrow but let it go. "I was good, good enough to be recruited by Reina, but not good enough to get me where I needed to be." He smiled at me, and despite myself, I smiled back. "I was actually pretty scrawny. Coach used to call me Jack the beanstalk."

At the mention of Coach Jensen, we both stilled, remembering. We weren't friends. We were on the opposite sides of this: for him, protecting his coach and his team. For me, getting justice against all of them for my brother.

Even though both of us were motivated by loyalty, it pulled us in two different directions. Jack was so, so sure he'd win. But I refused to let him. There was too much riding on it.

I took a deep breath, promising myself that even though I'd play his game, for now, I wouldn't lose sight of my greater purpose. He wouldn't destroy my mission, and he wouldn't break me. I wouldn't let that happen.

Jack Feldman didn't understand the enemy he'd made in me.

But I lifted my lips in a fake smile and said, "Open or closed?"

Jack watched me, and I tried to shut him out of my brain. "Open. We'll be here for a while."

Isaac thumbsed-up, busy chatting with the two girls from earlier who'd made their way over to us. But every few seconds, he'd glance over to where Tovah was busy serving the other half of the bar.

Now, *that* was interesting.

"Jack," the girl from earlier said. "I'm Lindsey. I'm a big fan of the team—and you."

"Yeah?" Jack looked at me. I purposefully turned away, taking orders from other students. Even though it was a Monday night, the bar had begun to fill up. Reina was very much a "work hard, play harder" type of school—unlike Stanford, which had been very "work hard, work harder, sleep."

Or at least it had been that way for me.

Don't you think you should start living for yourself?

Pasting a flirtatious smile on my face, I served student after student, cleaning as I went because Dick was too cheap to hire barbacks. I tried to ignore Jack's conversation with Lindsey, but it was practically impossible. He hadn't left his seat at the bar, just grinned at her. She giggled at something he'd said. It would be bullshit of me to not like her just for flirting with an objectively attractive guy. A guy who happened to have been inside of me only a few hours ago.

Fuck my life.

"Aviva!" Dick hollered from the back. "Get in here."

"But I have customers," I called back.

"Don't care. Tovah can handle them. Get in here."

Sighing, I dropped my rag on the counter, signaled Tovah, who rolled her eyes and shook her head. I walked around to the end of the bar and headed down the hallway to the back room.

I pushed the door open to find Dick, straddling a chair in front of his desk and, of course, leering at me. Revulsion filled me, but just like every other day I came into work, I buried it. I needed the money, he was my boss, so I was stuck hiding how I really felt and letting him push me around.

"What's up?" I asked him.

He tried to hide his leer under a stern look, but I saw right through him. Even if I hadn't been able to read his real thoughts on his face, his hard *weiner* told the story.

Ick. Ugh. Ew.

"I'm concerned about your performance, Aviva," he told me. "You're late all the time—"

Barely.

"—You're rude to the customers—"

The only customer I'd ever been rude to was Jack, and Dick hadn't been there to see it.

"—And you're not picking up the slack."

I worked my ass off, it was his ass that was lazy.

"I'm sorry. I'll do better." I forced out the words.

Dick smirked. "Unfortunately, better isn't enough. I think I'm going to have to let you go…"

No.

He couldn't. He couldn't fire me. The Stacks was the only bar in Gehenom or the surrounding towns that would hire me without a bartending license, and any other job would conflict with my classes. Work-study didn't pay well enough. The tips at The Stacks weren't amazing, but they were better than anywhere else I could work. What was I going to do?

Jack can help you. It was a bizarre thought. Jack was wealthy, but he didn't want to help me, he wanted to hurt me. I dismissed the thought, focusing on Dick.

"Please, Dick, don't fire me," I begged. "I need this job. I need—"

"I know Aviva, I know," he shushed me, and the sound slithered over my skin like a slug. I swallowed down bile. "We can come to an...arrangement."

He winked at me, and I wanted to die. I knew what he meant.

But as if I didn't, he placed his hand on his zipper. "You take care of Big Dick, and I'll let you keep your job."

Overcompensation. When someone exaggerates to cover up a shortcoming. Dick's macho bullshit was straight out of a psych 101 textbook.

I covered my mouth. I was going to laugh, or scream, I wasn't sure, but neither would serve me right now.

But I knew my answer.

No.

No, I couldn't do it. Wouldn't do it. I was already being sexually blackmailed by one man, I refused to let it be two. Let it become a pattern. I'd rather start an Only Fans than let Dick touch me.

But what made the difference between him and Jack? Why would I let Jack coerce me, but not my boss? Yes, I was repulsed by Dick, and not by Jack, but—

—oh god, was I into Jack, even though he was horrible to me?

"How about it, Aviva? You suck my dick good, and I'll even let you leave early."

I shook my head.

"Absolutely the fuck not."

Dick's face turned pinker than it had when Alex had given him shit earlier.

"Listen here, you little slut. I'm being generous with you. You don't do this, and I'll make sure you don't get a job *anywhere*. I'll—"

The door opened behind me, and someone cleared their throat. "I wouldn't finish that sentence, Richard Doyle," said Jack from behind me.

12

Jack

When my brother Micah re-entered my life, he had a lot to say. Micah thought he had a lot of sage advice, and although I'd never admit it to him, he was right.

One piece of advice was this: *If you let anger control you, it will destroy you. But if you harness it, you can use it to destroy other people.*

As I stood at the entrance to Dick Doyle's office and witnessed him leering at Aviva as he threatened her, I reminded myself about Micah's advice. It was difficult as hell, because all I wanted to do was plant my fist in the bar owner's face and punch him in the junk for good measure before carrying Aviva out of there. It didn't matter that she was the enemy, that I hated her for trying to ruin Coach's life. She was *mine*, and no one else in the whole fucking world got to talk to her that way. Only me.

I'd address the hypocrisy of that later.

But punching him in the face wouldn't get me anywhere,

except maybe kicked off the team for violence against a community member. No, as satisfying as it would be to hear his nose crack and blood explode everywhere, I had better options than my fists. I had power, real power—and I was going to use it.

Aviva stared at me. The relief on her face was obvious; her anger at being relieved was subtler, but I still saw it. She didn't want me to be her savior. Too fucking bad. I'd taken her virginity. She was mine now, when so little was.

"Jack—" she started.

"Jack Feldman?" Dick spluttered, eyes wide. "I'm a huge fan, son."

Only Coach got to call me son. He was the father figure in my life.

"Really?" I said, affecting a casual tone. "Because I'm not a fan of yours. I heard what you were saying to her."

"How?" Aviva asked.

"Through the door." I didn't even look at her. If I did, she'd be in my arms before I could stop myself, and I needed to focus on the worm in front of me, first.

Dick waved that away. "We were having a performance review."

"A performance review, huh? Pretty sure that most job performance reviews don't include harassing your employees or threatening to fire them if they don't perform sexual favors. But I'm sure the Gehenom Chamber of Commerce would love to hear all about it."

Aviva laughed but covered it with a cough. Out of the corner of my eye, I saw her shoulders straighten.

Dick glared at me. "Now listen here, kid, you have no idea what you're talking about, and no one would believe you. I'm a pillar of this community, and—"

"Are you, Dick? Or are you just some pathetic college

dropout who lucked out that his dad died and left him a successful bar?"

"How dare you—"

I rolled my eyes. "You don't want to know what else I'd dare to do. Like, for instance, inform the Gehenom police that you've been selling Vixen and Vice here, and the only reason no girl's been roofied or raped is because you have good, responsible staff. Like *Aviva*."

For a moment, Dick stopped breathing. If he had a heart attack right here and died, the world would be a better place.

It wouldn't hurt to make that more likely, would it?

I'd never murdered anyone, but I was angry enough to, now. Besides, murder and violence ran in the family; I'm sure I could figure it out.

Striding toward him, I grabbed him by the throat and lifted him out of his chair so I could stare him right in the eyes.

Dick flailed.

"You're going to want to listen to me, Richard, because I'll only give you this warning *once*. You're going to apologize to Aviva, and then you're going to leave her the hell alone.

You won't touch her, you won't threaten her, you won't harass her, you won't come near her other than to pay her— and you're going to give her a raise."

Dick coughed.

I squeezed, determined to get my point across.

Dick gasped.

"Jack!" Aviva said. "Jack, stop. You're going to kill him."

Fuck.

The red haze began to clear.

I'd lost control of my anger for a second. But her voice alone, solid and strong, calmed me.

Exhaling slowly, I released Dick, who dropped back into the chair with a yelp.

"Do you get me?" I asked.

"I—I got you," he wheezed.

"Don't you owe someone an apology?"

He glanced over at Aviva. "I'm sorry, Aviva."

"Good," I said. "Aviva's done here for the night. Oh, and Dick? If I find out you used Vixen on anyone, if you start harrassing your other female employees, I'll be back to see you—and you'll like my second visit even less."

He nodded.

"C'mon, pr—Aviva."

Aviva gaped at me.

I walked to her, grabbing her by the hand and tugging her from the room. "You either walk out of here with me, or I'm throwing you over my shoulder and carrying you out."

She rolled her eyes but let me lead her out.

"Remember what I said, Richard," I called over my shoulder at the sniveling, pathetic worm of a man behind me before I slammed the door.

I didn't speak, fully focused on Aviva behind me, her harsh, surprised breaths. Her hand was soft, smooth, delicate. Fully surrounded and protected by mine. An unfamiliar feeling, one I'd only ever experienced with my siblings, filled me.

Protective. I felt protective. Aviva was a flame, magnificent and dangerous, and at risk of being extinguished.

I didn't want to extinguish her. I wanted to protect her, even if it meant we both burned.

Fuck *even if*. I wanted to protect her *because* it meant we both would burn.

Possessed by some wild urge, I intertwined our fingers.

"Jack, what are you doing?" she hissed.

I glanced over at her. There were gold striations in her brown eyes; I had missed them before.

"Taking you home," I told her, briefly captivated.

"I mean, what the hell were you thinking, following me? Barging into my boss's office? Threatening him?"

I stopped, backing her up against the wall. We were at the end of the hallway; one more step and it would spit us back out into the bar. Light spilled in, illuminating her rosy skin and making it glow.

"I was thinking that you're mine for as long as I want you to be. I fucked your untouched cunt, and that changed everything. Your body's mine, your pussy's mine, your decisions are mine. Everything about you is mine, *and I protect what's mine.*"

"I'm not yours," she argued. "And making this about my virginity is barbaric."

I didn't even bother responding to her nonsense. Instead, I wrapped my hands around her head, positioning her where I wanted her, and swallowed her protests with my mouth. She fought me, pushing at my chest with her hands, but I had her right where I wanted her, and I wasn't letting her go anytime soon. I was too invested in the taste of her, the apples and honey smell of her, the feel of her soft skin under my hands, the soft gasps as I kissed her. Possessed once again by those urges I couldn't make sense of, I softened the kiss, slowing it until we were molasses together, sweet and thick and difficult to tear apart.

I could've kissed her forever this way, held her in this space forever. Time could've stopped, and I wouldn't give a fuck. Not when I held this girl in my arms, this furious and caring, vulnerable and strong, wise and brave girl. But Aviva must have felt differently, because there was a sharp sting on my lower lip.

She'd bitten me.

Again.

I pulled back, releasing her head to touch my lower lip with my thumb. It came away wet with blood.

I gazed at my thumb, then her.

"You want it rough?"

She glared. "Don't kiss me like you like me."

"Oh, princess. I don't *like* you. I *like* watching the Winter Olympics. I *like* my Classics advisor. Like is too gentle of a word for how I feel about you."

"That would sound romantic if I didn't know what an asshole you are," she said, her voice hoarse with anger.

I stared at her. It wasn't romantic.

So I continued. "Don't interrupt me. Like doesn't cover all the ways I'm going to defile you, ruin you. *Destroy* you. But you're forgetting, so I'll remind you: you don't decide how this goes. I *do.*"

In case she didn't understand how serious I was, I leaned over, pushing my right shoulder against her soft stomach, before standing again with her over my shoulder.

"What the hell!"

I slapped her ass. "Quiet, little fighter. I told you I'd carry you out of here if you weren't amenable."

"You said if I didn't walk with you! I would've walked with you!"

I laughed, but it was harsh, hard. I'd lost my mind there for a bit, feeling soft toward someone I couldn't be soft with. Aviva hadn't earned that from me, didn't deserve it. She didn't deserve my protection, either. The most she deserved was to be the receptacle for my cock and my come. No more, no less.

Then why do you want to wrap her soft body in wool and take her somewhere where she's safe—even from you? Why are you so impressed with her strength, bravery, compassion and loyalty if you truly hate her?

I fucking hated my inner voice.

Carrying her back into the bar, I stopped in the center of the floor. The place had filled up since I'd followed her into the back office, students sitting at tables, sharing pitchers, others gathered at the bar itself, waiting for drinks from a harried and overworked Tovah.

"Oh thank god, you're back—what are you doing with her?" Tovah asked, spotting Aviva over my shoulder.

"Put. Me. Down." Aviva ordered.

"Put her down, or I'll make you put her down. I swear to god, Feldman—" Tovah ranted. I ignored her.

"Bro," Isaac warned, from his perch on the same bar stool. One of the girls from earlier was sitting on his lap.

I lifted my chin at him, and he shook his head but dropped it.

Placing my hand casually on Aviva's ass, I turned in a circle so even hanging upside down she could see everyone —and everyone could see her.

I raised my voice, making sure everyone could hear me. "Sorry, Tovah, I'm taking my cumdumpster home for the night. She has a more important job to do."

There was silence at first as people digested my words. Then laughter rang out, almost haunting in its mockery.

Isaac shook his head. "Too far, man," he said.

For a moment, I felt guilty, but the emotion was quashed by satisfaction. I'd done two things at once:

Successfully humiliated Aviva.

And made it absolutely clear to everyone that she was *mine.*

"I hate you," I thought I heard her say.

It was okay, because as I'd said, I didn't like her. An emotion this big? It had to be hate.

Had to be.

Galvanized by the catcalls around us, I carried her out the door and down the block to my BMW XM, setting her roughly on the ground and gripping her hip to keep her in place while I unlocked the car.

"Get in," I told her.

"No."

"Aviva, get the *fuck* in the car or so help me god, I will strip you naked on College Ave and make you suck me off in front of *every goddamned person who walks by*, and if they have a penis, I'll make you suck them off, too. Those are your only options."

Glaring at me, she pulled the passenger side door open with a jerk, and I couldn't hold back my wince when the bottom of the door dragged across the curb.

"Do that again, and I'll spank your ass so hard, my hand-print will be embedded in your ass until the day you die," I warned.

She didn't say a word, just got in the car. I leaned down, making sure to take care of her seatbelt for her like she was a child before closing her door. Going around to the driver's side, I shut the door, starting up the car. Matt Maeson started playing as I pulled out of the spot and made a u-turn, headed toward her apartment.

"Where are you taking me?" she asked.

"Home."

She sat up straight. "How do you know where I live?"

I glanced at her.

"Princess, you still don't seem to get it. I know more about you than you can even imagine. Don't worry your pretty little head though; I'll know everything soon."

She shook her head. "Jack, it doesn't matter how much snooping you do. Until you realize I'm not a liar, you won't know me at all."

With that shit-stirring statement, she went silent, and didn't speak a word to me for the rest of the drive.

She was lying.

She had to be.

Because if she wasn't, then she wasn't the one living in a house of cards.

I was.

13

Jack

"What the hell's gotten into you?" Isaac huffed at me as we skated lines.

"Not fucking talking about it," I muttered.

It was a week after the night at The Stacks when I'd threatened Dick Doyle, gotten into it with Aviva, and then called her a cumdumpster in front of everyone. Since that night, I'd thought about texting her—I'd already tracked down her number—but I'd been too busy with hockey practice and training. And, honestly, I felt a little dickish myself for going from forcing her to give me her virginity to humiliating her publicly, all in the same day. And although there was a part of me that wanted to blame her for it, since she'd been the one who'd pulled away when I'd softened toward her, I knew that was just victim blaming. Everything I'd done to her was on me.

The louder, stronger part of me was satisfied as fuck that I'd been first. Just like I'd told her, her virginity was mine, her pussy was mine, her whole body was mine—she was mine, period.

And I protect what's mine.

But I hadn't done a very good job of that, had I?

"Jack," Isaac said harshly, pulling me out of my brooding.

Coach blew his whistle. "Feldman! Jones! What the hell are you two old ladies doing there, gabbing away?"

"Sorry Coach," I said, immediately ashamed of letting him down—even for a second.

Coach had us doing a bag skate for the past hour, because he was paranoid that we weren't ready for our first game of the season, which happened to be against Tabb. The game wasn't for two weeks, but none of us were willing to start our season with a loss, least of all me.

"You're full of shit," Isaac said, usual dimples missing in action as we skated back and forth across the ice. "You've been distracted and moody—moodier than usual. And erratic as fuck. First you call that girl a," he scowled, "a cumdumpster, which is one of the douchiest, foulest words in the English language—"

"I don't think it's actually a word," I interrupted, trying to seem casual even as my insides knotted. I refused to feel bad about it.

"Whatever," he scoffed. "When you said you wanted to go to The Stacks that night, I was surprised because that's not our spot. But nowhere as surprised as when you staked a claim and humiliated her in front of everyone. And then your mercurial ass warned us 'if any of you call her that, I'll make sure you ride the bench the entire season.'" Isaac imitated me.

I had done that. The idea of any of these bastards calling Aviva that made me sick.

"And since then," Isaac continued, "you've barely spoken a word to any of us. So once again, I ask, *what the hell has gotten into you?*"

I groaned. "Have you ever fucked a virgin?"

Isaac almost tripped over his skates. "Shit. Really?"

"Really," I said.

He wiped sweat off his forehead, picking the pace back up as we sped back and forth from line to line. Football and basketball players thought they were the only ones who had it bad when they had to run suicides, but try doing it on skates. And nothing, absolutely nothing, was as brutal as one of Coach's bag skates.

My body ached, my chest heaved, and I welcomed the exhaustion and pain. Anything to distract me from *her*. Every night, I'd gone to sleep imagining her smell, her taste. Every morning, I woke to the memory of her in my arms, her virgin cunt clenching around my cock. I felt guilty and angry and fucking confused as hell. No one had ever twisted me up like this before. No one had ever made me *feel* like this before. Obsessed, possessed, out of control. Like even I had no idea what I would do next.

Isaac was quiet for a moment. He got like that sometimes. Publicly, he was the life of the party: affable, charming, easygoing, talkative. Privately, he was quiet, studious, and not nearly as much of a fuck boy as he pretended to be.

Finally, he said, "I've never fucked a virgin because I don't want the responsibility, and I don't trust that I'd be careful enough. Treating her right—that's important. And I'm taking it from last week's show at The Stacks that you didn't treat her right."

"Not at all," I admitted. "Although I didn't fucking *know*. If I had..." I trailed off.

One of the assistant coaches blew his whistle. "Take five, get some water. And then get back to it."

Groans all around. Isaac stopped skating but ignored them, focused on me.

"If you had, what. You would've been nicer to her?" he raised an eyebrow.

I ripped my gloves off, and then peeled my shirt, suddenly overheated. Because I wouldn't have been. I still would have fucked her as hard, still would have subjected her to humiliation after she'd rejected my softer side.

"Fuck, man," I groaned. "I don't know what the fuck to do. And you don't even know how it started, what she tried to do to us."

Isaac had picked up a bottle of water and was about to chug it, but he paused.

"What she tried to do to *us*?" he asked.

The same assistant coach blew his whistle again. "Alright, scrimmage time. First line against second line."

More groans, this time from the younger guys on the team. The rest of us were used to being worked so hard.

And as team captain, it was my job to get their heads in the game.

"Listen up, all of you," I said, shoving Aviva to the back of my mind and skating out in front of them. "We've got two weeks until the season starts. Now is not the time to be tired, to groan, to call home and whine about how hard Coach and the team is working you."

I turned a circle on my skates, careful to look each player in the eye.

"If you're worn out this early, you won't make it through the season—and you don't belong here. Get off the ice, turn in your jersey, and go play club hockey. Got me?"

Not a single one of them moved.

Good.

"Good," I said out loud. "So you're all here, and you're agreeing to work. To *commit*. To put your all into the game, and the season, because your team is depending on you. Let's play."

Cheers broke out as I suited back up, relieved. My Aviva-related distraction hadn't impacted my ability to lead my team, at least.

We lined up for the scrimmage. As Isaac skated past me to take his spot for the face-off, he patted my shoulder with his glove—hard enough that I could feel it through the pad.

"Nice work, captain. But the Aviva conversation? Isn't over."

AFTER OUR LINE WON THE SCRIMMAGE, WE HEADED BACK INTO the locker room. My throat went tight as my gaze fell on the cubby where I'd cornered her and put my hand around her neck, the bench where I'd tied her down and eaten her sweet pussy. She was everywhere, always; I couldn't get away from her if I tried.

I didn't want to get away from her. Ever since I'd spotted the blood on the condom and realized what it meant, I'd had the insane idea of permanently handcuffing her to me.

"Jack," Isaac said.

He, Judah, and Levi crowded around me, Levi wiping off and putting his glasses back on, Judah pulling the elastic out of his hair and shaking it loose.

"Okay, Jason Momoa," Levi mocked his twin.

"I'm hotter than Jason Momoa," Judah protested. "Hotter than you, too."

Levi raised an eyebrow. "We're identical twins, idiot."

"I'm still hotter."

Before they could start a slap fight, Isaac interrupted. "Stop it, you two. Jack here has something to tell us."

Scratching my neck, I sighed. "It's about Aviva."

Judah snorted. "Of course it's about Aviva. She's the only girl you've ever staked a claim on, publicly, or threatened your teammates over." He chuckled. "What, you like her or something?"

I shook my head. I didn't fucking like her. "The opposite."

"Sure doesn't seem like the opposite."

Isaac held up a hand. If I led by example and kept everyone in line and motivated, Isaac led by the nature of his calm focus and "good guy" status.

Judah and Levi shut up.

"Jack, why did you say 'you don't know what she tried to do to us' earlier?"

I sighed. "You're going to hate her for it as much as I did."

As I started to tell them about what had happened between catching her in the locker room and now, they kept interrupting.

"Wait, so does she know how involved we are with Vice and Vixen?" Levi asked.

I shook my head. Of course they'd be concerned; Judah was the muscle, and Levi was the threat. "No, it's not about Vice and Vixen, although I thought that originally, too. No, she's Asher's sister."

"Shit," Isaac said. "That's fucked."

"And," I added, lowering my voice, "she was trying to frame Coach for," I swallowed, the words almost getting stuck in my throat, "sexually abusing Asher."

"What the actual fuck," Judah said.

Levi's eyes narrowed and darkened, but he let his brother speak for him.

"What a fucking bitch," Judah continued.

I gritted my teeth, reminding myself that Judah was my friend, and that punching him for calling Aviva a bitch was a bad call. Instead, I continued with my story, filling them in on blackmailing her for sex, and then blackmailing Professor Dylan Johnathan into letting me switch into the Deviant Psychology class so I could be—

"Closer to her," Isaac said.

"Keep an eye on her," I corrected.

"Not sure making a virgin fuck you is 'keeping an eye' on someone, but your definition may be different than mine," he said.

"I don't understand what the hell you have over that guy," Judah said.

"He's one of Vice and Vixen's number one buyers," Levi told his brother.

And the second I got wind that his recreational sharing of it wasn't consensual by both parties, I was going to kick his ass. It made me a hypocrite, but I didn't give a fuck. As I'd once told Mason Calloway, there was a difference between drugging a girl to get your rocks off like a fucking incel, and using Vixen to get her to acknowledge how she really felt about you.

Which gave me an idea.

I finished my story, catching my friends up to now and then filled them in on my new plan.

"That's fucked," Isaac stated.

"It is." Judah flashed a grin. "I like it. Let's all show that bitch who she's messing with."

Don't punch your friend in the face, I reminded myself.

"No," Isaac said. "Jack, you do something like this—you can't come back from it. Not with her, and not with yourself. *Trust me.*"

I wasn't sure what he meant, but was distracted when Levi opened his mouth. "In fact, I think we should all have a turn with her."

Judah laughed. "Sounds fun."

None of you are fucking touching her. Not unless you want me to rip your hands off your bodies.

Isaac was right. What the hell had gotten into me?

But all I said was, "Maybe. If you fuckers behave."

"Oh, we'll behave," Judah said, slapping his brother's hand. "We'll behave so hard, she won't walk for a week."

He held his hand up for Isaac, who refused, instead staring at me, not a dimple in sight.

"You sure about this, captain?"

"Positive," I said, swallowing.

Because I wasn't. I wasn't sure about anything, not anymore.

14

Aviva

Over the next week or so, Jack's declaration that I was his "cumdumpster" followed me everywhere. On campus, everyone I walked by went silent, only to explode into laughter once I'd passed them. In the cafeteria, I was surrounded by guys in Kings jerseys—either members of the team or team groupies—who did the slut cough, except they'd exchanged "slut" for "cumdumpster" when they fake coughed. Tovah made the mistake of posting a picture of us on Instagram and tagging me. Her comment section exploded with people saying what a trashy slut I must be for Jack Hat Trick Feldman to announce publicly that I was nothing to him but a set of holes. And someone had the balls to graffiti the study carrel I'd rented with the delightful word on it. The library was replacing it, but who knew how long that would be?

Cumdumpster. I thought I'd hated princess because of my past, but I'd had no idea how bad it could get. I avoided talking to everyone but Tovah and my professors, called out sick from work (Dick hadn't fought me on it), and counted down the days until the weekend. I planned to hide out in our apartment and watch *Ted Lasso*, like I should've done last weekend instead of going to that godforsaken party. Luckily, Jack had disappeared. Maybe this time, he *was* done with me.

I could only hope.

Jack confused me. He'd defended me to Dick, protected me, kissed me like I mattered to him. The tenderness had fucked with my head so I'd bitten his lip, but it was like my small action had triggered something in him and brought out the cruel asshole he really was, not the protective boyfriend type he'd pretended to be for five seconds.

Tovah, for her part, was livid. She'd ranted all week about "doing a murder, just a small but painful murder," and begged me to let her go after Jack "in any way I possibly can." In fact, she'd written an op-ed in *The Daily Queen* asking, "Do We Let Our Campus' Hockey Gods Get Away With Too Much?" The editor-in-chief had pulled her aside and told her no way were they running the article; the Kings were their biggest advertiser.

I told her it was okay, that I was okay.

And in some ways, I was.

Under normal circumstances, the bullying would have destroyed me. And I wouldn't pretend that being under such a malicious microscope didn't hurt, because it did. My anxiety was through the roof, my nerves were shot, I was sleeping like shit, and there were even times I had to force myself not to burst into tears. But these weren't normal circumstances. I had more important things to care about than my reputation at a university I'd never intended to be at in the first place.

All that mattered was proving that Joshua Jensen had

abused Asher so I could help Asher get his life and his future back.

Since hacking into Joshua's cloud account hadn't worked, I had to pivot to other tactics. I completely doubted that Asher was the coach's first victim, and I couldn't imagine no one had talked, so I spent the week diving deep into college hockey Reddits and other college sports forums, searching every version of Joshua Jensen's name I could think of to see if there was a single whisper of misconduct.

All I found was a single, buried post: *JJ's a real dick, and only thinks with his dick.* But the user, *motherpucker22,* had disappeared off of Reddit and deleted their account. I searched for them on every other social media site.

Nothing.

I was frustrated and desperate. This had to be a lead, so then why couldn't I find anything? I felt like I was failing my brother—and myself.

Unfortunately, my focus on justice meant other things slipped my mind. Namely, the semester-long partner project for Deviant Psychology.

Until one day, more than a week after Cumpdumpster-gate, I was rudely reminded of said project with this text from an unknown number:

> Hey, study buddy, when are we doing this thing?

My stomach dropped out of my body and through the earth. It probably landed somewhere in hell.

It had to be Jack.

> doing what thing

> Not even asking who this is?

> the red flags that popped up on my phone
> made it pretty obvious

He sent back a smirking emoji. I hadn't even know there *was* a smirking emoji.

> Meet me at the hockey house in an hour so
> we can figure out what our topic is.

Like I was an idiot. I wasn't going near the hockey house.

> meet me at M Libe

Ellipses danced across my phone's screen, before he finally responded.

> Sure, princess. If you think being in public
> will keep you safe from me, I'll play your little
> game. You win.

> For now.

I stared at my phone, uneasy. There was a part of me—a small part—that felt, if not happy, then excited that he hadn't completely disappeared. I hated that part. Jack and I were adversaries, and I had to keep my guard up around him. The only games we'd played so far were his, and I'd lost all of them. And maybe in Jack's eyes these were games, and I'd won this one, but I knew better. We weren't playing a game. We were fighting a war. And I needed to win.

MALEK LIBRARY, OTHERWISE KNOWN AS "M LIBE", WAS THE oldest building on Reina's campus. It was a large, dark, gothic structure, covered in climbing vines. Inside, it was dimly lit, aided by the soft glow of Tiffany lamps. Large oak tables and small study carrels filled cavernous rooms, surrounded by books that looked more for show than research.

I tried to find us a table on the first floor, hoping that all the quiet students would keep Jack on his best behavior, but there was no room, so I was forced to find us a table on the third floor, which, although not completely empty, was much less crowded. The one silver lining was that everyone was too focused on studying to take much notice of the most infamous girl on campus.

I practically jumped out of my chair when someone squeezed the back of my neck.

"Careful there, princess. You might hurt yourself," Jack chided, but he sounded more amused than concerned.

And of course he did. Why would he be concerned for me? Sure, he'd stood up for me to Dick and threatened him, but moments later he'd humiliated me in front of everyone. I was nothing more than a hockey puck to slap around the ice until he got bored of me.

"Don't do that," I said. "You scared the complete fuck out of me."

He raised an eyebrow. "Did I?"

He must have showered right before meeting me. His short, dark, straight hair was damp, and he smelled like lemony soap and that musky Jack scent that tempted me to lean into him. It didn't help that his white t-shirt and faded jeans stretched across his broad chest and powerful thighs, respectively.

He settled into the chair across from me, eyes probing my face.

"We should get started," I told him.

He ignored me. "How are you?"

I glared. "Really? You're going to ask me how I am? You painted a huge target on my back. Everyone here is shit talking me, in person and online. I can't go anywhere without being whispered about or laughed at. Or cat-called, propositioned..."

His jaw worked, and there was a look in his eyes I couldn't read. "Cat-called? Propositioned?"

"Every guy on campus thinks I'm easy. And they've had no problem with letting me know it."

He growled.

"I'll take care of it," he said abruptly. "No one is going to be fucking propositioning you anymore."

My eyes widened. "Why?"

He shook his head. "I already told you why."

You're mine.

"And yet here you are, in public," he mused.

"Here I am."

He looked closer at me. Was that admiration in his silver-gray eyes?

"You know, most people would have cracked under the pressure. Being mocked, torn apart online—"

"Don't remind me," I muttered.

"—ostracized...it would have broken most people. But you—you've held your head high and it hasn't distracted you from your priorities. I don't understand, how are you this strong?"

My cheeks heated with the praise. "Because I've dealt

with so much worse in my life," I told him. "It's not that it hasn't affected me, but I refuse to let it break me. I refuse to let *anything* break me. There are things more important than my reputation."

"So strong," he murmured. "So brave."

And then he leaned over the table, raising a hand to stroke my cheek. A shiver broke out, lighting up my spine.

I flinched away. "Don't," I said, my throat tight. "Don't mock me."

"I'm not mocking you."

Someone shushed us. I turned to see a student at a study carrel glaring at us. They looked at Jack, blushed, and looked back down at their computer.

"Sorry," they said, like they were the ones who'd broken the rules. It was truly amazing how being around a celebrity —and Jack was a celebrity—warped people's minds and values. Parasocial relationships were wild.

I cleared my throat. "We need to decide on a topic for the project." I squared my shoulders. He was going to hate what I said next. "I was thinking we could do it on the connection between power and sexual narcissism."

He shook his head, a shark's grin flashing on his gorgeous face. "You don't give up, do you?"

"Never."

"Strong, brave, and tenacious," he murmured. "Too bad though, because that's not what we're doing."

"Oh, you have an idea?"

"Yeah. I think we do our project on the symptoms of sexual repression and shame around sex. Sound familiar?"

"I'm not repressed," I hissed. My cheeks heated.

He hummed. "Are you sure, princess?"

"Don't call me princess."

His eyes, warm a moment ago, hardened. "I'll call you

whatever I want, Aviva. And I've changed my mind. You're right, we should do our project on sex and power—specifically the psychology behind giving up power in sex, the freedom in submission and consensual nonconsent. That feels...apt."

I swallowed. The room, once chilly, grew sweltering. "Submission isn't deviant."

His eyes were intense. "No, but it is considered divergent behavior."

"And what's between us isn't consensual."

He shrugged. Once again, I couldn't read the look in his eyes. "You're right. It's not. But you still want it, don't you, princess? Even though you tell yourself you don't?"

"Jack." I glanced around. "Not here."

It was like waving a red flag in front of a bull. I'd dared him, and as he shook his head at me before slowly disappearing under the table, I regretted my words.

"Jack," I hissed again. "You can't—"

But he either didn't hear me, or didn't care, because a moment later, my leggings were being pulled down, and my panties followed. And then my thighs were being pushed open and his mouth was on me and his tongue was drawing gentle circles around my clit and he was sucking it between his lips and working it and working me and I had to cover my mouth with my hand and trap my long, desperate, helpless whimper so everyone around us didn't figure out what he was doing to me.

He fingered me as he licked and sucked, one finger, then two, stretching me. The ache felt so good. I was still new to this, new to sex, and as he played with my pussy and lit up my whole body with pleasure, a thought came to me: Jack was shaping me around him. Around his own need, his own desire. My body was his Pygmalion as he molded me into exactly what he wanted me to be. Until I craved him, craved this so badly, I worried I'd never want anyone else.

And then I wasn't thinking anymore because he'd bitten down, because I was too busy coming, on his face, his fingers, completely out of control around strangers. I couldn't care as the sharp, brutal pleasure took over my every thought and feeling. I shook apart into pieces, my thighs caught in his grip as he feasted on me. It was too much, but he wouldn't stop, just worked my clit more, worked me harder, faster, and I fell apart all over again. And then again. And then again.

Finally, he released me, dropping a kiss on my mound so tender I almost cried. It was in complete opposition with the rest of his treatment of me. All these quick but sweet moments threw me, and I expected that was the point.

He pulled my underwear and leggings back up as I slumped back in my chair, drained. Moments later, he reappeared from beneath the table, his mouth wet with me.

"You can't tell me you didn't want that," he murmured. "I can taste how much you want it. Don't deny it or deny me, princess."

I tried to say *don't call me princess*, but my body was too buzzed.

Especially when he stood up from his chair, came around the other side of the table, and leaned down to kiss me. I tasted myself on him as he poured intensity into the kiss, into my mouth, and he was right, because I wanted it, wanted him.

And I didn't know how to make it stop.

When he pulled away, he lifted my chin with a finger, staring into my eyes. "If you like that, you're going to love what I do next."

His words chilled me. Not only because of the threat in them, but because I believed him.

I stood, gathering up my old crappy laptop and notebook as I stared up at him, refusing to be cowed. "I won't love it, because there's nothing you do that's loveable, and there's nothing about you that's loveable, Jack Feldman. I wish I'd never met you, and I can't wait for the day you're finally out of my life for good."

With that, I stormed out of the library.

But I could feel his eyes tracking me the whole time.

And part of me—a part I hated as much as I hated him?

Liked it.

15

Aviva

After Jack got me off in the library, I threw myself into finding evidence against Coach Jensen with renewed vigor. And although I hated to admit it to myself, I knew it was in part to avoid thinking about Jack, or how I'd responded to him. Although at night, I'd have dreams about him touching me; in the morning I'd feel desperate, frustrated, forced to get myself off with my fingers as I fantasized about him tying me up again.

Since the Reddit angle hadn't panned out, I turned to Tovah for help.

"What about seeing what Lucy or Leslie know?" she asked.

Lucy and Leslie were students at Tabb, and friends of Tovah's, even though they were both freshmen. I'd met them through Tovah a few times, and since Leslie was engaged to Tabb's hockey team's left wing, Mason Calloway, and Lucy's guardian was Tabb's hockey coach, Blake Samson, they might be able to find something out. Although I had my doubts Coach Samson knew anything. From what Lucy had reluctantly told us, he was a stickler for rules, decorum, and respect—something that pissed Lucy off to no end. Mason, however, was possibly as unhinged as Jack, but would do literally anything to make Leslie happy.

Part of me worried about saying anything to either girl. They were Tovah's friends, not mine, and Lucy especially seemed like a talker. I'd made a promise to Asher not to tell anyone anything, and I'd be breaking my promise and his trust by saying something. But I was running out of ideas, and I hoped they could help.

Feeling guilty, I texted my brother.

> im coming home for october break

He responded immediately.

> you don't have to. flights from california to NY are too expensive

His words made me feel even worse. I couldn't tell him I was only a few hours away by train; Gehenom wasn't that far from our aunt's home—our home—in Queens.

> im coming home. i miss you. how are you doing?

> you asked me that yesterday

> and the day before

> and the day before that...

> because I care about you, and i want to
> make sure you're doing okay. did you get
> the orange juice with the pulp in it?

> yes. and before you ask, i've been seeing
> the counselor twice a week, and it's helping.

Relief filled me like a cool drink of water for a parched throat.

> im glad you're going. kendrick lamar is
> headlining the super bowl half time show,
> did you see?

I watched as the ellipses danced on the screen. Finally:

> haven't been online. don't wanna see
> anything about hockey or reina

What could I say to that?

> you really don't have to come home.

> im coming home

I was. I'd find the money somewhere.

> ill see you in a couple weeks. love you,
> buttface

> not as much as i love you, farthead.

I smiled. Asher hadn't called me by his other childhood

nickname for me in a long time, and it was a sign he was doing better, even if only a little.

But he was still avoiding hockey. The thing he loved most, other than me. I wiped away the tears that spilled down my face.

I was going to get it back for him.

And make Coach Jensen pay.

Someone knocked on our door.

I padded over the door in fluffy socks, opening it.

No one was there, but there was a small package on the ground. I hadn't ordered anything, so it must be Tovah's.

Going back into the apartment, I glanced at the package.

My name was scrawled on it in big, block letters.

Filled with foreboding, I considered tossing the package in the trash, but curiosity got the better of me.

Opening it, I retrieved a small baggie, containing one white, nondescript pill.

Fuck, was it cyanide? Was he trying to kill me now?

There was a note on top.

TAKE ME.

Yeah fucking right. I wasn't an idiot.

My phone buzzed, and I glanced down. I'd saved Jack's number as "Jackass." It gave me a tiny bit of satisfaction, even though seeing his name appear in my texts made my heart skip and then stutter to a halt.

> Did you get the package?

> > im not taking your pill

> > for all I know, it's poison

> It's not poison.

Sure it wasn't.

> what kind of sociopath texts in full properly punctuated sentences anyway

Being grammatically correct doesn't make me a sociopath, princess. Ignoring societal mores and so-called ethics to get what I want and what I know other people need? That makes me a sociopath.

Speaking of which, we should meet up again to work on our project.

> nah, it's the capitalization

> and the rapeyness

He was relentless.

Take the pill.

> what is it

Vixen.

> i thought you said you weren't a drug dealer

> and i'm not taking your date rape drug

I'm not a drug dealer, I happen to know who deals. And it's an aphrodisiac, not a date rape drug.

> still not taking it

You think you have a choice? When are you going to learn?

this is going too fucking far Jack

it's one thing to let you...do things to me, fully conscious

Do "things" to you?

ykwim

I do know what you mean. You mean me fucking that tight little innocent pussy whenever and wherever I want, because you aren't allowed to tell me no, remember?

Or I'll go directly to the administration and tell them Asher Gold told his sister, Aviva Gold, to break into the hockey locker room and plant evidence against Coach Jensen.

And then Asher can say goodbye to ANY future in hockey, and you can say goodbye to a college degree. Going to be hard to become a psychologist without one, isn't it?

My teeth grinded together at the text. I hated him so much. He was taunting me, and I knew it. Because I had no way of winning against him. But I wasn't taking his fucking aphrodisiac-roofie-bullshit.

maybe ill go to professor johnathan and tell him what you're doing

There was no response. My heart pounded faster. Had I actually found a way out of this?

Don't you ever use that sleezy moron
against me.

Besides, my brothers have leverage against
him, and his entire family. He won't do
anything against me, even if he wants to.
How do you think I switched into your
seminar in the first place?

I stilled, staring at my phone screen. It explained so much, but it also meant I had no other option.

Take it now, and come to the hockey house
tonight. Or I'll ruin yours and Asher's lives.
Don't test me, Aviva.

Dress nice. We're having a special party.

And you're the guest of honor.

That same foreboding from earlier washed over me. Chills broke out over my skin. I could guess what sort of party it was. But Jack was right. What choice did I possibly have?

And with foreboding, a tingle all over my body that I couldn't deny. Excitement. I was excited. I was sick in the head, because the idea of taking an aphrodisiac, only to be at Jack's mercy, turned me on.

I didn't respond to the text, but opened the small baggie and located a bottle of water.

"We're all mad here," I muttered, before placing the pill on my tongue and swallowing it down.

16

Aviva

I t would've been better if the pill had been poison. Because right now, I wished I were dead.

I was hot all over. So hot. My skin *ached*. I wanted to be naked, and what's more, I wanted—no, needed—to be touched. I craved hands all over me, stroking, pinching, circling, rubbing, playing. I was soaked, my thighs covered in my own wetness. My nipples were so cold they burned, like someone had rubbed them with ice. And that thought was so kinky, I wanted to scream. Wanted to beg someone, anyone, to do that very thing to me.

No. Not someone, not anyone.

Jack.

The walk over to the hockey house was so uncomfortable, I sobbed the whole way. With each step, my thighs rubbed against each other. Even in jeans, the movement sent sharp sparks through me like someone was setting off mini fireworks in my pussy.

Finally, I arrived at the hockey house. I stumbled, my vision blurry from pleasure-pain, falling to my knees.

That's how they found me, on my hands and knees on their front porch, moaning like a wild thing.

"Jack," Judah—or Levi, I couldn't tell—yelled. "Your party guest's here."

There were footsteps, and then I smelled Jack's familiar scent—ice, spice, and whiskey—as he bent down and scooped me up in his arms like a bride.

"C'mon, princess. Your carriage awaits."

I moaned, curling against him like a cat seeking pets.

"It hit you hard, didn't it?" His laugh rumbled in his chest against my ear. I wanted to burrow into the sound. "Don't worry, I'll make you better." He paused, and I might have realized how sinister he sounded if my brain wasn't already blown with need. "Or worse."

All I could do in response was whimper.

"Fuck, that sound is so sexy," he growled.

He could talk. His growl made me wetter. I wanted to rub up against it, so I settled for rubbing up against him.

We were moving through the entrance, down the hall, around the living room where we'd danced with each other, past the kitchen where I'd first seen him, until we reached a room I hadn't seen before. Big and dark, with a huge wood table in the center of the room. And then I was being lowered onto the table, slowly, gently, on my hands and knees. I stretched like a cat, and I think I must have purred? Or something, because laughter echoed through the room, and it wasn't only Jack's.

No. Even in my mindless state, I recognized the twins and Isaac. There were others in the room, guys I recognized from the research I'd done on the team before transferring. I should've cared, I should've been worried. Nothing good could come from me being on the table, surrounded by strange men. This was the stuff of nightmares. I should've run, but all I could do was moan at how cool and hard the table was under my hands and knees.

I felt hands on me, big hands—Jack's hands. My sneakers and socks were removed, then my jeans were unzipped and peeled off, until I was bare below my waist.

Jack stroked me where I needed him, and I shivered.

"Fuck, already so wet," Jack groaned.

And then there was a thick finger pushing inside my pussy. I moaned. It was exactly what I needed, and yet somehow, not enough.

"Jack," I whined. "Please."

He leaned over my body, his mouth on my ear. "Please what, princess?"

"Please, I need you."

"Need me how?"

"Need your hand, your mouth, your cock. Need you to fuck me. Please, Jack, please, fuck me," I begged.

Later, I would be horrified by the way I'd acted, but the Vixen had buried the part of me that rejected sex and was ashamed that I got off on Jack's force and control. Right now, I was free to stop judging myself, or him, and just feel.

I luxuriated in it, in him. His big body behind mine as he leaned over my back and thrust his fingers in and out of me, rubbing exactly where I needed it. I came, for the first time that night, and even though it was a momentary relief from the endless need, it barely sated me. Instead it stoked the fire.

More.

"More?" Jack asked.

I must have said it out loud. But I nodded.

"Uh huh."

"Alright. More it is."

And then his fingers and body disappeared, and there was a wet mouth on me, licking, sucking. I came again, and this time it was both better and worse. Better, because the orgasm was bigger; worse, because when it ended, I needed the next one *more*.

More.

More.

More.

I must have said that word so many times. Screamed it, begged it. The mouth wasn't done. It hummed against me, sucking my clit between its lips and worrying it with its teeth. *It*, because at the moment, it was just a mouth. I didn't know if it was Jack's or not, it could've belonged to anyone, and even though part of me hated that, the not knowing, the other part of me reveled in it. Reveled in my orgasms, the freedom in my loss of control, the way the table grew slippery with sweat and my desire, the way my mind receded and my body took over.

More. More. More.

You sure? You sure you want more, princess?

Yes. Please, please. Yes.

Alright, but then you're going to give me what I want.

And then that mouth was back on me, and someone was lifting my arms, and my top with its high neck was being lifted off of me, too. And I knew, on some level, that was wrong. They couldn't see, no one could see...

No, I begged.

The mouth broke away. *Yes,* it growled.

And then the mouth was gone, and there was movement behind me as someone who smelled like ice, spice, and whiskey climbed up on the table behind me, and there was a cock, thick and curved and familiar, pushing inside of me.

Something was missing and I wasn't sure what it was, because it wasn't only my shirt.

Damn, that's hot, someone said, and then there were hands on my breasts, pulling and tweaking. I cried out at the cold-heat, the pleasure-pain, the fear-freedom of it all.

Don't touch her, someone barked.

But you said...

I don't give a flying fuck *what I said. You don't touch her. None of you touch her, or I'll fucking kill you.*

The voice was growling, but his hips were still moving, pushing inside of me at some perfect rhythm I couldn't follow but loved just the same.

Yes, yes, yes, more, more, more.

I'll give you everything you need, little thief. And then his hands were on my breasts, instead, pulling and tweaking and circling. And this was wrong, there was something wrong with this, that he was touching my bare breasts, that they were bare, that he could feel me, that he could feel—

A thrust so deep I lost my track of thought and screamed, coming again.

Deep male laughter.

But no more words. I expected to hear them still, and was almost disappointed. They were like a quiet Greek chorus, or maybe they were judges scoring me for my performance. I wasn't sure, and I didn't care.

Not as the man behind me with the perfect spice, ice, and whiskey smell and the big hands hammered away at my pussy, hitting the right spot every time and making fireworks, big ones now, explode inside me, and behind my eyelids. I shattered again, again, and again, only for him to remake me into someone else, someone new and unrecognizable. And then that version of me was broken, too, by the next orgasm, and the next.

Until finally, with a loud roar, he came. I felt him, felt the wetness of his release fill me up, and the heat of it, the rawness of it, made me explode again, one last time.

I would've collapsed against the table, except his big hands caught me around the waist and pulled me backwards with him still inside me, me on his lap, him still hard, even though he'd just come. He bounced me on top of him, his cock sliding in and out, and this was familiar, too. I curled against him and let him use me this way, content to be nothing more than...

My little fuckdoll.

Yes.

My little sextoy.

Yes.

Mine. All mine. You hear me, Aviva? You're fucking mine.

Yes!

I came again, one last time, and he came with me, and I couldn't tell who was who and where he left off and I began, and once again, I reveled in the tangle of the two of us together, the confusion of all of it.

He softened inside me, and my pounding heart slowed. His arm was around my waist, and his other hand was holding my breast.

My bare breast.

My bare...

It came back to me.

Why I couldn't be bare on top.

My scar.

He could feel my scar.

They could see my scar.

It was like I'd been drowning, and the realization pulled me above the surface. Blinking, I looked around me.

Jack had me cradled in his arms, resting his chin on my

hair. Surrounding us were men, so many men. Three I recognized: the rest of the Core Four. The others, from his hockey team. *Oh god.* Was Coach Jensen here?

And they could see all of me. They could see—

I screamed, the animal I still was wild with anger and grief and shame. The one thing I'd hidden, I'd kept to myself, and now they all knew. Now they all knew, and it was Jack's fault, all Jack's fault, and he'd done it because he hated me, and he wanted to punish me, and I hated him, hated him, hated him.

"What the fuck?" Jack growled, sounding confused, as his arms wrapped around me. I fought him, scratching and hitting, completely feral with my rage.

"That's some scar," someone said.

I cowered in on myself as I sobbed, but I had nowhere to go.

Behind me, Jack stilled. Squeezed.

"What scar?" he asked through gritted teeth.

17

Jack

I wasn't the type to make mistakes. The decisions I made were clearly motivated and my plans were prepped and well-executed. But I'd sorely misjudged this situation. After Aviva had physically rejected me, I'd been angry, and so I'd carefully planned my retaliation.

There's nothing you do that's loveable, and there's nothing about you that's loveable, Jack Feldman. I wish I'd never met you, and I can't wait for the day you're finally out of my life for good.

Her words haunted me. At the time, I'd refused to feel regret over what I'd done to her. Making her take Vixen and lose all of her inhibitions had been a great plan; letting my teammates participate so we could all humiliate her together had seemed even better. Judah, especially, had egged me on once he'd learned what she'd try to do to us. And making her so desperate, so horny, that I finally got her shirt off? Getting to see that part of her, and her knowing she'd played a role in it by taking the Vixen in the first place? Perfection.

Seeing her tonight, so broken and so free, had woken something feral inside me. Touching her, playing with her, watching her writhe on the table with an audience surrounding us had been equal parts hot and horrible.

But when it came down to it, when Judah and Levi had reached out to play with her tits, I'd lost my everloving mind. And I hadn't gotten it back.

No one else was going to touch her. No one else should've seen her. As I thrust inside her from behind, as I bounced her on my cock, as I finally got my hands on those sweet, soft tits with their hard, fat little nipples, as I felt her come around me, again and again, as I fucked her raw, there was only word in my mind, on repeat:

Mine.

Which meant that it had been a mistake, letting any other man see her naked.

It wouldn't be happening again.

I tried to recover, but my breath had gone missing along with my mind. Inhaling and exhaling deliberately to slow my heart rate, I caressed Aviva's bare breasts, enjoying the ripples of her aftershocks. Indulging myself for a moment, I nuzzled her hair and considered my next steps.

As my fingers traced her chest, I encountered skin that felt raised and a little rough. Before I could explore further, Aviva let out a bloodcurdling scream and began to fight me like a wildcat. Confused, I grabbed her around her waist, ignoring the scratching and hitting. Finally, she cowered against me, arms wrapped around herself, like she was terrified.

I shushed her, rubbing her back. The come down from Vixen could be fairly drastic. Although Mason Calloway, my counterpoint at our rival school, had drugged his girlfriend with it, and she'd gone to sleep after.

Dave Lawson, the goalie who'd replaced Asher, cleared up the mystery of the bump on Aviva's skin.

"That's some scar," he said, snapping me out of my own Vice-induced haze.

Everything in me froze solid.

"What scar?" I asked.

At that, Aviva screamed again, struggling against me like a cornered animal. I gathered her tighter.

"How could you? I hate you!" she railed against me.

I ignored her. "What scar?" I demanded again.

Nick McPherson, *my* backup, raised his chin. "See for yourself."

Dread skittered in my chest. Aviva used my distraction to shove away from me, crawling down the table. Before my brain could catch up, I grabbed her by the ankle and dragged her back toward me.

"You aren't going anywhere, princess," I told her, but I was gentle as I flipped her over onto her back and dragged her arms away from her chest.

I saw it. There was no way to miss it, now that she couldn't hide it with a high-necked tanktop or turtleneck. The scar was a long, dark, red-brown raised line of bumps and ridges. It ran from her sternum, up her cleavage between her breasts, ending below her right collar bone. Whatever it was from, it was old. A part of her body, and a secret she'd hidden from everyone. From *me*.

Until now.

Now, not only did I know her secret—all these mother-fuckers did.

Guilt replaced the dread inside me, but instead of skittering around, it stabbed me directly in the gut.

"I hate you, I hate you, I hate you," Aviva was still saying. Soft sobs shook her body, and tears filled her open eyes. She didn't close them, maybe because she wanted me to see how hurt and angry she was. It didn't matter that in this moment, she was deeply broken—she'd never been more beautiful.

And all these motherfuckers were witnessing it.

Not for any longer.

"Shut your fucking eyes," I ordered.

All of my teammates shut their eyes—except for Judah, Levi, and Isaac.

"You, too," I said, and all three did. Isaac was the last to do it, glancing at Aviva with sympathy and me with derision before closing his own.

Knowing they couldn't see Aviva in her naked pain anymore slightly relaxed me. Raising up off her, I slid off the table, pulled my shorts up over my softening cock, and scooped her into my arms like a bride before carrying her out of the dining room and up the stairs.

The whole way to my bedroom, she continued to sob, beating at me with her tiny fists. I let her. When I reached my room, I readjusted her slightly so I could type in my key code. 1113. November 13, the day I signed my letter of intent from Reina. The day I knew for certain that I was getting away from the nightmare that was my childhood home.

With a beep, the door unlocked, and I kicked it open, entering with Aviva still in my arms.

"I don't know what you think is going to happen now, so I'll tell you. I'm going home," Aviva informed me. The way her voice shook broke something in my chest, the heart I thought was long dead. She was so strong, so brave—and so, so vulnerable.

I'd hurt her. I'd been hurting her this whole time, but not like I had now. I'd taken something from her, more than her virginity. I'd taken her secret and aired it out in front of all those assholes. Would she ever forgive me?

"I'm going home!" This time, her voice cracked. Tears wet my shirt and I imagined they scalded my skin with shame: hers, and mine.

"Shhhh," I crooned to her gently as I shut the door with my foot and approached the king bed. I'd made it this morning, the fire red cover and ash gray sheets—Reina's school colors—still smooth and straight like I'd left them. I'd never had a girl in here. I usually fucked downstairs somewhere, or in Isaac's room. To have a girl I wanted so badly in my private space messed with my head. I ignored the urge to straighten up the room more for her, and placed Aviva gently on my bed.

She stood up to leave, and I stopped her by climbing onto the bed with her and pulling her into my arms.

"At least let me put clothes on."

"No."

Her apples and honey scent soaked my senses, and I buried my face in her wild, tangled hair, breathing her in. Her body was thick and soft, pliant in my arms. My cock stirred.

"That's why I'm here, then. So you can fuck me again. Humiliate me more." Her voice sounded dead tired. "Fine. Do it. Fuck me. Humiliate me. What choice do I have? You've made that clear, haven't you, Jack? *You. Win.*"

But I hadn't won. I didn't know what winning meant anymore. Aviva had a scar, which she'd been hiding from me, but I didn't know what it was from or why she hid it. There was so much I didn't know, and I usually knew *everything*.

"Princess," I began, before trailing off. What the hell was I going to say?

Sorry would be a good start.

The word got stuck in my throat.

She buried her head in the pillow, ignoring me.

Uneasy and unsure what to do with myself, I got up from the bed and bent over to retrieve a few water bottles out of the mini fridge.

Dropping them next to Aviva on the bed, I rejoined her, pulling her against me and stroking her hair.

"What can I do to make it better?" I asked, hating the urgency in my voice.

"Leave me alone."

The three words stabbed me in the gut. But the last thing I was doing was leaving her alone right now, not when she was this shaken up, this distraught.

This destroyed.

"Not that," I told her. "Tell me what to do that includes me being here with you."

"Nothing," she murmured into the pillow. Her voice sounded as broken as my heart. "There's nothing you can do to make it better."

With that, she fell silent. I rubbed her back as she sobbed, feeling desperate and lost, hating myself as much as she hated me, maybe more.

Finally, her sobs quieted as her breathing evened out. I held her in my arms for longer, until I was sure she was asleep.

I desperately needed air. Needed a drink. I wanted to rip my own hair out. I hated leaving her, but I couldn't lie here anymore. Kissing her on the forehead, my chest tight, I gruffly, quietly, finally said, "I'm sorry, princess." I shut the door behind me and hit the lock button.

When the beep announced the lock had engaged, I sank to the floor, burying my head in my hands. Humiliating her that way and getting to the bottom of what was under her shirt were supposed to make me feel amazing. Prove I had won, prove I was still in control. I hadn't won, I'd lost every vestige of control, and Jesus Fucking Christ, I'd barely even taken a look at the breasts I'd been obsessed with seeing since I'd met Aviva.

"Jack."

I looked up. Isaac's voice was soft, his blue eyes watchful, usual smirk nowhere in sight.

"Yeah," I said.

He shook his head, like he was disgusted with me. "Come downstairs. We need to talk."

Part of me wanted to argue, to stay camped out on my floor outside of my bedroom, like a guard dog. But Aviva was safe, and couldn't go anywhere because I'd locked the door from the outside. And sitting here on the floor like a pathetic fuck wouldn't do anyone any good.

Isaac held his hand out and I took it, using his help to stand on my own two feet before following him down the stairs.

The first floor was empty. The rest of the team had cleared out, probably on Judah and Levi's orders. Judah and Levi were in the media room, Judah's hand down his boxers as he played NHL 24 one handed. Levi was cleaning his glasses while staring off into space like the lunatic he truly was.

They both looked up when they saw me.

Judah paused the game, shaking his head, hairs escaping his man bun. "Dude."

"I don't want to hear it," I said, dropping onto the opposite couch.

"You don't even know what he's going to say," Levi pointed out, logical as ever.

Isaac joined me, slinging an arm around the back of the couch but not saying anything.

"Fine, what were you going to say, Judah?"

"You've got it bad, man. Down bad."

I laughed. It sounded hollow. "I didn't need you to tell me that. Or Taylor Swift, for that matter."

Judah rolled his eyes. "I know you said she's a lying, conniving, bitch and is trying to take down Coach and the team—"

Anger pulsed through me, and I started to stand before I even realized it.

Isaac put a hand out to stop me. "Jack."

Exhaling, I forced myself to slump back against the couch.

"This is what we mean." Levi took over. "You claim to hate her, say all these horrible things about her that *should* mean you don't give a shit if anyone else says or does anything cruel to her. But if we do, you go apeshit. It was your idea to bring her to the house and fuck her in front of all of us."

"Nonconsensually," Judah interjected, his jaw tight. "Which we didn't realize until the way she fought you once we all saw her scar."

Levi pinched the bridge of his nose. "I don't even want to touch that part. What's even more fucked is that you invited us to join in, remember?"

"I never invited you to join in," I protested, feeling sick.

"Maybe not verbally, but when we asked, you didn't say no. And then the second we touched her, you freaked out. Fucked her like a goddamned animal, and—"

"It was hot as fuck to see though," Judah interjected again. "And I hate what that says about me."

Used to his brother's interruptions, Levi ignored him. "—acted like it was the two of you alone in that room. Why invite us, if you didn't want us there, Jack? Why ask us to watch, only to blow up when Dave sees something you didn't? What's your end game here? You always used to know—do you now?"

"I know exactly what I'm doing," I argued. "She needs to pay. Needs to know her place."

"Does she, really?" Levi asked. "Even if she is a lying, conniving, bitch—"

"Hey!" My voice was sharp.

Judah chuckled. Levi's lips twisted in a smile.

"You clearly like her," Judah said. The insightful asshole added, "You don't react that strongly to someone who you only keep around for a good fuck. Don't be an idiot, Jack."

I swallowed. "I'm worried that I might push her too far, and lose her."

Judah raised an eyebrow. "Worried you *might* push her too far? What do you think you just did? A different woman —she would've broken in ways even you can't repair."

With those chilling words, both twins stood, Judah fixing his man bun and turning off the TV before they both left the room.

I turned to Isaac.

"You've been a quiet bastard," I noted.

Isaac sighed. "I never should've told you about that."

"Well?"

"I saw you, Jack. You insisted on going to The Stacks that night, you followed her even though I told you not to. I know what you were doing that night when you embarrassed the shit out of her. It wasn't 'cumdumpster' that was important, was it? It was the modifier. 'My.'"

I was surrounded by too many insightful assholes. "We never should've let you major in English."

"Hey, the English majors are the best fucks," Isaac smirked, then sobered. "If she's yours, then treat her like she's yours. It doesn't matter what she did or planned on doing to us. I know Coach means everything to you, but come on, Jack. That poor girl doesn't deserve this."

Fuck. He was right.

He held out his fist, and I fisted my own hand, tapping it against his.

"I need some sleep," he said. "And probably to rub one out. Because Judah is right. Even though that was a shit show, it was still hot as hell."

"Don't you dare fantasize about her," I growled.

He shook his head. "This is what we mean."

With that, he left me with my thoughts.

Pulling my phone out of my pocket, I told Siri to call Micah.

After two rings, my brother answered—on FaceTime, because he was a dick like that. It was dark, and he must have been asleep—it was late.

Even in the dark, the asshole looked good. Married life suited him—or whatever approximated married life when you were in a permanent relationship with three other people. His dark blonde hair had grown out a bit. And although his eyes were as astute and working as hard as ever, his face seemed more relaxed somehow.

Happier.

Fucking crazy that anyone who'd grown up in a home like ours could be *happy*.

"Yacob, what's going on?" he asked me, his voice scratchy with sleep.

I stiffened.

"It's Jack," I reminded him.

It wasn't the first time I'd had to remind him, and Micah never forgot shit. He did it on purpose. Why, I wasn't sure.

His voice cleared. "Jack. Right, sorry. What's going on?"

"Talk to me about Kara."

His tone went hard. Protective. "What about her?"

"There's no threat," I reassured him.

He visibly relaxed. "What about Kara?"

"When did you know it was more than a fuck for you?"

Micah looked behind him, then turned back to me and smiled. "Subconsciously, I knew the first time I saw her. In reality, it took walking away from her and missing her to realize how much I—we—needed her in our lives. You don't realize you're complementary puzzle pieces at first. But when you do, you don't let go. No matter what."

A hand—a woman's hand—appeared in the frame. "Baby, who are you talking to?"

"My little brother," he told her.

Kara's face appeared in the screen, soft with sleep. "Jack, what's going on? Is everything okay?"

The pretty redhead always called me by the right name.

"Jack here is having woman troubles," Micah told her.

I stiffened. "I've got it handled."

"Do you?" Micah asked.

"When you say you don't let her go no matter what, you mean no matter what she wants." I didn't even ask.

Kara snorted. "He does."

"Have you fucked her yet?" Micah asked.

"Micah!" Kara chided.

I didn't answer him. But by his eye roll, it was obvious he knew.

"Two words, kid. *After care.*"

"I think that's one word," Kara told him.

"I provide the aftercare, I think I know how it's spelled."

There was a groan behind them, then a very loud, "Unless our world is ending, hang up, and go the *fuck* to sleep."

"Shut up, boss," Micah said fondly to Conor, one of their other partners. To me he said, "One word or two, don't forget to do it."

"Aftercare is one word," I said. "And she—" I had started to say *doesn't deserve it*, but that would've been a damn lie. She deserved all the comfort in the world, and I hadn't given it to her. She'd been shaking, quiet, in shock. I'd hurt her, badly, and then I'd *left her alone.*

Bile rose in my throat. I moved to hang up the phone, but my brother spoke.

"Wait one second. You don't really think she doesn't deserve it, Yacob," he said, because the fucker was basically a mindreader. "If you did, you'd have to be a fucking fool, and you're no fool. Get off the phone with me and go fix whatever you fucked up."

"Goodnight," Luke, their other partner, called.

Micah sighed. "We're going to try to make it to one of your games this season. Have some jobs to complete, but I'll let you know when. Marcus is coming, too."

"Whatever." I couldn't admit to the hope that bubbled up. I could trust Micah and Marcus when it came to advice, but not much else. I doubted they'd actually show. They hadn't been there for me in the years I'd actually needed them. That had been Coach.

Who Aviva was still trying to destroy.

That poor girl does not deserve this.

I pressed end without saying goodbye.

Stretching, I pocketed the phone and wandered down the hallway, picking up Aviva's clothes from the dining room. The house was quiet; everyone had gone to sleep.

Another woman would have broken.

Had I gone too far? Aviva was strong, remarkably so— she'd proven it tonight when she'd still stood her own against me. But even the strongest tree could crack if lightning hit it right. Was Judah right? Had I broken her?

And who was I, to be so confused, so torn? Not Jack Feldman, that was for sure.

Stopping in the kitchen, I heated up some water and made hot chocolate. Aftercare involved chocolate, right? A little late, but still seemed like it would help. I was both anticipating and dreading what would happen when I got back up to my room.

Once I was upstairs, I entered the code, slowly opening the door, expecting anything. More screaming, more crying, maybe projectiles thrown in my direction.

Nothing. The quiet was punctuated by soft breathing from the bed. I made my way over, switching on the flashlight on my phone so I didn't trip over anything.

Aviva was asleep on the bed above the covers, curled into a protective ball, pillow between her thick, beautiful thighs, brown curls covering her soft, heart-shaped face. Gently, carefully, I moved her hair off her face. Even in sleep, she seemed troubled, eyes moving under eyelids as if she were having a nightmare.

"No," she begged, "No. Don't look, please."

"Aviva? Princess, are you awake?"

She didn't respond.

She was dreaming. Was it about me? Was the nightmare because of what I'd done to her?

Guilt returned. I set the hot chocolate on the nightstand, stripping down to my boxers before climbing into bed behind her. I wrapped my arms around her waist, pulling her back against my chest. Immediately, I relaxed. I'd never slept with a woman in my arms before, but I didn't hate it.

Not at all.

"You're okay," I murmured as I leaned over her and stroked her hair. "You're okay."

Slowly, she relaxed, her face smoothing out. I released her waist to remove the pillow between her thighs, replacing it with my leg. Truly tangled together, and satisfied in ways I couldn't fully explain, I soaked up the feeling of her in my arms, shutting my eyes and picturing a life where this was every night for me.

When you realize, you don't let go. No matter what.

I might not trust her, I might not like her, but I was obsessed with her.

And she deserved better. She was stuck with me, but that didn't mean I couldn't treat her better.

"You aren't going anywhere, little thief," I murmured into her hair. "But I am sorry."

She'd stolen something from me, something I couldn't entirely describe. My control? My equilibrium? Something worse? Maybe we were even now, since I was stealing her, but it didn't matter.

She'd pay. Forever, if I had a say.

But then why did I regret what I'd done?

I closed my eyes, but as good as holding Aviva felt, sleep wouldn't come. Guilt and fear had run off with it. Because what if Isaac, Judah, and Levi were right? What if Micah was? Had I pushed her too far? Was I going to lose her? Had I lost her already?

18

Aviva

My bed had magically become more comfortable overnight. Instead of a stiff, thin Ikea mattress, supportive memory foam cradled my body. A pillow, softer and cooler than I'd maybe ever felt in my life, was under my head. And I was warm. Too warm.

What's more I felt safe, protected, cared for. Maybe it was because of the strong pair of familiar arms wrapped around me, one holding my belly, the other cupping my breast.

My *bare* breast. I could feel fingers directly on skin...and touching my scar.

Jack.

I was in his bed.

He'd fucked me last night in front of his entire team while I was high on Vixen, and taken off my shirt and bra, and I'd let him. Everyone had seen my bare chest, everyone had seen my scar.

He'd humiliated me, stolen my privacy, was witness to my tears, and then the asshole didn't even let me leave. And now he was cuddling me in sleep?!

I slapped at his hands. They squeezed my stomach and breast tight, and I gasped despite myself.

"Good morning, princess," he crooned in a sleepy voice. "Do you like to play rough in the mornings? If so, I'm game."

He pushed his hips against me, and I could tell he was growing hard, could feel it between my ass cheeks. An unwelcome tingle crept over my skin.

"I also brought you hot chocolate last night. I thought the sugar might...help the crash, but I didn't want to wake you. I can get you more," he said, nuzzling me.

It was almost cute that he thought that would win him brownie points. *Almost.*

"Since when do you make hot cocoa for your *cumdumpster*?" I spat. I needed to get the hell out of here. I wasn't safe here, my sleeping brain had tricked me. This was the quiet before the storm. Jack was either:

- Fucking with my head by being sweet so that it would hurt more when he was cruel again later.
- Completely unaware or uncaring of my feelings, and liked having a human pillow in his bed with him; an emotional support woman post heartrending fuck.

Or both. Both was accurate.

"You are my cumdumpster. You're also my princess. My little liar, my little spy, my little thief. You're all those things. But you know the common thread here?" This time, he pinched my nipple—hard—and didn't release it. I cried out, surprised by the action, the sharp pain, and the resulting pleasure.

"Mine," he finished, releasing my nipple. An ache started in the tortured bud, spreading to my whole body. "You're all those things, but mostly, you're mine."

"You keep saying that," I countered, doing my best to ignore the desire he'd stirred up. "But it doesn't mean what you think it means," I quoted.

"*The Princess Bride*?" he laughed into my ear. "Fitting, I guess."

"How do you know *The Princess Bride*?" I asked, curious despite myself. It was super old, after all.

His voice sounded...sad. "It was my mom's favorite movie."

Oh, *shit*. "Was?"

He sighed. "Could still be, for all I know. I haven't spoken to her since I left for college over four years ago." He changed the topic. "How do *you* know the movie?"

"It was my great-aunt's favorite."

"Was?" he mirrored.

"Was. She died my freshman year. Left us the house, at least, but not much else because there wasn't much else."

"Poor princess," he said, sounding genuine, nuzzling me again. His empathy scared me more than his cruelty.

"Alright, story time is over," I said. "I only belong to myself. And if I ever *do* belong to someone else, they'll treat me a hell of a lot better than you do."

He froze behind me. "I deserve that."

I froze, too. "Does that mean the bullying and torture will stop?"

"What will you give me, if it does?"

"What do you want?"

"The story of how you got that scar, for one thing. For another, you promise to stop trying to destroy Coach's life and the team's chances at winning the Frozen Four this year."

I would've shaken my head if it wasn't still pressed against the pillow. Instead, I laughed. *My* laugh was bitter. "You don't *deserve* to fucking know. And *he* doesn't deserve leniency."

Jack stroked my hair, and I shivered at his touch. "This is always going to come between us, isn't it? I hurt you last night, and I'm—"

"What, sorry?" I spat.

"Tell me about the scar, princess."

"Don't call me princess!" Something in me broke, like the shock from the night before had worn off and the hazy nightmare of last night was coming clear. "Just fuck me, Jack. That's what you want me for, isn't it? That's all I am to you, right? Stop with this pillow talk half-assed apology bullshit and fucking fuck me already."

His hand on my hair stilled.

Then:

"As you wish," he said, and something about his quoting *Princess Bride* in such a dark moment made me want to cry.

Until he rolled me over onto my stomach, pressing his entire body on top of me. "Is that what you need, little thief? To be fucked? Will that make you feel better, to be used that way?"

Jack forced my thighs apart and my hands above my head. I felt him moving behind me, the sound of fabric sliding off, and then he was tying my wrists together with his boxers. He shoved his hips against me again, and this time I felt his bare skin, cock hard and hot again and wet with precome. Like I'd fantasized about, masturbated to.

Oh, god, what had I done? What was I *doing?* Did I want this?

Shock, my inner psychologist supplied. I was in shock. Last night had been too much, and so my brain was protecting me by keeping the worst of the emotions at bay until I could process them. It was using sex as a distraction. That was all this was.

"Jack, *no*," I said, even though I didn't believe it.

"Aviva, *yes*," he said, just as firmly. "You need this, even if you don't want to admit it, little liar. Need me to be the villain, so I'll be the villain. Your villain.".

And then he was pushing my thighs apart and his cock was at my entrance and the tip was entering me and—

"Jack! Put on a condom. God knows who else you've fucked."

"I get tested regularly, I have no STIs. I've never been with anyone bare. And you've only ever been with me."

"But I'm not on birth control—" I started to protest.

He cut me off, pushing my head against the pillow as he slowly shoved his cock inside me. Even though I was already wet, it still hurt. He felt thicker this way, longer, bigger—and that feeling only increased when he shoved my legs back together with his thighs.

He sighed as he bottomed out, kissing my neck. "Perfect."

I hated it, hated him, hated my own body, hated myself. Because in that moment, it *was* perfect. I felt so full, surrounded by all sides, and the shame I'd felt before was gone. This wasn't my fault, none of it. I had no control, so I couldn't be blamed. And if my body liked it, well, I couldn't be blamed for that, either. That was only biology.

Maybe he was right, maybe I did need to be fucked.

As if he'd heard my thoughts, Jack began to croon his

approval in my ear. "Such a good girl, accepting you don't have any control. Such a good, sweet little cunt, accepting the cock it was made for. It's okay, princess, let yourself feel. You're not doing this, I am. You aren't at fault, the big bad hockey player is. And doesn't it feel good, letting someone else be in charge?"

Oh god, it did. It *did*. I clenched around him, and he growled.

"Fuck, that's it, yes. I can feel you drenching my cock. You're going to come like this, just from the sound of my voice. I'm not going to move at all. In fact, I might not move ever again. Would you like that, little thief? Being trapped here forever, forced to take my cock every single second until we both die?"

Oh, *fuck*. I clenched again, everything in my body going tight from his words and the picture he drew.

He growled again, lower, harsher. "I think I *will* keep you here. Tie you spread eagled to my bed, keep the door locked. Feed you whenever you need, fuck you whenever I want. Make you completely reliant on me. Your entire existence will be to serve my cock with all three of your holes. I'll come in you, over and over, until you don't know what it feels like to not be wet with it inside you, until you crave me every second I'm not inside you...my perfect, beautiful, brilliant little whore." He bit my ear, lowering his voice, his breath tickling my neck. "You drenched my cock again. That vision appeals to you doesn't it? Aviva Feldman, Jack Feldman's little fucktoy..."

It was the slip up, him giving me his own last name in this godforsaken fantasy, that did it. I cried against the pillow as a soft but powerful explosion went off in my body, my pussy clenching and pulsing around him as incredible pleasure took over.

"That's it. You come on *my* fucking cock," he groaned, and then wet heat spilled into my pussy as he came, too, his cock pulsing inside of me. I trembled, overwrought and overworked from his words. I came again from the feel of him, the knowledge that he was bare, filling me up, *and there was nothing I could do about it.*

The second orgasm was better and worse than the first one—bigger, sharper, cutting me deep so all of my pent up emotions came out: The lust and the loathing and the incredible *relief*, not only from the physical release, but from knowing I didn't *have* to do anything right now, have to make decisions, that all I had to do was feel.

Finally, he relaxed, letting me feel his entire weight. I expected him to pull out, but he stayed where he was, even as he softened inside of me. Come spilled out, on his balls, between my thighs, all over the bed.

"I really wish we *could* stay like this forever," he sighed. "But you should go pee so you don't get a UTI." Muttering to himself he said, "See, I know aftercare."

I snorted. Making sure I peed wasn't aftercare; cuddling me last night *almost* was. But I wasn't about to correct him and risk a repeat—or worse.

He untied my wrists, before taking each in his hands, rubbing them to bring life and circulation back to my hands. And completely disconcerting me when he dropped a gentle kiss on each of my pulse points. With that, he climbed off of me, releasing me.

"Where are my clothes?"

"You don't need your clothes," he said calmly.

My thighs clenched. "What, you want to fuck me again?"

He sighed. "I always want to fuck you, Aviva. But no, right now I'm going to hold you and we're going to talk and then I'm going to feed you breakfast."

Breakfast. Like we were boyfriend and girlfriend, not bully and...

...victim.

I'd become a victim. His victim. But I wasn't a victim. Refused to be. He'd tried to break me, almost succeeded, but I was stronger than that. I wouldn't give up, wouldn't give in. I didn't care how hot it was, how good sex felt with him.

"You took things too far, Jack. When you made me drug myself and took off my shirt in front of your *entire goddamned team.*"

Anger felt good. Anger felt strong. Anger felt *healthy.*

"Where are my clothes?" I asked again.

Silently, he stood up off the bed and went to the closet, coming back with my clothes, carefully folded.

I sat on the edge of the bed, pulling my pants and top back on, twisting my knotted hair into some semblance of a bun. I'd never done a walk of shame before, and the fact that I'd have to, in broad daylight on a Saturday morning, pissed me off. Knowing my scar was visible in the daylight pissed me off. Everything about this, about him, pissed me off. Moments from last night played in my mind: the way I'd lost myself while everyone had watched, Dave Lawson noticing my scar and announcing it to the room, Jack carrying me up the stairs as I fought him. It had been degrading and devastating, and I needed to be done. I'd said that before, told myself that before, but Jack had a crossed a line last night that neither of us could come back from. If I continued with him, if I *let this continue*, then I would become someone I didn't recognize.

Had I already become that person? I didn't want to be a stranger to myself.

No. This was it.

I.

Was.

Done.

I'd apologize to Asher when Jack destroyed our lives. I'd find another way to get him justice and take Joshua Jensen down. But I couldn't take any more.

Jack watched me as I dressed. I refused to turn away, to lower my gaze, to give him any satisfaction in my submissiveness or fear. No, I stared him straight in the eyes, like I had last night while I'd cried. I wouldn't cower in front of him.

No more.

I wouldn't let him hurt me again.

We stayed like that, me seated on the bed, him by the closet, staring at each other. Neither of us spoke, but the silence spoke for us. There was so much ugliness between us, anger on my side, something—could that be fear?—on his. But I couldn't fall into the trap of trying to figure out what he was feeling. And the stabbing in my chest that felt like sadness, like regret? It had to be a hangover from the Vixen.

"Jack?" I asked, injecting sweetness into my voice.

"What's up? You want to stay? I make a mean pancake." He grinned at me, but it didn't reach his eyes.

"I wish I'd never met you. No amount of justice is worth the hell you're putting me through. I never, ever, want to fucking see you again."

His face turned to stone.

"As you wish, princess," he said.

With that, he pressed a button on the door. The locks beeped as they disengaged, and he stood to the side, arm held out to guide me out the door.

Slipping my feet into my frayed sneakers, I ducked out of the way of his arm, determinedly walked out of his door—and hopefully, out of his life.

Just as I reached the hallway, he stopped me with four chilling words:

"See you in class."

19

Aviva

I spent Saturday and Sunday on my couch buried under blankets, rewatching *Ted Lasso* with a concerned Tovah. She'd begged me to tell her what was going on, but I knew if I did, she'd go directly to the police. What's more, I was worried she'd be ashamed of me, and that I'd put up with Jack's behavior for so long.

But no longer.

My phone was silent; no packages were delivered. It was a relief, even though I knew I hadn't seen the last of him. I even went so far as to research if I could drop out of Deviant Psych this far into the semester without it impacting my transcript; unfortunately at this point I'd fail the course.

My only option was to beg Professor Johnathan to let me switch project partners.

Monday rolled around, and I forced myself to get up, shower, put on clothes—careful to cover my scar. As I wrapped a scarf around my neck and tucked it under my top, I froze, staring in the bathroom mirror at the dark circles under my eyes.

What if someone had taken a picture with their phone? What if someone had recorded the whole thing? What if it already was online somewhere?

What if Friday night had ruined my life in ways I couldn't imagine?

Walking into the living room, I called to Tovah, who was making us both coffee.

"Tov?"

"What's up?"

I swallowed. "There haven't been any...posts about me on social media, have there? Can you check?"

She eyed me. "Do you want to tell me why?"

I shook my head, and she sighed, picking up her phone and scrolling.

"Nope, nothing. But I swear to god, Aviva, you need to tell me what's happening. You don't have to go through whatever this is alone."

I blinked tears away. "You're the best, have I ever told you that?"

She reached forward, hugging me. "No, you're the best. The strongest, the bravest, the loyalest. But you don't *have* to be."

Even without any posts about what had happened at the hockey house, I still couldn't relax. Just because it hadn't been posted yet didn't mean that it wasn't coming. Or that they hadn't created a fake Only Fans account and shared it there. I resisted the urge to text Jack and beg him not to post anything, and to tell his team the same thing. That would only give him ideas. I prayed that he hadn't thought of it yet, and no one else had, either.

I made my way to class slowly, knowing I was going to be

late, but reluctant to be there. I didn't want to see Jack, and I didn't want to be back in the room where he'd first fucked me. There were too many memories and they weren't all horrible ones.

By the time I got there, the door was locked. I had to knock, which was embarassing enough. Worse was Professor Johnathan's concerned face when he saw me.

"Aviva, you're late. You're never late. Is everything okay?"

His voice carried through the hallway; everyone in class must have heard him too.

I forced a smile on my face. "Everything's fine. Overslept."

He gaped at me. "It's four p.m., Aviva." His face turned stern. "I'd expect better from you than to be partying so hard on a Sunday night."

Someone inside the classroom chuckled.

The professor sighed.

"Come on in. There's been some rearranging I'll go over."

There was one free chair by the window. Jack wasn't next to it like I'd expected; instead, he sat beside another girl.

I did not care. I would not care. Jack Feldman meant nothing *to me.* Nothing.

Shaking myself mentally, I went to go sit in the only empty seat, pulling out my beat up laptop and paying attention to the professor and only the professor.

He cleared his throat. "Before you got here, Aviva, the class decided they wanted to do some rearranging of partners for the project. Jack and Katie are now working together—"

Was there anywhere lower my stomach could fall? Through the floor maybe? I inhaled deeply, forcing my expression to stay blank.

"Does that mean I'm working with Sebastian?" I asked, naming the student who'd wanted to work with me before.

Professor Johnathan looked guilty. "Sebastian wanted to stay with his current group."

"No I didn't," Sebastian muttered.

Wait, what?

Professor Johnathan coughed. "You'll be working alone, Aviva." He brightened. "But you're welcome to come to office hours whenever you like if you want to talk through anything."

I glanced over at Jack. He looked unconcerned. This, if anything, solidified my hunch that he was done with me.

What a goddamned relief. It was over. And hey, I could do my project on power and sexual narcissism after all.

But I wasn't relieved. That stabbing feeling in my chest? Not relief.

Why wasn't I relieved? Had that motherfucker wormed his way into my heart, even as he'd tormented and tortured me? I hated him, I refused to be sad he'd moved on.

My phone buzzed. I checked it when Professor Johnathan wasn't looking at me.

It was Lucy.

> tovah said you wanted to talk?

Oh, thank god. I'd meant to reach out to Lucy myself, but I'd felt like such shit this weekend I hadn't had the energy to. I was grateful Tovah had.

> i need your help with something
>
> how much do you know about coach jensen

jensen? the kings coach?

that's the one

not much, only that blake hates him

My skin tingled. Someone hated Joshua? Someone who knew him?

blake's tabb's hockey coach, right

yup

also my warden, guardian, jailor and general pain in the ass, but that's besides the point

I tried to play it cool.

why does he hate him?

idk, but blake's face gets all tight and mouth all square and pissed if his name comes up

ill bug him about it, its fun to bug him about things

why?

Before I could respond, Professor Johnathan cleared his throat.

I looked up guiltily, hiding my phone under my desk.

"Ms. Gold, I would appreciate it if you paid attention to class and not to whomever you're texting."

"I'm sorry, you're right," I mumbled.

The class laughed. Jack raised an eyebrow.

I raised an eyebrow right back.

I wasn't going to get caught up in his games. Not when it looked like I finally, *finally*, had a lead. And without the distraction of Jack's torment and torture, I was free again. Free to get justice for my brother. And god save *anyone* who got in my way.

Including Jack Fucking Feldman. Anger, righteous and energizing, filled me. So did determination. I wouldn't let how he'd hurt me at the hockey house destroy me. Wouldn't let it distract me from my true purpose at Reina. I wouldn't take his bullshit bent over anymore. Even if a fucked up part of me craved it.

As if he could hear my thoughts, his eyes narrowed.

I narrowed mine right back.

Because if Jack thought he was still calling the shots when it came to me?

Then he had another think coming.

20

Aviva

"I can't believe he thinks he can boss you around like this," Tovah said. She was sitting on my bed, eyeing me as I got dressed for the hockey game. "What, he ignores you for a week—thank god—and then sends you a box with his jersey in it, tells you to wear it to the first game of the season, and expects you'll...do it? Does he know you at all?"

"He does," I said.

That was the problem. He knew I didn't like being bossed around, especially by him. He also knew that when it came to sex, I craved it from him—because he'd fucked up my brain when it came to sex.

And maybe when it came to everything else.

Earlier that day, I'd been surprised by a box at our door. Inside was Jack's jersey with instructions to come to his game "or else." Apparently he wasn't done fucking with my head, after all.

At first, I'd considered ignoring it entirely. I'd tossed

the jersey in the trash and was about to text "fuck you," to him, but that didn't feel like a big enough statement. No, I wanted my fuck you to be impossible to ignore or misunderstand. He'd humiliated me publicly, now it was my turn.

"Well," Tovah said. "Should we make a sign that says "JACKASS FELDMAN" and cheer every time Tabb scores? Lucy and Leslie said they'd sneak over to our side of the arena for part of the game, so at least we can cheer with them."

I couldn't wait to see them. Not only because they were fun and I liked them, but because Lucy had promised to grill Coach Samson about Joshua Jensen. I hadn't told her why, but Lucy, who was loyal in ways I understood and appreciated, had said, *I get it, girl code.*

I eyed her. "The sign sounds cute, but it's not enough." An idea came to me. "Any chance you have another player's jersey?"

Tovah blushed. "Um, as it so happens..."

She opened her closet.

I blinked.

There were easily eight hockey jerseys hanging inside, surrounded by dresses and sweaters. I knew Tovah was a hockey fan, but this was a little...extra.

I moved forward and started going through them.

"Wait, I think—" Tovah started.

Jones, 37

Jones, 37

Jones, 37

Jones...

"Why do you have four of Isaac's jersey?" I eyed her speculatively, pulling one of the jerseys off the hanger and waving it in front of her.

"They were on sale. Probably because he sucks," she said, her cheeks turning pinker.

Hmm.

"Anything you want to tell me?"

"Nope." She popped the P. "And since you're leaving a lot of shit out about Jack and you, I'd say we're even." She nodded toward the closet. "There are other players' jerseys in there."

The next jersey said *Lawson 10.* I ran my fingers over the 1 and 0, a tingle going through me. The number was apt: 10 was the year my life had fallen apart.

The number belonged to Dave Lawson. The goalie, who'd spotted my scar on the night I refused to think about, had once been Asher's backup before taking over his position.

Dave had also been a friend of my brother's at one point. Until Asher was kicked off the team and Dave ghosted him.

A lightbulb went off in my head.

Wearing Dave's jersey would serve dual purposes–and I was nothing if not resourceful.

First, since he'd replaced my brother he might know more about what had happened, might even feel a little guilty about taking Asher's spot. It was also possible that he'd be more tight-lipped because he'd benefited from Asher being kicked off the team, but I refused to leave that stone unturned. He may not notice me from the ice, but Jack fucking would, and I hoped Jack noticing would mean Dave would notice, too.

Which brought me to my second purpose. Because what could be a greater "fuck you" than not only wearing another player's jersey, but also wearing the jersey of the player who'd cemented my humiliation by pointing out my scar? Wearing Dave's jersey would prove how little I cared about what Jack and his teammates thought of me. How unaffected I was. It was like saying "you don't and never mattered to me."

It also was like waving a red flag in front of a bull—apt, given that Reina's colors were red and white. But if this exploded in my face, I'd make sure that Jack got hit by all the shrapnel, and didn't escape unscathed.

Holding the jersey alone made me feel like I'd gotten my power back.

Power I'd lost ever since he'd caught me in the Kings' locker room, backed me up against his locker, and wrapped his hand around my throat.

That night felt like so long ago. I'd aged years, become someone else I didn't fully recognize, but I was going to get the old Aviva back.

I pulled the jersey over my head.

"I look okay?" I asked Tovah.

"You look like you're about to be sacrificed on the funeral pyre of Jack Feldman's crazy, but you'll look hot as you burn," she said.

"Well, as long as I look hot," I joked.

She shook her head. "I like this Aviva, and how kickass, take-no-names, fuck-all-the-haters she is. But I've gotta admit—she's scary."

"Perfect," I said. "I like being scary."

Looking in the mirror, I tossed my curly-wavy brown hair over my shoulders, squaring them as I prepared for battle.

A battle I was going to fucking win.

THE ARENA WAS PACKED. TOVAH HAD ASKED THE SPORTS editor at The Daily Queen for a favor, and they'd gotten us great seats—center ice.

I tried not to stare at Jack as he warmed up, but it was impossible, especially based on the way his ass moved as he practically humped the ice. At least he couldn't see me staring.

But I was distracted from Jack stretching when an older man with blond hair walked out on the ice. He was busy staring at the tablet in his hands as he talked to a player. If you didn't look closely, he looked kind, dignified. *Normal.*

But I knew better. I knew Joshua Jensen, the true one, even if I'd never spoken to him. The bespoke suit and commanding nature couldn't hide the narcissist underneath. Often, the worst of humanity hid their horrors behind a friendly smile, because they'd learned how to imitate friendliness and manipulate people in order to set them at ease. Powerful men especially used their charisma and seeming respectability to hide whatever evil inclinations lay beneath.

But peel the suit back, and people would see the weak, pathetic, power-hungry abuser. I'd make sure of it.

"You okay?" Tovah asked beside me. "You've got that 'take no prisoners' look in your eyes."

"I'm fine," I growled.

She glanced over to where I was staring.

"You can't kill him," she said immediately. "I know it would be fun, but I don't want to visit you in prison."

My teeth ground together. "You'd get used to it."

The buzzer sounded the beginning of the first period. Isaac faced off against Tabb U's center, and the second the puck dropped, he stole it and sent it wide to Jack, who hit it up the weak side. Tabb's defensemen slammed him into the boards, but he pushed the puck between the boards and his stick so that he kept control. Once the other winger had shoved the defensemen off of him, Jack continued toward the goal.

And that's when he spotted me.

My heart pounded as he stared up at me from the ice. He didn't lose track of the puck for a second, and reluctantly, I marveled at him. Even with his focus on me, he still managed to fake out the defenseman and pass the puck back to Isaac. A moment later, the horn sounded, signaling a goal. The scorebox changed: 1 Reina, 0 Tabb. I barely paid attention, unable to look away from Jack as he skated toward the bench, his eyes never leaving mine.

I could read his lips from where I sat.

What the fuck are you wearing?

I winked at him.

Take it off. Now.

I shook my head.

He shook his, then drew a line across his neck, before pointing at Dave. Dave hadn't noticed either of us.

"Here we go," I murmured.

The buzzer sounded, signaling the end of the first period.

Jack skated over to Dave and said something. This time, Dave's head turned toward me. I sat up straighter, hoping the number on the jersey I'd borrowed was visible. Even though I couldn't see his face through his goaltender mask, I could imagine the conversation going down.

Why the fuck is Aviva wearing your jersey?

I have no clue, Feldman.

You better have some clue. If I find out you touched her—

Why the hell do you even care if I touched her? You treat her like—

Like a whore?

Exactly.

Do. Not. Touch. Her.

I swear, Jack, I have no idea why she's wearing my jersey. Maybe you should ask her.

Jack raised his stick midway, and for a moment I thought he might try to hit Dave in the junk with it. Even with layers of clothes between Dave and Jack's stick, it could still be painful.

I waved.

"*Super* scary," Tovah said.

Energy fizzled beneath my skin. I hadn't felt powerful in so long. I also had never felt this reckless, but hey, high risk, high reward, right?

Joshua Jensen yelled something at Jack and Dave that I couldn't hear. Jack ignored him, advancing toward Dave. Isaac skated over, touching Jack on the shoulder, who shoved him off. And then, shocking even me, Jack broke the cardinal rule of "protect your goalie" and smacked Dave on top of his mask, *hard*.

Shouts broke out, Jack's teammates skating toward them to break things up before it turned into an actual fight.

"Jack!" Joshua Jensen barked. "What the hell are you thinking?!"

Well, that I could hear.

"Holy shit," Tovah whispered.

"Holy shit," I agreed.

As Jack skated toward the coach, he stopped, turning to look at me one more time.

I swallowed, my mouth and throat suddenly dry. The cold disappeared, the rink and fans disappeared, until it might as well have just been him, and me, alone in space, no gravity, no nothing, the only thing keeping me from floating away the heat of his gaze on mine.

He broke my trance.

Run and hide, he mouthed through his helmet.

And even though a part of me wanted to, I lifted my head and stared at him, staying where I fucking was. I refused to back down, to cower in front of him like a punished puppy. To let him win.

He shook his head, saying something to Joshua before disappearing down the tunnel.

I exhaled, feeling dizzy.

"Well, that looked intense," a chirpy voice said.

I glanced over to see Lucy and Leslie standing there, both in purple and gold Tabb jerseys, staring at me in amusement and shock, respectively.

"Omg, hey!" I said, momentarily forgetting Jack Feldman —or at least trying to.

We all hugged. Tovah and I scooted over, making room for Lucy and Leslie.

"I can't believe he hit his *goalie*. You don't hit your goalie. Your goalie is sacred," Lucy said, awed. "What the hell happened?"

"Yeah," Tovah asked. "What do you think happened, Aviva?"

"Wait," Leslie said. "Aren't you with Jack? Why are you wearing Dave Lawson's jersey."

"I'm *not* with Jack."

"That's not what I heard."

"Not what I heard, either," Lucy added.

"We're not together. He's been bullying the shit out of me," I clarified.

"Because he's an unhinged asshole," Tovah added.

Leslie coughed. "I know something about unhinged

assholes, and I hate to be this person, but sometimes he *does* bully you because he likes you."

Lucy's laughter pealed out. "You would know, wouldn't you, *butterfly*."

Leslie blushed, but smiled dreamily. "I'm not saying that what they do isn't terrible, but—"

"—Pretty fucking terrible," Tovah interjected.

"—but it all ends up working out. At least in my case. You have to show them you'll give as good as you get."

"And she should know, she gets *it* pretty good from Mason," Lucy teased.

Interest piqued, I asked, "Mason bullied you?" This I hadn't heard.

Leslie nodded. "At first, for sure. He was a real asshole, but I refused to like, be a doormat and put up with his crap. When he followed me to Tabb, it turned into more." She flashed the diamond on her finger in front of us. "And well, here we are."

"Even though he's her stepbrother," Lucy pointed out.

Leslie swatted at her. "Whatever."

"Oh right, right. I forgot. You don't 'stepbrotherfucking care.'"

Leslie laughed but rolled her eyes. "It's like you want me to get you in trouble with Coach Matthews."

"Don't you dare!" Lucy sounded worried.

"Well, I *do* stepbrotherfucking care that Jack is targeting Aviva," Tovah broke in.

Lucy eyed me. "You look like you're handling it okay, but then I'm not surprised. You've always seemed like the type who doesn't melt under heat."

Tovah smiled proudly. "She doesn't." Then she sobered. "But that doesn't mean I don't worry she won't get burned."

Leslie played with her ring. "Sometimes these

douchebags have a way of surprising you," she told Tovah. "At least, mine did."

As Tovah and Leslie chatted, Lucy leaned in closer to me. "So I talked to Blake."

My heart raced. Was this it? Was I finally going to get justice for my brother? And why did the possibility of fulfilling my mission for him make me feel a little...sad? Why did Jack's face pop into my head?

I shook my head, trying to dislodge the feeling. "And?"

She shook her head, frowning. "I'm sorry, I couldn't get anything out of him. The second I said 'Jensen' he clammed up. Told me I needed to stop sticking my nose in places it didn't belong, and to 'stay away from that jackass.' I kept trying, in every way I could think of—and then some—but he refused to say another word about him."

Lead filled my chest.

Blake Samson knew something. I refused to give up on this lead so easily. It hurt, knowing in some ways I was so close to my goal, and in others, I was no closer.

What was I going to do if I couldn't get the evidence on Joshua Jensen that I needed? How could I even face Asher, knowing that I'd failed? What would I do if I had to watch him live his life without hockey, when he used to live and breathe it?

"Can you try harder?" I asked Lucy.

She tilted her head at me. "You know, I don't know anyone as persistent as you. It's definitely admirable, but I'd love to know why."

"Not my story to tell," I said. "Please, keep trying with him."

Lucy lifted a shoulder. "I would, but Blake hasn't returned a single one of my texts or calls. I'll have to do something...drastic to even get him to talk to me." She looked thoughtful. "Like, get myself kicked out of Tabb drastic, which I'm not entirely against, but—"

"No," I interrupted. I couldn't be the reason Lucy got expelled. She'd told me she'd always dreamed of being a veterinarian, and she deserved to accomplish her dream.

And what about your dreams? A little voice asked. *Justice is one thing, but what about what you want? Beyond your psychology degree?*

Once again, Jack's face appeared in my head.

Once again, I forced it away.

"You sure?" she asked.

"I'll find another way," I told her.

"Well, like I said, girl code. I'm happy to help in any way I can," Lucy said.

"Butterfly!" A man yelled. Leslie looked up. The players were back on the ice. Mason Calloway was watching us, Jack next to him. Jack did seem calmer, although no less intense.

"Did you get lost?" Mason asked Leslie pointedly.

"Ah crap," Leslie said. "Lucy, we need to get back to our seats." She waved at her fiance and with a quick goodbye hug, headed to the other side of the stands, tugging Lucy after her.

Text me, Lucy mouthed at me.

I nodded.

Jack still stared, eyes burning into my body and mind. I felt shaky, buzzed, excited, disappointed. Powerful but helpless, focused but out of control.

So close to getting what I wanted, but so unsure of how to destroy the walls in my way.

Watch out, princess, Jack mouthed.

Princess.

I was so fucking sick of that nickname, the way it made

me feel, both bad—and good. So sick of Jack Feldman, and the way *he* made me feel, both bad—and good.

I desperately needed air.

The horn for the second period started, and Jack was once again focused on the puck. Feeling like I'd been released from prison, I turned to Tovah.

"I need a drink, and a snack." *And maybe a lobotomy.* "You want anything?"

She shook her head, focused on the game.

In the main corridor, I exhaled, leaning against the wall. Even separated by glass, Jack's energy was overwhelming. And watching him play... there was nothing like it. Asher was amazing on the ice. Jack was a *god.* He owned the ice, the puck, the entire game. And we, the spectators, were only lucky enough to get to experience him in his prime.

Hockey was everything to him. That was clear. And if I succeeded, I was going to take that away from him.

I got in line, ignoring looks from other students and fans. Jack's interest in me had gotten around by now, and by wearing Dave's jersey...

"Look, it's Hat Trick's slut," some guy said.

"You mean cumdumpster," one of his friends supplied, and the whole group of them laughed.

Fuck this. Between Jack's pissed off attempts to piss a circle around me, other students' mockery of me, and my fear that I wasn't going to be able to help my brother, I'd reached a breaking point. I felt angry, reckless, like a newly lit, unsupervised fire in a forest that hadn't seen rain in too long.

I wanted to burn.

At that moment, someone put their hand on my shoulder. I practically jumped out of my skin.

"I didn't take you for a hockey fan," Professor Johnathan commented, smiling down at me.

I rolled my eyes. "I'm not."

I was. I used to be.

"Then why are you here?"

"Why are you? I didn't take you for a hockey fan either, professor."

"I told you, call me Dylan."

"Okay, Dylan," I said. "But only because we aren't in class."

"Please," he looked around. "You're destroying my cover."

"So are you? A hockey fan?"

He shrugged. "I'm not usually a fan of the sport. Too much aggression, too much power. Too easy for it to be... misused."

He looked at me meaningfully, and my heart pounded. Did he know something about Coach Jensen? Could he help?

Was it worth the risk of telling him what happened, when Asher had begged me not to tell anyone?

High risk, higher reward.

"Professor—" I started.

"It's important to me to support my students," he said quietly. "In whatever ways I...can."

Was he saying he wanted to help me? Or was it something else? The hairs on the back of my neck rose, a physical warning that something was wrong.

It only got worse when Dylan put his hand on my lower back and guided me away from the line. Even through the jersey, his touch burned, like recrimination or punishment. Like I'd done something wrong. Like letting anyone other than Jack near me was a mistake. It was bullshit. I didn't belong to Jack. I didn't belong to anyone.

"Where are you sitting?" he asked.

I hesitated. I wanted to say an even bigger *fuck* you to Jack, but something about the professor felt...off somehow.

Men in positions of authority, my mind whispered.

But what if he could help?

"We're right behind the penalty box. Want to join me?" I offered.

He bestowed a bashful smile on me. "Thought you'd never ask."

When we got back to our seats, Reina was up another goal, and Jack had the puck.

Tovah glanced over at me, then did a double take, eyes widening.

"Um..." she said.

"Tovah, this is Professor Johnathan. Dylan," I corrected, glancing over at him. He smiled, but his eyes were on Jack as Jack stole the puck back from one of Tabb's defensemen before passing it to Isaac. "He teaches my Deviant Psych seminar. Is it okay if he sits with us?"

"Dylan Johnathan?" she said, like the name meant something to her. "Not often that we get to hang out with the cousin of dead or imprisoned billionaires."

I stared at her in shock. "Tovah!"

Dylan chuckled. "I wasn't close to my family, don't worry. And Tovah Kaufman, right? I'm a fan of your articles."

Tovah, who was susceptible to flattery when it came to her writing, smiled. "Sure, he can sit with us."

As we sat, I was aware of the professor's arm against mine. But unlike when Jack touched me, Dylan's nearness didn't send tingles running up and down my spine. Instead, a low-grade revulsion filled me.

"Aviva," Dylan said, drawing my attention away from the game. "I've been worried about you. Something's been going on. Is it Jack Feldman?"

I cleared my throat. "I'd rather not talk about Jack."

Jack, who was currently flying across the ice.

"Oh?" Dylan asked. "So then what is going on?"

I cleared my throat, forcing out the next words. "Professor—"

"Dylan," he corrected, placing a hand on my elbow.

"Dylan," I said, putting my hand on his to remove it from my body. "If you found out that an...authority figure on campus had sexually abused one of his students..."

Dylan's hand tightened on my elbow, squeezed.

"Who have you been talking to?"

"What?" I stared at him, momentarily forgetting about the game. "Do you know about Coach—"

"Aviva, you should know better than to spread rumors. Really, I expected better from you," he tsked, not releasing me.

"Why are you touching her?" Tovah was *pissed*.

Dylan released me immediately. "Forgive me, I was concerned."

Even though he wasn't touching me anymore, I could feel the ghost of his hand on my elbow. I felt sick. I didn't want his patronizing ass near me. I should've listened to my gut. I'd made a mistake, and now—

There was a loud *thump* as someone slammed into the glass. I looked down, expecting to see a fight. Instead, Jack glared up at us.

He slammed the glass again.

"Move, *professor*," he yelled.

Everyone in our vicinity turned to look at us. Some began whispering. I felt my face heat.

"Jack!" Coach Jensen yelled in frustration.

Dylan shook his head.

Slam.

"I. Said. Move."

It was like the entire arena had gone silent.

"Shouldn't you be playing a game, Mr. Feldman?" Dylan taunted, a small smile playing at his lips.

He'd done this on purpose. Was taunting Jack on purpose. Whatever Jack had on him, it had pissed the professor off, and now he was using me to get back at him.

Powerless men always need to feel powerful, my inner voice mused.

"You don't want to play games with me, professor. And you certainly don't want to use Aviva in your games, unless you want everyone to know why you had to leave Yale."

Dylan—Professor Johnathan—blanched.

"Now, *move.*"

And then the professor was standing, dusting himself off, and trudging up the stairs, and it felt like I could breathe again in his absence.

I glared at Jack.

"You okay?"

Confusion filled me. Was this possession, or protection?

It didn't matter. Either way I hated it.

I hate you, I mouthed.

He slammed the glass one more time.

"*Mine.*"

It felt like the word echoed through the arena.

It certainly echoed through *me.*

"Well," Tovah said. "Shit."

I sat back down, aware of dozens, maybe hundreds, of eyes on me.

"You can say that again," I muttered.

"Well. Shit."

21

Jack

I was starting to think of life as Before Aviva and After Aviva. Before Aviva, I rarely got angry. Micah said that anger was a wasted emotion, and I agreed. But ever since I'd met her, anger had become an unwelcome companion. Before Aviva, I never felt possessive or territorial. Now, my body was consumed with the need to mark her, brand her, prove to the world—and her—that she belonged to me.

And make sure creepy fucks like Dylan Johnathan kept their goddamn hands off of her.

Somehow, even with my mind as fucked as it was, we managed to win the game. As the team celebrated, I looked up at the stands. Aviva was gone.

Hell no.

I followed the team back into the locker room. I saw her everywhere; on her knees in front of me, on the bench as I ate her. Would I ever be able to be in here without remembering that first time with her?

Fuck. I *missed* her. I'd changed partners in psych class partially to punish her, and mostly to get a response out of her. I barely had, of course, because Aviva wasn't the type to let something like embarrassment or rejection distract her from what was important to her. Namely, her brother.

What would it feel like, to be that important to her?

"Jack." Isaac shoved me. "Wake the hell up."

"She was sitting with *him,*" I said.

"I know. The whole fucking school knows, plus everyone from Tabb will hear about this soon. You know Mason and Emory can't keep their damn mouths shut. We'll handle Dylan Johnathan. But you realize everyone now knows you have a weakness, right?"

"Bullshit."

He shook his head. "You literally yelled *mine* in front of the whole arena. You may as well have stood with your back to a firing squad. You're fucked. And if you're fucked, it means we're all fucked."

I rubbed my face in my hands. He was right.

"So what the hell do I do?"

"Go fuck her until she can't see straight and you get your equilibrium back," Judah said, coming up behind us and slapping me on the shoulder.

Isaac groaned. "I was going to suggest *apologizing.*"

"I don't even know where she went," I growled.

Judah laughed. "You might want to do something about that in the future. For now, you don't have to worry. We asked Mason to stall her."

"He agreed?"

Levi gave me a pointed look. "Says he owes you."

He did. I was the reason he and Leslie were together, after all. And I'd delivered some much-needed advice at the right time. The least he could do was keep Aviva right where I wanted her.

"Feldman!" Coach stomped into the locker room. "My office. NOW."

Shit.

Levi cleaned off his glasses before putting them back on and staring at me. "How are you going to handle this?"

I groaned. Some of my anger had left me. "No idea."

I followed Coach into his office, closing the door behind me, aware the rest of our team could see me.

"What the hell got into you, Jack?" Coach asked.

I shook my head. I could feel how disappointed he was in me, and I hated it.

"I don't know."

"You don't know?" He snorted. "Well, that's great. I can tell the scouts who were here to see *you,* the administration, 'sorry, no idea what happened, or why our *usually* level-headed star player almost beat up his own goalie and then threatened a tenured professor.'"

"He's not tenured," I muttered. And he wouldn't be getting tenure when I was done with him.

Coach shook his head. "What has gotten into you? Is it that girl? How many times have I told you not to let a girl get in the way of your goals and dreams? You've worked too hard for this, Jack. Your whole team has. *I* have. Don't let us all down because you want someone. There will be plenty of that later. *Trust me.*"

I swallowed.

He sighed. "I'm only doing this to help you. Now, go shower and clear your head."

With that, he pointed to the door, and I exited without saying anything else.

Oh, I was going to clear my head alright. And I knew exactly how.

I quickly showered and dressed. Before I left the locker room, I texted in a favor, then grabbed something out of Dave's locker and some stuff out of my hockey bag.

Outside the locker room, Aviva stood with Tovah, both looking bemused as Mason, his fiance, Leslie, and her best friend, Lucy, stood in front of her, Lucy chattering away as Mason smirked and Leslie placed a soft but restraining hand on Aviva's arm, keeping my princess from running off.

Mason caught my eye, and nodded. Once.

I nodded back.

Debt paid, the motion meant.

"Butterfly," Mason said, grabbing his fiance's hand where her ring glittered in the hallway's bright halogen lights. My eyes caught on the ring, and some inexplicable, undefinable emotion slammed into me as hard as I'd slammed into the boards earlier.

An image came to me—a big, glittering diamond on Aviva's finger.

A mark.

A brand.

A claim.

Jesus fucking Christ, what was wrong with me? I wanted to own her pussy, I didn't want to marry her. Coach was right; she'd dug her way into my head. I needed my equilibrium back. My *power* back. Control back.

But I forgot all about power and control when Aviva turned toward me, fire making her brown eyes turn gold. I expected a deer in headlights look; instead, she raised an eyebrow, daring me.

But of course she wouldn't look like a deer in headlights.

Aviva's strength, her ability to hold her own in front of me, no matter what I did to her, was one of the things I lo—

What the fuck?

I stuttered over the word that had appeared in my brain. I loved nothing about her. I wanted her submission and my power back, and I was going to get both.

"Aviva," I growled.

Aviva raised her chin.

Walking forward, I grabbed her around the wrist.

"Leslie, Lucy, Tovah. Mason. If you'll excuse us." To Aviva I said, "We're leaving."

"Uh, no you're not," Tovah argued. "She's not going anywhere with you Jack Feldman, I swear to god—"

"It's fine, Tovah," Aviva interrupted, not taking her eyes off me. "I'm fine. I promise."

"You better be," Tovah muttered.

I ignored their conversation, grabbing Aviva's elbow, then dragging her down the tunnel, back to the rink.

"Jack!" she protested.

I drew up short. The fucker had squeezed her elbow; I could still see it. "Did he hurt you?"

Her eyes widened. "Who?"

"Dylan Johnathan."

"Oh." She exhaled. "No. He—no. Is that all?"

I thought it would relax me, hearing that she was okay.

It didn't.

"Come on." I started dragging her again, this time by her hand.

"What the hell are you doing?"

"Teaching you a lesson you won't forget."

The ice was dark and empty, like I'd asked. Even without my skates, I moved easily. Aviva didn't. Although I had my hand on her wrist, she slipped and stumbled, until I had no choice to scoop her up and carry her across the rink to the single goalie net left. Beside it was my stick. I'd used this stick for a number of checks, assists, wins—even in fights. But I'd never used it the way I planned to tonight.

Depositing her on the ice, I turned her so she was facing the net, ripping the netting and wrapping it around her wrists until she was trapped, a fly in my web. They'd have to replace the net, but I didn't care.

I unbuttoned her jeans, lowering them and her black panties to her ankles, trapping her even further. Seeing her, bare, helpless to do anything but take what I gave her made my cock go stiff and hard, so quickly it almost hurt.

"I don't know what you're thinking," she started.

"Quiet." The word smacked against the ice, echoing in the huge arena.

Shocked, she shut up.

I stroked my right hand up her hips, the sides of her ribs, to the front of the jersey that still pissed me off. Locating the Swiss Army knife in my pocket with my left hand, I opened it, gripped the front, and started cutting.

That got her talking again. "Jack, what the actual fuck, I swear to god I'm gonna—"

Nope, couldn't have that. I quickly sliced through the tough polyester, all the way down, careful not to cut her pretty skin, until it hung open over her arms.

Bending down, I sliced through the leg holes of her panties. Once they were free, I balled them up and shoved them in her mouth. She tried to talk around them, to spit them out, but I'd stuffed them so deep, all she could do was mumble around them.

Much better.

Returning to my original task, I finished cutting the

jersey, slicing through the sleeves, until it fell off her body, revealing another high-necked tank top. Mostly satisfied, I picked up the pieces, walking around to the other side of the net, facing her.

Time for the next step.

Anticipation filling me, I stood in front of her and slowly sliced the jersey into ribbons. The knife slipped, cutting my thumb. Blood dripped onto the jersey, and my thumb burned where I'd cut it, the copper scent making me slightly nauseous, but I didn't care. My eyes were on Aviva's, which flashed a brighter fire than they had before.

"This is what will happen if you ever wear someone else's jersey again. From now on, when you come to my games, you wear my jersey, and only mine. Disobey me, and I'll slice up something worse." Like the player whose number she wore. "Got me?"

She yelled something through her balled-up panties, but they were an effective gag.

I let the warning sink in for a moment as the tiny pieces of nylon and polyester fluttered to the ground. She fell silent, watching as they gathered in a pathetic heap. Finally satisfied, I flicked the Swiss Army knife shut and dropped it on the ice.

Time for lesson two.

Picking my stick up off the floor, I tested it, taking a few practice swings. I'd never used it for this purpose before, so I had to make sure I got the angle and momentum right. I wanted to bruise her, not break her.

That was new. Before all I'd wanted was to break her.

Shaking my head, I zeroed in on my target. Her ass was round and juicy, framed by the dimples on her thighs. Pale, pink, and just begging for what came next.

"This is going to hurt, princess," I warned her, and then swung.

Thwack.

The blade heel made direct contact with her ass. The sound it made was satisfying, but nowhere near as satisfying as Aviva's shocked scream.

I pulled back and swung again.

Thwack.

Another shriek, partially muted by the gag.

Thwack.

Thwack.

Thwack.

My cock, already stiff from seeing her bare body, grew so hard it hurt. Seeing her cheeks turn red, hearing her cries and screams, was maybe the hottest fucking thing I'd ever experienced in my life so far—and I'd seen her gagging around my cock.

Thwack.

Thwack.

"Jack, no, no, stop, please—" she tried to beg around the panties.

"Fuck," I groaned, pausing to adjust myself. "Keep begging, princess. See where it gets you."

Thwack.

Thwack.

I got lost in the moment as her screams echoed in the cavernous arena, grounded by the cold scent of ice, the sense of invisible spectators witnessing her punishment. Everything about this girl was the hottest thing I'd ever experienced, and I was going to take her so much further into the dark, neither of us would ever find our way out.

Pausing again, I stepped closer, inhaling the scent of

apples, honey, and ... wet pussy. Caressing the heat of her reddened ass, I shoved my hand between her squeezed-shut thighs and slid my fingers over her cunt.

"Soaked," I groaned into her ear. "Who knew you were such a slut for pain, princess? Don't worry, there's more coming."

She shook her head wildly, rejecting the truth. I drew circles around her clit, part punishment, part reward.

Before I could think better of it, I dropped a kiss on her spine before backing up and continuing our session. I didn't think she could take much more—her begging had turned to hiccups and sobs, and her ass was so red, I was almost concerned. *Almost.*

"Every time you try to sit for the next week, you'll think of me, won't you, little thief? Remember that you're going to wear my jersey from now on, and my jersey alone?"

Thwack.

She sobbed some more.

"Say you're sorry, Aviva."

She shook her head, her shoulders rigid and straight.

Thwack.

"Say it, or we'll go all night, until the Zamboni driver shows up in the morning and sees you like this."

I raised my stick again, ready to continue—

She mumbled something through the panties. It sounded like "I'm sorry."

Good enough.

Dropping the stick, I fished the small bottle of lube out of my pocket, because one could never be too prepared. When I reached her, I reached around her hip, playing with her pussy for a bit, gratified by her helpless moans and the way need and lust ran down her thighs and my fingers.

Sticking them in my mouth, I licked the taste of her off them, temporarily tempted to eat her out. But I had bigger, better plans.

Pulling down my sweats, I popped open the bottle and squeezed lube onto my hand. I fisted my cock in my hand, spreading the lube everywhere.

"You're lucky," I told her. "I considered fucking this virgin ass without aid. Say, *thank you, Jack.*"

She turned her head toward me, eyes wide with anger, fear—and yes, need. She wanted this, my greedy, slutty little thing. She'd never been taken this way, but she wanted to be taken by me.

And even if she didn't...

I squeezed more lube on my fingers, before slowly pushing a finger into her virgin ass. Greeted by tight heat, I stretched her out as best as I could, then slid in a second finger, then a third. A low, desperate moan escaped her, music to my ears and my angry cock, that wanted to skip the preparation and be inside her *now*.

"It's time, princess," I told her as I lined my cock up with her delectable, untried asshole and slowly pushed inside.

Heat and pressure from her tight hole greeted me—and a feeling so insanely good, I forgot how to fucking breathe. I could usually take or leave anal, but as I continued to push deep inside Aviva, as she cried out around her panties, half in pain, half in pleasure, I decided that I was going to take it.

And take it.

And take it.

I was the only one. No one had ever had her this way before. Not that jackass Tom she'd dated, not anyone else. And no one else would ever have her this way. Not Dave Lawson, and certainly not Dylan Johnathan. Me. Only me.

Her asshole resisted my slow slide inside. It wanted me

gone as much as its owner did. But that wasn't right. I was its owner now. I was *her* owner now. And like Aviva, her ass would stop fighting me at some point, would discover how good it felt in to give in to me.

"Never," Aviva groaned against the panties.

At first, I thought she was saying no, but then realized that I'd spoken out loud. I was so caught up in how good being inside her sweet, tight ass felt, I'd lost control of my words.

Oh, well. She might as well hear the rest.

Gripping her hip to hold her in place, I narrated all of my thoughts to her, no matter how filthy or cruel, tender or vulnerable. I told her how good she felt, how hot, how tight.

How her ass gripped me so hard, it was almost painful.

How I wasn't even the whole way inside her, and I already wanted to come.

How I was going to fill her slutty ass with so much come, it would drip out of her for days.

How everyone would smell it on her and know exactly what had happened—and that she liked it.

How obvious it was that she liked it, my little pain slut; I could hear it in her moans, feel it in the way her body trembled, see it as her pussy grew sloppier and wetter the deeper I got.

How knowing I was the first one here was so satisfying, I didn't have a word for it, only a feeling in my bones and chest, a feeling that made a home for itself, permanently.

How I was going to be the motherfucking last person she'd ever feel here. How I'd kill anyone else who even tried.

How I couldn't imagine ever fucking anyone else, not after I'd had her.

How she was it for me.

I barely heard a word I said to her. I was listening to her moans, not the nonsense spewing from my mouth.

Finally, I bottomed out, my balls resting against her pussy.

"You're mine, you fucking lying thieving beautiful brilliant sweet perfect little bitch," I told her in one shallow breath. I needed more, to thrust, to feel her bare skin against mine. I ripped my hoodie and tee off my body, not giving a fuck where they fell, so I could layer my chest against her back.

I ripped the panties out of her mouth, too, needing to hear her as I pulled back and thrust back in.

"I hate you," she said on a guttural moan.

I kissed her neck, shushed her. "I know, princess, I know. I hate you, too."

"I hate how much I want you. How I can't get you out of my head. How you've burrowed so deep inside my skin, I'm worried I'll never get you out. I hate that when you do let me go, you'll still haunt me forever, and I hate how much I'll always wish you'd kept me."

Triumph filled me at her words, at the proof that I wasn't alone in this insane obsession, this need to be close to her forever. I stroked her hair. "I'll never let you go."

I released her, moving one of my hands to grip her soft belly. My other traced down the silky curls covering her pussy until I reached her clit. As I began to stroke figure eights on her clit—the eternity symbol—I continued thrusting, picking up my pace to match her guttural moans as she fought the ropes around her wrists, the jeans around her ankles. Fought, and lost.

And then finally, finally, submitted. She stopped fighting, relaxing into my arms, her moans no longer angry, but begging.

"Doesn't it feel good to give in?" My voice was deep. I was hanging on for dear fucking life, my balls like rocks, spine hot with the need to come.

"Yes," she moaned.

God, hearing the word *yes* from her made my cock so fucking hard, harder than I'd ever thought possible.

"You're going to come for me, Aviva. You're going to come, and I'm going to come, too, and fill you all the way up, mark you, own you."

"Jack, oh god, Jack," she cried.

Hearing my name on her lips was the last straw. Any remaining control I had snapped, and I powered into her, skin slapping against skin, words tumbling out of me once again, abandoning the figure eights to start spanking her directly on her clit *because you're going to fucking come for me, damn it, this pussy was made for me, it's mine, and it's going to come so hard for it's master—*

With a shriek so loud it bounced off the walls, she came, her ass clenching around my cock so tight it ripped the orgasm right out of me. I roared my release, my relief, vision blurring until all I saw was her, just her, only her, would only see her *for the rest of our goddamned lives, you hear me, Aviva? This is fucking it for you, for both of us, goddamnit what the fuck have you done to me—*

—mine— I think she cried in response. *You're mine too, Jack...*

Come poured out of me for what felt like forever, until finally I slumped over her, exhausted and satisfied. She slumped over too, against the net, and the entire contraption slid forward. My reflexes kicked in and I caught her around the waist before she fell headfirst into the ice. Reluctant to pull out of her, I stayed where I was as my cock softened, reaching around her to untie her wrists from the net and rub them gently to bring feeling back into them.

Aviva was quiet, trembling, probably cold from the ice because she didn't spend time out here like I did.

Finally, I pulled out, watching with unreserved glee as my words came true, my come dripping out of her ass and onto the ice.

"Do you think the Zamboni driver will notice?" I asked her, not even to be a dick, but because my brain had abandoned my body and my thoughts had become pure nonsense, like I was high for the first time in my life.

Hell, maybe I was. Had I ever experienced anything like that before? I'd know, right?

I dragged her jeans up over her legs and her bare pussy, before locating my hoodie, dusting off the ice shavings, and pulling it over her head. Aviva, for her part, didn't fight me, but submitted as I did my best to cover and warm her, before lifting her into my arms my favorite way and carefully walking us over to the penalty box. Sitting down on the bench with her in my lap, I cradled her in my arms, contenting myself with the smell of her hair and the way she burrowed into me, like I wasn't her worst enemy, but her protector.

"You're okay, I've got you," I murmured. "I've got you, Aviva. I'm here, princess, I'm here."

She settled into my arms, sighing, soft and sweet and overwhelmed. I kissed the tears on her face, my heart in my throat at how overcome she was, because after all, I felt the same way.

This woman was amazing, and she was mine.

What's more, I was hers.

I felt her slowly relax as she cuddled closer. Satisfaction

filled me that I could do this for her. My brother thought I didn't understand aftercare? *Bullshit.*

I may have still hated her, but I'd meant every unhinged thing I'd said to her out there on the ice. I'd broken her, and I'd put her back together.

We stayed like that for a while, and I lost track of time, soothed by the feeling of her in my arms, the sensation of caring for her, protecting her from the world, from everything and everyone but me.

I could've stayed that way forever.

"Jack?" she finally said, voice sweet as she reached up her small hand and gently cupped my face.

I nuzzled into her soft palm. "Yeah, princess?"

The sting was as sudden as the sound.

She'd slapped me. Again.

Temporarily shocked, I released her. "What the actual fuck, Aviva?"

"What, you think you can force your cock into my ass and then cuddle me and I'll be okay with it? That some soft words and touches erase every horrible thing you've done to me? Fuck you, Jack Feldman. Truly, go fuck yourself. Because you won't be fucking me, ever again. I'm not yours. You don't deserve me."

Her words ripped right into me, shattering my chest, my bones, destroying that feeling from earlier, the one I hadn't been able to name.

I knocked her from my lap, and when she thudded to the floor, I hated myself almost as much as I hated her.

"Sounds good, princess. It's been fun, but it's time for me to find a new toy. This one's...used."

I rose to my feet, determined to leave her there, to do exactly what I'd said. I stumbled more than walked off the ice, down the tunnel and back into the locker room, grabbing my stuff and heading to my car so I could get home and shower this whole fucked up experience off of me.

When I got to my car, I sat in the dark with my headlights off, waiting for her to leave, and then following her home to make sure she got inside her apartment safely.

I'd become a motherfucking simp for my enemy.

I hadn't succeeded in breaking Aviva.

But she'd succeeded in breaking me.

22

Aviva

I didn't hear from Jack after that night. He'd disappeared from my life, like he'd promised. I told myself I was happier this way. I repeated it so many times, I actually began to believe it.

The next week passed by quickly. It felt almost...normal, without Jack threatening me from the shadows. I used the time as best as I could—trying to track down Dave Lawson, who was proving elusive as hell—and digging deeper into that reddit thread to see if anyone else had said anything about Joshua Jensen.

Lucy texted a few times, saying that she'd tried again with Blake but he was still avoiding her. I thanked her, feeling dejected. What was I going to do?

On Friday, I took the train to the city for October break. I hated that I didn't have good news for my brother, hated even more that I was lying to him, but I was relieved to get to spend time with him. Being this distant from my twin was like an ache in my chest, and I needed to see how he was doing for myself.

Aunt Gladys' home was a small row house in Kew Gardens. I walked up the broken sidewalk with my overnight bag, staring up at the faded red siding, and pressed the doorbell.

A moment later the door opened, and a moment after that, I was swept up in a familiar hug.

"Hi farthead," Asher said affectionately, as he gave me a noogie. "I missed you."

I laughed in relief and swatted him. "Missed you more, buttface."

He grabbed my bag off of my shoulder and I trailed after him.

The old house was clean—unlike a lot of college boys, Asher wasn't a slob—but sad. Empty, even. Before, the walls in the front hall had been decorated with photos of Asher playing hockey, or the two of us goofing off. Now, all the hockey photos had been taken down. As I watched my brother drop my bag by my old bedroom and head down the hall, pulling at his frayed black shirt, I had a flashback to the days following my parents' deaths.

Once again, it felt like we were in mourning. For hockey, this time. For his dreams, and maybe for mine.

Uneasy, I followed him into the kitchen, pulling open the fridge to check the orange juice bottle.

"You must be starving after your flight," Asher said, watching me.

Goddamn it, was I going to spend this whole weekend feeling guilty for lying to him? I spotted the bottle, pulling it out.

Pulp.

Relaxing, I put it back. It seemed like a small thing, but seeing it back in the fridge filled me with a tiny bit of hope.

"I got something at the airport," I said.

My stomach grumbled, giving me away.

"What do you want to order in? Shwarma? Thai? Pizza?"

"Shwarma," I said. We took care of ordering food, and then sat across from each other.

"Tell me how you are," I said.

"I found a job," he said.

I brightened. Getting out of the house was good. "Doing what?"

"Coaching middle school hockey at the J."

Now I really brightened. "That's great! Do you like it?"

He shrugged, but he was smiling. "Yeah. The kids are fun, it's easy, and it's ... nice to get back out on the ice, even if I'm not the one playing."

Okay. Baby steps.

"Have you thought about playing?" I asked cautiously. "You could reach out to your old friends, see if anyone's around—"

He cut me off. "No."

"Asher—"

"No," he said again, emphatic. "I know you want to help, kiddo, but I can't. The idea of standing in front of the net again makes me want to hurt someone. I can work with kids." He swallowed. "Be better than *him*. But that's it."

"What does the therapist say?"

"She agrees with me."

I reached over to him, placing a hand on his shoulder. "I want you to be happy again."

His smile was sad as he covered my hand with one of his. "I know you do, kiddo. That's what you've always wanted. But have you thought about what will make *you* happy?"

Jack flashed in front of my eyes—the soft, gentle, tender version that had held me in his arms after punishing me.

"You being happy will make me happy."

He shook his head. "So selfless."

I changed the subject. "What do you know about Jack Feldman?"

His shoulders stiffened. "Why would you ask about him?"

I felt heat rise to my face. I knew it would be a tell. "Tovah was talking about him. I guess he's involved with Vice and Vixen on Reina's campus?"

Asher's shoulders relaxed. Slightly.

"Yeah, he oversees the dealing, although he doesn't deal himself. It makes him sound like a bad guy, but he does his best to ensure that it doesn't get used nonconsensually. They never have it at hockey parties."

Well, that had certainly changed. I kept my face blank.

Asher warmed up to his topic. "He's a good guy—volunteers with foster kids like we used to, takes care of his siblings the best he can. And always led the team. He wasn't the type to give a soft pep talk, but he'd still inspire us to do better. Straightforward, but not a dick."

That didn't sound like the Jack I knew. The Jack I knew *was* a dick, was cruel, callous, inconsiderate. I couldn't see him volunteering, or caring for anyone. Did I not know him as well as I thought? As orphans, volunteering with foster kids had been important to both of us, and was something I'd still done at Stanford. What motivated Jack to do so? It made me feel a bond with him, and I didn't want to.

Asher's expression had darkened. "I'd trusted him, but he didn't believe me about what Coach—what Joshua Jensen did to me. Fucking sucks."

"Yeah, it fucking sucks," I echoed.

Because I was right, and so was Asher. No matter where he volunteered, Jack wasn't a good man.

I had to remember that.

The rest of the visit passed by too quickly. We watched TV, walked around the neighborhood, caught up as best we could, given that I was lying to him. On the final morning, Asher insisted on driving me in our old, beat up car to JFK, where I'd pretended I had a flight. I'd winced at the fact that he was spending gas money we didn't have, but I couldn't tell him the truth.

Not yet.

After he pulled over at departures, he got out of the car. I hugged him tightly.

"Be good, yeah?" I asked.

He nodded. "I'll do my best. Do something that makes you happy, kiddo."

I blinked away tears. "I am," I lied.

After he'd pulled away, I entered the airport and headed over to the subway, taking it to the train station. The trip back to Gehenom was smooth, easy, leaving me alone with my thoughts: my renewed determination to make things right for my brother, my confusion over who Jack Feldman really was, and finally, Asher's words.

What would make me happy? I thought getting justice would, and psychology. But was that enough?

What did I want for me?

I closed my eyes, taking deep breaths to slow down my thoughts. They quieted.

Everything felt quiet, but some part of me knew it was the calm before the storm.

23

Aviva

The storm hit the Friday after October break at The Stacks. There'd been another home game that night. It had played on the TVs, and I'd done my best to ignore it. It helped that we were slammed. Although even I couldn't ignore the cheering that signaled another win.

At least Dick had been pleasantly un-dickish. I guess there was one thing to be grateful to Jack for.

Tovah and I barely spoke as we tried to keep up with drink orders. The music was pounding, the lights were low, and I was sweating through my bra. Since it was a Friday night, The Stacks had become Club Stacks: people grinding between tables and *on* tables. The bar itself was the only no go zone, although I'd had to kick at least three girls from the dance team off the table, and it was only 11 p.m. We didn't shut down on the weekends until 2.

"It's going to be a long fucking night," I muttered.

"I'll say," Tovah said, bumping shoulders with me. "At least The Weiner has been absent."

"Or he's shrank so small, no one can see him," I said.

Tovah giggled. "It *is* cold out."

I laughed, too. For a moment, one almost-perfect moment, I felt free.

And then the door to the bar opened, and that freedom died a swift death.

There stood Judah, Levi, Isaac, and some other members of the team I unfortunately recognized from the other night. Bile filled my mouth, and I forced myself to swallow it down.

Only for it come back up when Jack followed them through the door, wearing a backwards baseball cap, his arm slung around some girl's neck. She was thin, with straight brown hair and blue eyes. She was beautiful. And even though I rarely disliked my body, in that moment, I felt self conscious about my size, my shape, my hair that had frizzed from work and sweat, my scar.

I blinked.

Then I blinked again.

Maybe if I kept blinking, the tears that threatened to spill would recede entirely.

Seeing Jack with her hurt, and I hated how much it hurt.

"Aviva," Tovah said gently.

"I'm fine," I said automatically. "It's fine. He's inconsequential."

"You are fine, and it is fine, because this is a *good* thing. He's moving on from fucking with you to fucking with someone else. Halle-fucking-lujah," she said.

"Halle-fucking-lujah," I mimicked, but I didn't feel it.

"I can ask Alex to kick them out."

I shook my head. "There's no way we get away with that.

Rejecting the *hockey champs* will definitely bring Dick out here, no matter how he feels about Jack."

Alex glanced over at me as he scanned their IDs.

You okay? he mouthed.

I nodded.

Even though my gut cramped at the sight of Jack guiding the pretty brunette through the bar, his hand on her lower back, and her turning to smile up at him, stroking her hand down his cheek.

"Aviva. Hey."

Dave Lawson greeted me with a hand tentatively raised.

Shit.

I'd been looking for him, been trying to get his attention. It had worked, but it was happening at the absolute worst time. Even though Jack was with someone new, it didn't mean he wouldn't notice me talking to his goalie.

"You know my name…and I guess other stuff, but I don't know yours. Doesn't seem fair," I lied, looking at him from under my eyelashes. I of course knew his name; I'd studied the entire team before I'd transferred, plus Asher had talked about him in the past.

He ran a hand through his hair, seeming bashful, then held it out. "Dave."

"Aviva."

He chuckled. "We both knew that though, right? I heard you've been looking for me."

"Where'd you hear that?" I switched tactics. "And what do you want to drink?"

"Coors."

I pulled the draft, making sure to smile at him.

"My friends told me you were looking for me, for one thing. For another, well," he scratched his head. "You wore my jersey to the hockey game."

"Are you sure that was me?" I raised an eyebrow.

"Pretty sure. And I had the bruise on my forehead to prove it."

I winced. "Sorry about that."

He waved it off. "Occupational hazard. Look," he lowered his voice. "I assume you were looking for me because of what happened at the hockey house."

That was *not* why I'd been looking at him, but I nodded.

He inhaled. "Okay. Right. Well, I wanted to find you, but I know Feldman would have my head if I tracked you down when you were alone. Hell, he might have my head for talking to you, period."

Out of the corner of my eye, I saw Jack take a seat at one of the booths before pulling the girl onto his lap.

"I somehow doubt that."

Dave shrugged. "Anyway, I wanted to apologize for the... other night. I should never have participated, I just didn't know the—" he blanched, "—details."

I interrupted him. "Please don't mention that here."

He nodded. "Fair enough. Still, I wanted to apologize. There's no excuse for what any of us did."

My shoulders relaxed. I hadn't even realized they'd gone stiff. It was refreshing, hearing a guy apologize so easily. Yes, Jack had said sorry, but only after he'd almost destroyed me. Dave was only a bystander, and yet here he was, taking accountability for his actions and everything.

"There wasn't. Thank you for acknowledging it." This time, my smile was genuine. Lowering my voice—not that it was necessary based on the din of the bar—I asked, "Do you know if anyone took photos or..."

He shook his head. "Absolutely not. Before we all showed up, Jack warned us we'd be off the team if we documented a single thing. You're safe, Aviva." He rolled his eyes.

"Well, I guess I can't say that what with the way Jack has locked onto you. But your naked body won't be leaked online."

His ears turned red at his own words. It was almost cute. I should've found it cute, even attractive, but unfortunately I was only attracted to one person, who got off on making me miserable. And I couldn't even blame Stockholm Syndrome for my feelings about Jack, because Stockholm Syndrome wasn't real.

I focused on Dave. "You have no idea how relieved I am to hear that," I said, handing him his beer.

He put up a hand. "Don't mention it."

Okay, one thing handled. Now I needed to get close enough to him to find out what he knew about Coach Jensen. And if there was a part of me that felt disloyal to Jack? Well, his presence across the room proved how pathetic that was.

As we talked, I paused the conversation to take orders from other students, swipe their credit cards, and pass them their drinks. It made for a slightly awkward conversation, but Dave didn't seem to be going anywhere. Still, "Did you know that your coach was abusing my brother, and is that why you stopped talking to him," wasn't really something I wanted to ask in public.

As I pondered over how best to approach it, Dave cleared his throat.

"Listen," he said. "I shouldn't ask this, but do you want to maybe hang out sometime? I know that's presumptuous, but I swear I'm a good guy and you seem like you could use a good guy in your life."

I froze, almost dropping the drink in my hand. Dave caught it and set it down.

"I know you were with Jack. And I know he might kill

me for this. But I like you, Aviva. You interest me. And not only because you're a knockout. There aren't a lot of people who could've gone through what he—what *we*—put you through, and still served me a drink after with their head held high. Let me buy you a coffee or lunch or something one day. Yeah?"

Here it was. My chance. Get to know Dave, tell him I was Asher's sister, see what he knew and if he'd be willing to help. He seemed like a good guy, but—

—but it felt disloyal to Jack. God, Stockholm Syndome might not be real, but it had me tight in its fictitious grip, regardless.

Dave watched me. "Is it about Jack? Because I can back down..."

I shook my head.

"He's with a new girl now," I told Dave, the words sticking in my throat. "Unless he's the type to not like when other men play with his discarded—" I winced at my next word, "—toys, he's not going to care if you make a move on me."

Dave raised his eyebrows. "Usually I'd say that Jack wouldn't give a shit about his discarded 'toys', but everything about how he treats you is different than he's treated anyone else." He straightened. "I don't care, though. Jack doesn't control either of our lives. Let's do it."

I was in.

I felt sick.

"I guess you can have my number..." I rolled my eyes.

He grinned. "You really are cute. Hand me your phone."

I slipped it out of my pocket and handed it to him—

—only for it to be intercepted by a big, familiar hand. I knew the veins on that hand, the short, round nails, the slight discoloration of the pinky—probably from being slammed into the boards the wrong way during a game.

I looked up at Jack. He loomed over us, his hand wrapped around my phone. His muscles had swelled beneath his t-shirt. His hat was gone. Probably on the brunette's head. His jaw ticked.

"Lawson."

Dave twisted to look at my tormentor. "Jack. I believe that phone was meant for me."

"Did nobody ever tell you about not poaching?"

Dave drew himself up to his full height—which was still a few inches shorter than Jack. "It's only poaching when the person in question doesn't want to be poached."

Jack glared, moving in closer to Dave, and I considered turning the soda siphon on him.

Instead, I tried to placate him. "Jack."

Jack raised his hand, still holding my phone. "Not now, Aviva. I'll deal with you after." He lowered his voice, but if anything, that made his warning to Dave even clearer. "You don't want to test me, goalie."

The threat must have pissed Dave off, because he turned to me, winked, then turned back to Jack. "Feldman, didn't you ever learn how to share? You seemed like you understood that concept the other night."

The punch came so fast, I almost missed it. But the crunch of Dave's nose against Jack's fist was unmistakable. So were the screams.

Jack shook out his hand. Blood dripped from his knuckles, and from Dave's face.

"What the hell is wrong with you? How the hell are you going to punch your own goalie?!" I yelled, and this time, I did spray him down with the soda siphon, turning his gray t-shirt darker. It matched his eyes at the moment, which had also darkened with anger.

He didn't even flinch at the spray. "You're taking a break, Aviva."

I continued dousing him with water. "No, I'm fucking *not*. You're leaving, and Dave is pressing charges."

Dave turned to me. His face was a mess, blood everywhere. "I'm not," he tried to say. "I knew this would happen. My own fault."

"You. Don't. Talk. To. Her. Or the next punch will take out your teeth." Jack's growl set off some sick, Pavlovian response in me, because my thighs clenched.

"Alex!" I yelled. "Fight!"

Alex pushed up from his stool and made his way over to us. The wrestler grimaced when he saw Dave's face.

"Feldman, you're done. Get the hell out of here."

Jack shook his head. "Or what?"

"Or I call the police."

"You know the police won't do shit to me. Still, I'll leave. Party's getting stale." He patted his wet t-shirt, then glanced down at his hand. "Oh right, I'm taking this phone with me. It's *mine*."

The stress on the word mine was obvious.

"Jack, I need my phone!" I told him.

He shook his head. "I think this is my phone."

And then he was walking through the bar, nodding to his friends. They rose. So did the pretty brunette, wearing Jack's hat like I'd thought. She glared at me, before following Jack out the door. He pulled her toward him, and I watched, rage filling me with fire, heart in my throat, as he wrapped his arms tightly around her.

I looked away. I didn't need to see that. Instead I focused on Dave, locating a clean towel and pressing it to his face.

"I'm not going to press charges," he tried to tell me, but it was hard to understand him with the broken nose. "Wouldn't do anything, anyway. Jack's teflon. Even if the police wouldn't cover it up for him, his brothers would make sure nothing happened to him." He scoffed. "And Coach would be right there with them."

"Do you want me to take you to the hospital?" I asked.

"Nah, Matt will take me," he said, gesturing at one of the guys who'd come in with Jack, and was the only one still in the bar. "See you around, Aviva."

With that, he waved and walked out of the bar. He was shockingly blasé for someone who'd just been punched in the face, but I guess he *was* a hockey player. Even if goalies usually weren't the ones in fights, it didn't mean he hadn't seen a skirmish or two. Asher had certainly seen his fair share.

I took a deep breath.

"Tovah?"

She appeared next to me. "Are you okay?"

"I need to—"

"Take five. Of course. Take a break, I've got it."

I looked at the packed bar. "You sure?"

She waved me off. "You need it. Alex can help me."

Alex was already rolling up his sleeves as he headed behind the bar.

"Go," he told me.

I needed air, and the hallway wouldn't do it. Instead, I went out the back door to the alley. The chill October air was the relief I needed. I hadn't realized how overheated I was until this moment.

Leaning against the door, I inhaled, rubbing my hands over my face. My face felt sticky. When I pulled my hands away, I noticed dark drops on my thumb.

Great. I'd gotten some of Dave's blood on me. It felt metaphorically apt, since I felt partially responsible for him getting punched. I'd really thought that Jack flaunting another woman in front of my face meant he was done with me, for good. I was an idiot. Of course he wasn't going to let go of me that easily. I was his target, nothing more. He wasn't going to let me live my own damn life.

And I needed my phone back. Which would require tracking him down.

Exhausted, I shut my eyes for a moment.

"Is it safe to be out here alone at night?"

My eyes popped open. Jack loomed over me, blocking out whatever light filtered in from the street lamps.

"It *was*," I said.

He laughed. "Fair."

"What are you doing here?"

"Figured you'd want your phone."

I held my hand out for it, but instead of handing it to me, he grabbed me around the throat. He didn't squeeze, but like that first time, the threat was there.

"You don't talk to other men, Aviva. You certainly don't *flirt* with them. Especially if they're my teammates."

I shut my eyes. It was easier if I didn't look at him. It was too easy to get lost in his gray eyes. "You don't get to tell me what to do. Not anymore."

"Oh, princess. You're mistaken if you think that stopped."

"You found a new girl, you don't need to torture me. She can suck your dick from now on."

"Open your eyes, Aviva."

I didn't.

He squeezed. It was so slight, but it was enough. I opened my eyes.

"Let me get this through that beautiful little head. If I find out you've flirted with another man, I will lock you up in my basement and throw away the goddamned key. And him? They'll never find his body. Do you want that on your conscience, princess?"

I swallowed against his hand. He released my neck slightly, lifting his thumb to stroke my pulse point. It immediately took me back to that morning in his room, when he'd untied me and kissed my wrists. It would be so easy to get lost in him, but that was madness. He didn't give a shit about me. I was a sick game to him. Even if he was obsessed with me, even if he was messing around with another girl to fuck with my head, it didn't matter. I needed to *keep* my head around him from now on.

"Jack, for the last time, I'm not yours."

"You're still mine, Aviva. You really think that changed because I found someone new?"

I glared at him. "I hate you."

"You don't hate me. If you did, you wouldn't be so jealous."

He leaned in, like he was going to kiss me, and even though I hated myself for it, I craved the feeling of his lips on mine.

Except he paused a centimeter away, whispering, "Too bad I can't say the same."

I snorted. "What was that with Dave earlier, if not jealousy? What's all this 'mine' business, if not trying to claim what you think is your territory?"

He laughed, stepping away and releasing me. He'd been giving off so much heat, I'd forgotten it was cold out. "I'm not jealous. I just like making your life hell." He handed me my phone. "I'd keep this, but you'll need it to get home safe. And I'm nothing if not generous."

With that, he sauntered out of the alley, leaving me there in the dark and the cold, forced to face a painful realization. So painful, it was like being stabbed with the serrated edge of a bread knife. I wanted to sink to the ground over what I'd learned.

It didn't matter what Jack had said to me the night after the hockey game, when he'd paddled me with his stick and then taken whatever innocence I had left for himself. He claimed to hate lies but he was a hypocrite.

I'm yours, he'd said.

It was a lie.

Because I might've been Jack's, but he'd made one thing *absolutely* clear tonight:

He wasn't mine.

24

Jack

I should've been on top of the world.

We'd won. We'd not only won, we'd won again against Tabb, and I'd gotten three assists and a goal. And Coach told me there were recruiters from the Bruins and the Rangers watching the game. I should've been riding high, but Aviva's words were still stuck in my head.

No amount of justice is worth the hell you're putting me through. I never want to see you again.

I grudgingly respected her for standing up to me, but her absence from my life made me desperate; in a short period of time, she'd become as essential to me as breathing.

So I'd brought Marnie to The Stacks with the specific purpose of making Aviva jealous. Of getting a reaction out of her. Of making her think I didn't care. It had worked in class before October break; Aviva had tried to hide her expression, but she hated that I'd changed partners on her.

I'd done it partly to play hard to get so she'd realize she

wanted me, and partly to punish her for distancing herself from me. I should've felt bad for using Marnie, but then I should've felt a lot of things.

It had taken more threats against Dylan Johnathan to get him to agree to make her work alone, and I'd had to have words with him after about inviting Aviva to visit him during office hours. It helped that Marcus now owned the controlling shares of Johnathan Pharmaceuticals. Dylan wasn't getting by on a professor's salary alone. It also helped that Dylan had a history of inappropriate behavior with his female students. Seeing him with Aviva —seeing how uncomfortable he'd made her—had made me lose my mind, and he wasn't getting near her again. If I had my way, he wouldn't be *teaching* for much longer. Either way, the professor was in my pocket, and he didn't like it.

I parked a few blocks away from Aviva's apartment, just in case someone saw me, pulling my black hoodie over my head as I walked to her apartment. I'd cased the place earlier in the week: the lock on the gate to the complex was broken. I would've fixed it, but it served my purposes too well.

Seeing Aviva's reaction when I got to The Stacks and pulled Marnie into my lap had been especially satisfying. Even though I could've done without having her bubblegum scent all over me, it was worth it for Aviva's expression alone. What I hadn't planned for was Dave being a fucking idiot and going to talk to Aviva, or Aviva being pissed off enough that she'd flirt with him. Was she really trying to get back at me that way?

That wouldn't do.

I'd quickly used her phone to share her location with mine. I'd never stalked someone before, but I *was* the younger brother of a hacker; one short conversation with Micah, and I knew exactly what I was doing.

It wasn't enough. What if Aviva left her phone behind? What if she got a new phone? Or what if someone hurt her, and I couldn't find her? Even though I still wanted to punish her, the need to protect her almost overwhelmed me, and all three questions plagued me.

So I'd called in a favor, this time with Marcus, and now I was fully equipped for the next step in my mission: never let Aviva get away from me.

I stopped ruminating so I could make my breaking-and-entering plan. There was a huge oak tree right outside of Aviva's window. Even a guy as heavy as me could shimmy up it pretty easily as I continued to reflect on the night.

Shimmy up it I did, until I got to the thick branch right outside her window, and swung up.

Aviva left her windows open at night, even as it was getting colder. She was the type to need fresh air, which was fine with me. It was especially convenient tonight, as I pushed the window up higher and then eased the screen open. It was a tight squeeze, and I felt like some idiot parkour enthusiast as I dropped my backpack on the floor of her bedroom before somersaulting inside.

"The things I do for you, princess," I murmured as I stood and dusted myself off.

Aviva was curled up in the same position she'd slept in my bedroom. Her hair was covering her face again, and one leg was thrown on top of the covers. She slept in black cotton panties and an oversized t-shirt that bared her shoulder and part of her back to me.

Soft, almost innocent, although I knew better. Inside the soft sleeping woman was a spine made of steel. And I wanted her. I wanted the steel spine as much as I wanted the vulnerable sweetness she showed me at rare moments, like whenever I held her, or she'd fallen asleep in my arms. I had to stop myself from slipping into bed with her and holding her throughout the night.

Unzipping the backpack, I pulled out the equipment—a large syringe, and a tiny microchip in a plastic ziplock bag.

"This is going to hurt, baby," I murmured, leaning over and dropping a kiss on her hair. God, that apples and honey scent. I was addicted. Growing up, it had meant something else: a new year, a new chance for my family to not be a shit-show and my father not to be an abusive asshole. Every year, it became more clear that my dream would never come true. I'd come to hate the smell.

Until a few weeks ago, when this girl walked into my life. She'd brought me back to life in so many ways. Now, I was obsessed with the scent. I wanted to bathe in it, to drown in it. To drown in *her*.

All in good time. First, I had work to do.

Taking a page out of my brother's book, I injected Aviva with an anesthetic. It was supposed to last for about an hour, give or take. Long enough to insert the tracker without her knowing.

I snorted. I'd told myself when this began that the little thief was nothing more than a temporary extracurricular as I kept an eye on her and kept her from trying to ruin our lives. A way to get my dick wet regularly before I graduated and headed off to the NHL. But that was complete and utter bullshit. I could've gotten my dick wet easily without her. Instead, I had zero interest in any other woman. And I had a feeling I'd never be interested in another woman, ever again.

Aviva was it for me. This obsession—this need to

possess and keep her, and keep every other single fucking man away from her—wasn't going anywhere.

Which included always knowing where she was.

Busying myself with my task, I carefully pushed the plunger into her neck. She relaxed further, her sleep smoother. Easier.

I hoped she was dreaming of me.

Opening the little box, I pulled out the tiny tracker, no bigger than a tick, as well as a scalpel, needle, and thread. Covering my hands with surgical gloves, I ripped open a small packet and wiped antiseptic over her left shoulder. Hating marring her perfect skin, but needing it to be done, I sliced a small incision and placed the tracker inside before using Dermabond to seal it back up. That way, she'd never know what I'd done.

For a moment, I almost felt gratitude toward my father for his abuse. Almost. I'd become overly familiar with Dermabond over the years as I'd cleaned up my siblings wounds, and my own.

Rising to my feet, I stared at the Rubenesque goddess before me. She looked so beautiful, sleeping there, round and soft, her curved thigh and leg exposed. Everything was stunning, down to her unpolished toes.

An insatiable urge to get in between those thick, dimpled thighs overtook me. I didn't fight it. I wanted that pussy on my tongue and around my cock, and the idea of doing it when she was deep in sleep was so fucking hot. Maybe she would dream of me. She'd certainly wake to me.

Reaching down, I caressed her hip, her inner thigh, hooking my hand under it and dragging it open and over. She lay exposed, and I could see the outline of her pussy through her panties.

I dragged the covers off of her and slipped off her panties. Her perfect cunt was not prepared for me, clit hidden under its hood, no wetness to be seen.

Well, that wouldn't do.

Climbing onto the bed, I lifted her legs over my shoulders, leaning down to nuzzle her inner thighs and smell her. The apples and honey scent was still there, but overwhelmed by the raw scent of cunt.

My cunt.

Mine.

Just like I was hers.

It was a profound feeling, knowing I belonged to someone else. That I was making decisions for both of us now. I glanced up as I licked her, long and gentle. Her face was smoothed out in sleep, completely unaware of what was happening below. My cock grew hard at the knowledge that I owned her so thoroughly, I could even have her when she wasn't aware. She *might* take issue with that, but I didn't give a single fuck.

I licked again, and again, the taste and smell of her surrounding me as thoroughly as her legs. Got lost in her, in the sheer Aviva-ness of her, the uniqueness to her and this experience that no one else had provided for me, and no one else ever would. My gentleness turned into a ferocious need to dominate her. Something in me snapped, and I began eating her, biting her thighs, sucking on her clit, shoving my tongue inside her perfect pussy.

It could've been seconds, it could have been years, it didn't matter. I was attaching my mouth to her and never detaching.

And then a tiny sound. A moan.

And wetness drenching my mouth.

"Fuck yes," I growled against her pussy, determined to get her closer to orgasm before my now hard cock got its turn. My cock protested this, greedy and territorial, wanting to be inside her *now*.

I tried to find some control, but it wasn't easy, not when this delectable meal lay before me in the form of a girl that had taken over my every thought. A girl whose eyelids twitched as she moaned again, a word leaving her lips, a single, harsh syllable that sounded like my name.

Yeah, I couldn't wait any longer. Ripping off my gray sweatpants and boxers, I kneeled, grabbing my hard cock, lining up with her pussy, and slamming in.

Fuck, so tight. She was always so tight at first, even though I'd loosened her up with arousal. It was hard work, sometimes, getting all the way inside her. The reminder that she'd been a virgin until me was so fucking satisfying. I'd had her first, and I'd have her last.

Pulling out, I slammed in again, then again, the glide becoming easier each time. I gripped her ankles, lost for a moment in them; delicate, but much stronger than they looked.

Just like her.

Time passed, or froze, as I moved inside her, faster and faster, aided by her wetness as she soaked my cock, galvanized by her moans as they grew louder and quicker.

I needed her to come. Desperately.

Words spilled out of me, ones I had no control over.

"You gorgeous, brilliant little thing, you know I'm here, don't you. Asleep but dreaming of me. I'm everywhere, in your body, your head. Your fucking soul, when I get my way."

Releasing one of her ankles, I started drawing small, fast

circles over her clit, and when it peaked out from under its hood, I increased the speed, gentle in my control.

She was close. And oh fuck, so was I.

"Aviva," I growled.

On a moan, her eyes opened.

25

Aviva

I t took a while for sleep to come. I lay in bed, staring at the ceiling, scenes from that night replaying in my mind. The worst was seeing Jack with his arm around someone else. And his words after.

I'm not jealous. I just like making your life hell.

Although I knew he was trying to piss me off, part of me couldn't help wondering if he'd actually moved on from torturing me to someone else—someone he wouldn't torture, but may actually treat *well.*

And that felt like shit. So shitty, I had to flip over and bury my head in my pillow to keep myself from crying.

Jack Feldman wouldn't fucking make me cry, *ever again.*

Finally, I slept. Or must have, because I dreamed. I dreamed of a sharp pain, and then incredible pleasure—a mouth between my legs, and then a cock between my thighs, shoving inside me, fast and violent and *ohsogoodiwassocloseiwasgoingto*—

I blinked open my eyes. At first, it was a fog, some mist

between dream and reality, because my left shoulder itched, and there was a cock inside me, and that wasn't possible, because I'd gone to sleep alone.

Was I dreaming again?

Except there was Jack, staring down at me in the dark, his face hard with need and determination, his gray eyes black with lust, rage, or possibly both.

He slammed inside me again and I jerked away, crying out.

"Jack, what the fuck?! You can't be here."

"Do."

Slam.

"Not."

Slam.

"Tell."

Slam.

"Me."

Slam.

"What I can and cannot do when it comes to you."

He shoved deep inside me, then twisted and ground his hips. His cock hit places it never had before, setting off a domino effect of little explosions that I couldn't stop.

I tried to pull away. He just grabbed my hips, holding me in place.

"Get the hell out of here. Get the hell out of *me!*"

"No."

"Funny that you understand what the word no means when *you* say it," I gasped.

"I know what it means, I just don't care when you say it. Because you don't mean it, little liar."

Oh, this fucking asshole.

Rage filled me, battling it out with desire. Neither won.

"You're the fucking liar, Jack," I told him between moans. "Because you keep lying to yourself."

He froze for a moment, faltering in his thrusts.

"Bullshit."

He leaned over me and shoved three of his fingers in my mouth.

Punishment. Or to shut me up.

"I do not lie. I meant it when I told you we belonged to each other. You think you can get rid of me that easily, princess?"

I tried to yell at him, but it came out garbled. I tried to spit his fingers out, but it was impossible. And as he kept twisting and grinding his hips, his cock shifting inside me, I forgot what I wanted to say.

"Come for me, Aviva," he said harshly.

I had no choice. Not with the way the base of his cock was pressing against my clit, the curve of it was rubbing against my g spot, the absolute humiliating helplessness of his fingers shoved deep in my mouth, which shouldn't have been hot, but *was.*

With a gurgled, garbled scream, I came.

With an animalistic roar, Jack followed me over, shoving his cock so deep in me I swore I felt it in my throat. I felt his release, because once again, the fucker hadn't used a condom, and once again, I was too caught up in my own pleasure to care.

He'd broken me, and I didn't recognize the pieces that were left.

Finally, he sighed, pulling out and rolling over to his side. He tried to turn me and pull my back against his clothed chest, but the fight that had been missing in me when I'd first woken up finally appeared. Kicking, slapping, scratching, I fought him, trying to scramble off the bed. To do what, I didn't know. Tovah must not be home, because otherwise she would've barged in here already. Call campus security? Jack was as much a god to them as he was to the rest of Reina. Call the police? They were in Jack's pocket.

Call Asher?

My brother would get here as soon as he could, and he could probably take Jack in a fight, but I couldn't do that to him.

No, I was out of options.

"I'll go to U-Wire. To ESPN. I don't fucking know. I'll tell them everything I know, if you continue this," I threatened as I fought him.

I didn't get very far. Jack must have just been playing with me like a cat plays with a mouse, because suddenly I was yanked into his arms, the heat of his chest scalding my partially-bare back, even through his t-shirt.

"Aviva, you don't mean that." He sounded earnest. "You don't need a blackmail payout. I'll take care of your money problems. Whatever you need—whatever even your brother needs—I'll take care of it. Because I'll take care of you. You can let this all go."

His words were a blade, the insult cutting into my skin.

But it was nowhere near the pain of him abruptly releasing me and climbing off the bed.

"You motherfucking asshole," I spat at him.

He froze, the softness leaving his face. His jaw ticked, but he didn't say anything, just pulled on his boxers and sweatpants before stuffing his feet in his shoes and going to the door.

Just as it opened, I asked the question that had been plaguing me. "Who broke you? Who hurt you so badly you felt the need to pay the favor forward?"

He didn't even turn around. "You don't get to ask questions."

I never got to ask questions. I never got the upper hand.

I swallowed.

Maybe it would take something extreme, to get to the bottom of who Jack was. And while I shouldn't care, knowledge was *power*. What I learned about him could help me, right?

Are you sure you don't want to know about him, period?

It didn't matter. Either way, I needed to know.

Before I could reconsider, I ripped my shirt over my head, tossing it to the floor and rising to my knees to face him. Even though it was dark in the room, I saw his nostrils flare. Whether it was because of my tits, or my scar, I didn't know. I resisted covering myself. I was brave. I was strong. I could do this.

"If you tell me why you're so fucked in the head—"

He snorted. "That's nice."

"You're not nice," I volleyed back. "But if you tell me *why*, I'll tell—I'll tell you how I got this scar."

His hand froze on the doorknob.

Got you.

For whatever reason, Jack needed to know everything about me. I was some mystery to him—how or why, I didn't know—and for him, the scar was a puzzle piece.

For me, it was a last ditch attempt to get him to believe me, to understand why Asher was so important to me.

He turned around, leaning against the door and crossing his arms.

"Talk," he said.

"You first."

He shook his head. "Not how this works."

I sighed. I hated it, but he was right. I couldn't fight fire with fire, not this time. I had to put his out by pouring water over it, and the only way to do that was to expose my secret.

Exposure therapy was a good thing, right?

"I hate my scar," I told him. "Because it's a reminder of the night I failed."

"What do you mean?"

I closed my eyes, picturing it. The blood, the guilt, the pain. I could do this. I could force myself relive the worst night of my life.

"Asher and I were ten years old," I began.

26

Aviva, age 10

I jerked awake in my princess bed, pulling at the frilly cover and sheets as I sat up. I loved the bed—the headboard was shaped like a castle, the sheets had little tiaras on them. Even though he never called me it, my mother would tease that I was my dad's little princess.

Something had woken me up, and I wasn't sure what.

I strained my ears. The old, creaking house was silent. Weirdly silent. It was like our always "settling" house (which is what mom would say when I got worried about ghosts) was holding its breath and waiting to see what came next.

I wanted to go back to bed, to hide under the covers and pretend nothing was wrong. But I knew.

It's okay, Aviva, I told myself. You'll just go check on your parents and Asher, make sure everything is fine, and go back to sleep.

Climbing out of bed, I opened the door slowly, creeping down the hardwood floors in my bare feet, ignoring how cold it was. My parents were always so, so careful with money, they turned the *heat down low, even in harsh winters in upstate New York. They tried to hide we were struggling, but even at my age, I could tell.*

When I reached the end of the hall, I paused. My parents' bedroom door was closed, and I'd learned not to just burst inside. They loved each other, and I'd accidentally walked in on them before—it's how I'd learned what sex was. I tried to force myself to knock, but something stopped me. Something small and scared.

If you go in there, you'll never go back.

I shivered again, this time not from the cold.

I knocked, softly.

"Aviva, Asher, go away." My father yelled through the door.

I began to turn away, when I heard my mother crying.

"Please, please don't hurt them. We'll give you anything..."

Something was wrong!

Ignoring my dad, I twisted the knob and pushed the door open—

My parents were standing together near their bed, my father blocking my mom's body. Two men in masks were pointing guns at them, just like in the action movies my twin, Asher, made me watch.

I thought I screamed. I thought it pierced the night. I'm not sure.

One of the gunmen turned. His teeth flashed through his mask in the dark room, and then the gun was on me, freezing me where I stood. The other was trained on mom.

My heart raced.

"No!" dad yelled, glancing back and forth between us, and even in the darkness I could see the helpless horror in his eyes.

And then Asher was at the door, too. He was in sweatpants and his Wayne Gretsky t-shirt. . I'd always teased him for that, because the hockey player was so old now, but he was adamant that Wayne was the coolest, and if I didn't understand that, he felt sorry for me.

"Asher, run." My mother said in a choked voice.

"Don't you hurt my family," Asher said.

The gun shifted again, this time pointed at him

Wayne wasn't going to save my brother from a gun.

Bam.

Thud.

I jerked, looking at my brother. He still stood there, his face twisted in horror as he looked across the room. I twisted to see what he was staring at.

This time, I knew I screamed.

Dad lay on the floor, a dark pool spilling out from his head. His eyes were wide open in frozen fear.

Mom fell to her knees, sobbing.

One gun followed her. The other was still trained on my brother.

"What are you going to do, princess?" one of the masked men mocked. "Princess" sounded so ugly, so scary. "Watch your brother and mother die?"

There was a clicking sound—the safety, I knew from movies.

My body was moving before I even realized it. Thoughts flashed through my brain, startling as gunshots. I loved mom, but my twin was my whole world.

I dove in front of my brother, my twin, the most important person in my life, just as I heard a pop and my whole world exploded into pain.

There was a second pop. My mom screamed the scariest scream I'd ever heard.

And then everything went dark.

27

Aviva

"Aviva!"

Jack's voice, sharp and worried, snapped me out of the past.

I glanced up from where I'd been staring, unseeing, at my fraying pillowcase. His arms were no longer crossed, but clenched into fists at his sides.

"What happened next?" he asked, his voice disconcertingly gentle now.

I cleared my throat, trying to will away the tears choking it.

"When I woke up, I was in the hospital. Asher was alive, but both my parents were dead. We never talked about it, me choosing to save him instead of my mother. I don't like to think about it, and I've never told anyone everything—not even Tovah. Just you, now," I finished the story, picking at the threads on the pillowcase. I really needed to replace it— if I ever had the money for it.

"That's why you hate when I call you princess."

I nodded.

"And the scar?"

"The surgery when they removed the bullet. They have plastic surgery for it. One day, I'm going to save up for it and do it." I shook my head. "I hate it. Not only because Tom was so disgusted by it, that the night we tried to have sex, he couldn't even get it up. I promised myself then that I would only have sex with someone I knew completely respected me."

"Aviva," Jack interrupted, voice pained.

I continued, having to get the rest out. "I hate it because it reminds me of impossible choices, about how I couldn't save them both. I've tried so hard over the years to make up for it. Doing everything I could to give Asher the life he deserves. Working as a waitress under the table in high school, pinching pennies, begging family who hated us for help. It was exhausting. It is exhausting. I'm *exhausted.* But it doesn't matter what I do. I hate the scar, it proves how weak and selfish I really am." This time I couldn't keep the sob down.

Jack had fallen silent again, his eyes working. I had no idea what he was thinking, and I wasn't sure I wanted to. I'd given him so much ammunition against me. Was it a mistake?

But it was done.

And then he was crossing the room toward me in two big strides. He kneeled on the floor in front of me, his hands stroking up and down my bare calves. I wasn't sure who he was trying to comfort, him or me.

"No," he said. "Aviva, *no.*"

My real name. Not princess. It tripped over his tongue with ease, with a tenderness I neither wanted nor deserved.

"Aviva, it's not ugly. *You're* not ugly. You're beautiful," he said, reading me too well. That I'd let him see me—my scar, my insecurities—was terrifying.

I shook my head. "Don't lie to me."

"I'm going to find out where Tom is, and I'm going to destroy *him*," he said, his voice fierce in its softness. "He's full of shit. He was intimidated by how strong you are." Leaning forward, he placed his lips on the scar, right above my breasts and below my clavicle. "Aviva, you are the most beautiful thing I've ever seen. I hate it sometimes, it's so fucking overwhelming, but there it is: the truth." He dropped another kiss on the top of the scar before pulling back and looking at me. "If you want the surgery, I'll pay for it. I'll pay for it right now. I can't begin to imagine what it feels like to see it every day, but here's what your scar tells me, little fury: You're here. Alive. With *me*. That makes it the most beautiful part of you."

"Jack—"

He wasn't done. "Of course you're exhausted. Of *course*. I'll fix it, I promise. I'll take care of you. You'll never have to worry again, not about money, not about anything."

No one had ever spoken to me like that before.

No one.

Some part of me, long cold, warmed. And then I was pulling him on top of me, and he was kissing me and kissing me. He surrounded me, overwhelmed me. I felt safe, I felt like I belonged. I was lost again. This time, not in the past, but in Jack.

Mine, his kisses said. *Mine.*

And this time, I welcomed it.

Mine, my kiss said back.

Yours, his agreed.

Little fury, he'd called me.

And I liked it.

When he pushed my thighs apart, I let him.

When he put his mouth on me, I stroked his hair, encouraging him.

And when he rose up over me, and slid inside me, I welcomed him, my gaze never leaving his as he moved inside me and I moved with him, my arms clutching his back. And when he came, so did I, locked together in something more than the devil's bargain we'd made.

It wouldn't last.

But for now, for this perfect moment in time, I wanted it, I wanted him, I wanted to be his, I wanted him to be mine.

If only it could stay that way.

28

Jack

L*ittle fury.*
My little fury.

I clutched Aviva in my arms, my nose in her hair, taking her in.

She'd hated being called princess. She'd never told me why. Anger—at her parents' murderers, at *myself*—filled me, but I kept my touch gentle. She didn't deserve to be gripped too hard, like she hadn't deserved the ways I'd tortured her over the past weeks. I'd taken out my rage and my fears on her, my frustration at my lack of control when it came to her.

I had no more control than I'd had before. In fact, I felt the threads tying myself to my self control snapping. There was a crazed animal inside of me, scratching at its cage, howling to be let out. To hurt every single fucking person who'd ever hurt her.

Including me.

I didn't deserve her, but it didn't fucking matter. I was still keeping her.

I should've known what she meant to me. I'd had so much sex in my life, I couldn't even keep track. When I'd escaped the restrictive confines of my childhood home, I'd fucked everyone and anyone who would have me, men and women, young and old. I hadn't cared, beyond the release it gave me.

Aviva had been different from the beginning. The first time I'd kissed her, I'd lost. But if this was what losing felt like, I never wanted to win again.

She'd called me a liar. And she was right. I'd been lying to myself this entire time.

Light began to stream through the curtains. We'd fucked and fucked, for hours—sometimes slow and sweet, sometimes sharp and vicious. Every single goddamned second felt better than anything else ever had in my life...except, maybe, getting to hold her like this.

She yawned, soft and satisfied. "You said you'd tell me about—" she hesitated.

I swallowed. "What broke *me.*"

She hummed in agreement.

Sighing, I tried not to fall into the past. "My parents are...religious. Devout as hell. My father practically lives at his synagogue—or did. I don't know anymore, I haven't spoken to him in years. He never even worked, depending on my mom's small income to float all eight of us. Community members tossed us enough money that we managed to keep our home, and food on the table, but that was it."

"Eight?"

"I have five siblings. Well, six, if you include Marcus."

She digested this, so I continued, playing with a lock of her hair.

"My dad was abusive. Physically, verbally. Rarely to my mother—or at least if he was, he did it behind closed doors." The room was cold. How similar to him had I become?

"Jack," my little fury murmured, as if she could tell I was about to get stuck in the past and guilt. "Stay with me."

"My mother, for her part, never stood up for us. In retrospect I don't blame her. She was trying to survive, same as the rest of us. My brother, Micah, took the brunt of it. Until one day, he was gone. My sister Rebecca left after. I was third in line, doing what I could to protect my younger siblings, to be the buffer between my father and them. And even though I know better now—or try to know better—I felt abandoned. By my mother, my older siblings, the community. Everyone. No one looks out for you but you."

Aviva twisted around to look at me.

"Until Coach Jensen," she said, finally getting it.

"Until Coach," I confirmed. "The community center had a rink. The manager would pretend not to see me when I'd borrow skates and a stick, and go out on the ice. I owe her a lot. It was the only place where I felt safe and in control of my life. I'd go there after school, and stay until late. She even kept the rink open for me."

Mindy. I wondered how she was doing. If she remembered me. If she knew where I was. If she was proud.

She wouldn't be proud of the way I treated Aviva.

I wasn't proud of the way I'd treated Aviva. I'd raped her. There was no way around it. Something I abhorred, I'd done myself. And even though it had gotten me her, and that I didn't regret...I'd hurt the person who was quickly becoming the most important thing to me.

She was fire and she was fury and I'd tried to stamp that

out. Not because she'd threatened Coach, but because her very existence had threatened my control.

I cleared my throat. It hurt to swallow. "One day, a man approached me. Told me I was one of the most talented players he'd ever seen, especially for a teenager. He began showing up to train me. Let me join their team. Gave me free equipment. Taught me everything I knew—about ice skating, about what it meant to be a man."

I looked at her carefully, wanting her to get it. "He never once touched me inappropriately. Never even insinuated anything. He was—is—like a father to me."

Aviva opened her mouth, maybe to defend herself and her brother, but she must have thought better of it, because she said, "Keep going."

I shook my head. "There's not much else. I took my beatings, I began to fight back. The day I was stronger than he was, the day I threatened my real father—told him I'd kill him if he ever raised a hand to any of us again—that was the day he kicked me out. I went home on Saturdays when I knew he was out to check on my siblings, and now they're all safe, thank god."

Aviva pressed a kiss to my neck.

"It's okay, Jack. You're okay," she murmured, and I held onto her words—to her—like a lifeline.

After I'd calmed, she asked, "Is that why you volunteer with foster kids?"

I nodded. "How did you know?"

"My brother told me." She searched my eyes for a moment, then admitted, "I used to do the same thing. I miss it."

My chest ached with the sweetness of her words. In some ways, we were so similar.

"We can go together sometime," I said.

She nodded. "Tell me the rest."

I cleared my throat. Talking about this hurt. "Coach took me in, let me live with him, helped me with my applications. Helped me change my name from Yacob to Jack, because I wanted to leave my past behind. By that time, he'd gotten the job at Reina, and he made sure the recruiters knew who he was. We started around the same time, me as a rookie player, him as a rookie college coach. He was the one who convinced me to red shirt, pushing me until I became the player I am now."

"You're going to be first in the draft, aren't you?" she said.

"As long as I keep our winning streak going, take us to the Frozen Four, yeah. It's rare that a left wing gets picked first; NHL teams usually go for centers. But—"

"But that's how good you are," she finished for me. "I've seen you play."

I tugged her hair. "I remember."

A rosy blush covered her face, her chest. Probably from remembering that night on the rink, when I'd fucked her so hard we'd both changed. I'd refused to recognize it then, so had she.

But we were here now, thank fuck.

Or at least I was.

"Micah and Marcus showed back up in my life recently. Rebecca..." I shook my head. I had gotten two texts from her in the past couple of years, and relied on Marcus and his personal private investigator for news. "I think she ran away with the circus, or something like that. Marcus set us all up with massive trust funds, cars, helped get my younger siblings emancipated from our parents. But even with his financial support, even though his presence in my life means I have power, finally, I don't trust him."

Raising a hand, she gently brushed a hand through my short hair. "You don't trust anyone, do you?"

"How could I? Everyone leaves."

Except for Coach.

And maybe her.

"You don't trust anyone either," I pointed out.

"Except for Asher," she said.

"Right." Her fucking brother.

What would it be like, to have the same loyalty from her she had for him? I wanted it, badly. And I promised myself in that moment: I'd get it. Break my own rules to make sure it happened. Lie, cheat, or steal. Aviva would be loyal to *me,* and me alone.

She cupped my face. "I'd kill your father for you, you know."

Her words were a sweet stab, a knife dripping in honey.

"I will kill Tom, and those men who shot your parents. And you. Did you ever find them?"

She sighed. "No. It's more important to Asher than it is to me. It was a random robbery gone wrong—even though we had nothing to steal. I've got vengeance in my bones, but now it's for the living."

The look in her eyes.

You, it said. *You, despite every terrible thing you've done to me.*

"My little fury," I said, kissing her again, and she kissed me back, claiming me as much as I'd claimed her. There was no sweetness, no gentleness this time. We were both angry at each other's pasts, each determined to erase it. She scratched her nails down my back, I grabbed her arms and held her down. I shoved inside her, she bucked, still wet with her release and my come. I pounded into her and she fought me, but this time it was because she enjoyed it. At some point, I needed her, so I flipped her over onto her stomach and layered my chest over her back, entwining my fingers with hers. Daylight turned her brown hair almost copper. My cock hurt, almost raw from the number of times I'd fucked her, but I was too hungry for her to stop.

My world could've burned to the ground, and I wouldn't have cared.

As long as I was inside her wet heat, listening to her as she screamed from the combination of pleasure and pain, my name a litany on her lips, nothing mattered but her.

My little fury.

If Aviva wanted to burn the world down, I'd help her. If she wanted to burn *my* world down, I'd hand her the match.

Because from now on, she was my world.

29

Aviva

Things seemed to change after Jack's and my venture into somnophilia. That morning, he'd held me, made me burnt eggs in our little kitchenette, his eyes earnest as I'd forced myself to eat them.

I kept rubbing my left shoulder. It was bothering me.

"What's wrong?" he asked, an unreadable expression on his face.

"My shoulder itches, and part of the skin feels raised," I said. "It's kind of weird."

He walked behind me, lifting my hair to look at my shoulder, stroking his thumb over the bump and sending shivers down my spine.

"Looks like a bug bite," he said, before bending to drop a kiss over the irritated spot. "There we go, all better."

Straightening, he came around to stand in front of me, the kitchen bar in between us.

"How do *you* like your orange juice?" he asked, changing the subject.

I'd told him about Asher and the pulp.

I thought. "I don't know," I answered honestly. "I don't even know what type of juice I like, or if I even like juice. It's been so long since I felt like a kid, and it never occurred to me to figure it out.

He lifted my chin, kissing me.

"Then we'll figure it out together," he said.

It sounded like a promise.

He told me he'd see me later—and he did, insisting on driving me to work, staying there the entire night, and then taking me back to the hockey house after his shift, where he proceeded to give me so many orgasms I forgot my name.

He was no less brutal, no less demanding or controlling. If anything, he got worse. He seemed to be everywhere I was, all the time—except when he had practice, which he began dragging me to. I couldn't prove it, but he had to be stalking me. Otherwise how did he know when I was at my apartment vs. class vs. the library? If he even *thought* someone was checking me out, he'd stare them down until they looked away. And his animosity toward Professor Johnathan grew. I wasn't sure if we were going to make it through the semester without Jack beating the shit out of him, for nothing more than breathing the same air as me.

Thankfully, the slut shaming had stopped. Instead, I was treated with deference by other Reina students, as if I were Jack's girlfriend and not the target of his torture. I wasn't sure what to make of it, or of myself. I felt disloyal to Asher, and I didn't know what to do about it. I was incapable of resisting Jack, not when he was cruel, and not when he was tender.

My loyalties were shifting, and it made me uneasy. I'd never felt this way before.

I got breaks when Jack was at practice or training at the

gym, or at away games. I used them to work on other angles to get the evidence against Joshua Jensen I needed, attacking my mission with renewed vigor and the sense that the walls were closing in on me. Everything I did for my brother ran the risk of hurting Jack. I was being torn in two.

Since Jack had punched his *own goddamned goalie*, getting close to Dave and asking him what he knew was no longer an option. There was no way of talking to Dave without Jack finding out, and the goalie didn't deserve being punched again—or whatever worse thing Jack decided to do in retaliation. Besides, I doubted Dave even *wanted* to talk to me.

No, I needed something else. Tovah had done some recon, and discovered that Coach Jensen lived in a gated community with a code to get in, so breaking into his house was out. I couldn't figure out how to steal his phone. That left his computer in his real office. Not the one in the locker room, but the sports administration building: Hallister Hall.

Jack was supposed to be at practice late that night: he had a scrimmage. He'd told—not asked, *told*—me to come, but I lied and said I had a shift that night at The Stacks. I told him I'd meet him back at the hockey house after, and he'd accepted it without a fight, although he'd said something under his breath about me "not needing that fucking job." Worried that he wanted to turn me into a kept woman, I hadn't pushed the issue.

If all went as planned, I'd be in and out of Hallister Hall before Jack finished his scrimmage, and waiting for him in his bed before he got home. I didn't love what that said about me, but it was better than him figuring out what I was actually up to.

When I'd cased the building, I'd discovered that there was a back door on the first floor that led to a little, private courtyard—because didn't the coaches and athletic admin types deserve their very own courtyard, far away from the rest of us? The important thing was that the back door was never locked.

I threw myself over one of the hedges, landing on my ass. Embarrassing, if someone had seen me, but no one had. Standing and dusting myself off, I glanced around to make sure of that before trying the door.

Still unlocked.

My sigh of relief was the loudest thing in the night as I pulled the door open and headed inside the building. Coach Jensen's office was on the second floor in the east wing, a corner office that must have been a real get for him. I climbed up the old, wooden staircase, marveling at the grandeur of the building: cream colored walls lined with framed photographs of former coaches, players, and newspaper reports of historic wins. Although during the day it must have be a light, airy building, at night it was dark and almost creepy, as if all these former athletes' eyes were following me as I made my way down the hallway to Joshua Jensen's office.

When I reached it, I pulled the bobby pins out of my hair, unbent them, and got to work on the door. Jack was wrong when he'd called me liar, but he was right when he'd called me a thief. I'd stolen my fair share of food money out of my aunt's purse and "borrowed" her credit card when she was too sick or out of it to remember to get groceries. She'd always locked her door, so I'd learned how to jimmy a lock.

It was a good skill to have, and I was grateful for it as I twisted the ends of my bobby pins around, listening for that telltale snick that meant I'd released the locking mechanism.

...And there it was.

Triumphant, I went to turn the knob and open the door—

—only for someone to slam it shut and push me against the door.

Fuck.

I twisted my head, staring into Jack's angry eyes.

"You can't stop lying to me, can you, little fury?" he said in a voice filled with violence.

"And you can't stop lying to yourself."

"Maybe," he acknowledged.

Gripping my hips, he flipped me around, pushing me back against the door and wrapping a hand around my neck. The position was so similar to the first time he'd caught me breaking in somewhere, I had to take a beat to remember where I was.

Jack must have noticed, too. His smile was almost...sad. "Feels familiar, doesn't it? You couldn't leave it alone, could you? I told you, I'd take care of you and your brother. Is revenge for him losing his spot on the team really this important? Why can't you let this go?"

I stared up at him, shocked, angry, and, damnit, hurt. "Do you really still believe that? After all this time, after everything I've shared with you, everything I've *shown* you, you truly think I'm still this heinous bitch trying to take down your coach for nefarious reasons?"

He hesitated. "Aviva, I—"

"What are you kids doing here?" a gruff voice asked.

I peeked over Jack's broad shoulder to see an older man in a security uniform glaring at us.

Shit.

Jack turned around and cleared his throat. He was about to give me away, wasn't he? Visions of jail cells, the dean telling me I was kicked out of school and would never be able to go to grad school and become a psychologist attacked me. Never help other people heal from their grief. So did the vision of a depressed, lonely Asher, who could never play hockey again and would be reduced to shame and regret for the rest of his life.

"Jack, please—"

"Sorry, sir. Thought it might be fun to sneak into the nicest building on campus and, uh, have a little fun. You know how it is. Horny hockey champion and all that," Jack said in an aw shucks voice.

The guard shifted, his stern face relaxing into a smile. "Of course, Jack. Big fan. Huge fan. I'll let it slide, but you'll have to take your puck bunny somewhere else."

Jack's hands fisted. His voice was quiet, but the softness held a threat that scared me, even though it was directed elsewhere. "What did you call her?"

The guard laughed. "Puck bunny. Although maybe pussy is bet—"

My tormentor was across the room before the guard could finish his sentence. He reached out and gripped the man's collar, dragging him forward and up. I couldn't see Jack's eyes, but from the way the guard squeaked, it must have hurt.

"You don't call her that unless you want my fist through your face. Better yet, I'll let Coach Jensen know you've been drinking on the job."

The man squirmed in Jack's hold. "But I haven't—" he protested.

"Doesn't matter. Who are they going to believe, me, or you? Now apologize to her."

"I'm sorry," the man said in a choked voice.

"For what?" Jack asked in that soft, frightening voice.

"I'm sorry, miss, for insulting you."

Without a word, Jack released the man, who rocked back on his heels before scurrying away, leaving a small, yellow puddle on the ground.

Jack turned to me, the planes of his face even sharper in his anger.

He'd been defending me since the beginning, hadn't he? Even when he'd humiliated me, he'd threatened everyone else who tried to hurt me.

"Thank you," I said quietly.

He moved toward me slowly, before wrapping his hands around my upper arms. "No one talks to you that way."

"Including you?"

"Including me." He paused, correcting himself. "Except for when I'm fucking you. Degradation and possession gets you off."

I didn't protest. He was right.

"Does this mean you believe me?" I hated how small my voice was.

His eyes probed mine.

"I believe that you believe it's true," he said. "You're loyal to your brother, you wouldn't question him. But I know Coach—"

I shoved his hands away. He wasn't only clueless, he was intentionally clueless. "No, you're *loyal* to your coach, same as I'm loyal to Asher. Him taking care of you doesn't automatically make him a good guy. He can be good to you, and still have abused my brother. *It. Happened.* My brother has the emotional scars to prove it. He is not a liar, and neither am I."

"I know you're not a liar, Aviva. Not about this, at least. I'm sorry that I thought that for so long. But your brother—"

"My brother is telling the truth!"

"You don't know Coach the way I do, Aviva."

How did you get through to someone so set in their worldview?

"No, *you* don't know your Coach. You only think you do. I know you think you can read people so well, but you have this huge blind spot when it comes to him. And it makes sense, given your history with him."

No response. It was like arguing with a wall.

I pushed forward. "Men, especially men with power and authority, often put on a mask to keep society happy. All to hide the monster inside. You should know that better than anyone."

Jack's nostrils flared at the pointed accusation. But he *was* a monster, with a golden boy mask. How angry was he at me for pointing out the truth?

"Fine," he said. "You think your brother's telling the truth? Prove it."

30

Aviva

It only took a minute to unlock Coach Jensen's door, but it felt like a lifetime. Jack didn't speak, only stared at me. Finally, the locking mechanism clicked, and I turned the big brass doorknob, pulling the door open.

Jack waved his hand in front of him, a clear *after you*.

I paused, overcome, blinking rapidly to keep the grateful tears at bay. Even though Jack still didn't believe that his coach had sexually abused Asher, he believed *me*. He no longer thought I was a liar.

Not only that, he was helping. He'd never done that before, but here he was, guiding me into his coach's office. It had to be a betrayal. Was he choosing me? Could I let myself think that? Or should I be suspicious of this reversal? It was a new feeling, this tiny bit of hope, this wish to trust him. Like a seedling in the ground, desperate for sun, waiting to grow.

I shook it off and stepped inside.

The office was a cross between professor and sports bar.

Big mahogany bookshelves lined the left wall of the room, books like *The Art of War* and *How to Influence People* interspersed with trophies. On the right wall, framed photographs hung, of Joshua Jensen shaking hands with people: the university provost, the mayor, the former governor, and a number of fancy people I couldn't name. In the middle of the wall was a framed photo of a younger Joshua with a younger Jack, arms slung around each other, looking happy and caring.

Out of the corner of my eye, Jack swallowed, his right hand fisting again. Words tumbled into my mouth in a tangled heap, but I didn't release any of them. After all, what was there to say?

A mahogany desk stood in the center of the room. It matched the bookcases in its intimidating authority. I saw past it, to the computer on the desk.

"Jackpot," I said.

Jack snorted.

I walked around to the back of the desk, pushing the leather chair out of the way and turning on the computer. A moment later, it asked for a password.

"Jack, do you know—"

"Yes."

"Can you give it to me?"

He hesitated.

"Please, Jack, let me prove it to you."

Shaking his head, he said, "The password is Fr0z3n4."

I typed it in and hit return. A few seconds later, I was greeted by the desktop. I began scrolling through documents and files, looking for the damn videos.

Nothing.

Seized by an idea, I opened the "Taxes" folder.

And there it was, a small subfolder that just said "Asher."

"That's it." I practically choked out the word.

Here it was, my proof, my revenge, my brother's justice. What's more, it could mean justice for anyone else the coach had abused—and would prevent him from hurting players in the future.

So then why did the thought of breaking Jack's heart with the truth make my own hurt?

I steeled myself.

"Jack, come take a look."

He came around the desk, glancing at the computer.

"What am I looking at?"

"See the name of the subfolder?"

"It's your brother's name." He said it in a blasé way, but his jaw was tight, and his throat worked.

My hand shook. "Can you open it for me? I don't want to watch the video, I can't—"

He nodded. Grateful, I looked away, heard some tapping on the keys, a click on the mouse.

"Aviva, you can turn around," he said.

I did.

The folder was empty.

Not a single video.

Not a single file.

Jack sounded beyond relieved. "See, I told you there was nothing."

I stared at it. Yeah, there was no video, but why the hell would there be a subfolder with my brother's name in the Taxes folder?

"Click on the trash icon," I told him.

Jack shook his head. "You aren't going to find anything,

Aviva, because there isn't anything. Coach didn't do anything wrong."

God, I wanted to smack him so bad. But I'd probably slapped Jack Feldman enough in one lifetime. I wasn't sure how many more I would get away with.

"Are you sure about that?" I countered instead. "If there was nothing, why is there a folder with my brother's name in Jensen's Taxes folder?"

He sighed.

"Let me text my brother. He's a hacker."

Taking out his phone, he sent a quick text. A moment, later, it rang.

"Hey," he said. Then, "I'll tell you about it later. Can you —" his throat worked, eyes closing, like the guilt over betraying his coach this way was too much for him. "Can you access a computer remotely? See if you can find deleted files? Probably mp4s? They'd be labeled Asher." He listened for a moment, then said, "Yeah, it has to do with her."

A moment later, he hung up. "He's working on it," he said, but refused to look at me.

We waited for what seemed like forever, not speaking. The silence between us was thick with tension. Jack paced around the office, I closed my eyes and hoped.

Finally, Jack's phone buzzed. He checked it, then shook his head.

"Nothing."

I stared at him, my heart pounding.

"There can't be nothing." There was no way.

"My brother is a genius, Aviva."

"And he wouldn't lie to protect you?"

Jack glared at me. "Not about something like this. Do you want to check my text messages to him? Prove to yourself that this isn't some whole plot against you?"

The room began to spin around me. I was running out of options, and the knowledge made it hard to breathe.

Panic attack, my brain supplied.

A moment later, Jack was there, his arms around me. "I've got you, little fury," he said, stroking my back. "Inhale and exhale okay? Deep breaths. You're okay. You're going to be okay."

I let him soothe me, slowed down my breathing. But I wasn't going to be okay. Desperate, I began pulling open drawers and shutting them, rifling through papers and pens. Maybe there was a USB drive somewhere? Maybe the coach had another laptop, hidden away?

I started pulling out books and checking them to see if any were hollow. None were. Jack patiently took each one from me and put them back to rights.

"Aviva," Jack said, voice filled with pity. "I'm sorry, but there's nothing. And we should go before we *do* get caught."

"I'm not going anywhere," I said, resolute.

Not until I found the evidence I needed.

"You need to face the truth, little fury," he said gently. "You're looking for something that doesn't exist, when you really need to look closer to home. Asher is lying to you. It happens sometimes. I'm sorry, but that's the truth of it."

He grabbed my hand. I ripped it away.

"Don't touch me."

He raised an eyebrow, reaching for me again and capturing my wrist in his big hand. "Come with me to the alumni dinner next week. You can meet Coach, get a feel for him. Ask him yourself if he abused your brother, if that's what you need to get closure on this. You'll see what I see in him, I swear."

I couldn't believe the words coming out of his mouth. "You think I'll be your date to the absolute last place in the world I want to be." Not to mention, the closest thing I had to formal wear was the second hand, threadbare black dress I'd worn to my aunt's funeral.

"I want you there, princess."

Great. We were back to princess.

He must've seen the look on my face, because he softened. *Slightly.* "Come home with me tonight. And then we can go shopping for a dress tomorrow."

"No."

He shook his head, turning to go. "I'm not playing this game with you anymore, where you pull away and I retaliate. We're together now, and whether you come home with me or I sneak into your bedroom again, I'm going to bed with you and waking up with you. But I'm giving you a choice this time. It's up to you if you don't want to take it—if it makes you feel better to think you were forced."

He was right. I hated that he was right, that I wanted to go to bed with him and to wake up with him. I stared around the office.

"What kind of choice is that, if the result is the same either way?" I shot back.

He opened the door for me. "The only kind you'll get."

31

Jack

The next morning, I woke up before Aviva, who was curled up on my bed. For a little while, I laid there, listening to her breathe, letting it ground me. Finally, I reluctantly got up. She'd hopefully sleep for a while, long enough for me to go do what I needed to before coming back and taking her shopping.

For a moment, I considered locking the door behind me so she couldn't leave. But I'd be able to find her easily, thanks to the microchip in her neck, and I wanted to give her the semblance of freedom.

I drove to campus, my fingers tapping on the wheel. Last night had freaked me out and fucked me up in the head. I believed Aviva, but I didn't believe her brother. There was no real evidence—except that weird file with her brother's name.

I needed answers.

"COME IN," COACH CALLED THROUGH HIS OFFICE DOOR.

I twisted the knob, entering the same space I'd been in last night. I'd been careful to make sure everything was in its right place before we'd left. Seeing him sitting behind his desk was both reassuring and disconcerting. Was it my imagination, or was there a whisper of Aviva's scent in the room?

"Jack." Coach greeted me with a warm smile. "It's great to see you outside the arena." His smile turned to a look of concern. "Something's wrong. Why don't you sit down and tell me about it."

He gestured to the chair in front of the desk. I sat, and he steepled his fingers.

"What's going on?"

I swallowed. This was awkward as hell. "Why did Asher Gold leave the team?"

Coach sighed. "We've talked about this."

We had. But I needed reassurance. "Can you talk me through it again? It was a pretty...extreme accusation he launched against you, and—"

"It was, wasn't it?" Coach shook his head. "Asher Gold was—is—a troubled young man. Orphaned young, without much guidance in his life. And a huge chip on his shoulder. He felt entitled to his place on the team, and when it was in jeopardy by poor performance, he took it out on me."

"Yeah," I muttered, searching his eyes.

I'd always been able to pride myself on being able to tell when someone was hiding something, but my gut warred with my brain. Coach wasn't lying, and the discomfort I felt was because Aviva had put doubt in my mind, not because I was sensing lies.

Right?

Coach straightened. "You don't believe his accusations, do you, Jack? Because I have to be frank with you, after the relationship I've built with you over the years, that would hurt. I think of you like a son. I think of all my players as sons, but you in particular. For you to believe I could do something so heinous..." he trailed off, looking away.

I'd hurt him.

Because Asher Gold was lying. I might not know for sure, because I'd never seen him face-to-face, but I was positive.

I relaxed. "You're right, I'm sorry. I don't know what the hell got into my head."

Coach smiled a sad smile. "I'm assuming his sister did."

Now it was my turn to straighten. "You knew Aviva was Asher's sister?"

"After you had your meltdown at the opening game, I looked into her. Wanted to make sure she wasn't trying to manipulate you or screw you over. It was easy to put two and two together. Look, Jack, I'd never begrudge you a relationship. You should find someone who you care about, or at least takes care of your..." he coughed, "needs. But be careful, okay? Not everyone has your best interests at heart. Sometimes we want to see the best in people, even when they only give us their worst. And you're at a point in your career where a mistake like that could cost you everything. Your *team* everything. They need you to lead them, to stay strong and keep winning, okay?"

The insinuation against Aviva immediately made me want to defend her. Coach wasn't right about her, he didn't know her like I did.

"How about this?" Coach suggested. "Why don't we make a time for me to meet her? Dinner at my house. You haven't been over in a long time. That way I can feel her out, and she can see that I'm not a monster."

There was no way that would go well. Who knew what my little fury would do without witnesses.

"I'm bringing her to the alumni dinner," I offered.

Coach bestowed a warm smile. "That works too, son."

"See you at practice," I said, mostly relieved and reassured again.

As I rose and went to the door, Coach called my name.

"Jack?"

"Yeah?"

"I probably don't say this enough, but I'm proud of you, son. You've grown into the man I always knew you could be. Don't lose sight of what's important to you."

Any misgivings I still had disappeared. This was the man who'd always looked out for me, given me opportunities, rescued me from my heinous life when no one else gave a crap.

He wasn't an abuser. He was just trying to do the right thing.

Unlike me.

32

Aviva

Jack was gone when I woke up. We'd fallen asleep with his arms wrapped tight around me, one locked around my stomach, the other splayed across my pussy. I should've felt trapped, not safe. This morning, his absence should've made me feel relieved, not disappointed.

After using his toothbrush and trying to turn my sex-and-sleep mussed hair into some semblance of a topknot, I threw on one of his hoodies and headed downstairs to the kitchen. I was beyond thirsty, desperately needed coffee, and after...

...I didn't know. My brain wasn't functioning yet.

I skirted past the dining room, avoiding the embarassing but hot memories it brought up, and entered the kitchen.

Isaac sat at the island, scrolling through his phone. He glanced up when he saw me.

"Morning. Coffee?"

I'd expected awkwardness, but instead he seemed

normal, like he'd expected me here. Or maybe Jack always had girls wandering into the kitchen in need of caffeine. My stomach dropped like a stone at that thought.

As if Isaac read my mind, he said, "You're not the first girl I've seen in that hoodie—"

Oh, god.

"—but you're the first who he'd let keep it."

Oh.

Relief swamped me, so intense, I almost stumbled. It shouldn't have mattered, but it did.

"Coffee, yes, thank you," I told him.

Nodding, he got up, pouring a cup for me from the pot.

"What do you take?"

"Oat milk, but I can drink it black if you don't have—"

He walked over to the fridge and pulled it open. "Jack bought some the other day. He's never drank it before, so it must be for you."

Relief turned to warmth, and confusion. Jack and I had turned a corner in our relationship, but how did he know I was lactose intolerant, and why would he have made sure I could have coffee at his home? Was he that serious about me?

Adding oat milk to my coffee, Isaac passed it to me, before leaning back against the now closed fridge and crossing his arms.

"So. Aviva *Gold*."

"Yeah," I said.

"Any relation to the New York Gold family?"

Ugh.

The Gold family never came through for me and Asher when our parents died. Wealthy, elusive, exclusive, and possibly criminal, the Manhattan-based dynasty wanted nothing to do with us, and we wanted nothing to do with them.

"Distant cousin," I told him. "How do you know about the Golds?"

He smirked. "Let's just say we go...way back."

Hmm.

"What kind of way back?" I asked.

He shook his head, avoiding the question. "What's the deal with your friend?"

"Tovah?"

"Yeah."

I straightened, eyes narrowing. I didn't know Isaac well, but if he was friends with Jack, it possibly meant his ethics around consent were as skewed as my...whatever Jack was to me now.

"Off limits, to you," I told him.

He threw back his head and laughed. "You're cute. I get what Jack sees in you."

A throat cleared from the doorway. We both looked over.

Jack was glaring. "None of that," he warned.

Isaac shrugged, still chuckling. "Don't worry, I know it's a look but don't touch thing."

"No more looking. *Ever*," Jack said. To me he said, "C'mon, little fury, we have a dress to buy."

"I have dresses," I protested.

"Aviva, you'd be beautiful in a garbage bag. But I want to buy you something as beautiful as you, something new," he cajoled. "Don't I owe you at least that?"

He was trying to buy my forgiveness. Bribe me into softening toward him.

It worked.

"Fine," I said.

"Fine," he mimicked, holding out his hand for me to take. "C'mon, I scheduled you time at Pixie."

"Pixie?" The boutique was invite only. Dresses there sold for thousands of dollars. "That's unnecessary."

Impatient, Jack grabbed my hand and pulled me out of the kitchen. "I disagree. As much as I love you in my hoodie, wearing something I bought for you? Knowing when I take it off that I took care of what's mine by clothing you? It's very, very necessary."

PIXIE WAS A MISNOMER FOR THE EXCLUSIVE BOUTIQUE. I'D never been—not only because it was so far out of my price range it was ridiculous, but because I assumed, like the name, they'd only serve smaller sizes: not a 16-18 dress size like me.

I was wrong. Pixie was size inclusive, if not price inclusive. I gazed around the store, painted a pale gray with exposed beams and old, faded brick walls, with dresses of every color, style, and size hanging off racks made of old metal pipes. The store was funky and cool, but still very, very expensive feeling.

"Thank you," I said quietly to Jack as he guided me around the store with a hand on my lower back.

I didn't mean because of the prices; there was no way I was accepting this. But to keep my size in mind without making a big deal out of it? It made me feel seen and accepted in ways I never had before.

He smiled, like he knew what I meant. "I love your body, Aviva. I wanted to take you somewhere where I knew they'd do it justice."

I turned to kiss him, just a peck, but he took advantage, urging my mouth open and deepening the kiss. It was sweet, affectionate, tender—so many things he'd only recently become toward me. So I kissed him back in the same way; it felt like a promise.

"Let me help you!" I pulled back from Jack to see the sales woman make her way toward us.

"Aren't you pretty?" The sales woman fawned over me, although from the way she fluttered her lashes at Jack made it clear she was full of shit.

Jack completely ignored her, eyes burning into me as he issued orders to her. "She'll only want dresses with higher necks," he told her. He glanced back at me. "Right, Aviva?"

I nodded, once again touched that he'd know.

As he took a seat in a leather armchair, he murmured, "Unless you're ready to show people your scar. I wasn't lying when I said it's the most beautiful part of you—but if it's too soon, I get it. If it'll always be too soon, I get that, too."

It was too soon. I wasn't sure if I'd ever be ready for people to see it. Jack had sworn he'd pay for plastic surgery, and the care and consideration in that fierce promise had done something to me.

"Thank you," I said again.

His eyes were practically silver. "You never have to thank me for anything." He nodded to the changing room. "Now go. Try on dresses for me."

Once inside, the sales woman passed me the first dress —a black, tight, velvet number with a ruched waist and a high neck. I looked at the tag, preparing myself for an astro-nomical number, but there was no price on it.

"I doubt this means it's free," I muttered.

How wealthy did you have to be to not even care about prices? The thought made me nauseous. The second thought, that Jack had the kind of money to shop at a store like this—and wanted to spend it on me—made me dizzy.

I pulled the dress over my head, adjusting it before I went outside the locker room to show Jack.

He immediately shook his head. "Hot, but no."

The sales woman sighed, passing me another dress—this one royal blue with a huge, knee-length tulle skirt attached to a silk bodice. The neckline was sweetheart shaped, and probably would've been pretty, but I shivered as she handed it to me. Why wasn't she listening to Jack's specifications about the neckline?

"No," Jack barked, before I even tried it on.

I pushed open the door to the locker room to peek out.

"What did I tell you about the neckline?" he asked the sales woman.

She played with her hair, simpering at him. "This cut will look great on her. Don't you want your friend to look nice?"

"Girlfriend," he corrected, making my heart race. "And she wants a dress with a high neckline, so you'll bring her high necklines. Got me?"

Girlfriend. Is that what I was now? He'd blackmailed, fucked me less than consensually, treated me before like I didn't matter. Things had changed between us, but I hadn't known they'd shifted that much in Jack's brain. Did I want to be his girlfriend? More importantly, did I have a choice?

"Girlfriend?" I raised a brow.

"Yup." He popped the p. "Have a problem with that?"

Before I could respond, the sales woman caught me peeking and glared at me before flouncing off to find more dresses. She brought me a bunch on pretty beaded hangers before flouncing off again.

I tried on dress after dress, Jack shaking his head at each

and every one. Insecurity began to creep in—did I look so horrible in dresses that nothing would work? I'd worked hard over the years to not let my size get to me. I had enough to deal with the scar, I didn't need to hate my body, too. But moments like this could and would hurt, and I couldn't deny it.

I spotted the last dress—a knee length burgundy dress with a slit up the side, covered in delicate lace. I dropped it over my head and zipped it up, before admiring myself in the mirror. I loved this dress, but wasn't sure he would. And although it shouldn't have mattered, he was paying.

And I wanted him to love it. I wanted him to—

Nope. Not going there, I admonished my brain.

Pushing the door to the changing room open, I slowly walked out, standing in front of Jack, and preparing himself to hate this one, too.

Jack didn't speak. Just stared at me, throat working, gray eyes burning silver now.

"You hate it," I said, disappointed. I thought the burgundy lace was beautiful on me, but—

"I don't hate it," he said, voice husky. "No one's ever made me speechless before."

And then he was out of the chair and across the room, one arm wrapped around me, one in my hair, and kissing me like he'd never kissed me before. He didn't need to speak, his lips and tongue spoke for him. He wanted me, more than he wanted to breathe. Needed me more than he needed oxygen.

And I felt the same way.

"We'll take it," he called, pushing me into the locker room.

"Jack, it must be like a million dollars."

"Little fury, it could be a billion dollars, and I wouldn't

care. This dress was made for you, and I was made to take it off of you," he said, closing the door behind him and dropping to his knees.

"Jack—"

"Do you get to say no?" he taunted.

"Jack!" I protested, angry now.

"Shhh, we don't want her to hear us," he said, and then he was pushing the dress up over my hips and his mouth was on me and I lost the will to argue with him. In fact, this time *I* was the one who forgot how to breathe.

But who needed to breathe, anyway?

33

Jack

A week later, I was adjusting my tie in front of my mirror for the alumni dinner and thinking about Aviva in that dark red dress. About the taste of her pussy that morning, and almost every morning after. Things were...different between us. I'd called her my girlfriend because I'd meant it, although "girlfriend" was too tame a word for how I felt. But although things had stabilized between us, I wasn't sure if she'd be with me if she didn't have to be. We were still on shaky ground, and I couldn't help but feel like something bad was coming for us.

I jerked on the tie. It was too tight.

She was going to meet Coach tonight, face to face. And I, Jack Feldman, confident about everything, wasn't sure how that would go.

"Jack," Isaac called from outside my room. "We've gotta leave."

Time to face the fucking music.

AVIVA WAS WAITING OUTSIDE HER BUILDING WHEN WE arrived. The gate was broken. I hated that she didn't live somewhere safe. I'd need to have someone fix the gate, add extra locks to her door. Or take Marcus up on his offer to buy me a condo and move her in with me. That was an appealing idea. Absolutely insane, but appealing none-theless.

I put the car in park and got out of the car, going around and opening the passenger door for her. Judah, Levi, and Isaac were crammed in the backseat.

"Feldman, you're cunt-whipped," Judah quipped, but I ignored him.

Aviva watched me with wary eyes, worn gray peacoat wrapped around her, as she walked past me and I helped her into the SUV.

She needed a new coat. New York winters were cold. What if she didn't have something thicker? I was going to buy her a new coat tomorrow. No, ten new coats. She'd never ever feel a slight chill again if I—

"You didn't have to get the door," she said.

I shrugged, a little embarrassed at where my thoughts had gone. "I wanted to."

I wanted to do a lot of things, but those things required being alone. Worry filled me—everything felt like it was going to go wrong. Maybe I could skip the dinner, maybe we could stay home, maybe—

Except I was giving the opening speech before intro-ducing Coach. I wasn't a weasel, and I wouldn't be unreli-able. It would be fine. In fact, Aviva would *see* for herself how trustworthy Coach was, and drop this nonsense mission to get her brother justice he didn't actually need.

Reassured, I closed the door behind her, went back around the car, and got in, cranking up the heat on a chilly late October night and pulling out of the spot. Impulse overtook me, and as I steered one handed, I took Aviva's hand with the other, gripping it tight, so she couldn't let go.

If I got my way, she'd never let go.

THE BEGINNING OF THE DINNER PASSED BY IN A BLUR. ALUMNI approached me, wanting to shake my hand and take pictures with me. I gave them my best Jack Hat Trick Feldman, charming and funny and a little cocky, a little bashful. They ate it up. The whole time, Aviva stood beside me, her eyes on me, barely speaking. She was uncomfortable, maybe even angry, and I wanted to reassure her, but I didn't have time.

Finally, we were sitting at our table, being served dinner. I placed one hand on her thigh, forking dry chicken into my mouth with the other as I laughed with my friends.

"Have you even practiced your speech?" Levi asked.

Judah shook his head, spearing an asparagus. "Jack never needs to. He feels it here," he mocked, thumping his chest.

And then my name was being spoken up on the dais, and I was releasing Aviva's thigh, standing, straightening out my tie and approaching the stage. Coach sat at a table to the right of the stage, and winked at me before mouthing *proud of you.*

I got up on the dais and stared out at the tables of

wealthy alumni and important faculty and staff, noting that Aviva sat on one side of the room, Coach on the other. I felt divided between them, but I dismissed the feeling; I had a speech to give.

I cleared my throat.

"Not many of you know this, but Joshua Jensen saved— and changed—my life. I wouldn't be here today if it weren't for him. He spotted me as a young teenager, saw my talent, and patiently and painstakingly helped me hone it. But he's been more than a trainer and a coach, he's been a true friend, brother, even father figure to me—and to all of us on the team."

Looking down, I saw Coach smiling, and around the ballroom, my teammates nodding. But Aviva was playing with her salad and not even looking at me.

A frog stuck in my throat, so I cleared it again and went on. "He's always been there for us. Talking to us about private things you wouldn't think your coach would even care about—"

I paused, my eyes still on Aviva, stymied by my own words. Should a hockey coach be so involved in his players' private lives?

"—always available over text, day or night—"

Had that ever turned into something it shouldn't have? Why *was* he so available to us?

"And ready with advice or praise. His office door is always open, no matter what." I laughed, even though I didn't find it funny. "I can't tell you the number of us who've spent time in his office with the door locked, only to come back out reinvigorated to play..."

Had Asher been in there with the door locked?

What the actual fuck?

Sweat gathered on my neck, beneath my pits, on my

back. For a moment, it became hard to breathe, the room swimming in front of me so all I could see was Coach's concerned face, and Aviva's rapt one.

I wasn't going to lose it, here on stage, in front of all these people.

I shut my eyes for a second. People in the crowd began to murmur.

I spoke louder, stronger. "A team is only as strong as its weakest player, and Coach has always, always made sure that each and every one of us is strong. I've had the honor of leading our team for the past two seasons as its captain, and I can tell you all how strong and brave and committed each of my teammates is. The game means everything to us, but we mean more to each other. Commitment, determination, trust, loyalty—those are the things that make a good hockey team, and—" I looked at Aviva, "—a successful relationship of any kind. I'm proud to be captain of this commited, determined, trustworthy, loyal team—something I'd never have if it weren't for Coach Joshua Jensen. Thank you."

People stood, clapping. Including Aviva, who had tears in her eyes as she stared at me. It didn't feel like condemnation from her, it felt like pride and approval.

And then Coach was next to me, giving me a hug, slapping my back, and saying, "Thank you, son."

I went back to my seat and sat back down next to Aviva.

"You were great," she murmured, but she wouldn't let me hold her hand.

I tried to not let it bother me as Coach spoke. Most of his words were a blur, although he emphasized more than once how I was "like a son to him," that our team was "like family," and family always supports and encourages each other, that there's an unconditional love there, despite what may

happen. That "like Jack said," loyalty was the most important part of a team.

"These men, these strong, talented men, they know
loyalty. And I am proud to be their coach, their guide, their
father figure even—except for when they get up to no good,"
he said, and the room was filled with laughter. "Our future
here at Reina University is bright. It's setting up Jack for a
great career in the NHL, so he can accomplish every single
thing he's dreamed of since he was that scrawny teenager on
the ice. And I know, with Jack at the helm, we'll go to the
Frozen Four and the championship. Bright things lay
ahead!"

People rose, cheered raucously. I clapped, too, but all I
could do was look at Aviva's clenched fists on the table, and
the way she avoided my gaze.

I grabbed her wrist, forcing her hand open.

"Jack, what are you doing?" she whispered.

"You hold my hand," I ordered, also whispering.

She glared at me, but opened her hand, palm up. I took
hers, and felt immediately better—and worse, because I
could feel her mentally and emotionally pulling away.

34

Aviva

I t's setting up Jack for a great career in the NHL, so he can accomplish every single thing he's dreamed of since he was that scrawny teenager on the ice...

I sat next to Jack, his warm, strong thigh pressed against mine as he gripped my hand tight. I was reeling after his speech, and Coach Jensen's closing words. As much as I hated the topic of Jack's speech, I was proud of him. He'd stumbled a few times—why, I wasn't sure—but he'd given a passionate, eloquent, rousing speech. If I didn't know better, I'd begin to love his coach as much as he did, based on his hero worship.

Jack lifted my hand to press a kiss to my knuckles. I tried once again to pull away, but he just gripped it harder, nipping my middle finger with his teeth in reprimand. I looked over at him, his eyes were swimming with thoughts I couldn't follow. Anger and...confusion? Sorrow? Determination? I wasn't sure, because I'd never been able to read him as well as he read me.

"You did great," I murmured to him, unable to not share how proud I was of him, despite how upset I was.

... so he can accomplish every single thing he's dreamed...

I hadn't felt this at cross-purposes with my tormentor-slash-boyfriend since we'd first faced off in the locker room. God, that felt like years ago, and only yesterday, all at once. If I got justice for Asher, it meant taking Joshua Jensen down. But without their coach, with the scandal and resulting scrutiny, could Jack still take his team to the Frozen Four? Win the championship? Be first in the draft? *Accomplish all his dreams?* Or would I take that all away from him. Was I going to have to choose between my brother's peace and my boyfriend's future?

Suddenly, the room felt hot, claustrophobic.

I tried to tug my hand away. "I need air."

"I'll come with you," he said, rising from his chair, still gripping my hand.

"No!" The word was like a slap. Jack flinched, and I softened my tone. "Please, I need to get air alone. *Please.*"

He scanned my eyes, then slowly released my hand. "Okay, but when you come back, we're going to dance."

I nodded. I couldn't even worry about it, I needed air. Before, being around him meant I didn't care if I sacrificed breathing; now I couldn't go one more second without it.

I stumbled away from him, hurrying through the room, passing elegant couples on the dance floor as a small string band played a rendition of Chinchilla's "1:5" which was a weird but depressingly apt accompaniment to my current emotions.

Down a hallway, past Judah and Levi, who were talking about something in harsh whispers, and then out the side door into a small garden similar to the one behind Hallister

Hall. Once I was outside, I sat down on a wooden bench, gasping for breath.

Too much. This was too much. Angry, helpless tears fell. I understood the latter emotion, but not the former. Who was I angry with? The coach, certainly. Was I upset with Jack, who'd hurt me in so many ways but not more than when he refused to believe me? But who felt such obvious, understandable loyalty to the man who'd changed his life for the better and would help him gain everything he wanted in life? Or was I angry at myself, for falling for a man who should've been my enemy, and feeling torn when my loyalty should've been to my brother and my brother alone?

Because I *was* falling. Falling for Jack, with all his cruelty and kindness, terror and tenderness. He was the person who seemed to understand me the most but trust me the least. He knew the parts of me that scared me, had dragged them to the light, and had finally made it possible for me to let go of control. And in doing so, he'd stormed his way into my heart. I laughed bitterly, sniffing. He called me "little thief," but he was the one who'd stolen from me.

What was I going to do?

"Aviva?" The deep voice made my skin crawl.

I looked up to see Joshua Jensen standing in front of me, hands in his suit pockets. He smiled at me, but there was no warmth in it.

He was the last person I wanted to talk to. I stood up to vacate the bench—and the garden—when he raised a hand.

"You don't have to run from me, Aviva. I only want to talk."

"Is that the kind of thing you'd say to my brother?" I spat, wiping furiously at my tears.

The coach sighed, shutting his eyes for a moment. "Aviva, your brother is troubled, mentally. I'm sure you know this. It's understandable, the way you two...lost your parents."

I glared. "How do you know how we lost our parents?"

"Because Asher told me. Asher used to talk to me about everything. I was his confidant, a pseudo-therapist. That was a mistake because he attached to me in inappropriate ways..."

"Bullshit," I said. "You manipulated him, took advantage of his trust..."

The coach raised his eyebrow. "Like you're taking advantage of Jack's?"

"I'm not taking advantage of him."

"You may not mean to be, but before he met you, that boy had one focus, and one focus only—winning. Since he's met you, he's been distracted. Sure, he's playing fine, but I can sense him and his game slipping. Do you really want that for him?"

"You're so full of it," I snapped. "Who's really manipulating whom, here?"

He chuckled. "Smart. You're a smart girl. With a bright future ahead of you. Please don't let your brother's vendetta against me turn me away from that. All I wanted for Asher was for him to get everything he ever wanted. I still want that for him. I hope he gets the help he needs, Aviva. Are you getting it for him?"

I drew myself up to my full height. No wonder why Jack didn't believe me. Joshua Jensen was a smooth talker, able to twist the story and make you forget what was true in the face of his easy lies. If I didn't know better, I'd think he was actually concerned about my brother.

"You mean the help he needs because you assaulted him?"

He shook his head. "I wish you hadn't fallen for his lies, Aviva."

Joshua Jensen had a tell. There was a smugness in his stare, a smirk on his face. It could be misinterpreted as compassion, but I knew better. This was a man who'd taken advantage of his authority and power to take advantage of the boys who looked up to him. I'd been studying sexual narcissism for my deviant psych project: so often, sexual narcissists didn't groom, manipulate, or sexually assault their victims because they'd wanted them. They hurt them because they *could.*

"Do you believe your own lies, *Coach*?" I asked. "Have you convinced yourself you're a good man?"

That was the difference between him and Jack. Jack didn't pretend to be a good man. He knew who he was, and he accepted it. He'd never denied hurting me, never gaslit me. He was honest, and that honesty meant a lot to me, especially right now when I was faced with such an extreme liar. Jack, for all his flaws, was guided by his emotions, not his greed for power and dominance. He didn't want to make me feel small, the way the coach made my brother feel small.

It didn't matter. There would be no Jack and me after this. I ignored the pain of the realization even as it tore through me.

"If you'll excuse me, I owe Jack a dance."

Coach Jensen's hand flew out, gripping my bare upper arm. "Careful, Aviva. At the end of the day, I have his loyalty, you don't. You won't want to get on Jack's bad side."

Except I already had. And would again, after this.

I pulled away. "You ever touch me again, and I'll scream my fucking head off."

He shook his head, that smirk in place. "And they'll

think you're just like your brother. A liar. And we both know Jack *hates* liars."

I stormed past him, but he called after me, "Tell Asher I say hi," and the sinister taunt chilled me as I pulled the door open and re-entered the building.

I headed down the hallway to the bathroom, determined to wash the tears and my anger off my face. As I turned the corner, I almost bumped right into Jack.

"Whoa," he said. "Where are you going in such a rush, little fury?"

I shut my eyes, determined to hide my tears. "Not now, Jack."

Then he was closer, his hand tilting my chin up. "Have you been crying?"

I wrenched away from him. "No."

"Aviva, baby, look at me." He lowered his voice, stroking my face. "Tell me what's going on. Tell me what's wrong, and I'll fix it."

Willing away my tears with a deep breath, I opened my eyes and looked at him, really looked at him. Hoped he saw me.

"You can't fix it, Jack, if you refuse to believe me."

He inhaled. "This? I believe that you believe it. But it's not true, Aviva. Did you hear my speech at all?"

I swallowed down more tears. "Every word."

"Then you should understand how important he is to me."

"I do," I said to him. "I understand it, and I know it's hard to let that go, but Jack, if you care about me at all—"

"I do."

I do.

He thought he did.

But he cared about his coach and his worldview more.

Inhaling, knowing that his next response could break my heart, I said, "I'm about to tell you something, and I need you to believe me. Not about my brother. About me."

He swallowed but didn't say anything.

I continued, barely able to get the words out. "Joshua Jensen confronted me out in the courtyard just now."

Jack's eyes darkened. "And?"

"And he's guilty, Jack! You can see it in his eyes. He fucking smirked at me when he told me if I reported him people would think I was a liar—"

Jack cut me off. "You aren't a liar Aviva, but you have to let—"

This time, *I* interrupted *him*. "I don't mean report him for what he did to Asher. I mean report him for what he did to me."

Jack reared back, like I'd shocked him.

Good.

"What did he do to you?"

"Just now? He touched me."

"He. Touched. You?" Jack's voice was gravel, his eyes working. His fist clenched and unclenched. "How?"

"Your beloved coach grabbed me by arm and squeezed," I said. I shuddered from the memory of his grip. "You can probably see..."

But Jack was already relaxing, clearly relieved. "I'm sure he startled you, and I'll talk to him about it, but I'm sure he wanted to talk to you. He's like me, a little too aggressive at times—"

I gaped at him. "I'm sorry," I said slowly. "You lose your shit at your own goalie for talking to me, but your coach touches me and suddenly it's okay? Do you see how ridiculous that is?"

"He's a good guy, Aviva. I'm sure he'll apologize."

"How do you not see that he's manipulating you?"

Jack's eyes flashed. "He's not the one manipulating me."

I gasped, guttural and pained, hunching in on myself protectively. He may as well have punched me directly through the heart.

"You think I'm manipulating you?" I could barely get the words out.

Jack's jaw was set. "Coach said as much."

"So after everything we've been through, after you told me you knew I wasn't a liar, we're back to this?"

I shook my head in shock. My eyes burned. I wanted to be angry, but anger was a secondary emotion; I hurt too much to be angry.

"Maybe you don't mean to, but that's what you're doing, Aviva. You have a goal, and you're smart about people, about psychology, and you're utilizing it to get what you want out of me," he rationalized.

"What *I* want out of *you*," I said, then repeated it. "What I want out of you. All you've done Jack, is take, and take, and take. The one thing I've asked you for—to believe me, to support me here, to trust me—and you can't even consider the option. If there's no trust between us, then there's nothing."

We both stared at each other, my chest heaving from the effort to breathe, because it hurt too much to breathe. People had started to gather, whispering. I didn't care about a single one of them. All I cared about was that the man I'd started falling for, despite all the shit he'd done, was so set in his fragile worldview he'd decided to make *me* the villain.

We were at an impasse.

"I don't know where we go from here," I murmured, blinking away the tears that threatened to return.

His eyes flashed. "Don't say that."

"What else is there to say? Between him and me, you'll choose him, every time."

He shook his head like he couldn't believe me.

"And if it were between me and your brother, you'd choose Asher every time."

"So I guess this is it, then," I said, unable to fight off the tears anymore. They spilled out over my face.

"I guess so," he said. "Tell me one thing, Aviva Gold. Make me understand—what made you so hellbent on vengeance for someone else, you're willing to let go of the good thing right in front of you? That you'd give us up—for a lie?"

As if he weren't doing the same exact thing.

As if he weren't still lying to himself.

"Tell me, Aviva," he finished. "*Who hurt you?*"

I gave up the fight against the tears, and they streamed down my face.

"You did."

He reeled back, his face a kaleidoscope of jagged, betrayed edges. But he was the one who'd betrayed *me*. And he didn't contradict me. And how could he, when my heart was bleeding out on the floor in front of us?

We stood there, neither speaking, and even though physically we were so close, we were now worlds apart. Universes. Entire galaxies. Separated by our differing beliefs. It was a distance I couldn't cross, no matter what I did.

"Let me go, Jack," I said quietly, even though deep down I was begging *don't let me go, don't let this be over, don't believe him over me, don't choose him over me.*

Pain was etched across his features, his gray eyes dark, not with lust, but with a devastation that matched mine. His throat worked, but he didn't say a word.

I left him there like that, forcing myself not to look behind me, hoping despite myself that he'd follow. That he'd be his usual overbearing self, unwilling to let me go without a fight. Every other time, he'd chased me, caught me, brought me back.

But this time he didn't.

And that hurt most of all.

35

Aviva

It was pouring rain by the time I got home. I didn't
have the money to call an Uber, and Tovah was at
work, so I'd walked the whole way. I was soaked
through, my expensive dress was probably ruined, my feet
hurt from the high heels I'd walked almost two miles in, and
I was exhausted. All I wanted to do was shower, dry off, and
collapse into bed. I'd been crying for so long, I was drained.
Of emotion, of everything.

I'd left my broken heart on the hallway floor outside the
ballroom. My chest ached from the emptiness.

The hot water from the shower barely warded off the
chill. It didn't bring me back to life. I tried to wash Joshua
Jensen's words, the night, and my feelings about Jack away
until the hot water ran out and I finally gave up.

Wrapping myself in a towel, I exited the bathroom.
Someone was pounding on the door.

"Aviva!"

It was Jack. I wasn't sure what he was doing here, and

even though a part of me strained to open the door, I wouldn't let myself. Nothing good could come from it.

"Aviva! Let. Me. In."

I slid to the floor, burying my head in my hands and did my best to ignore him. I'd wanted him to follow me, but it was better if he hadn't. Better if this ended now, because if it continued, I'd only hurt more.

"Aviva, I swear to fucking god, if you don't open this door I will *break it down.*"

Sure.

I stood up on wobbly legs and went into my bedroom, collapsing facedown on my bed, covering my head with a pillow so I didn't have to listen to him banging and yelling.

A smashing sound, the squeak of hinges. I jumped.

Huh.

He'd broken down the door after all.

He stomped across the floor to my bedroom, and then I was being dragged up and off the bed, turned to face the mirror. One of his arms wrapped around my waist in a vice, the other locked around my throat.

"Look at us," he commanded. "Look. At. Us."

I looked. He was soaked through, like I had been, dark hair matted with rain, raindrops dripping off his long dark lashes, turning his gray eyes silver in the dark. His mouth was at my ear, his wet suit soaking through my towel, pressing against my bare legs.

"Do you see? Tell me you see." The order sounded as desperate as he'd sounded earlier. No, more desperate.

"I see my stalker broke into my apartment again and is restraining me against my will," I taunted, but it was half-assed. I was too drained to spar with him.

"No, I mean, do you see *us*. See how well we fit together.

How right we look together. How much we are *meant* for each other."

Oh.

I looked, really looked. His dark features and mine. His big, hard body, my smaller, softer one. My scar edging up toward his arm. And he must have been tracking my eyes, because he released his arm around my throat only to stroke the scar. "You see, don't you," he murmured. "I'm not letting you go, little fury. I don't care how much I hurt you in the past, I don't care if it hurts in the future. I. Am. Not. Letting. You. Go. Do you hear me?"

"All I hear is you claiming me as yours, without giving any of yourself back," I said, suddenly so, so tired.

He shook his head. "No, baby. No. I'm yours as much as you're mine. I'm sorry. I'm sorry I called you manipulative. I'm sorry I hurt you, I'm sorry I never gave you a choice, I'm sorry I made you feel like all you were good for was sex. You're so much more than that to me, little fury. You're *everything*. Let me show you."

He'd never said sorry to me before—not once. It hurt more than if he'd never apologized at all. I shut my eyes. I couldn't look at us anymore. I'd surrender again, and where would that leave me? I'd become someone else, not loyal, not strong, not...anything, but Jack's, until he decided he was done with me, too.

"Look at me, baby," he said, and then he had turned my head in his hand and he was dropping soft kisses on my lips, my cheek, my eyes. "Look at me," he murmured again. "Please."

It was the please that did it. My eyes opened. His own looked crazed. Pained.

"Please let me show you," he said.

I nodded, and even though I knew it was the last time, I wanted it, needed it. Needed him.

And then his arms were dropping and my towel was dropping and his suit pants were unzipping and he was tracing circles around my clit. I was wet, and not just from the shower, as if my body had known what my mind hadn't. Knew Jack was on his way here and had prepared for him.

"That's my girl," he murmured. "Wet for me already, because your body knows how right we are for each other. I was made for you, little fury. Made to keep you safe. Made to keep you happy. And you were made to keep me whole. Spread your legs."

I did, and then he was inside me, his arm once again wrapped around my waist to keep me upright as he thrust into me, slow and deep.

"Kiss me," he ordered, and I twisted my head in time for him to capture my mouth with his and swallow my protests, as if there had been any.

This was it. It had to be the last time, he knew as well as I did. And I was going to inhale every second of it. I'd be greedy for as long as I could, because the memories would have to stay with me once he was gone.

He groaned as he kissed me, as he pushed inside me slowly, like he was trying to soak up the moment as much as I was. I felt each ridge of his cock, his hard heat parting my folds and making a home for himself there like he had in my heart, as if he were promising to stay.

But I knew better. He wasn't. He couldn't. We were at cross purposes. Getting what I wanted—justice for my brother, and by this point, for myself—meant destroying every single one of Jack's dreams.

He's not the manipulative one.

Starcrossed. And it never ended well for starcrossed lovers.

"At least get a condom," I gasped as he hit a spot inside me I was starting to think of as his.

"No," he growled as he slid back out, still torturously slow. "Fucking you bare. Taking you raw. Nothing getting between us. *Ever*."

"Jack—"

"No," he said again, punctuating the word with a thrust. So deep, I felt him everywhere. "Don't argue with me, Aviva. Don't you *dare* argue with me. Don't you take this from me. Don't you take *you* from me. I won't fucking let you. Hear me, little fury. There is nowhere in this world you can hide that I won't find you, nowhere you can go that I won't follow. I will chase you down and bring you back. Every. Single. Time. So stop fucking fighting me."

He picked up his pace, his thrusts erratic, lacking rhythm or rhyme, like he couldn't control how badly he needed to be inside it. And I wanted it, I wanted it, but I couldn't. Couldn't have it.

"Why?" I cried out. "Why won't you let me go, when you hate me?"

"Hate you," he agreed on a grunt. "And you hate me too, don't you, little fury?"

"I do."

"Hate how good it feels to have me inside of you," he groaned.

"That," I agreed on a whimper.

"Hate how much you want me," he groaned.

"Yes."

"Hate how much you need me."

"Yes!"

He met my gaze in the mirror, his gray eyes dark, hard, desperate, pained. And his next words gave me vertigo.

"Hate how much you love me."

Assaulted by vertigo, I lost my footing, and he caught me, lifting me up so my feet dangled off the floor as he shoved deep in me and stayed there.

"No, Jack, I—" I tried to deny the words even as they sank their truth into me.

He interrupted me, whispering his next words brokenly into my ear. "Because believe me, I fucking *hate* how much I love you."

And then he was fucking me so hard I couldn't breathe, couldn't reply, couldn't be sure I'd heard him right.

"Hate you, hate you, hate you," he grunted in my ear, and all I could do was echo him as he pulled out of me and carried me over to the bed before throwing me down on it face first and following me down as he dragged me under.

36

Jack

She was trying to leave me.

She thought we were over.

I'd hurt her. I'd seen the devastated look on her face back at the alumni dinner, and a voice inside my head had gone, *there's no coming back from this.*

Every single fucking atom in my body rejected that. There was no way Aviva was leaving me, no way she was going anywhere. If I had to glue my cock to the inside of her pussy and remain inside of her until the end of time, I'd do it, if it meant keeping her. There were worse ways to spend a lifetime.

Her pussy agreed with me as it clenched around me at my words. Words I'd never meant to say, words I hadn't even known were *true* until this moment. I didn't love anyone, not anymore. So I'd never expected to love the little lying thief who was determined to ruin my goddamn life. But if love was the gaping wound in my chest that had appeared the moment she'd walked away from me at the alumni dinner and had only started to close once I'd shoved my cock inside her *where it motherfucking belonged*, then I loved her.

I hated her, too. I hadn't lied. I hated what she'd done to me. Hated what she was turning me into. I didn't recognize this guy, obsessed, practically possessed, letting my old priorities fall to the wayside when my priority had become her.

I couldn't let her go, I wouldn't, and if she burned my world to the ground, I'd make sure she burned up with me. Because I wouldn't let her go. Even in ash, we'd be together.

She struggled below me on the bed, fought me.

"You're fucking crazy," she cried. "We can't do this."

I ignored her, I had to, just pulled her back down onto my cock as she crawled up the bed and began hammering into her cunt, reassuring myself with how wet and hot and tight she was around me as she clenched. I shoved a hand below her and played with her clit, not bothering to be gentle or easy. I had one mission, and it was making her explode all over my cock. And then do it again.

"You close, little fury?" My voice was so hoarse, it sounded like a stranger's. "I am. I fucking love you, and you love me—you just clenched again. You might be able to lie, but your cunt can't, can it? She knows I'm right, she wants me to keep her." I continued strumming her clit, playing her, desperate for her to come. "I'll give this greedy, needy pussy what it needs until you can admit it. I won't stop you until you say it, Aviva. Tell me you love me, or I'll keep fucking you until we're both bleeding and raw."

"Jack," she whimpered but my words and touch had done it. Her whole body tensed and clenched around me, pulsing as she soaked my cock in her own come. The scent —apples and honey and pussy—surrounded me and I inhaled deeply, like it was the last time I'd get to smell it.

Bullshit. She wasn't going anywhere and neither was I.

I drove her into the mattress as I pounded my desperation and anger into her, over and over. My balls drew up.

"Tell me you hate me," I ordered.

"I hate you," she whined brokenly as she continued to come around me.

I felt the oncoming orgasm at the base of my spine as I continued fucking her, deep and hard and raw like I'd promised.

"Tell me you never want to see me again."

"I never—I never—" she broke off, because she wasn't able to say the words.

Good.

I withdrew from her pussy and flipped her over before shoving back into her, needing to see her eyes for what came next.

"Tell me you love me," I demanded but this time it was my voice that broke.

"I can't!" Her eyes were afraid.

"Tell me."

I thrust as deep as I could go and stayed there.

"I love you! I love you! I hate it so much, hate you so much, hate what you've done to me."

At her admission, a fucking supernova exploded inside me. I went blind for a moment, or maybe a century as the biggest, scariest orgasm I'd ever had took over my body and I lost track of who Jack Feldman had been, because all that existed was Aviva. She cried out, clenching around me as she came again, extending my own for an eternity.

Finally, I came down, was able to see again. Locked onto her eyes, which were filled with terrified awe.

I kissed her mouth hard.

"Same, little fury. Same," I groaned in that stranger's voice before kissing her again.

My heart refused to slow down, still pounding so hard, so loud I could barely hear her quiet, "I love you."

I pulled away from her lips. "Yeah you do, little fury," I crooned as my softening cock hardened again.

"Oh god, no more," she moaned.

"More," I promised.

I lifted her legs over my shoulders, leaning forward and bending her in half.

"You're not going anywhere," I threatened as I began thrusting inside her again, not interested in giving her a break. "You're going to take my cock like a good girl and keep taking it until *I* say we're done. Until you're so full of my come it's spilling out of you."

She shut her eyes and turned her head.

This time, it was anger boiling in my spine.

"Open. Your. Fucking. Eyes. And. Look. At. Me." I forced out as I made sure to hit her clit with the base of my cock.

Her eyes flew open, blurry with need and pain.

"I hate you," I told her again, because I loved her, and the two four-letter words were beginning to sound like the same thing.

I fucked her all night, her pussy, her throat, her ass. On the bed, against the wall, on the floor. I lost track of positions, of how many times she came, fuck, of how many times I came.

By the time the sun rose, my promise had come true. My cock and her pussy were so raw, there was blood on the sheets. I couldn't have fucked her again, even if I wanted to, so I contented myself by latching my mouth onto her pussy and refusing to stop making her come until her alarm went off.

Finally, I released her. We had an away game and I needed to get my shit together and meet the team at the bus. She collapsed against the bed, whimpering quietly. I reached for a bottle of water on her nightstand, opened the cap, and gently tilted her head up, feeding it to her. She drank, and that simple act of providing water for her made my practically broken cock twitch again as something sweet and satisfied settled in my cock.

The team could wait. I scooped her up like a bride—my favorite way to carry her—and brought her to the bathroom, turning on the shower and making sure it was hot and not too hot before setting her down inside and joining her there. I took my time, lathering up her hair with shampoo and rinsing it, careful not to get any soap in her eyes, before working conditioner through the tangles. I soaped up her body, drawing slow, gentle circles around her skin, chasing it with water and then with my mouth.

I wanted her, wanted to be inside her again, but I resisted. This was about her, not me.

She stayed quiet the whole time, although she let me take care of her. I told myself that was a good sign, but my gut didn't believe it.

After, I quickly washed my own body and hair, toweling her off slowly and me off quickly, before carrying her back to her room. "Take the day off of class and sleep. But come to the game tonight," I told her as I kissed her, lowered her to her bed, and tucked her back in. "I'll make sure you have a ride—it's only an hour away. And I'll get someone over here to fix the door."

"Jack," she said, or tried to say. She'd lost her voice screaming from all the orgasms I forced on her, and I couldn't help but be pleased about that.

"Yeah?"

"Can you believe that Asher is telling the truth? Can you help me?"

I paused above her.

Because the answer needed to be no. If it wasn't, I'd give up my entire world.

But then, wouldn't it be worth it?

And hadn't I started to doubt, anyway? I'd be lying if I pretended I wasn't.

"Just come to the game, little fury," I finally said. And then, even though it was a word I never used: "Please."

She murmured something that I decided was "yes," so with one last look at her, I dressed and left her apartment.

Aviva was right. I was a liar. I was lying to myself.

Because she hadn't said yes.

She'd said no.

37

Jack

Where the hell was Aviva?

As I warmed up on the ice, stretching out my hip abductors to the sounds of women cheering in the stands, as if we did it for them, I stared at the away team side of the arena. Aviva was nowhere.

The driver I'd hired told me she'd never showed, and last I'd checked the app on my phone, she was in the library. I'd texted her, but she hadn't responded.

Some people had showed. Micah sat next to her empty seat, eyebrow raised. To his right was Kara, a big fuzzy hat on her head, and to her right were my brothers' other partners, Conor and Luke. In the row above them, Marcus sat next to his friends and business partners—Billy, and some creepy, quiet guy they always referred to as "Doc" that I knew better than to cross.

Billy said something to Marcus, who laughed. Doc stared out at me. Kara waved.

Isaac skated over to me. "Looks like your whole family showed."

I sighed, pushing up with my arms and standing. "And then some."

"But no Aviva?" he asked, searching my eyes.

But no Aviva.

"You know, maybe that's for the best," Isaac said. "I never asked you what happened at the alumni dinner, but it didn't look good. And she's dug her hooks into you. Maybe it's time for you to let go and move on. There's easier pussy out there and—"

My fist connected with his jaw before I'd even realized I'd taken a swing.

"What the fuck, man?" Isaac stared at me in shock, blood dripping from his cut lip.

I shook out my hand. "Don't ever fucking call her pussy again."

"What the hell has gotten into you?"

"Feldman!" Coach yelled from the team's box. He never called me by my last name. "Come here."

I looked up. The stands had gone silent, as fans, ours and the opposing teams, stared at me. Then whispers broke out. I couldn't hear them, but I'm sure they were trying to figure out why Jack Feldman had just punched his own teammate.

I skated over to Coach.

"I—" I started to say.

Coach shook his head. "I don't care, Jack. You're out of the game. Go sit in the locker room. I can't look at your face right now, and the team shouldn't have to, either. I'll talk to you after."

The disappointment hung off him like a coat. As I headed down the tunnel into the locker room, I glanced up to see Marcus wearing a similar expression. Micah, however, looked thoughtful, eyes working as he watched me. Kara leaned over to whisper something in his ear, and he nodded.

Oh well. First game my brothers actually attended, and they wouldn't even get to see me play.

Fuck this.

Back inside the locker room, I paced. I wanted to punch something, or someone else. The wall, maybe.

Or Coach.

I was losing it. Isaac was probably right. I needed to let Aviva go. I'd told her I'd loved her, she'd said it back, and then the little thief had bailed. Maybe this wasn't love after all. Maybe I was so fucked in the head, I'd mistaken lust and hate for love.

Except I could see her, the way she'd looked at me last night, terrified and awed. She was strong and determined, loyal and loving, and I wanted that love and loyalty for myself. I was jealous of Asher, for having that loyalty from her. I was a fighter, not a quitter. But I didn't know how to break down the final wall separating us, when it was her mission and mine. We couldn't both win.

I would win.

But it meant I would lose *her*. And that, I was frightened to realize, was the biggest loss of all.

The door opened. I looked up, expecting it to be Coach, or maybe the team: I'd lost track and for all I knew it could be halftime.

Instead, my brothers and their partners filed in.

"Why are you here?" I glared at them.

It wasn't their fault I'd lost my shit at Isaac, but I was aching for another fight. The crack of my knuckles against Isaac's jaw had been satisfying, and I wanted that feeling again.

"I think the question, little brother, is why are you?" Micah raised an eyebrow.

Always calm, always ten steps ahead of everyone. He knew why I'd been banished to the locker room and where my head was at. The fucker always knew everything.

"What the hell were you thinking?" Marcus chimed in, much less chill. "Punching your own teammate, Jack? Did you learn a single thing we taught you?"

Micah raised a hand. "Yacob doesn't need to be attacked. He needs to be understood."

My hands fisted at my sides. "Don't fucking call me that."

"Micah," Kara chided softly at his side.

Micah ignored her. He stroked his beard. "Why not, Yacob? That's your name. Your *real* name."

And then I was across the room, staring him down from my slightly taller height, my hand gripping the collar of his pristine button down. "My real name is Jack. I left Yacob in the past years ago, in Teaneck. That kid is *dead*. He was foolish and needy—"

"And vulnerable," Micah interjected. He didn't even flinch, just stared up at me calmly. I was a few inches taller than him, and it should've made me feel stronger.

It didn't.

"And *pathetic,*" I growled.

Luke and Conor, his and Kara's partners, were at my side, glaring protectively.

"Get your hands off of him."

Micah waved them off. "It's fine. He's angry. Tell me, why are you so angry, little brother?"

"Because you weren't fucking there for me!" I exploded in his face. "Because you fucking *left* me there with *him*. And *her*. One day you were there, defending us, the next you were gone. And then Rebecca left, and who the hell was left to be a buffer for the younger kids? Who the hell took the brunt of our father's drunken rage while our mother ignored all of it? *Me. I was.* And you didn't give a single shit."

Micah sighed. "He kicked me out. You know that. And Rivka...she had her own demons to fight."

I didn't give a fuck. "You could've come back. Could've *fought* back. Instead you joined up and forgot us."

"Jack..." Marcus interjected.

I released Micah. The fucker didn't even stumble backwards. I whirled on Marcus. "And what about you? You show up when my life is finally together with your guilt and your money and your promise to make things right. But you didn't. The money is nice, *brother*, but it doesn't make up for the past."

"I didn't even know—" he started.

"Bullshit. You didn't even *care*. You know who cared? Coach Jensen. You know who rescued me? Him. So don't show up now and act like you want to help me. You're years late and dollars short."

I heaved air into my lungs, trying to clear the red rage out of my eyes. Blinking, because I was a man, and men didn't cry. That's what Coach always said when I was young. Tears were for the weak, and I wasn't weak.

Micah sighed, rubbing a hand over his short blonde hair, his tan face.

"You're right, Jack. I'm sorry. I was young and scared and angry, and I fucked up. I should've saved my family, but I tried to save the world instead."

Conor snorted. "And look how that went."

Micah gave him a look. "I built a new family instead of taking care of my original one. Marcus and I, we can't fix the past. But *you* can't live in the past, Jack, or it will eat you alive."

"I don't even think about the past," I told him.

He nodded. "You shove it away, right? Put it in a dark box and never crack the lid." His voice softened. "But by facing it, acknowledging it, you can release it. Ignore it, and all the demons inside will keep banging at its walls until they break it open." He looked at Marcus. "Something you should think about, too."

Marcus scoffed. "We're not here to talk about me. And I like my demons."

The Doc and Billy were the ones to snort this time.

I sat down on one of the benches, slumping over and burying my head in my hands. I hated that Micah was right. I'd held onto my rage too long. Channeled it into hockey and punishing anyone I felt had crossed me, or the only people I was loyal to.

Punished Aviva.

Hadn't trusted her for so long.

And even when I began to, I still didn't believe her.

Kara joined me on the bench. "Jack, why did you punch your teammate tonight?"

Micah smirked. "Because Isaac talked shit about his girl." He didn't even glance at me for confirmation.

"I've fucked up a lot," I said into my hands.

Kara laughed. "So did they," she said, meaning my brother, Conor, and Luke. "Sometimes love makes good men do bad things."

I didn't contradict her. I loved Aviva, but I wasn't sure she loved me.

"She's not loyal to me," I said.

"And are you loyal to her?" she asked.

I shrugged, picturing her face when I'd told her her brother was lying. She'd been sad, not angry.

"She thinks Coach..." I trailed off. "Did something fucking awful. But I know him, and he'd never—"

Kara gently peeled my hands from my face. "Jack, look at me."

I did. It was easy to see what had made my brother determined to have her. She was beautiful, with her red hair and big golden-brown eyes, but she also had this...I don't know. A steel spine surrounded by a soft joy. The first part reminded me of Aviva. The latter...I wanted that for her. Wanted to give it to her, like my brother had given it to Kara.

"I'm looking," I said gruffly.

"Don't look too hard," Conor called, clearly territorial over his woman.

Kara ignored him. "Sometimes good men do bad things for love. Often, powerful men do horrible things for more power. The charismatic ones? They hide it well. Take it from me—listen to your gut, even if you've been silencing it for a long time. Before it's too late."

Before she could say more, the door opened, and my team entered. Coach was the last one in.

Isaac wouldn't look at me.

"Uh," Judah said to Kara. "You're hot, but your entourage is unnecessary."

Luke growled.

"Eyes off," Conor barked.

Coach cleared his throat. "None of you can be in here."

Marcus straightened, staring down Coach, but didn't say anything.

Coach's face began to turn red.

"We were just leaving," Micah interjected.

He came over to us, reaching his hand out to Kara, who took it.

As all seven of them exited the room, Kara stopped, tugging on Micah's hand. She looked up at Coach. He towered over her, but for some reason, in that moment, he seemed small.

"The most outwardly powerful men are often the weakest ones. Isn't that true, Joshua?"

Now Coach turned full on red. "I don't know who you are..." he began.

Kara shrugged. "You don't need to. But I know who *you* are. Women like me, women who've been hurt like me—we *always* know.."

Micah looked back at me. "Save your loyalty for the people who deserve it, Jack. Call if you want to talk."

And then they were gone, leaving me with a confused, curious team and a pissed-off looking Coach.

Kara's words rang in my head. She saw something in him I couldn't.

Or refused to.

38

Jack

Intermissions in the away team's locker room were tense. Isaac still refused to talk to me as he patched his face up, placing ointment over the cut on his lip. He wouldn't be smirking for a while. Judah, man-bun askew, and Levi, glasses fogged, exchanged glances and did that annoying twin thing they did when they communicated without saying a word. Coach glared at all of us. Dave smiled to himself. The players I wasn't close to whispered to each other.

By the second intermission, the Kings were down by two, and I knew they all blamed me for it. Guilt swamped me. My team looked up to me, needed me, and I was fucking it up for them. But the guilt for letting down my team was nothing compared to the guilt I felt for what I'd done to Aviva. My brothers were right: I'd expected her loyalty without giving her mine.

I needed to talk to Coach. To get real answers this time. I'd ignored my gut, which usually detected lies, because if

I'd caught him in a lie, what would that mean about my life? What would being loyal to someone who potentially did something so fucking heinous mean about me? And yeah, I'd done some heinous shit to Aviva, too. I'd fucked her multiple times, forced her to fuck me. She hadn't consented, not at first. I hadn't cared. And if I were honest, I still didn't —not if it had gotten me her. I did care, however, that I'd hurt her, that I'd put that broken look in her eyes more than once. I wanted to roar at myself for what I'd done.

I wasn't pretending I was a good man, wasn't making excuses for myself. I'd wanted her, so I'd made an excuse to make sure I had her—any and every way I wanted. But as I'd once said to Mason Calloway, it was different if you gave a shit. Otherwise you were just a pathetic predator taking advantage of your power.

Had Coach cared about Asher? Or was he a weak man who'd wanted to feel powerful by subjugating someone he should've protected?

I needed answers.

The second intermission ended.

The team filed out.

"Coach," I called as he began to exit the locker room.

His shoulders looked tight. He glanced back at me, face impassive. "I'll talk to you later, Jack."

I shook my head. "I need to talk to you now."

He sighed, but waited. When the last player—Isaac— walked out, finally looking at me with a questioning glance, he shut the door and turned to me, hands in his pockets.

"I'm disappointed in you," he began. "I told you not to let that girl get in the way—"

"Why did you really kick Asher off the team?" I interrupted.

This time, his sigh was filled with annoyance. "This

again? Jack, I told you. The young man was troubled. Jealous. Of *you*. Wanted to take it out on me. That girl has gotten in your head."

I cleared my throat, an idea coming to me. "She finally admitted to me he was into some bad shit."

Was that a smirk on his face? Like Aviva had said?

He quickly hid it. "Yeah, some really bad shit."

"Like Vice and Vixen," I prompted.

Relief this time.

"Exactly, Jack."

Lie.

I felt it this time. If I were honest, it had always been there. Like Aviva said, I'd been willfully blind.

I hid my thoughts, nodding, and Coach continued.

"I didn't want you to know about it. No reason to ruin his reputation more than it was already ruined. I know you don't know much about those drugs—at least I hope you don't—but they are bad, truly bad. Make people go out of their minds with...lust."

That tiny, almost invisible smirk was back.

I nodded again. Coach had no idea just how much I knew about Vice and Vixen.

"You know, Aviva told me he was *dealing* it. It makes sense, he was a scholarship student—"

Coach cleared his throat. "Unfortunately, that's the truth. Asher was dealing Vice and Vixen to students at Reina and other schools, namely Tabb. We tried to keep it quiet because, as I said, there was no reason to destroy his future. But yes, he was a dealer. From what I learned, a very successful one."

Lie.

Even if my gut hadn't told me so, his words confirmed it. Although I didn't deal Vice and Vixen, I was the liaison between the people in charge of Vice and Vixen and the low level dealers on campus. Asher Gold had never had anything to do with Vice and Vixen, and he hadn't dealt it. I would know.

Lie.

Liar.

Coach had absolutely no reason to lie, to make up Asher being a dealer—unless he was hiding something. And what else was there to hide, other than the fact that he'd sexually abused Asher Gold? And who knew how many other of my teammates?

Rage—and regret—were so powerful inside me, I almost choked on them. Aviva had been right. She'd never once lied, and neither had her brother. Coach had groomed him, abused him, hurt him. And then when Asher threatened to tell, he'd flipped the script and ruined Asher's life in the process.

In order to protect his own ass.

Who else on the team had he abused? Who else knew?

The room spun around me, lockers and benches going blurry. I stumbled backward, dizzy.

"Jack?" Concerned, Coach moved toward me. "Are you okay?"

"Sick," I told him. I wasn't lying. I wanted to hurl.

He moved toward me, put his hand on my shoulder. I wanted to rip his hand away—rip it off his body—but I forced myself not to recoil and instead accept his "comforting" touch.

"Maybe you should head back early. You certainly aren't playing tonight. Go rest, think through what went wrong. And I'll see you at practice tomorrow morning."

I nodded. "Thanks, Coach," I said. "You always have our best interests at heart, don't you?"

He smiled. "I try to, at least. Now, I better get back to that game." He grimaced. "They don't play the same without you. Your team needs you, Jack. Don't forget that."

And then he was gone, leaving me alone with my thoughts. I grabbed my phone, checked the app to see where Aviva was, and then ordered a car to her apartment.

I'd fucked up, big time. Let my demons run the show.

I'd lost her because of my own stubborn idiocy.

I felt nausea roll through me, a burning stab in my gut, my heart, at the prospect of never being inside her again, having her in my arms, getting that rare soft smile and laugh from her.

No.

I wouldn't believe that. Couldn't. I'd meant what I'd said to her. I loved her, and she loved me, and I wasn't letting her go.

No matter what.

And Coach would pay. Not only for what he'd done to Asher, but for coming between me and the person who *truly* mattered most to me in the world. The person I couldn't—refused to—breathe without.

Oh, he'd pay.

I'd make sure of it.

39

Aviva

At least this time Jack had told the truth.

An hour after he'd left my apartment, workers showed up and repaired it without saying a word. By the time Tovah had gotten back from an allnighter at the newspaper, it was like Jack had never knocked it off its hinges.

Like he'd never been here, period.

It was for the best. On Monday, I'd ask Professor Johnathan if I could finish the semester up as an independent study. I doubted Jack would fight me on it. Even as he'd admitted he loved me, even as he'd fucked me into confessing it back, there was a desperation in his touch that made it obvious: he knew we were done, too.

Better for him to disappear out of my life altogether. I'd pick up the pieces.

Tomorrow. I'd pick up the pieces tomorrow.

I wasn't home when the car he'd ordered for me showed up. Tovah had sent me a text:

there's a car here?

for you?

to take you to the hockey game?

????????

CAN I FINALLY MURDER HIM?

I'd ignored her texts.

Just like I'd ignored Jack's texts and calls. Instead, I'd hidden out at the library, trying to focus on classwork. It was impossible. I kept picturing the look on Jack's face, the feeling of him inside me, as he told me he hated me and loved me with an intensity I'd never heard before. Terrifying, exhilarating, both at once.

But he still didn't believe me, and even though it hurt, hurt, hurt, *ohgodithurt*, I had to put Asher first. Had to focus on school and completing my mission to get him justice. Not worry about what it would do to Jack, because Jack was done and we were done and—

The words in my textbook swam in front of my face.

I wasn't getting work done.

I was bone tired, and all I wanted was my bed. Even though it smelled like him, and maybe because it still smelled like him.

I trudged home, checking the hockey score on my phone. The Kings were behind by two points. It was weird. I doubted Jack was playing shitty because of our...breakup, or whatever it was. He was too focused on the game, too determined to win, to let some girl he thought he loved but didn't believe throw him off. I loved that truth, and hated it at the same time.

The door was unlocked when I got home.

Weird, because Tovah had a shift at the bar tonight.

Shit.

Had someone broken in?

I glanced at my phone, not sure who to call. Who could help? Asher was too far away, Tovah wouldn't see her phone, I didn't trust the police, and Jack was at the game and might not help, anyway.

Double shit.

No way was I going into my apartment when god knew what could be waiting for me.

I turned, and someone grabbed me around the waist.

I screamed.

"Shh, little fury. It's me."

I smelled him, his spice, ice, and whiskey scent. Felt the terrible comfort of his arms.

But how was he even here?

I craned my neck to look at him. He looked terrible—eyes bloodshot, face almost haggard.

"Shouldn't you be at your game?"

He shook his head. "I got penalized before it even started. Kicked out. Sent home. But not before my brothers talked some sense into me."

What did that mean? Why was he penalized?

I started to ask, but he stopped me with a hand on my mouth. "Can we go in your apartment? It's better we talk in private."

He was asking? Not demanding?

"I'd rather be in public with you," I told him. Even through my shock, I knew nothing good happened when we were alone in my home together.

He shook his head, and then I was up in his arms, bride style once again.

"Jack, put me down."

"I like carrying you like this," he said. "It's good practice for our wedding."

Okay.

None of that.

Especially not the way his words made my heart race.

"Jack, stop. Put me down. You're being completely crazy again. You can't say shit like that to me and—"

He silenced me with a kiss. It was sweet, tender, and maybe even...

...sorry.

And then we were inside my apartment and he was shutting the door with his foot and carrying me over to the couch, lowering me onto it...and kneeling in front of me.

My heart froze.

"Jack, what the hell."

"Aviva, little fury." He swallowed. "I've only ever apologized to you, but once again, I'm so, so sorry."

I gaped at him. In some ways, they were almost more shocking than him telling me he loved me. And settled something inside me.

"Sorry for what?"

"For not believing you."

I couldn't speak for a moment. So he did.

"I should've believed you about the Co—about Josh Jensen. You were right. Your brother wasn't lying. He was. I'd ignored it, like you said. I fucked up, and didn't give you what I so desperately wanted from you—your loyalty. And for that, I'm sorry."

He captured me with this gray eyes, wet pools of silver. I stared at him.

"So you believe me."

"Yes."

"And Asher."

"Yes."

"And understand that just because the coach treated you with dignity and care and respect doesn't mean he wasn't capable of hurting someone else."

"I know that, little fury, believe me, I know that. And I believe you. I'm sorry I didn't."

I didn't know what to say. I'd never expected an apology. Desperately wanted one, but never thought it would happen. Instead I asked, "Why do you call me that?"

"In Greek mythology, they were fierce and determined to see justice, and so glorious, so beautiful, it hurt to look at them. I won't call you princess because I know how much it hurts you, and I refuse to hurt you anymore. I can't tell you how it felt, when you told me that I hurt you. I won't do it again. Not to you, not *my little fury*." His face went hard. "And anyone who has hurt you will pay."

I swallowed, cupping a hand around his cheek. He leaned into it, and the physical connection between us was everything I'd ever needed. Filled me with hope.

"Including you?" I asked.

He turned his head, kissing my palm. "Including me. I donated eight million dollars to a charity for young men who've been abused. In yours and Asher's name."

I startled. Eight million dollars? I couldn't imagine that much money. Couldn't even imagine what it would feel like to part with eight thousand dollars, much less eight million.

"Why? That's so much money."

"Because you deserve it yourself, but I know you won't take it from me. So I did the next best thing. I'll do whatever I have to do to show I'm sorry."

I stared at him. "What are you sorry for?"

"I'm sorry for everything—except for keeping you."

It was hard to breathe. Hard to believe. Hard to trust that this was real.

He wasn't done. "Oh, and I called your brother and apologized to him, too. Told him I'd make sure he got his spot back on the Kings and his scholarship back. And I mean it, little fury. If I have to use up every favor I have to make sure it happens, I'll do it." He grinned. "By the way, he's pissed at you for not telling him you'd transferred. I told him I was keeping you safe."

My eyes got big. "You didn't."

"He's coming up this weekend to see you. I think it'll be good for him to be back on campus, don't you?"

It would be. Exposure therapy and all that. But I was still stuck on the fact that he'd called Asher at all.

"Why would you even call him? That can't have been comfortable."

"It wasn't comfortable. I don't give a shit though. Your brother is important to you, which means he's important to me," he said simply. "Everything that's important to you is important to me. It's going to be that way for the rest of our lives."

"Our lives?"

"Fuck yes. I know I messed up, did terrible things, hurt you, but I am not giving you up, Aviva. I meant what I said last night. You're mine, and I'm yours. Forever."

"And you're sorry."

He nodded. "I am."

"On your knees? You've never been on your knees for me before."

My heart was in my throat. This man, who never apologized to anyone, had told me sorry. He kneeled for no one, but here he was, kneeling in front of me. He'd hurt me, bullied me, doubted me, forced me to have sex with him so many times.

And gave me more pleasure than I'd ever known. Allowed me to be myself. Admired me. *Protected* me. Used all his power to give my brother his life back. And now—

"I'd crawl on glass if it meant keeping you safe and happy," he told me.

God. This man.

"You can call me princess," I told him, because it was true. I'd hated that I loved it, but I loved it. "It's different when you do it."

He kissed my hand again. "Good. Because you're my princess and I'm going to treat you like one from now on." He smiled. "Outside of sex, at least. I'll still fuck you like you're my whore."

My thighs clenched at his words, but I forced myself not to get lost in lust. It was time to broach the harder subject, to see if he was for real.

"So if you believe me about Coach Jensen, what does that mean?"

"It means that he's going down. Anyone who hurts you..." he shook his head. "I don't really know him, can't trust him. I let my past cloud my instincts. And since he hurt your brother, he hurt you. I'm right, aren't I? This isn't just for your brother, this is for *you.*"

I swallowed. "Yes."

He was right. I'd told myself for so long I was doing this all for Asher, but it was for me, too. My family had been hurt so much over the years, and I couldn't take any more. I'd had to prove to myself that I was powerful enough to stand up to the injustice in the world—and win.

"Who else hurt you, Aviva? Tell me, and I'll rip them apart."

So many people. The men who'd murdered my parents. The Gold family, for never helping us. The world at large, for making me feel so small.

He watched me. "Tell me. Who *hurt* you. Besides me."

If he truly wanted to know, I'd tell him. "I don't know. Society? The patriarchy?" I stared at him, needing him to hear the last part. "Institutions that put men in positions of authority and never hold them accountable for the terrible things they do. Take your pick."

He didn't say anything for a moment, and I worried that I'd crossed a line, it was too much, that even with all we'd been through, this was when he'd walk away.

Instead, he stared at me, his eyes so silver, I almost gasped. There was love there, trust, determination. *Loyalty.*

"Then let's burn it down together, princess."

40

———————

Jack

The next night, I'd become a full on liar.

And I was okay with it.

I hadn't meant it when I'd said "together." We'd go to the cops together. Show the world what Coach—Joshua Jensen—had done together. But in order for me to take him down, I needed to go to his house, and I refused to bring Aviva with me. Something told me it wasn't safe, and I trusted my instincts. I wasn't risking her safety, even if she got pissed at me over it.

She was pissed at me. She sat on her bed and glared at me with those big brown eyes.

"Do you know how beautiful you are when you're angry?" I asked her, a little entranced.

"You can't sweet talk your way out of this, Jack Feldman," she said. "What happened to burning down the world *together*?"

I shrugged. "We can do that after. For now, you're going

to stay here and Lucy and Leslie are going to keep you company."

"What if it's not safe? I don't want you to go alone."

Her worry for me warmed me to my very soul. "I'll be fine. Coach—Joshua—trusts me."

A sliver of guilt slid inside me at the thought of betraying Joshua's trust, but I forced myself to ignore it. I'd spent years looking up to the man, of course it was going to be hard to let go of it. But exposing the truth—and giving Aviva what she wanted—mattered more.

"Jack, I swear to god, I will not—"

I shut her up with a hard, brutal, claiming kiss. I owned her mouth with mine, demanding entry, not giving a fuck that my friends were watching. She moaned and let me in, and I tasted her, got lost in her.

Remembered that I had justice to carry out for her.

Reluctantly, I pulled away, satisfied by the dazed look in her eyes.

"I love you princess. Be a good girl for me."

She threw a pillow at me but I ignored it. She was going to have to get used to me making the decisions and imposing my will on her. That was how it was going to work, even if she hated it. Because she loved me.

COACH—JOSHUA JENSEN, THAT WAS, BECAUSE I COULDN'T think of him as Coach anymore—lived in a large colonial about five blocks from Reina's campus, in a gated community with a code. Fortunately, I knew the code and had keys to his house. I parked about a block away from the gated community so I couldn't be placed at the scene of the crime, just in case. I'd walk through the gate instead of driving through it.

As I parked, I noticed the souped-up SUV behind me. Isaac had followed me here.

We both got out of our cars, staring at each other..

"Feldman."

"Silver."

He flinched. I was one of the few people who knew his real last name.

"Why did you follow me?"

He shrugged, walking toward me. Under the street-lamps, I could see the healing scab on his lip from where I'd hit him. "You've been acting erratic, so I followed you to Aviva's, and then followed you here. If you're about to do something stupid, I'm not going to let you do it alone."

"So I have my own stalker," I joked. Relief poured through me. I lifted my own chin in acknowledgement.

He chuckled. "Hey, you give it, you should be able to take it." Then he sobered. "So what stupid shit are we doing?"

I sighed. "Breaking into Coach's house."

He raised an eyebrow. "Why?"

"Because he groomed and sexually abused Asher Gold, and I need to find the video he took of it to prove it," I said succinctly.

In the dark, Isaac blanched. "I thought that was a lie."

"No. I caught Coach *in* a lie, though."

"Fuck man, I'm sorry. For you and for Asher. Where do you think the video is?"

I explained what had happened at Coach's office in Hallister Hall, and seeing the empty folder marked Asher. "The videos must exist somewhere," I finished. "I figure he would've saved them on his home computer or personal laptop instead."

Isaac nodded. "How are we getting in?"

I pulled the small metal object out of my pocket. "I have a key."

Isaac followed me up the stairs to the porch, waiting as I unlocked the door. "You know Aviva's a Gold, right? A distant cousin, but..."

"Yeah," I said. "Small world."

"The smallest."

I tried the key in the lock, relieved when it worked. "Quiet, we have to make sure he's not home."

I entered the silent house, noting the photos on the plain white walls—me and other teammates, a lot of Coach himself.

"Coach?" I called.

Silence.

Good, he was out like I'd thought.

Isaac followed me up the carpeted stairs, past the guest bedroom I'd crashed in before my freshman year started. Something stabbed me in the gut—I was doing the right thing, but it hurt, knowing that in a way, I was betraying the only father I'd ever known.

And then I imagined Aviva's face when I'd told her I believed her and was going to help her, and kept going. She was more important than any false father figure.

Outside Coach's office, Isaac stopped me. "Are you positive you want to do this, Jack? Once you know, you can't unknow."

I nodded. "I need to. For her."

I turned the knob and entered the office—an almost exact replica of the one in Hallister Hall.

Coach's personal laptop was nowhere in sight.

"Fuck," I muttered. I'd really thought I'd get the evidence this way.

My phone buzzed in my back pocket. I pulled it out.

Levi calling, it said.

I answered. "Everything okay?"

"No Jack, it isn't. Judah and I went to check on your girlfriend and her friends, bring them food. Apparently, your girlfriend snuck out the window. She's gone."

"What?!" I exploded.

Isaac eyed me, concerned.

"What is it?"

I put my hand up.

Visions of her falling, breaking her ankle, her fucking *neck*, paraded in front of my eyes. I shook my head to clear it. "And she's gone?"

"Yup." Judah must have grabbed the phone. "No idea where she went."

Without another word, I hung up on him, sliding open the tracker app.

And there were Aviva's two dots—from her phone and her neck—heading across the quad toward Hallister Hall.

Where Coach probably was.

"Fuck!"

"What's going on?" Isaac asked again.

"We need to get back to campus. Aviva's about to get her ass into trouble, and we need to be there before anything bad happens."

I texted Judah and Levi to meet us at Hallister, telling myself it would be fine.

But as we raced out of the house, down the street, and hopped into my car, my gut churned. I was lying to myself. It wasn't going to be fine. Not if I didn't get there fast enough. I needed her, needed her safe—from everything.

I sped down the streets, running every single red light on the way to campus.

It didn't matter.

We were still too late.

Because when we arrived at Hallister Hall, there was smoke pouring out of the windows of the building.

And according to the tracker app, my little fury was inside.

41

Aviva

"Maybe we should watch something," Leslie said cheerily. "Don't you guys like *Ted Lasso?*"

"Maybe we should tranquilize her," Lucy muttered. "It might make her stop pacing."

"Aviva, take a deep breath," Tovah ordered, watching me with concerned eyes.

All three girls were in Tovah's and my apartment. Lucy and Leslie had been sent to keep me company by way of Mason, and Tovah had come home as soon as I'd texted an S.O.S.

"I'm worried," I explained.

I wasn't worried, I was terrified. Not only because there was so much riding on Jack finding the evidence. I'd seen the kind of man Joshua Jensen was. The DSM didn't have a code for evil, but it leaked from his eyes all the same. If he caught Jack, what was to say Joshua wouldn't hurt him—or worse?

Tovah scoffed. "Please elucidate on how we went from 'Jack Feldman's an abusive bully who belongs in prison' to 'Jack Feldman's my boyfriend, I love him, and I'm scared he'll come to harm." I'd caught the girls up on *some* of what had happened.

I sighed. "If I tell you everything, you'll hate him more."

"That doesn't fill me with confidence, Aviva."

Finally sitting on the couch, I explained everything, sharing the whole story—minus some of the more salacious details. Tovah listened without speaking, but I could see the anger, the judgment, on her face.

"You don't have to worry about the coach hurting him, because I'm going to," she announced when I was done.

Leslie and Lucy looked at each other.

"Here we go again," Lucy giggled.

Leslie was gentler. "Tovah, as someone who's been there...you don't understand it unless you're *in* it."

Tovah, skeptical, raised an eyebrow. "I'll take your word for it."

I scooted around to look at her. "Jack's so much more than his early actions. He loves me, and yes, his love is brutal and intense, painful and all-consuming, but he's gentle, too. Tender, too. He wants me safe, and happy, and unlike other men—he'll do anything to make sure both happen. He sees me, and he loves what he sees, and we understand each other. I know you don't get it, but please, at least accept it. And if loving him is crazy, then I don't want to be sane."

"Fine." Tovah threw up her hands. "I'll accept him, but I reserve the right to kick his ass."

I cracked a smile. "I'll let him know."

"So *Ted Lasso*?"

I nodded. "*Ted Lasso*."

As they settled in, my phone buzzed. I pulled it out, hoping it was Jack.

But it was from an unknown number.

> I have that evidence you're after.

My stomach dropped.

> who is this?

> You know who it is, Ms. Gold. Come—alone—and I'll give you the evidence.

I snorted. Like I was going to fall for that. I didn't know how Joshua Jensen had figured out what I was looking for, but I wasn't going to let him get me alone, or he'd hurt *me*.

But if Joshua Jensen knew, what did that mean for Jack? I texted him.

> did you find it? coach jensen texted me, I think he's onto us

No response.

Another text appeared from the unknown number.

> If you're trying to reach Jack, don't worry, he's with me.

> Or maybe do worry, because he's with me at Hallister Hall right now.

> If you're not at my office in twenty minutes, then Jack gets the fate I was saving for you.

My heart began to race. I wanted to puke. He had Jack. What was he going to do to him?

> why would you hurt him? you care about him!

I care about the team more. The Kings need me, and I won't sacrifice that—or them. For anything or anyone.

Clock's ticking, Ms. Gold.

I texted Jack again.

No response.

I called him.

It rang through to voicemail.

"Aviva, what's wrong?" Tovah asked sharply. "You're pacing again."

"Nothing, just want to talk to Asher," I said, hoping she couldn't hear the tremor in my voice. "Feel free to start the show without me, I've seen them all a million times."

I headed down the hall to my bedroom, thinking through my options. But it came down to one thing:

I knew it was a trap.

I didn't care.

Nothing would happen to Jack. I wouldn't let it. If it meant sacrificing myself for him, then so be it. I'd do it willingly, to protect him—just like he'd protected me so many times, even when he'd thought he hadn't wanted to. It was my turn now.

I swallowed. What did they say about bravery? That it wasn't the absence of fear, but acting in spite of it?

Maybe Jack and Tovah were right. Maybe I was brave after all. I'd have to be.

I'm on my way, baby, I thought. *Please be safe.*

Please let him be safe.

I LEARNED THE HARD WAY THAT THERE WAS NO EASY WAY TO climb out of a window.

I fell on my ass, and something in my ankle hurt. I must have twisted it.

I had to hurry. Nauseating visions of what the coach could be doing to Jack flipped through my head like a horror story. I practically ran to campus, trying to ignore the sharp pain in my right ankle. I'd deal with it later.

Campus was quiet, empty in the dark night. Students were at the bars, partying at frat houses, studying at the library. No one would be at Hallister except me, possibly that security guard who hated me, Coach Jensen and Jack.

But then Jack's face flashed in my mind's eye. The earnest look on his face when he promised to crawl over glass to make me happy—I couldn't lose that. Couldn't lose *him*. He'd fought so hard for me, put himself at risk to give me what I wanted. It was my job, now, to make sure he was safe. I'd do more than crawl over glass, I'd fight through fire. Like anyone desperately in love would do if they were in my shoes.

Said shoes traipsed their way into the unlocked building, up the stairs to Joshua Jensen's office.

The door was open.

And Jack was nowhere to be seen.

Inside, Joshua sat behind his desk, watching something raptly on his laptop.

"Ah, Aviva," he said. "Come here, I want to show you something."

"Where is he?" I demanded.

The coach's lips quirked. "Ah, I may have...fibbed a little."

Fuck.

I turned, ready to run, but to my horror, the door shut behind me—and locked with a resounding click.

"A little birthday gift from Jack. He thought it was funny, me being able to close the door with a button. Comes in handy sometimes. Now, come take a look."

My throat went tight.

"I'm not sure I want to see whatever it is," I told him.

"Are you sure? It's your evidence."

Bile filled my mouth at the insinuation, burning my throat. The idea of seeing my brother hurt in real time...

Reaching into my pocket, I typed in the passcode and swiped up on record. If something happened to me, at least whatever the Coach said would download to the cloud. Maybe I'd still get justice that way.

Maybe Jack would find out what had happened to me.

It was the most I could hope for.

"Evidence for what?" I asked, playing dumb.

He glanced at me, shaking his head, smile still in place. "Evidence for having sex with your brother. I did, by the way. He wasn't the first, and he won't be the last."

"You didn't have sex with him," I said, glaring. "You assaulted him. Raped him."

He shrugged. "If that's what Asher's saying to make himself feel better. All I did was help myself to what I already deserve."

"What do you mean by deserve?"

"I've saved these young men. Trained them. Given them everything, so they'll have everything. I'm a leader in this community, and a well respected one. So why shouldn't I get to have a ... slice of pie every now and then? Who does it hurt?"

"My brother," I spat, disgusted. Joshua Jensen thought he was above right and wrong, above the law. That he was owed sex with his players, like droit du seigneur. But he was no king, just a pathetic, greedy man who'd smelled his own bullshit too often and was drunk on the fumes.

"Are you jealous, Aviva? Do you want what your brother got? I'm willing to give it to you."

He winked at me. I shuddered.

"You'd assault me like you assaulted my brother?" I asked, calmly and clearly, even though my heart was racing. I just needed to get him to admit it on the recording.

"Yes," he said, eyes flashing, grinning in an almost macabre smile. "And like your brother, you'll like it."

Got him. I'd done some research before I transferred: New York was a one-party consent state. Even though the coach didn't know I was recording him, it would hold up in court.

If there even was a court case. If he ever got caught.

I had to believe he would.

But Jensen's eyes narrowed on my hand, still in my pocket.

"Are you recording me, you little bitch?"

And then he was up out of his chair and standing in front of me. I didn't know how he'd moved so fast.

"Give me your phone."

"Go to hell."

He reached for me. My heart sped up. I tried the door again behind me, but it was still locked. I tried to duck past him—even though I had no idea where to go—but he caught me by the wrist and dragged me forward. Sliding his hand into my pocket, he pulled out my phone, dangling it in front of my face; a taunt. "I'll be taking this with me. You, however, are staying."

I fought him. I really did. I scratched and clawed. He slapped my face, punched me in the stomach. I doubled over in his arms, but I wasn't losing that easily. I bit his ear, tasting blood.

Angrily, he tossed me across the room, and my head smacked against one of the nearly-empty bookshelves. A book toppled and fell on top of me, and, dazed, I was bemused to realize it was *The Art of War.*

As my ears rang, he approached me, dragged me across the floor, and then he was tying my arms together and looping the rope around one of the feet of the huge, mahogany desk. I struggled weakly but it was no use, I wasn't going anywhere.

Oh god.

What was he going to do to me.

Jack, I thought. *I need you.*

But Jack didn't come.

"What are you doing?" I managed to croak, although part of me knew.

Jensen confirmed it when he began pouring a bottle of whiskey on the floor, around me, all over his office. The whiskey made my clothes stick to my skin, a tease of future horrors.

"Why? Why do this?" I managed to croak. Speaking felt like chewing on sawdust. "Why hurt me? It's one thing to be convicted of sexual assault, another of murder"

I thought I saw him shrug. "I have your phone. I'll use it to send a suicide email. You were so distraught over learning your brother's lies, you decided to burn down the building, and got caught in the flames. I'm a leader in this community; no one will suspect me."

Oh god.

He continued to pour out the whiskey as he talked. "It wouldn't have come to this if you had only let this go. But you were too committed to your little crusade. Tried to ruin not only my life, but Jack's and my team's as well. I refuse to let you hurt those boys—or me. They're too important. Their futures are too important—especially Jack's."

"You don't care about them," I told him angrily. "You don't care about *him.* If you did—"

"People are complex, Ms. Gold," he said. "It's something you would have learned as you grew older—unfortunately, you aren't going to get that chance."

"Jack won't believe you," I said desperately. "He'll get justice for me. He—"

"Jack's young," he interrupted calmly. "Still malleable. I've been the most important person in his life for years, he'll listen to me. You're so hellbent on your so-called justice, you think everyone else will be, too. But people aren't as pure of heart as you think they are. I know Jack, I know what matters to him. It's hockey. Not some girl he liked to fuck."

But he didn't know Jack, not really.

I did.

"You're crazy if you really think that will happen."

He chuckled. "Maybe I am."

He moved toward the door and opened it, pulling something out of his pocket. "Have a nice life, Aviva. For however short it is."

There was that macabre smile again. True evil.

I heard a click. Through my blurry vision, I thought I saw a lighter. Flame. Thought I saw him drop it on the ground.

The door opened and shut.

The flame burst out on the wooden floor, grew, and spread. Heat surrounded me as the fire spread, and I could barely see through the smoke.

It couldn't end this way. I wasn't going to survive this. And all I wanted was one more chance to tell Jack I loved him.

"Wait!" I begged the closed door. "Please."

From outside the office, a key turned in the door.

And locked it.

42

Jack

When I was a kid, I was obsessed with fire. If I got my hands on a match, I'd burn anything I could: Rebecca's hair scrunchies, Micah's notebooks for school, my father's newspapers. I could sit and watch the flames forever.

Until the night my mother "forgot" to turn the burners off on the stove. A paper towel near the stove caught fire, setting off the smoke detector. We'd had to file out of our home late in the night and wait for the firemen to come. Fortunately, they were able to put the fire out. I took the blame, not wanting my father to hit my mother, even if she never stood up for us. He took it out on me; it was the only time he almost put me in the hospital.

The house survived, and my mom repainted the kitchen, but I swore I could smell smoke every day in that kitchen until the day I left home.

I could smell smoke now. And even though I *hated* fire

and wanted nothing to do with it, I was about to confront it head on.

"Jack, what the fuck do you think you're doing?" Isaac stared at me in shock and fear. "You can't go in there."

I pulled my hoodie up over my head. "Too fucking bad."

Aviva was in there. I could see both tracker dots somewhere inside the building, right on top of each other. The building that currently had smoke pouring out the windows as a fire alarm blared from somewhere inside.

Parents with kids at Reina complained a lot that the fire station was manned by volunteer firefighters. Firefighters with other jobs, who were known to arrive late on the scene here. A frat house had burned down a few years ago for that very reason.

How long could someone inhale smoke before they had permanent brain damage or died? What if she was trapped? I couldn't take that risk.

"Call 911," I told Isaac. "And when Judah and Levi get here, see if you can figure out a plan to get her out."

"*Her* out?!" Isaac was furious. "What about you, man?"

I didn't answer him, just said: "Look, I'm sorry about what I did. I—"

I couldn't finish the sentence. With one last look at Isaac, I ran into the building.

HALLISTER HALL WAS CHOKED WITH SMOKE. WOODEN FRAMES had caught fire; a wooden bust of one of the university founders was engulfed in flame. I looked down at Aviva's dots on the app, ignoring how my overheated phone burned in my hand.

She was on the move.

Toward me.

"Oh, thank fuck," I breathed. Relieved, I ran toward the stairs, which she seemed to be heading down.

And then paused.

One of the dots was moving.

The other one was still.

What the fuck?

I stared at my phone. Fear choked me more than the smoke did.

"Jack? What the hell are you doing here? We need to get out!"

I looked up. Joshua Jensen was running down the stairs, one hand covering his nose. His ear was bleeding. But if he was here, where was Aviva? And why was one of the dots still moving toward me?

No.

I swallowed.

The asshole had her phone.

"What are you doing here, Coach?" I asked.

He shook his head. "Work thing. But come on, we need to leave. *Now.*"

"Were you alone?"

He looked me over warily. "What's that supposed to mean?"

I dropped the act. "Where is Aviva, Josh?"

"Jack—"

"Don't even," I spat. "Where. Is. Aviva?"

So did Joshua. "So you do know. She'd said as much, but I'd hoped—"

"*Where the fuck is Aviva*?!" I roared.

"That girl has gotten into your head," he said. "Look at

you, standing inside a burning building when I'm trying to save both of us."

"I know you lied about Asher Gold," I told him. "I know he had nothing to do with Vice and Vixen, because *I run the Vice and Vixen game.* What else are you lying about, Coach?" I sneered the word.

He threw his hands up. "He wanted it! He liked it! Liked me! Was always around after practice, asking for extra training, being helpful when he didn't have to be. Always had a question for me about 'improving his game.'" Joshua scoffed. "He didn't need help with his game. Kid's practically one with the ice. But *he* wanted *me.*"

I stared at the coach in horror as the lobby grew hotter, smokier. How had I never known him at all?

"What the actual fuck, Josh? How can you think that's okay?"

"What, are you going to let this ruin me? I made you, Jack Feldman. I was there for you when the rest of your family wasn't! I am your family."

I shook my head. "Aviva's my family, not you."

"That little bitch? She was practically begging for it earlier."

I froze as red filled my sight—and not from the flames.

"What did you just say?" I asked quietly.

"She was all over me earlier. Looks like she was trying to trade up." He said. There was pity on his face, false pity.

Aviva was right. My past had made me blind to who he really was, had gotten in the way of my lie detection. I'd been so fucked in the head when it came to him...and to her.

Aviva...

I took a step toward him, ignoring the fire surrounding me. "If you so much as touched her, Joshua Jensen, you will regret it. I will tear you apart, limb from fucking limb. You hear me?"

He shook his head. "You're crazy."

He had no idea. So I let him see just how crazy I was, staring at him, unleashing the madness inside of me at the thought of him laying a hand on Aviva. And where the hell was she?

"Where is she?" I asked. "You obviously have her phone."

"Jack," he pleaded. "Come with me. You don't need her. Choose me, choose your future. Choose her, and you can say goodbye to not only our relationship, but your future in the NHL."

Maybe what he was saying made sense. Maybe it didn't. I had no idea. The red haze hadn't cleared, and my whole body went stiff with tension.

"I'll kill you," I told him quietly, sure he could see the flames reflected in my eyes.

"Crazy," he said again, but this time he sounded afraid. "Well, I'm getting the hell out of here, Jack. One more chance to choose me and not be a complete idi—"

With a crack, a beam fell from the ceiling, dropping directly where he'd stood a moment before.

He screamed, trapped by the flaming piece of wood.

"Jack, help me! Help me, son! Get me out of here, I'm going to die! You can't leave me!"

But I was already moving past him on the stairs. Aviva had to be in his office.

Oh, shit.

Stopping, I walked toward him.

"Oh thank god," he coughed.

But I was reaching in his pocket to fish out his keys.

"I'm not your son," I told him—for the first and last time.

And then I was running up the stairs toward his office, heart racing. How much time had I lost arguing with him? Was Aviva still alive?

I couldn't think that way. I'd give up everything—my team, the Frozen Four, the draft, my future in the NHL. My motherfucking life. As long as it meant she was okay.

As long as it meant she *lived*.

Behind me, I heard a man's screams.

Ahead of me, I heard what sounded like a woman crying out my name.

I left him behind, racing toward her, hoping I wasn't too late.

43

Aviva

I was going to die here.

I was going to die in this fucking asshole's office, tied to his desk. Would I die of smoke inhalation first, I wondered distantly, or would I burn alive? I'd never thought about it before, but maybe the way my parents had died was better. At least it was over fast. At least they hadn't had to stare their death in the face with nothing to do but think about how they were leaving behind their loved ones to mourn them.

I knew Asher would mourn me. I wasn't sure he could take another hit. But would Jack?

At least I'd kept him safe.

At least I'd gotten the chance to tell him I loved him.

If only I could tell him one more time...

I pictured him in my head: his dark hair with the short, tight curls, his piercing gray eyes, his little smirk when he knew he'd backed me into a corner I couldn't get out of. The way those eyes turned dark with lust, or pain—silver with anger...or love.

He loved me.

He'd told me.

He'd move on and meet someone else and be happy.

"I want you to be happy," I whispered into the burning room. "Please be happy."

The smoke made my tears sting.

I shut my eyes. I didn't want to die, but it looked like once again, I didn't have a fucking choice. At least I could distract myself with memories of Jack until it was all over.

I shut my eyes.

I love you, I thought.

"Aviva!"

Pounding on the door.

I had to be imagining things. He was at the coach's house, wasn't he?

More pounding. "Aviva, goddamn it!"

Maybe I wasn't imagining things. I coughed.

"Here," I tried to say, but my throat hurt so much I could barely get the word out.

I couldn't hear anything over the roar of the flames. Had he left? Thought I was somewhere else?

Oh god, I was going to die. And so was he. The fire had to have spread so far...

Except there he was before me, whole and coughing, towering over me like an avenging angel.

I ignored the heat of the flames, staring up at him as he stared down at me, throat working.

"You're here," I tried to say, but my words turned into coughs.

"Holy fuck," he said. "Did he tie you up?"

"Yes," I tried to say.

"Did he touch you?"

I shook my head.

"Let's get you out of here."

He kneeled down, ignoring the flames around us as he worked on the tight knots.

"Fuck, it's not working," he growled as he rose, going to the desk and rifling through it. "Hang on."

"Don't have much other choice," I joked on a rasp.

He kneeled back down, holding scissors. "Don't move."

Quickly but carefully, he sliced the blades through the tie around my wrists, and then I was free.

Jack gathered me up in his arms, covering my face with his hoodie sleeve as he walked determinedly toward the door.

He grabbed the knob before I could tell him not to, only to stumble back with a yell.

"Fuck, it melted."

He placed me down on the floor gently, before throwing his body against the door, again and again. I watched him, tears burning their way down my face.

"I can't," he heaved, "get the door open."

Something on fire fell from the rafters.

"Jack, don't—"

"We don't have much time!" he yelled over the roaring flames. "I'm getting you out of here."

"With you," I cried.

He shook his head, picking me up in that bride carry he liked so much, making my heart shatter into tiny pieces.

"No, little fury," he said sadly. "I don't think I can get us both out of here."

"What do you mean?" he was carrying me over to the window.

"Like I said, not enough time."

"You're coming with me," I insisted. "I'm not leaving you."

"Aviva, you are. I refuse to let you die in here with me."

"I'm not leaving you!" I screamed. Or tried to. "You don't get to make that choice!"

"You are not dying. What did I say to you before, little fury? You don't get to make the decisions anymore. I love you."

And then he was breaking the window, with the same shattering sound as my heart, and pushing me out of it.

I turned my head at the last moment—just as another flaming rafter dropped...

...right on top of him.

"No! Jack!"

I fell, and fell, and fell.

Even after I saw the rafter fall, I still expected him to follow.

He *had* to follow.

But he didn't.

"Jack!" I screamed again, as I was caught by a pair of strong arms and carried away.

I looked up. I was surrounded by Isaac, Judah, and Levi.

"We have to go back!" I yelled at them. "We have to go back for him."

Isaac shook his head, jaw tight, as he took me away from the fire. Away from Jack. Away from the only man I'd ever truly loved.

"We have to go back," I sobbed.

"He made me promise to take care of you. So that's what I'm doing. Taking care of you."

"Where are the ambulances?" Judah asked.

"On their way," his twin replied.

I tried to fight Isaac, but he was as strong as the rest of

them. He held me easily as we both stared at Hallister Hall. The old athletics administrative building was engulfed in flames, red and orange burning bright against the night. I willed the door to open, for Jack to stumble out. But the doors remained closed, and Jack remained absent. I sank to the ground, screaming, sobbing, I wasn't sure. Was that shrieking, keening, wailing sound me?

I'd lost him.

I'd truly lost him.

I hadn't even told him I loved him one last time.

"It should've been me," I whispered. "It should've been me."

But all I could do was stare at the burning building that had become my true love's funeral pyre.

44

———

Jack

Love was fire.

Love was flame.

Love burned, scalded, turned everything else to ash.

Aviva.

I could see her in front of me.

Aviva.

Aviva, my little fury, what will happen to you without me? Who will protect you from the bullies, tormentors, terrible men, if not your own bully, tormentor, terrible man?

Aviva, I love you.

Aviva, I'm sorry.

45

Aviva

Love was ash.

Love was dirt.

Love hurt, blinded, charred, turned anything and everything into dust.

Jack.

I could see him in my mind—like a ghost. An apparation. Not real.

He would haunt me forever.

Jack, my love, how could you leave me like this? How will I survive without your special brand of loving torment? How will I go on?

Jack, I love you.

Jack, I'm sorry.

46

Aviva

I cried until there were no tears left. Until my eyes were as hot as the burning building before me.

The fucking firemen hadn't arrived, and it was too late.

I'd tried, more than once, to run back into the building. Jack's friends had stopped me. I got the sense they didn't want to, that they would've preferred it was me caught in there and Jack fighting to go save me, but they weren't doing anything about it.

I agreed with them.

I wished they would.

I closed my eyes, unable to stare at the building anymore. It hurt too much.

I wanted to die. Without Jack, life seemed meaningless. I hadn't known what made me happy, until I had him, and now he was gone.

Gone.

Another sob, sharp and blistering, broke out of me.

Gone.

"Holy fucking shit," Isaac said, pulling me out of my grief.

"Jack?" Judah asked.

My eyes flew open.

A man, covered in ash and soot, stumbled out of the building toward us. And even though his gait was unsteady, even though I couldn't see anything below the soot and ash, I knew. I knew it was him.

With a cry, I stumbled toward him, too. And then his arms were wrapped around me, and we were sinking to the ground.

"How? How?" I asked.

"Turns out the doorknob hadn't fully melted. Got it to turn, managed to find my way out of the building," he choked.

I lifted his hands. One was mostly fine, but the other had a gaping red wound on it.

"Oh god," I said.

"Hurts," he told me. "But not as much as the thought of never seeing you again."

And then his hot, ash covered lips were on mine, and all I tasted was Jack. Jack and fire. Jack and flame. Jack burned me and burned me and I didn't care, didn't care, because he was alive, alive, we were alive, and I held him in my arms and he held me in his and we were together and I *lovedhimlovedhimlovedhim...*

"I love you too, little fury," he rasped. I hadn't realized I'd spoken out loud. "I couldn't lose you. Would never leave you. Remember? I told you I'd chase you down, always find you, always bring you back. Would crawl on broken glass for you, so what's one measly fire? You're stuck with me for the rest of our lives, so get comfortable."

"I love you, and I'm not going anywhere," I said.

"Promise?"

I looked at him, brushing a hand over his burned hair. "Promise."

A thought occurred to me. "The coach?"

He grimaced. "Dead."

"I'm sorry." But I wasn't. Not really.

He shook his head. "I'm not." He cleared his throat. "I love you, little fury. So much, I'd cheat death, steal you—and lie, if it meant keeping you."

I swallowed. "I love you, Jack Feldman. And I'd cheat, steal, and lie to keep you, too."

Kneeling, he took my hand in his uninjured one, and together we watched as the rest of the building burned down.

In the distance, I heard sirens.

And then there were first responders there, wrapping us in blankets and asking us urgent questions like was there anyone else in the building? Jack and I shook our heads, saying we didn't know, but a few of the firemen went in anyway.

They came back out, carrying something. A body.

My stomach roiled.

One of them seemed to be saying something to another. There were more sirens—cop car ones, this time.

"Aviva Gold?"

"Yes?" I croaked.

"Jack Feldman?"

Jack glared at them, moving closer to me. "Yes?"

"We're taking you both to the hospital. The police are waiting for you there—they have questions."

Before I could say anything, they were ripping us apart, dragging me into one ambulance and Jack into the other, and as they shut the doors on mine, I heard Jack roar.

47

Jack

I lay in my hospital bed, seething.

They weren't letting me see Aviva.

After we were taken away—in separate goddamn ambulances—we were rushed to Gehenom Hospital. I was hooked up to an IV and given fluids and food, all my vitals were taken, and they'd seen to my hand. I should've been worried, since I needed my hand healed to play hockey— but all I cared about was seeing Aviva.

"Let me go see my girlfriend," I demanded to my nurse.

He tsked at me. "You can't leave your room in your state. And neither can she. You're both being treated for sustained smoke inhalation and burns. Honestly, you're lucky you survived. Don't push it."

"Do not tell me what to do when it comes to her," I said through gritted teeth, even though it made my jaw ache.

But the nurse couldn't be intimidated. "Jack Feldman, I've seen a lot worse than you over the years. You don't scare me."

It hurt to smile. Everyone caved when it came to me.

Except Aviva.

At that moment, as if I'd summoned her, the door opened.

She was standing, fragile and pale, wheeling a mobile IV next to her.

"Aviva Gold, I don't care how scary *your* relatives are. You shouldn't be out of bed," my nurse scolded.

Aviva glared at him. "Do not tell me what to do when it comes to him."

The nurse sighed. "Peas in a pod, the two of you. Fine, I'll pretend I didn't see you. But let him *rest*."

With that, he walked past Aviva and out of the room, softly shutting the door behind him.

Aviva stared at me, trembling.

"Little fury, come here," I said, as gently as I could.

"You're hurt."

"I'll hurt worse if you don't come here and let me hold you," I wheedled.

She wheeled her IV toward me, sitting carefully on my hospital bed.

"Jack, your hand!"

"It's fine. The doctor told me it would heal okay and I'll be able to play hockey. And even if I couldn't—" my throat worked, "I wouldn't care. I have you, and that's what matters."

Tears filled her eyes. Finding strength I didn't knew I had, I pulled her down against me with one arm.

Thank fuck. Having her in my arms immediately healed a wound inside of me the hospital hadn't managed to mend.

Burying her head in my chest, she inhaled.

"I was so scared," she whispered.

"Me too," I said, inhaling her scent, too. She smelled like

smoke and hospital, but I'd rectify that as soon as they let us leave. Shower, feed her, fuck her—so she smelled like me and only me.

Tugging her hair gently with my good hand, I pulled her back so I could look at her face.

"Should you even be down here?"

She stared at me, eyes working. "You don't want me here?"

"Don't ever ask a question like that. I'm worried that you are out of bed when you should be resting."

But I was greedy for her, and selfish, and glad she was here anyway. She'd fought to see me. She'd made it clear that she would fight for me, no matter what. And I hadn't realized I'd needed that from her until now.

I buried my nose in her hair. I might've been imagining it, but I thought I caught a whiff of apples and honey.

Which reminded me.

"What the hell were you thinking, leaving your apartment and going to meet him?" I tried to keep my tone even.

"Coach Jensen texted me that he had you and was going to hurt you. I knew it was a trap, but it didn't matter. I couldn't risk losing you."

This woman. My heart—that organ I was sure had died when I was a kid—beat steadily in my chest, so fucking content with the world. With *her*. Aviva was brave, loyal—and finally her loyalty was mine, the way I'd craved since I'd first gotten to know her.

That didn't mean I'd allow her to risk herself.

"You're not doing anything like that ever again. You don't sacrifice your safety for mine—"

She interrupted me, staring me down with her big, beautiful brown eyes. "You almost sacrificed your *life* for me. I know we didn't start this way, but hear me, Jack Feldman—

we're equal partners in this relationship, now. And it means we need to give, equally. I love you too much for anything else."

I stroked her hair. "Understood."

I got it now, why so many people lied. To protect her, I'd lie through my teeth for the rest of my life, and never lose sleep over it.

"I don't know if you know how much I love you," I said, quietly, solemnly. "I don't even have words for it. I don't think there are words for it. I love you fiercely, obsessively, relentlessly. I love you in my heart, mind, soul, in my fucking bones, until the day I die, and then I'll love you still. There's no heaven or hell for me, little fury—just you, forever."

Eyes glistening, she kissed me, softly, a promise. "Those are great words. Especially for a Classics major."

I laughed, and kissed her back, content in the feel of her lips against mine.

With a start, she pulled back. "I forgot to ask—how did you even find me?"

I wasn't about to tell her about the trackers. "Intuition," I said smoothly.

She narrowed her eyes, about to question me more.

Thankfully, the door opened, and my brother Marcus entered, dressed in a bespoke suit.

"Oh, good, you're alive," he said.

I rolled my eyes. "Nice to see you, too."

His eyes passed over Aviva, lips quirking. "This must be the girlfriend."

"Fiancée," I corrected.

Aviva stared at me. "Have you lost your mind?"

"Never had it in the first place, princess." I grinned at her.

"You never even proposed to me," she pointed out.

"Don't need to. Proposing implies the option of saying no, but you don't get to say no, remember?"

"Jack—"

"Fiancée," I repeated to my brother. Changing the subject before she could argue more, I asked, "Why are you here?"

"I have eyes and ears everywhere. I found out what happened, and decided it was a good idea to beat the police here."

Aviva sat straight up. "The police?"

Marcus nodded. "They aren't accusing you of anything, but they have questions. Namely, how you both ended up at Hallister Hall during the fire—where the head hockey coach was found dead on scene."

I swallowed. I'd known he couldn't have survived, but I hadn't processed it. I was sad, angry, relieved. But truthfully, the man I had known had died before the fire—when I'd finally accepted who he actually was.

Sensing my mood, Aviva brushed a hand over my cheek, searching my eyes.

"Are you okay?" she asked quietly.

I nodded.

To Marcus I said, "If they need someone to pin it on, pin it on me."

"Absolutely not," Aviva protested.

Before I could argue with her, Marcus cleared his throat. "We're not pinning it on anyone. My lawyer is on her way, and you aren't saying a word to the police without her."

Someone knocked on the door.

"Ah, Ilana must be here," Marcus said.

A moment later, a no-nonsense looking woman entered with a briefcase. "Hello, I'm Ilana Brandeis and I'm your attorney. Neither of you will say a word to the police without clearing it with me, first, alright? Now, what's the story?"

Aviva began to speak.

Ilana shook her head. "Do not tell me anything remotely incriminating. I want to know the *story*."

Aviva and I looked at each other, before explaining everything. I didn't mention Aviva's tracker, of course—or the fact that I left Josh to die.

I should've felt guilty.

I didn't.

Ilana listened, then asked, "Do you have any proof?"

Fuck.

I started to say no, but Aviva spoke up. "I recorded the coach's confession, and his threats. He destroyed my phone, but it should've sent to the cloud."

Awed, I kissed her again. "My brilliant fucking fury," I said against her lips.

She melted against me.

Ilana clapped her hands. "None of this. The police are waiting outside. Again, you do not say a word before clearing it with me first. Ready?"

Gripping Aviva's waist, I nodded.

WHAT FELT LIKE HOURS LATER, THE POLICE WERE DONE grilling us. They were sympathetic, concerned, but I still didn't trust them. We stuck to our stories, and they accessed Joshua Jensen's confession through Aviva's cloud account.

One of the police shook his head as he left. "Sounds like a tragic accident, but I'm glad you two are safe. Sometimes the best seeming people hide the worst crimes."

The other police officer didn't look quite as sure. "It's an interesting story, I'll give you that," she said.

Neither Aviva nor I said a word.

An hour or so later, we were discharged and on our way back to the hockey house in Marcus's town car.

"If you're engaged, then I assume it means you'll let me buy you a condo," Marcus said easily as he scrolled through emails.

"I can buy my own condo," I told him.

He shrugged. "I can buy you a better one."

Aviva bit her lip, trying to hide her laugh.

"What do you think, princess?" I asked.

She rolled her eyes. "I don't really want to live in the hockey house," she grumbled. "But I can't leave Tovah—"

"We'll talk about it later," I said, not mentioning that Tovah was going to be distracted for a while.

Once I was sure Marcus was ignoring us, I asked, "Do you love me?"

"Of course I do."

"Then marry me."

"Fine," she grumbled. "As if you're giving me a choice."

I smiled and bent my head to kiss her hair. "I'm not."

48

Aviva

"Aviva. Wait."

I paused on the quad, outside of the building where Deviant Psych took place. It was a month after the fire, and I was on my way to class to give my final presentation—the one I was doing on my own after Jack had swapped partners to piss me off.

Jack was supposed to meet me. He had practice. After Joshua Jensen had died, and the truth about him had come out, campus had been in an uproar. The athletics department put out an urgent call for a new head coach, finally finding someone that they offered a disgusting amount of money to to break their contract and come to Reina. The new coach, Bill Matthewson, was "tough as hell" according to Jack and the rest of the Core Four. Worked them until they were exhausted, sore messes, accepted absolutely no bullshit—and was as respectful as they came. Jack had done his "lie detector" test over Coach Matthewson multiple times, and even had his brothers look into him, but he seemed clear.

Fortunately, Jack's hand had healed well, and he was back to playing just fine. And when he wasn't using his hand to play hockey, he was using it to torture me into orgasm after orgasm, or to bring me presents I didn't need—books, flowers of all kinds (because I told him I didn't have a favorite), even a puppy we named Psych—all ways of saying sorry for the past.

A past that was, thankfully, beginning to dim, making way for the bright future ahead of me.

But first I had to deal with whoever was calling my name.

I turned to see Dave Lawson standing there, hands in his pockets.

"Hey," I said, startled.

"I owe you an apology."

I looked him over, confused at how contrite he seemed. "For?"

He looked around to make sure no one else was listening. "I knew what Coach Jensen did to your brother. Knew it was true. Almost walked in on them, once. I'm sorry."

Anger, bright and fast, filled me. "You fucking—"

He lifted a hand. "I know. Believe me, I know. You and Asher deserve to rip my head off. I wanted his position on the team so badly, so I convinced myself it was consensual, and didn't say anything."

I processed his words.

"If you want to kill me, I get it. Or sic Jack on me. That works, too."

I considered retribution for a moment. We'd needed his help, and instead of telling the truth, he'd used my brother's pain for his own benefit.

"Who else knows?" I asked.

"Just me."

I exhaled slowly. I could sic Jack on him. Could do worse.

But these days, revenge and justice didn't carry the same weight they used to. My brother had his position on the team and his scholarship back—if and when he was ready. Joshua Jensen lay six feet under, worm food, something I didn't lose any sleep over. Destroying Dave—what would it do, except reopen old wounds that were finally healing?

"I called your brother already. Apologized to him. He swore at me and hung up."

I smiled faintly. "Good."

"Aviva," Dave said. "I truly, truly am sorry. I'm sorry for everything you went through, and if I can ever make it up to you—"

"You can," I said. "The next time you see someone take advantage of their power, you'll act on it. You hear me?"

He nodded. "No matter what."

"What are you two talking about?" Jack asked as he approached us, eyeing Dave with distrust.

"I'll tell you later, baby," I said, standing on tiptoe to kiss him. "But we need to get to class."

With that, I put Dave Lawson behind me, in the past, taking Jack's hand and pulling him toward the present.

THERE WAS A STRANGE WOMAN SITTING IN PROFESSOR Johnathan's seat when we arrived.

I gaped.

"Um..."

"Hi, I'm Dr. Maria Peters," she introduced herself. "I'll be replacing Dylan Johnathan for the remainder of the semester."

I turned to Jack. "What did you do?"

Jack smirked. "Pulled some strings."

I hissed at him as we sat. "Tell me now."

He sighed. "Turns out that Joshua wasn't the only authority figure at Reina abusing his power to take advantage of his students. Dylan was caught with Vixen, and the administration fired him immediately."

I narrowed my eyes suspiciously. "And how was he caught?"

Jack placed a hand on my face. "He fucked with you. Made you uncomfortable. Probably intended to do worse. You're not the only one who can dole out justice, little fury."

Our new professor cleared her throat. "From what I've learned, you all have presentations to give today." She consulted a paper with students names on it. "Ms. Gold, would you like to go first?"

I glared at Jack. "We'll talk more about this later."

"Like we'll talk about whatever Dave was telling you?" he asked.

Sighing, I rose to give my presentation. I talked first about sexual narcissism, and then, with a look at Jack, moved onto how sexual deviance was seen and treated generally.

"When someone uses their power to control and manipulate someone else sexually, it's considered deviant behavior. There are a variety of treatments, although not everyone agrees that it's pathological—"

Jack raised an eyebrow.

I winked at him.

"—there is a school of thought that it can be cured, and

the sexual deviant will no longer be interested in sexual control and taking someone else's power to buff up their own. In fact when there's behavior that's considered inappropriate by society—"

"Cured?" Jack interrupted.

"Cured," I said.

He shook his head, rising to his feet. "No curing this, princess."

"Mr. Feldman!" interrupted the new professor. "Let her finish."

He ignored her.

"I'll show you behavior that's 'inappropriate'" he warned. Suddenly, he was crossing the room and throwing me over his shoulder.

"Jack! I'm not done!" I protested.

"You are now," he said, and with that, he carried me out of the room to the sound of the classes shocked laughter.

As he carried me down the hall, I started giggling.

"You did that on purpose," he accused.

"Eh, I can be a little manipulative sometimes," I admitted.

He slapped me on the ass—hard. "It's okay. I like it."

I'D EXPECTED JACK TO TAKE ME HOME TO OUR NEW apartment. Marcus hadn't bought us a condo after all—Jack had pointed out we'd be moving soon once he was drafted, so it made more sense to rent for now.

"And when we do, *I'll* buy us our damn place," Jack had said.

But that was the future. Our future.

In our present, Jack was carrying me through the arena into the locker room.

The empty locker room.

He locked the door.

"Um," I said.

Setting me down, he cupped my face with his right hand, kissing me.

Pulling away, he said, "Whenever I'm in here, I think of you. Standing up to me, calling me out on my shit. The first time I felt your tight throat—" he winked, "Or got a taste of that apples and honey pussy of yours. Even when I thought I hated you, it haunted me. Now, the memory of treating you so badly haunts me."

I nuzzled into his hand, not speaking.

"I want to make new memories of us in here, so when I'm getting ready for a game, I can see me worshipping you instead of torturing you. Let me worship you, princess."

"Yes," I said.

He closed his eyes. "You have no idea how good the word 'yes' sounds coming from your lips."

He kneeled down, sliding off my sneakers and unbuttoning my jeans before pulling them down, followed by my underwear.

Then his lips were on my pussy, and he was kissing— soft, gentle kisses that felt so good, I melted against the wall next to his cubby. He licked, sucked, played, winding me tighter and tighter.

"Love this pussy," he said, looking up at me, his mouth covered in my wetness. "Love you."

And then he was back at it, working me, playing with me, guiding me slowly and tenderly into one sweet climax after another.

"Enough!" I cried out.

"One more, little fury," he said. "For me."

His mouth was on me again. I didn't say no to him. Couldn't. Not when it felt so good, not when he was trying to heal our past with our present like this, with his tongue drawing circles around my too-sensitive clit, licking his love into me.

I came again, sagging and sliding down the wall.

Jack rose, catching me, lifting me into his arms and balancing me with one arm while he unzipped his own jeans with the other.

He pushed into me, slow, steady thrust after slow, steady thrust, hitting me in the perfect spot as he watched me.

"I love you," he said.

"I love you back," I told him, and he was kissing me again, his lips as gentle with my mouth as they'd been with my pussy. I tasted myself on him, and sharing that intimacy, that love, broke something open inside of me.

"Fuck me harder," I whispered into his ear, biting him.

He caught my hair in his fist and pulled. "Yeah, princess? You want it rough?"

He'd asked me that, too, the first time. But this time, it wasn't taunting, it was giving.

"As rough as you can give it to me," I told him.

"Grab the wall behind you, don't you dare fucking move your hands," he growled, a switch flipped.

And then he was powering into me, again and again, hard and fast, bouncing me endlessly on his cock.

"That feel good, princess? Does my thick cock feel good in that tight little cunt?"

"So good," I moaned.

"I'm going to get so deep inside you, you'll feel me for

days. Fill your pussy up so when I carry you to our home, I'm spilling out of your cunt. Hell, maybe this time I will make you lick it up off the ground."

With a cry, I came again, clenching around his cock.

Something in him snapped and he drove into me so hard, it hurt. I welcomed the pain. Welcomed the madness. Because even though Jack fucked me violently, like he hated me, he stared at me like I was something precious and priceless, something deserving of worship, like I was a gift he'd never expected but wasn't giving back.

"Loveyousofuckingmuch," he growled, the words coming together as he bottomed out inside of me, filling me up with his come like he'd promised.

Finally, he relaxed, pulling out of me and lowering me to the floor. He stared as his come spilled out of my pussy, down my legs, onto the floor.

"Fuck, that's always so hot," he groaned, scooping up some come off my leg and feeding it to me.

"You're so hot," I teased breathlessly.

"Am I?" his eyes were lazy. "Get on your knees and use your mouth to clean me off, princess. Show me how hot you think I am, so I can fuck you all over again."

And so I got on my knees, taking him in my mouth, licking off the taste of both of us. He grew hard, filling my mouth, filling me, and I reveled in it, in the submission and the lack of control, letting it consume me as he pulled me off his cock and put me on my hands and knees before shoving back inside me and showing me how much he loved me, loved me with his violence and his tenderness, his full, unbreakable focus, and mostly, with his neverending, relentless, undying obsession.

And I showed him.

Right.

Fucking.

Back.

THE NEXT MORNING, I WOKE UP TO AN EMPTY BED.

Walking out into the kitchen, I saw a shirtless Jack—surrounded by bottles upon bottles of juice. There was orange juice: pulp, pulpless, some pulp, freshly squeezed, even the blood orange kind. And not just orange juice. I walked around, touching each bottle, reading the labels: mango juice and coconut water, guava and cranberry, a million different versions of apple mixed with something else, regular lemonade and pink lemonade. There were kinds that he must have had to special order from other countries. There was even Fanta.

My eyes wide, I walked around the kitchen island, tracing each bottle, taking it all in.

He came up behind me.

"Why did you do this?" I asked. "Why juice?"

Wrapping his arms around my waist, he put his lips to my ear. "Because you never took the time for yourself to learn what kind of juice *you* like, and I want that for you. I promised you we'd figure out your favorite, and that's what I'm doing."

I turned my head to look at him.

"Are you going to fulfill all your promises to me? Because this is a little extra, even for you."

"Every single promise that keeps you safe, happy, and mine," he said, and that was a promise, too.

I forgot about the juice, turning to kiss him, because his

mouth was my favorite taste of all. And I made sure he forgot about the juice, too.

Turned out, freshly squeezed orange juice was my favorite—and Jack made sure I had it every morning, for the rest of our lives.

Just like he'd promised.

EPILOGUE (ONE)

Aviva

The arena was packed.

Fans—students, professors, and random townies—sat closely together, cheering for the Kings as they skated across the ice and took on their opponents. They were tied two to two, it was the final period, and as I sat between Tovah and Asher, my eyes were locked on Jack. I wanted this win for him. I wanted it so badly, I'd steal the title for him if it made him happy.

As if Asher heard my thoughts, he snorted. "He's not going to play better because you're beaming love rays at him."

It had taken a lot to get my brother to come to the Frozen Four championship game. Even when I'd told him the truth —or some version of it, he was still hesitant. Coach Jensen's death—and the truth about what he did coming to light— had helped Asher a bit, but it was his new, better therapist that had pushed him to come to the game.

He was finally getting back on the ice again, thank god. Not yet, not with the Kings. But Jack had convinced him

I looked at my brother: his dark eyes, his big frame, the way his hands clenched as he watched his former teammates move across the ice. There was longing and pain on his face.

"You know," I said, "There's no reason to be embarrassed. The team knows what happened, and they support you."

They did. The videos had been found, and even though no one had seen them, their existence was enough to turn the remaining players over to Asher's side. Judah, for his part, had joked "I guess Gen Xers and Boomers still don't understand how technology works."

Jack hadn't laughed. He'd squeezed my hand instead, and I'd squeezed his back. I knew losing the coach—and the pretend version of him he showed the world—was hard on him. A lot of things were hard on Jack now. He had nightmares sometimes, waking up and gripping me tightly.

I couldn't find you, he'd say. *I ran and ran through the fire, and I couldn't find you. Couldn't get there fast enough.*

And I'd hush him, comfort him, with my body when he needed it, with my voice when he didn't, until he finally fell back to sleep. I'd expected to have nightmares, but I didn't. And neither of us dreamed about the coach. I should've been worried, how little guilt we both felt over his death, but then, I knew there was something dark and wrong about me—if there wasn't, I wouldn't be marrying Jack.

Asher glanced at the huge, shining rock on my hand. "I know your fiance pulled strings to get me back on the team—"

"He didn't pull strings," I argued.

"—But I'm just not ready. I will be, I promise. But I'm not."

We watched as the opposing team's goalie froze the puck.

"That's illegal right?"

"Delay of game," Asher murmured. "They're getting desperate."

An official blew a whistle, calling it.

Jack took advantage of the break to skate over to us where we sat in the stands above the team's bench.

"Asher," he called.

"Jack," Asher said back.

After Jack had apologized for not believing him—and Asher had gotten over his anger—they'd formed something of a friendship. They weren't close, but they were getting there. Asher refused to speak to Dave, which Dave seemed to accept.

For now.

Jack turned to me.

"Princess, you ready? Because I'm going to win this one for you."

I grinned at him, happy.

"I know you are."

"You look good in my jersey."

"I know I do," I teased.

Behind me, Marcus coughed. "Get a room, you two."

Beside him, Micah chuckled. "I'm sure they will. *After* the game."

Jack ignored them, but I knew he was glad his brothers were here. I was glad they were finally mending their relationships.

"God, do you have to make jokes like that?" Asher

complained. "She's my sister. It's disgusting," he said, turning to me. "You're disgusting."

I giggled, punching him in the shoulder.

The horn sounded and the game started back up, and we were busy watching Jack and his team move across the ice like they shared one brain. Jack stole the puck from the other team's defensemen, passing it to Isaac, who ragged the puck and then passed it back to Jack.

The defensemen must have exchanged a look, because they ganged up on Jack and slammed him against the boards.

I was up on my feet, yelling. But Jack had already shoved both defensemen off him, regaining control of the puck. He deked to the left, and the defense fell for it. Then, as the crowd watched in enraptured silence, Jack executed a snap shot—a combination of a wrist shot and slapshot.

The puck flew straight into the net, past the goalie.

The horn sounded.

I stood there frozen.

They'd won.

The Kings had won the championship.

And Jack had scored the last point that got them there.

Then I was yelling in joy, as the crowd cheered and absolute bedlam ensued. I ran down the steps toward the ice, and Jack was there, lifting me into his arms and skating around with me in circles.

"You did it," I said, kissing him.

"I did it," he replied, kissing me back. I expected him to look shellshocked, but instead he looked smug. "We did it, actually. But then I knew we would. How could I not, when I have you?"

"You're cheesy as fuck," I told him.

He sobered. "None of this matters, Aviva, without you. You know that, right?"

I kissed him again. "I do."

"Good," he said, skating me back to where his team was celebrating. "Let's go home so I can fuck your pretty little pussy until you beg me to stop. How does that sound, princess?"

It sounded pretty perfect to me.

EPILOGUE (TWO)

Isaac

She was late.

I'd agreed to this bullshit interview for the Daily Queen, partly out of loyalty to Jack's girl, partly out of curiosity, and partly for my own purposes. But I had plans tonight—plans that involved very enthusiastic triplets—and I didn't have time for little journalists who couldn't even keep track of time.

As I rose to leave the bar, she came running in. Her hair was in her face, her shirt was partially unbuttoned. Her cheeks were flushed. She looked freshly fucked. A growl rose in my throat, but I immediately tamped it down. I didn't get jealous, or territorial. Especially over girls that got around like Tovah Kaufman did.

So then why did the idea of some other douchebag fucking her make me want to throw this pitcher of beer against the wall?

"I'm sorry I'm late," she said. "Something distracted me."

I looked her up and down, aware I was leering. "I'm sure it did."

She glared at me, but didn't defend herself.

"I agreed to this interview under the impression that you'd be respectful of my time," I told her.

She sat, ignoring the glass I pushed toward her. "You know, you come off as this easy going charmer to everyone else. Why do I get this grumpy asshole whenever we talk?"

I grunted in response.

"See!" Her eyes flashed in triumph. "I don't know what I did to hurt you, Isaac, but—"

Her mere existence hurt me. Knowing she breathed the same air as me, after what she'd done—*that* hurt me. Seeing her face at night, in my dreams, when I jacked off in the shower, when I was fucking some other nameless, faceless girl or woman—*that* hurt me.

And she was going to pay.

"So what's the content of this interview? You never sent me questions."

"I didn't want to give you a chance to figure out a lie."

My hackles rose.

"What would I have to lie about?"

"Why you're pretending your last name is Jones, for one."

My heart roared in my ears. No one but Jack knew my real last name, who my family was. It was the deal I'd made with my father; I'd take over the family "business" if he gave me these four years at Reina without interfering. The strings of the deal that I'd tried to ignore tightened; I could feel them around my throat.

I narrowed my eyes. "If you know my real last name, you know better than to threaten me, little journalist."

She puffed up her chest. "I don't know who you're calling little, Isaac Sil—"

My hand shot out, covering her mouth. The feel of her breath against my palm made my skin go tight and my cock harden. Tovah growled, and then bit me.

I didn't release her. "You like to play rough, huh? Or at least, that's what I've heard about you."

She glared at me.

With my free hand, I dragged her chair closer to mine, dropping a casual arm over it. My hand closed around the back of her neck.

I squeezed.

She shuddered.

Fuck. My cock turned into a rock.

"You might know my last name, little journalist, but that doesn't come close to what I know about you. That's right," I stared into her angry, defiant, terrified eyes. "I know your secret. And while you revealing mine would be an...inconvenience at best, if I revealed yours, it would blow up your entire life, wouldn't it? I could take it to the police, to the dean...even tell Aviva."

She shook her head back and forth in negation.

Of course she did. She didn't want me telling the world what she'd done.

"After all, if you know my real last name, it's helpful that I know yours...Tovah *Lewis.*"

I could practically hear the *dun dun dun* in the silent bar, echoing in her head.

I glanced at the mirror behind the bar. My grin was terrifying—a shark about to take a bite out of its prey.

Focusing back on her, I released her mouth to tuck her hair behind her ear. The way she shivered beneath my touch? It pleased me.

"Now," I began. "Here's how this is going to go..."

THE END

WANT TO KNOW WHAT HAPPENS NEXT WITH ISAAC AND Tovah? Preorder their book now!

*

This is the end of Jack and Aviva's story, but not the last time you'll see them. They'll make appearances throughout the rest of the Kings of Reina U series, and pop in other books as well. AND if you want to see how they're doing after college, you can read a bonus epilogue here.

*

Curious about Jack's older brother, Micah? He has his own story, out now. Get the first book in the *Bad Heroes* trilogy here.

*

Intrigued by Mason and Leslie? You can read their story in *Butterfly*, out now!

*

Want to know more about me, and get publishing updates, sneak peeks, and other news? Join my newsletter here!

AUTHOR'S NOTE

It should go without saying, but I feel the need to say this anyway: Queer people are by and large, not groomers, sexual abusers, or perpetrators of sexual assault. In fact, queer people are more likely to be victims of said crimes.

I say this because a part of me worries that the point of Joshua Jensen's character may be misunderstood, when what he is is just another powerful but pathetic man in a series of powerful but pathetic men who think their wants, needs, and desires supercede everyone else's. Men who use their power, not to help, but to harm—because they can.

In case it hasn't become crystal clear from any of the books I've written, I really, really loathe men—anyone really —who use their power to abuse others. I've been the recipient of many a "powerful" man's attentions over the years, and if you don't think it's created a well of rage inside me, I suggest you go back and reread this book from page one.

Now, you may say, "Hey, Jo, isn't that what Jack does?" and I will reply, "Yeah, you're kind of right, and I'm talking it through with my therapist."

On a more serious note, because yes, dark romance is

fiction and what we enjoy reading doesn't mirror what we actually like (and dear god, I would absolutely love if dark romance readers and authors could stop having to have that conversation), I did struggle a bit with what Jack does, given what Joshua does. But as I forced myself to sit and listen, really listen to my characters, here's what Jack told me:

We readers (and authors) are messy, and complicated, and hold multiple truths in our heads, and all of us know that we can root for Jack to end up with Aviva while we root for Joshua to get his just desserts. Maybe not everyone wanted Joshua to be burned alive, but not everyone contains the anger that I do (and Aviva and Jack, by proxy).

At the end of the day, what Jack does to Aviva is absolutely inexcusable. He knows that, we know that. And he loves her. And she loves him. That's just a circle you can't square in reality, but in fiction, it allows for so much: a safe place to explore fantasies and kinks, catharsis from our own traumas and wounds, and, finally, the ability to confront some uncomfortable truths about power and the lack of justice head on. To force an entitled, gorgeous, wealthy, powerful king (because what is a hockey champion, if not a king?) to realize how much he *hurt* the person he cares about, and atone. Not redeem himself, not make amends, but atone. And to do that by helping her burn down the patriarchy, even a little symbolically? Mama, put that shit in my veins, every fucking day.

I'm publishing this at a time when the future looks scary —for some of us, maybe for all of us. At a time when burning unjust systems to the ground maybe feels less like a fictional plot point and more like a place our enraged imaginations take us to. But here's the thing, the future also looks hopeful: the same way a man's beautiful gray eyes may look when he commits to helping you with your cause, whatever that might be. The same way I know we all have more power than we think to stand up to bullies, be them individuals or institutions. And to systems that seek to hurt us, to divide us, to destroy us.

You know what Jack would say:

Let's burn it down together, princess.

ALSO BY JO BRENNER

Bad Heroes

You Can Follow Me

Lose Me In The Shadows

Meet Me In The Dark

Tabb U

Butterfly

ACKNOWLEDGMENTS

First, thank you to Skye Warren. This book wouldn't be what it is without your guidance and support.

Poppy and Sabrina: Thank you for holding my hand through all this madness and giving my ass the tough love it needs. RFC: Thank you for being the best authoring sounding board a girl can have.

Jasmine: I couldn't do this without you. Never leave me.

Brittney, I love, miss, and appreciate you. And miss you. Did I mention I miss you?

Alex and Liz: If this is the best you can do, then I'm lucky AF.

Mikaela: Thank you for going above and beyond with this one, you sports romance queen.

ARC and Influencer team: Y'all are incredible. Truly. Words cannot express how grateful I am for all you've done to help with this book's success. If I could hug each and every one of you, I would.

And to my alphas and betas: Y'all were instrumental in turning this book from good to great, and I'm deeply grateful to each and every one of you:

Angela, Justine, Jasmine, Mikaela, Brittney, Tori, Alexia, Tamara, Carly, Candace, Jennifer, Kayla, Jenni C, Sara, Mariah, Jennifer, Karin, Amoy, Kaitlen, Jessie, Britty B, Beccs, Claire, Alexis, Jasmine M, Brianna, Blair, Emily, Alyx, Carly M, Desiree, Emma S, Erin, Miya Christina, Ashley, Madison, Love Letter Library (and anyone I possibly missed!)

And finally, to my readers: There are so so many books out there, so every single time one of you picks up mine, it makes my heart so big I don't think it will fit through doors anymore. Thank you, truly. You make this whole thing worth it.

ABOUT THE AUTHOR

A lover of dogs, mountain adventures, and HGTV, Jo Brenner writes romances that are little bit twisted, a lotta bit sexy—and always have an HEA.

Stay in touch and get the latest publishing updates, book teasers, book recommendations, and more by joining her Facebook readers' group, Jo Brenner's Bar, and by subscribing to her newsletter!

facebook.com/AuthorJoBrenner

x.com/jo_brenner

instagram.com/jobrennerbooks

tiktok.com/authorjobrenner

goodreads.com/Jo_Brenner

amazon.com/author/Jo_Brenner

bookbub.com/profile/jo-brenner

Printed in Great Britain
by Amazon

60951460R00241